Lessons in French

HILARY REYL

Simon & Schuster

New York • London • Toronto • Sydney • New Delhi

Simon & Schuster
1230 Avenue of the Americas
New York, NY 10020

First Simon & Schuster hardcover edition March 2013

SIMON & SCHUSTER and colophon are registered trademarks
of Simon & Schuster, Inc.

For information about special discounts for bulk purchases,
please contact Simon & Schuster Special Sales at
1-866-506-1949 or business@simonandschuster.com.

The Simon & Schuster Speakers Bureau can bring authors
to your live event. For more information or to book an event,
contact the Simon & Schuster Speakers Bureau at
1-866-248-3049 or visit our website at www.simonspeakers.com.

Designed by Esther Paradelo

Manufactured in the United States of America

1   3   5   7   9   10   8   6   4   2

Library of Congress Cataloging-in-Publication Data
Reyl, Hilary.
Lessons in French / Hilary Reyl.
    p.   cm.
1. Americans—France—Paris—Fiction. 2. Women college graduates—
Employment—Fiction. 3. Women photographers—Fiction. 4. Psychological
fiction. 5. Domestic fiction. I. Title.
        PS 3618.E947L47   2013
    813'.6—dc22   2011045815
        ISBN 978-1-4516-5503-2
        ISBN 978-1-4516-5504-9 (ebook)

For Charles, mon grand amour

one

They say I have no accent and that this is a gift. Sometimes, people can detect a lilt in my voice, which makes them wonder which rural part of France I come from, or maybe which Scandinavian country. But no one can hear that I'm American. And yet, because I am not French, I show almost no signs of belonging to any group or class. In Paris, I am virtually transparent. A gift, perhaps. *Un don,* so to speak, *voilà.* But, when you feel invisible, there is no end to the trouble you can get into.

My trouble began in 1989, on a wet September morning at Charles de Gaulle Airport, when I decided to splurge on a taxi into town. The worn smells of leather and tobacco were deeply reassuring, the precise blend of odors I craved at the edge of the unknown.

But I probably shouldn't have taken that taxi. Mom claimed that you had a much higher chance of dying on the way to or from the airport than you did on the plane. However, you had more say about how you traveled on the ground. You could go by car, bus or subway. You could slow down, look both ways, watch your back. On the ground, you could take responsibility. In the air, worry was nothing but a production.

I had just graduated from college, and was trying to ignore most of what Mom said, but I was secretly proud of her, pretending to be as callous as she would have been to any signs of fear in myself as my plane flew to Paris.

The driver asked me where I was returning from. Where had I been on my *vacances*?

I told him I hadn't been on vacation anywhere. I had been a waitress in New Haven all summer. That was a town on the East Coast, near New York.

Ah, New York!

But I was returning to Paris for the first time in ten years. Though I wasn't French, my grandfather was, and I lived here once, for two years, with cousins, in the Nineteenth Arrondissement.

He laughed. Today, he wasn't driving me to the Nineteenth but to the Sixth. A much more chic *quartier*. More central. Mademoiselle was moving up in the world!

We glided through the industrial ring around the city. We had just permeated its first layer when the taxi was rear-ended at a stoplight. There was a shock, a screech, swearing.

I felt so vindicated for Mom that I was strangely overjoyed by this accident, proof-positive of her theories of relative danger. I sidelined the fact that she would have told me to take the Métro because it was cheaper, and safer. I had wanted a driver to be my own personal shepherd into my new life.

This was my moment in the sun. So what if it was drizzling? Experience was going to transform all.

The driver punched the steering wheel—"*Merde!*"—as I flew into his headrest.

"*Ça va?*" he asked, rubbing his own forehead. "Are you hurt?"

No, no, I was not hurt, and I would wait uncomplainingly on the sidewalk of this outer arrondissement for him to exchange the necessary information with the woman who had hit us.

We were by a news kiosk. I had forgotten that the news kiosks here were green and suppository-shaped, that the newsprint was denser than ours, that there were Chupa Chups lollipops and Hollywood gum for sale, a magazine called Figaro Madame, headlines about a pop star named Johnny Hallyday, erotic ads for coffee and chocolate, small posters for chamber music concerts in Ste-Chapelle, dog shit. It was all coming back.

Looking hard at the familiar candies and magazine covers, I saw their colors and meanings bleed into lines and shapes. I pulled a sketchbook and pencil from my bag, keeping half an ear to the words between my driver and the offending woman. He wrote down her details. She lit a cigarette.

Because I sensed the conversation wrapping up, I did not put pencil to paper. There was too much to draw in a few moments, and I hated resorting to quick symbols and tricks. I was uncannily good at reproducing what I saw, but only in the fulness of time. If I couldn't do it right, I would rather simply stare. I slipped my sketchbook away.

The drizzle was lightening into the gray gauze I recalled well but hadn't thought of in years.

In Germany, the Berlin Wall was about to come down. A photo on the front page of *Le Monde* showed a rock band playing a concert in front of big bright graffiti on the West Berlin side. I looked into the crowd that filled out the *Le Monde* photo. People were dancing ecstatically, sensing the coming demolition, except for the photographers, who were still, their flashes going off.

I scanned the photo for my new boss, Lydia Schell, the woman I had come here to work for. She was a photographer, a famous one. Mom had not heard of her, but once I was able to prove her credentials, Mom was impressed that I would have the opportunity to be the Paris impresario to someone with such a name. "Impresario" was Mom's term. When I had interviewed with her in her Manhattan town house a few weeks ago, Lydia had called me her assistant.

Now she was in Germany capturing the momentous happenings. There was a chance, wasn't there, that she was in that crowd, peeking through her lens at me in welcome?

"You made it," she would say, if only I could spot her. *"Bienvenue!"*

two

My dented taxi stopped on a beautiful street that flowed toward the Luxembourg Gardens, stonework giving way to rich green. This was a new angle on Paris for me. *Le Sixième.* Even the cigarette smoke was elegant here, twirling above well-groomed bodies in a velvet calligraphy quite foreign to the noxious haze of my youthful memory. There was no confusing this cigarette smoke with car exhaust just as there was no confusing the clatter of high heels on this pavement with the street sounds outside my cousins' subsidized building. What had those sounds been again? I couldn't remember. They were muffled now by the luxurious revving of a Citroën's engine, by the calm rustle of nearby leaves, by the voluptuous exhale of an impossibly petite woman in two-toned heels, which even I knew were Chanel, her shoulder pads broad enough to soften any blow.

The taxi was gone. I was outside No. 60 with my suitcase, forgetting the exorbitant fare as I looked down my new street, repeating the building code, 67FS, which I would have to punch in order to open the door to the interior courtyard, "a hidden gem," according to Lydia, "although my husband Clarence likes to complain that it's dark and depressing." As I was preparing to punch the keys that would work this magical door, it opened by itself.

"*Ah, c'est mademoiselle Katherine?*"

"*Madame Fidelio, je vous reconnais de votre photo!*" It was true. I recognized her overhanging brow from a photograph of Lydia's.

4

Her plumpness did nothing to soften her sculptural face. I knew that skull, those imposing eyebrows. She was an intimate, the Portuguese concierge who also helped with Lydia's housework. *"C'est vous, non?"*

"Oui, c'est moi. Enchantée, Mademoiselle." She gave a short laugh, overshadowed and outlasted by the suspicion in her eyes. Was I going to be a slut like so many of Madame's other assistants? Was that what she was looking to know from my brown ponytail, pale pink lip gloss, jeans, leg warmers, t-shirt frayed and ripped to reveal one shoulder?

I wanted to tell her that she had nothing to worry about. I was a serious young woman who could not afford to be careless. I needed this job. I still wasn't quite sure what it entailed, but whatever Lydia's "little bit of everything" was, it would become my mission because Lydia was my first step into a real future. I had no intention of being a disaster, of dragging strange men up to my maid's room or coming to work hungover. This wasn't throwaway time for me like it had been for the other, more privileged girls. This time was real, Madame Fidelio.

"You have no accent." Her tone hovered between mistrust and admiration.

"I lived in Paris when I was younger. I had cousins here, cousins of my father's. My grandfather came from France to America but his brother stayed here, and his children were my dad's favorite relatives. His only relatives really. I stayed with them for two years."

"They will be happy to see you again, no?"

"They have retired and moved away. They were teachers in Paris, because they were sent here by the school system, but they always knew they would go home, to Orléans. So, I'll have to take the train to visit them sometime."

"That is a good thing, to be attached to your roots. My husband and I, we return to our family in Portugal every August."

Watching Madame Fidelio's slow understanding nod as she spoke, I was struck by the force of my cousins' nostalgia. As a kid, I never thought much about the fact that Solange and Jacques were always scrimping and saving to build a small retirement house in a development outside their native town despite the fact of forty working years in Paris. It was simply the state of things. But it now struck me as incredible to have so concrete a vision of the future guiding your every youthful move, to know you will go home again, to live your life in a loop.

I thought Madame Fidelio might begin to tell me more about herself, perhaps her own plan to return home someday for good, but instead she said that I was prettier than the last girl and repeated that my French was *impressionnant*.

Relief sunk in. Along with gratitude to my cousins for their patient teaching. When Lydia arrived, she would learn from her faithful concierge that I had told the truth about my fluency back in New York, and our first bond of trust would be forged.

But, even more striking was the fact that I had impressed the impressive Madame Fidelio. I must, in fact, be someone.

She looked at me, smiled.

I read my substance in her eyes.

"I do not know if the young *monsieur* is awake yet," she said. "Perhaps we should not ring the doorbell. I have a key to the apartment, of course. *Allons.*"

It took me a few seconds, as we walked across the interior courtyard toward a staircase at the back, to mentally match "young *monsieur*" to Olivier, boyfriend of Lydia's daughter, Portia, who was a couple of years younger than I. Olivier was going to show me around the apartment before he left later today for the final leg of his European trip. Madame Fidelio's hushed and reverential tone suggested a prince.

"Does he like to sleep in?" Although I had quite forgotten his existence until now, my curiosity was suddenly acute.

"He is often pale. He has many *soucis,* I think. But he is *charmant.*"

"*Ah, bon.*" What kind of *soucis?* What troubles?

I could see why Lydia had said the courtyard was precious. It was cobblestoned and planted with manicured trees in ornate pots, with dignified doors and tall windows rising all around. The building's inner walls formed a plush lining to this jewel box, known only to its owners and their secret guests. I felt a thrill of initiation. I also saw Clarence's point. There was almost no sunlight. It was indeed a little dark and depressing.

The apartment was on the ground floor. As Madame Fidelio turned her key, I recognized the firm, if vaguely tender, expression from the final plate in Lydia's latest book, *Parisians*. It was a book of portraits that began with the famous literary critic Jacques Derrida, in a bathrobe, in front of a bowl of coffee at the white plastic table in his suburban garden, and ended with this Portuguese concierge. The book had been criticized. They said Lydia Schell had lost her edge. *Parisians* was a mixture of Who's who and *noblesse oblige*. But it had sold better than anything else she had done.

We came into an entry hall half-painted a color I could only call eggplant. The painting work must have stopped suddenly because the last brush-stroke of purple dripped down the creamy primer.

Madame Fidelio clucked at the unfinished walls. *"Pauvre Madame Lydia,"* she said cryptically. Then she signaled me to follow her down a long paneled hallway with many doors, some closed, some ajar enough to give me clues as I passed, a swatch of fabric, the pattern of a rug, the flicker of a mirror.

Only one door was fully opened. I saw an unmade twin bed with a pale blue ruffle in the same fabric as the drapes. I could not tell whether there were flowers or little figures on the fabric, but something was going on, something delicate and complicated. There was a dressing table strewn with bottles and tiny baskets.

"C'est la chambre de la jolie petite."

La jolie petite must be Portia. I thought of the fine-boned blond girl in the red leather frame back in the dining room clutter of the Greenwich Village house. As I wondered how Madame Fidelio might describe me, I tried to tread lightly down the hallway, a girl accustomed to bed ruffles that matched her drapes. A girl with a dressing table perhaps.

After a time, the hallway forked. That door down to the right, said Madame Fidelio, was Monsieur Clarence's study. We veered left into the kitchen, which, on first glance, was less substantial than Lydia's kitchen in New York. The appliances here were white, not stainless, and they appeared half-sized.

On the wall was a framed series of Lydia's magazine covers. There was a *Rolling Stone* cover of Jim Morrison and one of Yoko Ono crying, holding a single wildflower in Central Park. There was a *Time* cover of Nelson Mandela. There was a *Life* cover that was probably the March on Washington. Martin Luther King was moving in a sea of signs. "Voting Rights Now!" "End Segregated Rules in Public Schools!" The March on Washington took place in 1963. That would make Lydia about my age when she took this photo. I wondered if she had felt young.

"Ah, monsieur!" Madame Fidelio smiled appreciatively, a woman who approved of men.

Young Monsieur was sitting at the kitchen table. He was tousled, and there was a fresh warmth to him, a waft of the morning bread from the *boulangeries* I could remember from my childhood.

He must have just emerged from that soft rustled bed I had glimpsed from the hallway, Portia's bed. Without being able to look straight at him, I knew he was the most attractive person I'd ever seen. He was reedy and lithe. His hair tumbled like light over features of brushed elegance, light brown eyes, cheekbones curved and quick as the paws of a cat.

"Bonjour, Madame Fidelio." He had an American accent.

There was a flicker of annoyance in his face, surely at the invasion of his last private moments in the apartment, but the flicker disappeared as his gaze lit on me, and in the lifting of Monsieur's irritation I felt myself uplifted, blessed, sun-kissed.

"You must be Kate. I'm Olivier."

"Sorry to bother you so early." It was just before ten o'clock. "Lydia says you're leaving for Italy today. You probably have a lot to do."

"Tomorrow, actually." He smiled. "I don't fly to Venice until tomorrow morning. And I'll be back in a couple of weeks to pick up most of my stuff before I head out for good. So, I'm mellow." He flung a wave of brown curls out of his eyes and looked at me again. Then he rose and put the kettle on. "Tea? Madame Fidelio? Kate?"

Madame Fidelio said she would leave us. Here was my key to the main apartment. Here was the key to the maid's room on the sixth floor where I would live. But not the sixth floor on this staircase. The *escalier de service*. Monsieur would show Mademoiselle, please.

"*Pas de problème, Madame Fidelio,*" he said.

"*Merci beaucoup, Madame!*" I added. "*Vous êtes gentille de vous occuper de moi.*"

"*Bonne journée, mes petits.*"

The three of us smiled indulgently at one another. Again, I felt a certain pride in sensing I had made a favorable first impression on regal Madame Fidelio. I had passed through my first gate.

"How do you like your tea?" Olivier asked once she had gone.

"I like milk, if there is any."

He took a carton from the small refrigerator.

My cousins' refrigerator had been an even tinier affair, drawerless, without a working light. But I had bright memories of the food packages inside, and they were revived in a flurry by the box in Olivier's slender hand. It was *longue conservation* milk, the kind everyone here drank. It could sit in that box for months until you snipped one of the corners and began to pour. It had a chemical smell that used to make me nauseated. I hated it. I had never told Mom because she had had more important things on her mind at the time, but the milk here was terrible.

"I got some honey at the farmers' market on Boulevard Raspail. Would you like some in your tea?"

I had forgotten I liked honey but was suddenly longing for it.

"Sure. Honey would be great. I've never been to the market on Raspail. Is it wonderful? I haven't been to Paris in over ten years."

"Where did you get that accent? You sounded totally native talking to Madame Fidelio just now."

I fell back on well-rehearsed lines. "I think the timing of when I learned was perfect. I was here between the ages of nine and eleven, young enough to get the accent and old enough to intellectualize the language."

"No, you must be gifted. I've spent years here on and off and my mother's French and I sound awful."

"I doubt that."

He laughed gently. "Spend some time with me then."

I felt brave enough to glance into his eyes.

"So you're fresh off the plane," he said. He made my freshness sound like the quality of a flower or an apple. "Lydia says you're a painter. Is there anything you want to see today, any art, anything in particular in Paris?"

"She told me you'd only have a few hours before you caught your plane and you'd barely have time to show me the alarm and the washing machine and such."

She told me you were charming.

"But I don't leave until tomorrow, remember? I love Lydia, but she has a lot on her mind. We can't expect her to remember other people's schedules. I have a whole day. I thought maybe I'd just walk around. I have to pick something up in the Sixteenth. Figured I'd go to the Marmottan. You know, where all the Monet waterlilies are? I haven't been there this trip. I know it's not very cool or contemporary, but I'm a nostalgic person." He sighed. "I'm about to start a job in New York. Investment banking. I doubt I'll have time to *flâner* in the foreseeable future. So I'm open. What do *you* want to do?"

"Can we get a croissant?"

three

At the *pâtisserie* on the corner, Olivier asked what I would like.

A plain croissant, please.

He bought it for me, and ordered a pain au chocolat and a pain aux raisins for himself.

We wandered over into the Seventh Arrondissement. On the rue du Bac, we passed the luxurious grocery store Hédiard, and I smiled inside because Hédiard had been a joke in my cousins' house. When Étienne and Jacques would refuse second helpings of Solange's food, she would say, "If this isn't good enough for you, *changez de restaurant! Allez chez Hédiard!*"

I wondered now if Solange knew that Hédiard wasn't a restaurant, but a famous store with Art Nouveau windows framing pyramids of fruit and pastries against a luscious depth of cheeses and exotic teas in red-lacquered drawers. But what caught my eye, as we floated by, was a silver tray of croissants à la crème de marron. I loved chestnuts, and imagined chestnut cream to be something otherworldly. These chestnut croissants, with their dusting of powdered sugar, struck me as the most delicious things I could possibly eat, but I wasn't sad that I didn't have one at this moment. I still had half of the plain croissant that Olivier had bought for me, and I knew I could wander to Hédiard on my own anytime from now on. I lived nearby.

My lack of covetousness toward today's uneaten treasure was so marked that I wondered if I hadn't become a new person. So often I was defined by what I could not have.

Olivier veered away from me into Hédiard. I moved to follow him, but he told me to give him a second. When he reappeared, it was with two of the chestnut croissants. "Second breakfast." He winked.

When we reached the Seine, I gazed across to the Grande Roue, the giant Ferris wheel that comes to the Tuilleries a couple of times a year.

He saw me staring. "You'd like to ride in it too, wouldn't you? It's a great way to get the lay of the land if you haven't been to Paris for a while. Let's go."

We had a compartment to ourselves. Our knees grazed in the metal seat. Whenever the wheel stopped, we rocked into each other, pretending not to notice, talking too much.

After the ride, we were altered and unsteady. We walked quietly along the Right Bank all the way to the Sixteenth, where we picked up a small paper bag that he said was for Lydia.

"I get along with her pretty well," he ventured. "But she's complicated. And the family is complicated. You're in for some interesting times. I hope you've been taking your vitamins."

I wanted more information about Lydia and her mysterious family, but I also didn't want to be reminded that this boy across this café table from me sipping Belgian beer, drawing glances from all around, belonged to them.

I reminded him that he had mentioned the Marmottan museum with the Monets.

"Are you sure you want to go?" he asked.

"I would love to."

"That didn't sound entirely convincing." He looked at me with an attention I had rarely felt. "Are you being polite?"

"No, no, I'm strange about the Impressionists, the style. I don't have my own style yet, so I get a bit wary, and impressed, so to speak." I giggled lamely. "But I'd like to go. I'd like to look at the actual paintings. I've seen so many reproductions."

"You can't not have a style."

"Think about mirrors. No style, right?"

"You're funny," he smiled, making my funniness into an appreciable quality, a style of its own.

He told me his mother used to take him to the Marmottan on trips to Paris when he was a boy. It was her favorite museum because it was small and perfect, a *bijou*. He always made at least one pilgrimage when he was in town. "She loves the place and the paintings, and it's hard for her to travel these days. Her circumstances aren't what they used to be. Hopefully, I can start bringing her back once I'm working and I can afford it. Anyway, her favorite thing about this museum is the series of footbridges over the lily pads. I think you'll see why."

As we walked uphill to the end of the rue de Passy and through a dainty park, Olivier's eyes gleamed with what I took to be memory.

"What are *your* parents like?" he asked.

"Well, my dad died when I was eleven. While I was living in Paris actually. The whole time he was dying of cancer, he kept writing me letters about how happy he was that I got to be here, living with his cousin Jacques whom he adored, and learning French. He never really got fluent in French. His own dad didn't speak it to him—I guess he wanted him to fit in in America—and Dad had this idea that my learning the langauge would somehow make my life complete."

"You must miss him."

"I think about him all the time, try to guess what he would say if he could see me, especially here."

"I'm sorry," he said.

I shook my head. "It's okay."

"So, did your mom bring you up? I mean, after?"

"Basically. I guess you could say my mom is wonderful. I mean, she was supposed to have another kind of life. My dad was an up-and-coming movie director when she married him. She probably thought she was going to have fun, but ended up taking care of him when he got sick and then working hard as a secretary, an executive secretary in a law firm, but still a secretary, when she could have done something truly interesting with her life. She's slaved all these years to send me to good schools and she's proud of me. It's been just the two of us since I came home from France. She lets me do these things that make her seem almost liberal, like coming to Paris to work for Lydia, but it's because she believes in some form of well-roundedness to prepare you for life. Actually, she's obsessed with me becoming a corporate lawyer because what she wants for me more than anything is security, and she knows that you can't rely on anyone but yourself for that. And I feel terrible about not wanting to be a lawyer. But I really don't. I don't think that way at all. Logically, I mean. I don't think logically. It would be torture."

I was suddenly embarrassed. Had I been talking this whole time? Did I seem disloyal to Mom? Was I?

"You know, Kate, I've only just met you, but you appear to me to be many things at once. So, you may not have the luxury of diving into your dreams right away. Almost no one does. I've thought about this a lot. Not everyone can do everything in the ideal order. That's what children of privilege don't have to face."

I imagined that he too dreamed of the freedoms of privilege and I felt intensely jealous of Portia, but only for a second because the next thing he said was, "They get so hedonistic sometimes, it makes them soft. Portia and Joshua have their good points, but they are incredibly spoiled. They just don't get it like we do."

At the mention of Joshua, I was startled into recalling that Portia had a problematic younger brother. I felt the onrush of all I had yet to know.

We stood in a room full of different colored impressions of the footbridge in Monet's Japanese garden at Giverny. Olivier explained that his mother had told him that it was impossible to know that this was a bridge from looking at only one of the paintings by itself. You needed the series of views superimposed in your head for the true image to take shape.

"I see what she means," I said. "It's a beautiful trick. Pretend

14

you don't know what they are supposed to be and walk around until the bridge comes out at you."

These paintings were gorgeous, but they made me uncomfortable. Even though they had become classics, they took an intimidating leap of faith, painting the light instead of the contours of the thing itself, letting the subject slowly emerge on a magical surface. I was convinced I could never do such a thing. I was too literal. I loved the Monets, but I didn't entirely trust them.

In a nearby tearoom, over the tiniest and most expensive of tomato tarts, which Oliver treated me to, he finally told me what was in the bag he had just gotten for Lydia. "Papaya extract pills, probably mixed with speed. She gets them from a diet guru up here."

"Why are *you* picking them up?"

"She likes to involve people she feels close to in her fetching and carrying. It's an emotional thing. She'd never ask Clarence because she would feel too judged, but I'm sure she'll want you to do it. She starts by asking you to pick something up somewhere without telling you what it is. But she always ends up blurting it out sooner or later. She can't not confess eventually, but she controls her timing."

"Maybe that's what makes her such a great artist."

"Yeah, that's what you have to remember when you're tempted to make fun of her for wanting to funnel baguettes and cheese all day, then sending you out for these damn pills. She's amazing at what she does."

We made our way back across the Seine and over to the Sixth with a detour through the Rodin Sculpture Garden, where we sat on a bench and watched children feed ducks in the shadow of Balzac. How lucky to grow up here, we agreed.

I asked him about the signet ring on his finger.

It was a *chevalière* with the coat of arms from his mother's side of the family. He wore it for her.

"Is that castle on there your long-lost château somewhere deep in the Dordogne?"

"The Loire, actually." He laughed. "But you're right, it's long-gone. The land is gone too. They sold it when my mother was a child. The only piece of it left is the 'de' in her name. It's my middle name. I'm Olivier de Branche Craft."

Suddenly, I felt light among the statues in this venerable garden. Amid all these voluptuous stones straining toward life, just short of breathing, here I was so very alive without even trying. The simple stupid joy of it was overwhelming.

I stole a glance at Olivier. I felt my throat catch. I had to say something to make sure that I could still speak.

"Olivier *de* Branche," I said, with emphasis on the particle, and I reached to touch the golden ring. "Maybe you'll be able to rebuild the château for your mother one day."

"You're sweet, but I'd settle for a *pied-à-terre* in the Sixth."

I pulled my hand into my lap.

Back at the apartment, we sat in the half-painted living room and drank Lydia's white wine infused with a crème de pêche. She had gotten Olivier hooked on her peach Kirs while they were here together last month. Olivier had been traveling in Europe all summer, mostly without Portia, who I gathered was interning at a fashion magazine in New York and was now headed back to college for her junior year. I wanted both to picture her and to block her out, so that I had a filmy image of her as a drowned princess or a girl frozen in a magazine.

Being in the Schells' living room, among their many possessions, cast a sheen of formality back over Olivier and me, and we started conversing seriously. I tried hard to ignore the fact that each of his words was a little drumbeat between my legs.

"Lydia and I were good roommates," he said. "She got me on this routine of starting with her Kirs around five."

We looked at an ornate clock that had been taken down by the painters and was leaning against a striped silk ottoman. A fraying wire connected the clock to a hole in the wall above the mantel. It was quarter to five.

"We're knocking off early," I tried to laugh.

I had to stop myself from drinking too quickly and asking too many questions. My curiosity about this household was intense, but so was my awareness that Olivier was completely bound up in it.

After three Kirs with no food, I began to feel dizzy. Struggling to my feet, I said I had to go to bed. I couldn't even count the hours since I had last slept. The jet lag was catching up to me.

Didn't I want some dinner?

"No thank you." Mom had taught me what a waste of time it was to long for the unattainable.

"Goodbye, then." But I couldn't quite close the door. "Maybe when you're back between Italy and the States? Are you staying in Paris for a day or two then?" I hoped I sounded nonchalant. "Will you stay here?"

"I'm not sure that's such a good idea."

I blushed.

He smiled sadly. "But I might not be able to help myself," he said. Flecks of green melted in his brown eyes as he leaned in for what I realized in the nick of time was a double-cheek kiss. The curls that only this morning had seemed such a rare vision actually brushed my neck, and then it was over.

I stumbled backward.

"Not sure of my exact dates yet," he whispered, "but I'll see you in two or three weeks."

As soon as I reached my own tiny space, I knew I was too tipsy and tired to unpack. But I did manage to rummage for a half-eaten turkey sandwich I had leftover from the plane. My first dinner in Paris, alone, staring out at a sea of blinking windows. I had no idea what I was doing here. This was not the Paris of Jacques and Solange, bound by all the limitations of decency, where I first discovered how faithfully I could draw in the illustrated letters I sent home. This was a city whose shapes were still unclear. I had no idea what tomorrow would look like, except that it would be empty of the only person I thought I needed to see.

17

I forced down a final chalky bite.

I wondered what Olivier might have whipped up for me in the kitchen downstairs. A recipe of his mother's? Of Lydia's?

In a couple of weeks, he would pass through my life again, on his way back to Portia, whom we had hardly touched upon all day. Slender Portia of the toile and the bed skirt. Portia who was not me.

four

Lydia had told me that my sixth-floor maid's room, the garret that came attached to "every Paris apartment," would have a view of the Luxembourg Gardens. When I woke that first morning to the alarm on my digital watch, I looked out to the promised sliver of green visible through rain-glossed rooftops.

I had not told Lydia that my cousins had not had a maid's room, or a *cave* for their wine for that matter, nor had I told her that it might be a problem for me to pay the $400-a-month rent for her maid's room out of my salary. I had said that, of course, I understood, and I had implied that I was among the lucky few who did not have to worry about such things. The world was elitist, and this was a funny if slightly embarrassing fact. Common knowledge. The *chambre de bonne* with a view, *c'était normal,* normal at any price.

The rooftops and the little corner of Luxembourg trees in my line of sight were glossy and trembling. The room was spartan, but I took my time in arranging it with my few things. I had an hour before Lydia was to call me with my first instructions.

On an old trunk, I made a neat pile of books next to a framed black and white snapshot of my mother and father with me as a plump five-year-old with short hair, outsized eyes and an unsure smile for the camera. Dad was already sick in the picture. His own smile was strained, but he was still trying. Mom had unimaginably long hair and a roundness to her that I couldn't actually remember, but the firm set of her mouth was the same as today.

I put my clothes on wire hangers on a bare metal bar, next to the single futon on the floor.

"We bought the futon for the last assistant because the springs in the old bed were simply gone," Lydia had said. "It's so comfortable that I'm a little jealous. Maybe we'll get one for Portia. Can you imagine? Portia on a futon on the floor? She'd probably love it. She's always saying she hates her bedroom in Paris, that it's too precious."

My bathroom was tiny and strange, a shower stall with a curtain that didn't quite reach the floor and an electric toilet that made an alarming suction sound. The door was plastic and folded like an accordion. The sink was outside, next to a camping stove and a tiny refrigerator. In the cupboard by the refrigerator, I found a few dishes and a box of verveine tea bags. There was still sugar in the sugar bowl, but otherwise there was no sign of the disastrous assistant who had preceded me.

The string of events that led me to this garret was so tenuous that I believed it might snap at any moment and send me hurtling back across the Atlantic to the nothingness from which I'd come, to Peter, the noncommittal boyfriend who finally called it off, to the professors who told me that I had to outgrow my delusion that accurate contour drawing was art, to the mother who said she would hire me an LSAT tutor if I promised to get my act together.

It was only this past May that Lydia called me at school to say she had gotten my letter and résumé. She liked the fact that I had been a volunteer lifeguard in Nicaragua. Was my French really fluent? She needed to fire the assistant she had in Paris because she wasn't working out. "I am far from uptight, but this girl has no morals." Her voice was hoarse and breathy. So could I take the train into the city as soon as possible to meet with her? "I'm in the Village," she said.

"Of course. I'll come tomorrow."

I was stunned that she had responded to me.

20

One of my college roommates had told me about the job with Lydia Schell. "I used to be friends with her daughter, Portia. They're both kind of crazy, mother and daughter, but pretty brilliant. She always needs an assistant in Paris and it's probably an interesting gig. Write to her. You can use my name."

So, I had gone to the library and found books of Lydia Schell's photographs. I had quickly learned that she had been a part of everything that mattered in recent history. I had written to her.

Lydia had made her name photographing the Civil Rights Movement and Vietnam War protests. Now she traveled all over the world, but she was based in Europe as a magazine correspondent, mostly for *Vanity Fair* of late. She was famous for a framing device whereby her pictures looked like they were from the point of view of one of their own subjects. They felt very intimate, but they told far-reaching and important stories.

After initial skepticism, Mom had been suitably impressed by my reports of Lydia Schell's fame to support my effort. This was why she had sacrificed to send me to a good school, so that I would have this kind of opportunity. But I shouldn't simply drift on it. I should make sure I always knew where the opportunity was taking me because people like us could not afford not to be practical.

"So, you're telling me she's in the big leagues," said Mom, with the beginnings of approval.

"Mom, she probably won't even answer my letter."

"Well, then it won't have been for you, will it? And you can use your French in a law firm. Max said he would be able to get you a paralegal job in any major city in the world in a heartbeat." She took a rare pause. "But they do say," she went on, "that law schools are looking for variety these days. Think about how that week in Nicaragua helped you get into college. You wrote such a great essay about it, remember? So your law school application may end up stronger if you work for this woman."

"Is that why you let me go to Nicaragua? To give me a better shot at college. Well, Mom, don't get your hopes up."

But when Lydia did answer me, I took the train from New

Haven into New York City the next day and found my way from Grand Central Station to the Christopher Street subway stop. I had only been to Manhattan a handful of times, had no mental map of it, and did not picture it this cozy and leafy. The streets were sun-dappled and people looked friendly.

Lydia's New York home was a four-story townhouse. I rang the bell and was let into a foyer by a maid who turned quickly away. It smelled like wet paint.

"Hello! Is this color terrible?" Lydia came toward me, hand outstretched. She swallowed audibly and looked alarmed at the lavender walls. There was a slight bulge to her eyes that made them catch light like fruit in a still life. They glistened with the sheen of the fresh paint. Although I did not know what color the insides of townhouses were supposed to be, my instinct told me that she was displeased with the lavender and that I should be too.

"It might be a little too Eastery," I ventured, "for a first impression of such a great house."

"I couldn't agree more. My husband has no eye for color. But this is far from the worst of it. You have to come see what he's done in here." She led me into a living room with tarps over the furniture and gestured to the walls. "This looks like a melon, doesn't it? The man wants me to feel like I'm living inside a melon."

"You think it's on purpose?"

"So you agree that it looks like a goddamn cantaloupe in here? We see eye-to-eye on this? I have to know so he doesn't think it's just me being difficult."

"Well, it's definitely fruity. Maybe a little darker than a cantaloupe, though? Maybe you could tell your husband it looks like a papaya."

"Don't get me started on papayas. Have you heard about this papaya diet? The enzyme that's supposed to make you lose weight? I'm going to start again as soon as I get back to Europe. Have you ever done it? It's disgusting, but it works."

"I like papayas."

"Well maybe we can do it together, then. You and me and

Portia. We'll do it when she comes during her school breaks. Then it won't be quite so miserable. Anyway, I'm sorry the place is such a shambles. Let's go into the dining room and sit down. They haven't started on this room yet. It's not going to be green anymore. Green is supposed to be an unappetizing color. I don't know what we were thinking. We haven't painted in about ten years. We're going to do red this time. Maybe you could take a look at the swatches on the table. And there's a menu there. I hope you like Chinese food. I was going to order lunch." She began rummaging through papers on the dining room table. "God, I can't find it! No one puts anything away around here." She walked to a doorway and yelled up a mahogany staircase. "Joshua! Joshua! Where's the Excellent Dumpling House menu?"

No answer from Joshua. Lydia's eyes shone a sad pale green. "I think I know what happened," she said. "The maid is on the rampage against us ever since Portia's boyfriend started sleeping over. It's breaking her heart. She's been with us since before Portia was born, and suddenly I'm a terrible mother in her eyes and my lovely daughter is turning into a slut. It's more than she can take, I think. She can't keep track of anything. And she's throwing stuff out right and left as though she owned the place."

"Is this the menu?" I asked.

"You godsend, you. So have a seat and tell me what you'd like and then we'll get down to business."

Not wanting to seem indecisive or difficult, I read out the first dish I spotted under the lunch specials. "Beef with broccoli."

"Are you sure? The orange beef is better."

"Orange beef is probably more interesting. I'll try it."

"It comes with spring rolls. Do you want spring rolls?"

"Absolutely!"

"Because if you don't want them, my son Joshua will eat them. I'm going to give him mine. Spring rolls are one of the few things he'll eat. He's in a phase."

"I'm sure I don't need my spring rolls. Chinese food is always so big."

"Yes, but in a few weeks we'll be living on papayas, remember? Give me a second."

She went through a swinging door into a kitchen with a big island in the middle, stacked with magazines and newspapers. Cast iron pots hung dangerously over her head as she dialed the Excellent Dumpling House.

I looked around the dining room. An arrestingly pretty and delicate blond looked out at me from a red-leather-framed picture on the sideboard. This must be Portia. I took a step toward her, saw that she had her mother's overround eyes and that there was a bitter undertone to her smile. She had a golden dusting of freckles, which made me think the picture had been taken during the summer, on some exotic vacation. I had always wanted freckles.

Lydia ordered our lunch without ceremony and came back to me.

"So I take it you know nothing about photography, which is good. I'm not looking for an apprentice. That's part of the problem with the girl I have now. She wants to be me and she can't believe it might take a little work. That and she acts like she was raised by wolves. Wakes up with a different boy every morning. But anyway, you're a painter? You have an eye?"

"Not really. Not that kind." My eyes skidded over the green walls. In my letter to her, I had written that I was interested in fine arts, in all that Paris had to teach me. I hadn't been specific. But she had paint on the brain, and besides I was twenty-two and I ought to have an ambition by now. Something beyond the simple love of drawing. By this point in life, you had to want to be something, even if it was going to change. You needed direction.

"I do dream of being a painter," I stammered. "But I love photography too. I mean I appreciate photography. I could never do it myself. I'm inspired by it though. I think your work is amazing. And your writing about photography. Your books. Everything. I grew up with *Changes* and *Human Landscapes*. So, I feel like I know you. And through you, ever since I was little, I feel like I knew Martin Luther King."

"What a lovely thing to say. So, were you really a lifeguard in

Nicaragua? I was down there, you know. I did some great work on the Sandanista Literacy Campaign."

"I saw your photo of Ortega getting the Nobel Prize for vaccinating so many children."

"You liked that shot? My family hated it. They thought it was creepy."

"I thought it was moving. And something about the angle—I can't explain it—it felt like it was taken from the perspective of a young child."

"Nice to know somebody notices things. Anyway, what about your French? It has to be good, you know. All my business in Europe is done in French. All the important agencies are French now. I need you to promise it's decent."

I thought about breaking into French, but decided not to because something told me that hers might not be so great, even though she was a genius.

When our lunch came, we ate on Limoges china that she said she had just inherited and was on the fence about. The china was kept in a piece of furniture that was called a hutch, I learned. I did not touch my spring rolls.

"I'll put these away for Joshua," she said, then she yelled up the stairs again, "Joshua!" In the ensuing silence, she cleared her throat. "He'll be down to forage after dark. So, do you have any questions about the job? As I say, it's a little bit of everything."

I had no idea what she meant, but I wanted it. "It sounds fantastic."

"But I haven't told you about the money yet, have I? Condé Nast is so cheap—and they're my only steady client these days, because you can't count on the agencies for anything—that I'm embarrassed to say this is the kind of job you can't take unless you have another means of support. Jesus, it's so elitist to talk like this I should be shot, but you know how it is."

I nodded.

"So, they give me a hundred and fifty a week for an assistant. But they only pay part of the rent on my Paris apartment and the assistant has to rent the maid's quarters, you know the *chambre de bonne* up on the sixth floor. It's a great little garret, very romantic, with a sublime glimpse of the Luxembourg through a dormer window. You'll love it. That's about four hundred a month, which doesn't leave a whole lot. So, you'll need help from your family."

"That shouldn't be a problem," I lied again.

Lydia told me the house in Paris was being painted too and would surely look like Beirut. She might not be there when I arrived in September to begin work, but her husband, Clarence, surely would because he was taking a sabbatical this school year to write in Paris. She hoped I would stop him from doing anything too hideous with the walls.

five

It was ten-fifteen. The phone was beside me on the kitchen table. I kept touching it.

I sweetened my tea with Olivier's honey.

With my first sip, the kitchen grew a shade homier. The Washington marchers lowered their eyelids toward me, less imposing than intimate despite being on the cover of *Life*. I felt the flicker of their benevolence. Even Jim Morrison was beginning to know me. But my place in this wonderful web was tenuous. If I messed up this phone call, I might "not work out," and then what would I do?

It was ten twenty-two.

The phone rang. I picked up and gave my cheeriest, *"Allo?"*

"Listen, Katherine, I'm pressed for time, but you arrived okay? Was Olivier still there when you showed up?"

"Just barely."

"Madame Fidelio was decent? She takes a while to warm up. The last girl quite threw her. I've told her you're vastly different, but she'll take her sweet time. Anyway, I have a meeting in two minutes, but here's what I'd like you to do. Can you clip and précis anything in *Le Monde* or *Libération* on Germany for the next few weeks? There's a box of petty cash in the far right drawer of my desk to buy the papers with. Don't forget to put all your receipts back in the box. Start today. I have to keep a time line for the photos."

"A time line? What exactly—"

27

"Use the files in my office. Start a new one for the Wall. And you can clip *Le Canard enchaîné* too, but only if you see something interesting. I find it so hard to follow, don't you? Oh, and did Olivier mention a package for me?"

"There's a bag in the kitchen with your name on it."

"Could you look inside?"

"It's a bottle of what looks like vitamins."

"What does the bottle say?"

"*Extrait de papaye.*"

"God, that's a nice accent."

"Thanks."

"I'm going to have to have you make all my French calls. Anyway, you're sure that's what it says? Good. What about the paint?"

"It looks like the entryway and the living room are about half-done."

"Listen, do me a favor. When Clarence shows up tomorrow, do a walk-through with him and get him to tell you the names of the colors. He won't tell me, but I'm sure he'll tell you and I need to know what he's up to."

"The names of the colors?"

"Yes. Find out what he thinks the colors are. Find out what is going on in his mind. Then you can tell me what they really are, but right now I have a very important meeting. I don't mean to be abrupt, but you're fine, right?"

"Great, I'm great. Thanks for everything."

"Your *chambre* is clean? She didn't sabotage it?"

"No, she left me tea and sugar."

"I'm sure she didn't mean to. Anyway, Olivier didn't say anything in particular? Nothing going on?"

"I barely saw him. He had to leave right away."

"Well, good. I'm glad you're settled. Now, call your mother. She'll want to know you've landed. Do you know how to make a collect call from France?"

"Sure. I just have to wait until it's late enough in California."

"Listen, my German translator has shown up. Tell Clarence,

when he gets there, to expect a call from me tomorrow evening, around five."

Clip and précis. Knowing the definition of the words didn't illuminate Lydia's meaning. How did one keep a time line? How could she trust me to synthesize international events and to fathom her husband's ideas about paint color? And which part of my job was the more important? All the tasks she listed sounded equally urgent. "A little bit of everything."

I went into Lydia's office, off the main hallway, to investigate. The room's two windows framed the small interior garden, one degree further removed from the street than the quiet courtyard, the gem within the gem. Almost no one ever saw this garden, with its pleasantly overgrown geometric plots, outlined in pale stone, and its wrought iron table with a glass top where someone, Olivier surely, had left a china cup that must be full of rainwater by now.

Despite its harmonious view, the office was unsettling. Its topography was like nothing I had experienced. There were piles of papers everywhere. There were file cabinets, an enormous desk with a giant computer, an armoire full of supplies, a Rolodex. There were envelopes from Condé Nast and from a photo agency called Maxim. There were proof sheets full of people I had never seen and places I did not recognize, all marked up in white china marker, in a mysterious and beautiful code of circles and X's and arrows.

I picked up a magnifying glass from Lydia's desk and looked through it. At first, all I saw was a close-up of a boy in a knit hat with a faraway look in his eyes. Then I noticed a guitar strap over his shoulder, then a tank rolling behind him. There was a Post-it above the boy that read, "learning English from Bob Dylan records, hopes to go West."

There was another sheet of soft circles of light over shadowy-colored backgrounds. It proved to be a candlelight vigil on the West Berlin side of the Wall. A bearded man held a white candle up in front of a silver-gray vulture with clenched claws and an alarmingly focused downward glare. A baby in a pouch slept in the glow of her mother's candle, behind them the word TRACE spray-painted a ghostly outline over layers and layers of bold block letters. There was a couple sharing a candle by a soaring Japanese manga boy, with a lean muscular chest, white wings and red hair whipped upward by the wind into the shape of a flame. There were German names and cartoon animals bathed in candlelight. An old woman smiled behind her candle, her teeth sparkling from the depths of her shawl. So this was how people looked in Berlin.

But what about clipping and précising?

In the top drawer of the first file cabinet I opened, I found a manila folder labeled "Germany Time Line." I smiled. On the front of the folder was a magazine cutout of a pillared monument. On closer look, there was a rushing bronze chariot on top. I didn't recognize anything about it until I read a quote below: "'The German Question will remain open as long as the Brandenburg Gate is closed.'— JFK. The Brandenburg Gates."

Mom had a recording of the *Brandenburg* Concertos that she had played during breakfast on almost every morning of my childhood in order to make me smart. Now I realized where those concertos came from. I opened the Brandenburg file. There were Xerox-ed clippings and a date-by-date summary of the articles. The summary ended a little over a week ago, when the last girl must have gone. A time line. Perhaps I could be trusted after all.

I took some cash from the box in Lydia's drawer, went out, found a news kiosk, bought *Le Monde*, *Libération* and some strawberry Hollywood chewing gum.

It had stopped raining.

The German story of the day was about a hundred arrests at a demonstration in Liepzig. Helmut Kohl, the prime minister of West Germany, had denounced them.

Back in the office, I turned on the electric typewriter. Lydia told me not to touch her computer. It was easily sabotaged, she said.

I found the scissors in a mug that said VOGUE.

I took a moment to feel impressed by my new boss. She was creating art that would refract for years through millions of eyes and brains and hearts. Even though she was probably driving some poor translator in Germany crazy right now, she was giving meaning to her times.

My own mother back home, what was she doing? She was smoothing things over for a powerful man, a lawyer who was not her husband. She was organizing lives, his, mine, hers to some extent. But what was she making? What did she mean?

I stopped cutting *Libération* and picked up the proof sheet closest to the computer, all close-ups of a half-smiling man labeled "Portraits of Salman" in red crayon.

Even I knew who Salman was. Muslim extremists had put a price on his head for "offensive" passages in his novel *The Satanic Verses*. In these images, he appeared quiet and resolved. I gazed into his sympathetic eyes.

My communion with Salman Rushdie was short-lived. When the phone rang, I dropped the pictures, leaped to the ringer on Lydia's desk. It was touch-tone. Modern.

"*Allo?*"

"Who is this?" It was a young woman's voice, soft and faintly accusatory.

"This is Kate. I'm Lydia Schell's assistant. Can I help you?" I asked, pleased with my imitation of professionalism.

"I'm Portia, Lydia's daughter. My mother is very busy right now so she has asked me to call you with some instructions for the house."

"Hi, Portia."

She came back quick and breathy. "Hi, listen, my mother asks that you call the plumber—his name is Monsieur Polanski and you'll find him in the Rolodex—because the toilet in her bathroom is running and also to tell Madame Fidelio to have the window washer come as soon as possible. Apparently the windows in my bedroom are filthy. Also, look out for a delivery for me from Maud Frizon."

"Maud Frizon?"

"Shoes"—she sounded as though she could barely mask her surprise at my ignorance. "Boots actually. A pair of boots I ordered last time I was in Paris. They're finally in."

"What should I do with the boots?"

"Oh, send them please. They're fall boots. I won't be in Europe before Thanksgiving."

"Sure."

"Thank you. That's very kind. Really. Listen, nice to meet you."

"Nice to meet you too."

So, Olivier dated a girl who liked her windows clean, who summoned window washers even though she lived on the ground floor, or rather had her mother's assistant summon them by way of her concierge.

Olivier must have been the one to tell her the windows were "filthy." After all, he had spent the last few nights in her ruffly room. Despite what he'd said about being an outsider like me, he must really be on her aesthetic plane.

It was all I could do not to hate her.

six

Nobody had told me that Clarence was British. Olivier's use of "pompous" to describe him, which I quickly found inaccurate, was probably meant as a synonym for British, but I had not caught on and was startled by his accent.

"Lovely to meet you. What do you go by, Katherine? Kate?"

I liked him immediately. "My friends call me Katie."

"Katie it is. I hope you were welcomed. Madame Fidelio can be a bit daft, but I trust she hasn't been too hostile. You are settling in?"

He was gangling, but with a fleshy face, full quivering lips and unruly curls that were turning silver. There were specks of dandruff on his glasses.

"Oh, Madame Fidelio was quite nice to me, and I'm fine. I absolutely love it here. It's unreal."

"Lydia will tell you it's a bit of a shambles, but I adore the place, even if the courtyard *is* sunless. How long have you been here now?"

"A week today. It's such a fantastic neighborhood." Could I sound any more like I had never left Southern California? Why did I always revert when I was nervous?

But he didn't seem to mind. My enthusiasm swept across his face. As he smiled almost youthfully, his glasses hopped. "So, I trust you're finding your way around?"

"I've been doing some exploring. Paris is the greatest city to walk in. I guess that's a cliché, but I mean it. It's the best city to wander around alone because it's so beautiful you feel like it's hugging you."

"An embrace, yes. Nicely put. These are the most satisfying streets to experience on one's own. And even when one arrives at this empty apartment, one feels welcomed, despite the vicious Portuguese sentry!"

We laughed.

Right away, I was comfortable with Clarence. Having spent long stretches of my adolescence imagining what life with a father would be like, I was emotionally primed for this man with his ripe, knowing face, as he took off his blazer in his half-painted entryway and ushered me into his living room with a gallant "please."

The leafy motif of his ascot matched the celadon stripe in the cushion where he rested his elbow as he settled into an armchair. The cushion was of the same striped fabric that covered the ottoman. I was beginning to notice patterns in the apartment where before there had only been striking, singular images. Was familiarity like this?

"Lydia said you teach comparative literature and that you're on sabbatical writing?"

"Did she happen to say what I was writing about?"

"Well, I don't know if she mentioned it, but I—"

"Oh, bloody hell!" His calm rippled furiously, then resettled.

"What's wrong?"

"Nothing, it's nothing. Just that ridiculous old clock. It's rubbish, but Lydia is very attached to it. I suppose it's valuable rubbish if such a thing can be. Expensive rubbish anyway. Why did the painters put it on the floor like that? Bloody idiots, all of them."

I had only looked at this clock to check the time with Olivier while we were drinking. I had not noticed that the clock face was set in a black tree ornamented with Rococo branches. Wrapped around the tree was a polished snake. And beside the tree, standing on the bronze base, was a fairy, fondling the snake with one hand and offering it a drink from a half-shell in the other. The snake was arching into the fairy's caress.

"It's not ticking, is it?" Again, a slight erosion of calm, then he chuckled. "But it serves her right. It's so hideous, that object."

"You're right, it's not ticking. I think it must have stopped. It was working when I got here. Last time I checked. A week ago."

"It's appalling-looking, don't you think? I mean, didn't it strike you as hideous when you first entered the room? That's not to say that it's uninteresting, historically. It's probably very revelatory of the 1830s, but that doesn't mean we need it in our living room, does it? For goodness sake, swastikas are revelatory."

"Well, it's not my taste, but there is something very French-looking about it."

"You're kind. Lydia did say that about you, that you seemed like a kind person."

"Goodness, thanks. So, what are you writing about?"

He looked at me as though he were about to pull a big box of chocolates from behind his back. He may have even winked.

"In a word," he said "'fashion.'"

I glanced at him, ascot askew in the collar of a rumpled Oxford shirt, brown cords, old-man shoes, a white flake on the glasses.

"Wow."

The telephone rang.

"That will be Lydia." He picked up a cream-colored rotary phone from a black-lacquered side table.

"Hello, my dear. Are the Huns brandishing their pickaxes yet?" He began to pace within the limits of the phone coil. "Yes, she's fine. . . . Yes, Olivier appears to be gone, thank God. And he doesn't appear to have murdered Katie or stolen or ransacked anything, although I did have to rescue a piece of your faience from the garden. He'd left one of your cups out there to the mercy of the elements. It was full of rainwater and dead leaves. Selfish twit . . . As I say, Lydia, she's fine. Why don't you ask her yourself?" With a meaningful look at the stopped clock on the floor, he put his finger to his lips. Then he handed me the receiver.

Lydia sounded awash in happiness, but a happiness that had nothing to do with Clarence and me and everything to do with faraway events. The Wall would break soon, she said. There was monumental pressure from both sides. That was all anyone was talking about. She was getting unbelievable shots. She kept interrupting herself to say "hello" and "wonderful to see you" so that our conversation was populated by prominent German ghosts. She told me that her Paris printer would be stopping by tomorrow to introduce herself and that the two of us should have a coffee—"keep the receipt"—because we would be working together from time to time. "She does all my black and white work in Europe." There was a loud social rumble. "Thank you!" she said away from the receiver, and I heard a clink and a cool rivulet down her throat. "Listen, I'll call you from somewhere quieter tomorrow, but I have to know, have you told Clarence about Yale yet?"

"About Yale?"

"He can't stand the Deconstructionists. They're his nemesis. He'll die when he finds out that I've hired a Deconstructionist from Yale to come work in the apartment. He'll just die. He'll moan that there's a traitor in his midst."

"But—"

"Just tell him. It's a joke, sweetheart. He's trying to be a Historicist."

"Of course, yeah." I giggled nervously.

"Listen, the prime minister has just arrived. I'll call you later."

Deconstruction was a joke? The form of literary criticism I had felt so terrible not mastering in college, hell, not even grasping, except to understand that all language pointed nowhere but back upon itself, which wasn't very helpful. This concept that had walled me out with its jargon, these lit majors who had hurt my feelings so many times, this momentous testament to my lack of sophistication was really a gag. Here in the land of jet-set intellectuals, it was a mere farce between husband and wife. I felt my world gelling anew as if I had finally found the right prescription for a pair of glasses. So, this was the point of view of choice. Deconstruction was not glowering and intimidating. It was funny.

"What's so amusing?" Clarence asked. He was annoyed, but not with me.

"Lydia wanted me to pretend I was a Deconstructionist because I did some literature at Yale. I was an art major, actually, but I did try some theory courses because you kind of had to in order to know what anyone was talking about. She said you would think it was funny because you're a Historicist."

"I hope she said I was a 'New Historicist.'"

"I'm sure she did."

"Probably not, but it's not your fault. Anyway, is that her idea of a joke?"

"Well, she said the Deconstructionists were your nemesis, that I was the enemy."

He practically spat. His trembling lips were a comical version of Portia's gorgeous pout from the leather frame.

"Where is the woman's sense of nuance? My nemesis indeed! She likes to pretend I'm some sort of reactionary. I am a cultural critic. I incorporate deconstruction into my work. I appreciate the text-only approach for what it meant to its time, but it's passé, you understand."

"Not exactly."

Clarence explained it to me in fatherly tones. He said that it was simply the jargon that got you. Most critics should be shot. Their writing was rubbish.

"Can you believe that Derrida was the first photo in Lydia's last book?" he asked. "You must have seen it. A travesty. I nearly convinced her not to do it, but you'll learn how stubborn she can be. Anyway, I can help you sift through the jargon if you're interested. Then you'll see how easy it is to move beyond it."

My perspective adjusted again. So, deconstruction wasn't a joke exactly. Instead, it was a historical phase that I would master because this lovely professor, whose eyebrows did not frown and who did not assume I knew what hermeneutics were, was going to help me. Yet another vista to take in. There were cocktail parties where the German chancellor was giving you the inside scoop on when the Berlin Wall would come tumbling down and a room full of Monets that made your mother sigh as though she had once possessed them in her boudoir. There was faience abandoned in a secret garden, chestnut croissants at Hédiard.

The doorbell rang. Clarence jumped out of his seat, then sank back.

"Who could possibly be here now? Are you expecting anyone?"

I shook my head.

"Shall we go see?"

We were just intimate enough by now for me to know perfectly well that he knew perfectly well who was at the door.

seven

"Are you sure these people aren't exploiting you?"

"Mom, it's a different world here. Things don't work like that. It's not like I'm punching a time clock and they aren't paying me for my overtime. It's a full situation I've moved into. You should see this place. I'm in the heart of Paris, Mom. Henri Cartier-Bresson stopped in yesterday for tea. This world-famous old man just dropped by the house. He's a friend of Lydia and Clarence's. Apparently, Lydia has already mentioned me to him. She told him I was an artist in the making. He asked about my work because he's started to draw as a second career. He said he likes the exertion. He's questing, Mom, at his age, and doing something he'll never be nearly as famous for only because it's interesting. He looked at my Paris sketchbook and said my work was beautiful, almost without flaws, he said. People like this are talking to me. They like me."

"I'm sure they do. What's not to like? All I'm saying is that you're paying a ridiculous amount for one room and you have almost no salary and you're transcribing notes for the husband and running errands at all hours. You have to learn to protect yourself. I don't want you to get to a year from now and feel like you've wasted your time."

"It's not wasting time. It's experience. This is what experience is. I've only been here a couple of weeks and I've already learned so much."

"I'm telling you, if you're not careful, you'll be a dog-walker before you know it."

39

"The dog isn't even here yet. Clarence is getting him from the country tomorrow. He's been boarding at some farm in Normandy. Nice, huh?"

"You mean there *is* a dog? I was kidding, darling. It was a manner of speaking. Listen, if this Lydia person says that her fancy magazines can only pay you so much, then she asks you to walk her dog, she should supplement your salary. And if you end up working for her husband, then he should pay you too."

"Mom, you're being cynical. These people aren't petty. I'm telling you, it's not a tit-for-tat world. They feed me and it's not like they send me bills. Clarence and his friends even take me out to eat with them sometimes, and I know Lydia will too when she gets here. She already said there are all these places in the neighborhood where we'll be regulars. I could never afford that if it was just me working in an office. And it won't be so bad to walk a dog in Paris, anyway. I can take him to the Luxembourg."

"So, you *are* going to walk the dog. You know that already. They've prepared you to walk their dog. It's part of the deal. Admit it."

"They bought the dog for their son, and he doesn't take care of it anymore and the whole thing breaks their hearts. So, he's become sort of a family project. Everyone pitches in. I will too. Apparently he's cute. He's some big sheep dog. And, by the way, if I worked in a law firm, I'd pick up dry cleaning and make coffee and do all kinds of stupid errands. You know I would. Only they'd be boring."

"You'd be paid for it and it would lead somewhere. I don't want you to get exploited and hurt. I'm not denying that these people are interesting. I'm just saying they're fishy. Watch out. Now, have you called your cousins?"

I reddened. I fingered the brown suede of Portia's Maud Frizon boots, which had been delivered several days ago but which I hadn't managed to send. They lay in their open box on Lydia's desk.

Jacques, Solange and Étienne knew I was here. Before I had arrived, they had written to say how thrilled they would be to see me again. They would be confused by my silence. How could I explain it?

"I haven't had a whole lot of time."

"Well, I've called them for you. Solange told me they are worried about Étienne in Paris. They'd love it if you reconnected. Maybe you could let them know how he's doing. It sounds like he's losing touch."

"Mom, Étienne thought I was the biggest loser he'd ever met. I'm sure he has no desire to talk to me."

"That was over ten years ago. Give him another chance."

"He always walked way ahead of me in the street on the way to school and pretended not to know me."

"You said he was nice to you in private. He asked you if you weren't sad about your father."

"Once or twice."

"Well, Solange tells me they are worried about him and would you please call? We owe them a lot, you know."

"Of course I know."

"I have Étienne's number for you. They feel very cut off from him in Orléans and they would appreciate some news."

"Mom, you don't pronounce the s in Orléans."

"I'm too old to start pretending I can speak French, dear. I have other skills. Do you have a pen for the number?"

eight

In the three weeks between Clarence's arrival and Lydia's appearance, life was Clarence and me and Orlando, the brown dog with the giant yellow eyes that looked like Métro headlights, with constant visits from Claudia, the passionate graduate student who had been at the door that first day when Clarence pretended not to know who was there, and the friendly Moroccan housepainters cracking the windows so that the late September breezes mingled with the music of a tape of Lemchaheb, playing over and over.

Claudia, who was half-Moroccan and half-French, was writing her dissertation for a professor at Berkeley about comparative dream analysis. She was petite, although her dramatic clothes and elaborate shoes could make you forget it. The first impression she made was one of strange and striking beauty, but once you looked at her for a few minutes and all the signs fell into place, you realized that the one beautiful thing about her, the thing that instantly stood for everything else, was her long straight black hair.

She had rented a cheap studio apartment in Montparnasse, which she could not stand to work in, but it was all she could afford. Ever since meeting Clarence at an anthropology and literature conference at Harvard, she had had trouble staying away. Most mornings, she showed up to work before breakfast time and stayed into the evening. Clarence would read over her work, discuss it with her endlessly, feed us both.

42

Her thesis covered a year she spent in a Moroccan village, keeping a dream journal. She was interpreting her dreams both from a Freudian point of view and a traditional Moroccan one. Clarence was not working with her in any official capacity, but he was a brilliant student of culture, she said, and it helped her to write in his house, to be able to talk things over with him as they occurred to her, because she couldn't stand her adviser back in the States.

"He is the worst kind of imperialist," she said one evening, the day's paint fumes fading, Orlando napping at my feet, Clarence opening a cheap bottle of wine that Lydia would never notice missing from the cellar. "The man stumbles along in benevolent self-interest." Not so Clarence. She gulped her wine. "Clarence is a theorist, not a critic, you understand. He can see that the position of my dreams in this thesis is like a horizon between east and west. He gets that it is both a dividing line and also a joining place. Clarence, he knows so much, he is so wise and yet he has such a youthful mind. Nothing is set in stone for him. Nothing is fixated. Not language. Nothing. He is truly agnostic, this man, which takes so much more strength than dogma, you know. It is so easy to be dogmatic. But *you* grasp that, Katie."

Clarence excused himself to see about dinner and Claudia continued. "We can both tell, Clarence and I, that you are a very open-minded young woman."

I blushed. "I feel like I'm made out of hot wax and I'm taking impressions of you guys."

"Oh, no, there is more to you than that. Much more. I can see it and Clarence can see it. You have a complex moral structure."

"I do?" No, I wanted to say, but being in the room with you two makes me look good. It's like hitting with skilled tennis players. I'm not even sure I know what a moral structure is.

"Of course, he sees your complexity and your lovely intuitiveness. You have such instincts. You draw with perfect pitch and he makes the analogy to your character. You are gorgeous and this reflects an inner beauty."

I tried to protest, but she waved me silent.

"Yes, he is very understanding in his way." Here I thought she looked at me woman-to-woman. "Now, some things he does not comprehend and it frustrates me, right? Sometimes he has a colonialist bent that he doesn't recognize. For example, take the women in Morocco. He does not grasp their nuances. He can't see how privileged they are to be left alone among themselves. He has the Western prejudice that they are miserable and somehow can't see it, as though they were thick in the head. But he is coming to see the bias. I keep explaining to him, and he listens. You've heard us discussing it? He is so very open-minded for a man with his stature. It makes him sexy, no? That kind of intelligence?"

Clarence came back into the room to say the lamb was almost done. He was attempting Lydia's gigot recipe, with a mustard coating.

"You see," Claudia smiled. "He is interested in everything. No meal is too low, no theory too high."

"Not everyone would agree with you, Claudia," Clarence laughed.

Clarence had recently published an abstract of the book he was working on about fashion as the nexus of high and low culture in the late nineteenth century, "fashion as horizon if you will." Some imbecile had written that the abstract was "jargon-heavy" and he hoped the book would lighten up, considering its subject matter.

"Such a fool, that critic!" Claudia's gaze flickered between us. Whenever she defended his work, she jumped up in a flame of bright clothes and dancing hair. "What is jargon? It means nothing. The word 'ego' is jargon. 'Original sin' is jargon. 'Soufflé' is jargon!" She turned her fire decisively on me. "You just wait until the book comes out! Clarence writes so elegantly that he will bring the so-called jargon into the street and the street will never be the same."

"I know, I know," I flushed. "It's going to be a great book. I've been hearing bits of it." Clarence had a hand-held tape recorder that he slipped to me every morning so that I could transcribe his thoughts for the book when I had time, and only after I was done with my work for Lydia, of course, and with the various tasks that Portia called with on her behalf.

The toilet was fixed now. The windows were clean. The boots were sent. The Thanksgiving turkey was preordered from the butcher. The new linens to match the toile were on Portia's bed. The tulip bulbs had been planted in a row of stone pots in the garden. Since the gardener was not "entirely trustworthy," I had personally counted eighty bulbs, which was exactly the number Portia told me had been ordered from Holland.

Was I sure? Yes, I was. Had I remembered to reserve La Coupole for her mother and father on October 12, their wedding anniversary? Yes, I had.

Clarence's chuckle brought me back to the living room. "I wouldn't quite say I'll be bringing anything to the street per se, not with my book anyway, Claudia, but I will say there's nothing wrong with a little pleasure in your seriousness. Always remember that, my girls." Here he refilled our wineglasses.

When he had to leave the room to take a call from Lydia, Claudia confided in me that she worried Lydia might not be the kind of woman who could value Clarence. "She is very conventional in her fame, you know, very utilitarian, very puritanical."

"Her photos don't look puritanical to me."

"No, no, you miss my meaning. She thinks that anything that doesn't work or sell or have immediate impact is a little sinful. She's materialistic in that way, that insidious American way. They call it pragmatism. She's too American for him. He deserves a European sensibility."

Clarence came back into the room flush with the excitement of his long-distance conversation. There was a whirl of names and terms—Perestroika and Walesa and Stasi and Ostpolitik—all meant to show how the German uprising had been building for years, all twirling, bright and somewhat abstract in my head, like the first leaves of fall. I knew what they were, but indistinctly.

"You realize," said Clarence, "now is the most exciting time to be in Germany, right before the East Germans go west. Because it is going to happen anytime now. The Wall is coming down. I mean, East Germany has essentially collapsed. They've got fifty thousand people 'on vacation' in Hungary, going through to Austria. It's all on the verge."

Claudia and I hung on his words.

"People," he continued, "can watch their revolution on TV as it happens, and it excites them no end. The image of progress engenders progress. It's all about the image. Last time Lydia was there, she took a whole series of a family in Leipzig one evening watching the day's protests on an illegal satellite channel. It's one of the best things she's ever shot."

Claudia's eyes were sweeping the living room. "Such an ugly clock," she said.

But Clarence was not done with Germany. "No, no, no, don't you see that Germany is her moment to flourish again? She's got a chance to save herself here because it's not as if the demolition of Germany as we know it is going to be some kind of disaster and she's going to be called a sadist for looking on at the beauty of the destruction. It's not as if she'll be filming children dying of starvation. It's not exploitative or colonial at all. She's going to be able to show how Germany is our shared destiny, even if we aren't there with her. She's got to seize this opportunity to reconnect and to redeem her career."

"What do you mean 'redeem'?" I asked. "Redeem from what?"

"Oh, that last book about the Parisians. People are saying she's become a celebrity-watcher and that she's lost all sense of responsibility for her point of view. I mean, to lead with Derrida? To put Naomi Campbell facing a striking English coal miner? I think she was trying to make some comment on the death of photojournalism, but the point is she doesn't truly believe photojournalism is dead, nor should she. So the whole thing came off as disingenuous, and the criticism from people she cares about was brutal. Magnum almost didn't publish it."

"But it sold, right?" I tried to sound as if I weren't sure.

Claudia flashed her eyes at me as if to ask, why was I so afraid of allowing what I knew?

I promised inside to do better.

"It didn't sell as well as Lydia would have you think. But I'm more worried about her career as an artist, and the work she's doing now in Germany is so good, so bloody good. I want her to keep at it and not get sidetracked by this Rushdie rot. That man is simply another celebrity tangent and I don't want her to fall for him. That Olivier character, little star-fucker, got her all excited about Rushdie. He has some crackpot theory about Rushdie's significance. He's stopping by tomorrow by the way, Katie. From what I gather, he's finally leaving Europe." Clarence's face melted into a sneer. "He wants to come around noon to pick up his things from Portia's closet. I won't be here. I'm meeting Henri for an early lunch. Can you make sure he leaves behind his keys to the apartment? I don't like the idea of him having keys to my home. He has some nerve, that twit."

Olivier rose in me, freshly bright. He hadn't even bothered to let me know he was in Paris. Yet the news that he was here set my inner sky aflame.

I had lost my focus on Clarence. He was saying something about Salman Rushdie again, about Rushdie being beside the point of the Muslim question. Then he was onto Germany and the moment of tension right before the collapse. How poetic such a moment was.

I found it in me to nod.

Claudia nodded too. Her hair undulated.

After she left that night, as Clarence and I were finishing the last of the dishes, he said, "You know, Katie, your father would be very proud of you."

"You mean for going to a good college?"

"No, no, that goes without saying, my dear. The point is that you are adventurous, intellectually adventurous. You're not after a way to turn your education into quick money. You've taken on something rather difficult and unwieldy, and you are doing a beautiful job."

"But I don't really understand what the job is." For the first time, I felt safe admitting this.

"Of course you don't. If you thought you did, you'd be an idiot."

I laughed with relief, said goodnight, climbed the stairs to my attic, turned my skeleton key, saw at once the red envelope slipped under my door, my name written big across the front.

nine

"Dear Kate, So looking forward to seeing you tomorrow. *À bientôt,* Olivier."

Even though I had no way of getting one to him, I composed several versions of a short answer. Letters were my main means of communication, the phone being so expensive, and it was impossible not to respond to one, even in my imagination.

"I hear you are coming at lunchtime. Perhaps we can grab a tomato tart. Can't wait to hear about life on the Venice canals."

"Look forward to seeing you too. Hope you won't feel too land-locked."

"Don't let me forget to take your keys. Clarence made me swear to get them back. By the way, why does he hate you so much?"

"Will be good to have closure tomorrow before you go home to Portia. It's been nice knowing you."

"*Mon cher,* I have such trouble not smiling and laughing that I will surely be pleasant when you stop by, but know, even in the fantasy space of my writing, that you abscond with a little piece of my heart."

I couldn't sleep. At one point, I sat up and sketched my left hand with devilish accuracy, getting every skin crease, every suggestion of bone, leaving nothing undrawn, with the fantastic idea that I would give it to him as a keepsake and a proof that, despite my ramblings, I had consistency. Then I lay down and spun more lunatic words under my breath. Somehow I made it to morning.

Noon passed. It was almost twelve-thirty. I had looked into the courtyard several times to see the door to the street as shut as a sleeping eye. Twice, I noticed Madame Fidelio peering from her own curtains. Had she also been alerted to Olivier's arrival? Was she too waiting for his return from Italy and his final farewell? Did she also long for closure?

Roaming the empty apartment, I fingered my precious note.

Again and again, I returned to Portia's closet, where, beside a neat stack of shoe boxes, I stared at his duffel bag, unzipped, his neatly rolled socks, a swatch of soft gray sweater.

Above the bag hung the three shirts Portia had had me pick up from the *pressing* on the rue de Vaugirard. "You can put them in my closet. You should see a duffel there. Hang them above it." I had detected a wisp of melancholy in her tone, as if she might somehow intuit how left-out she made me feel, as if she might be human.

With all these possessions here, Olivier couldn't not show up. I took comfort in the socks, the sweater, the worn leather luggage tag whose writing matched the writing in my hands. Even if it was going to make me feel terrible, I *was* going to see him again.

The doorbell rang. The hallway pulsed as I moved toward the entryway. I opened the door. He had grown a beard, golden and slight. It tickled when he leaned in for the double kiss.

"I'm going to have to shave it off in a couple of days." He laughed. "And I guess I should probably cut my hair."

"How was Italy?" I managed.

"Amazing. Are you going to let me in?"

I realized I was frozen in the doorway. I let him pass, followed him into the kitchen.

"Anyone else around?" He cast his eyes about. "Clarence here?"

"No, just me. Would you like something to drink?"

"No thanks, let's get out of here. Can I take you to lunch?"

"Sure."

Lunch. It must be okay to get lunch. Lunch was only a moment. Why not enjoy it?

Olivier said he didn't like to stay in the apartment while Clarence was here so he was in a hotel room in the Marais. Did I know that part of town, the winding old Jewish quarter that was getting so funky? He could show me around if I had time. He was going to be here until Friday.

So not just a few more minutes. Two more days.

He took me to a narrow Italian restaurant called the Cherche-Midi. Our table was so small that our knees almost touched underneath.

We shared a tomato and mozzarella plate. Then I had spaghetti with baby clams and red pepper, which I tried to eat as neatly and prettily as I could.

"It's such a pleasure," he sighed, "to be with a woman who actually eats. So many women just play with their food."

I flushed as the specter of impossibly delicate Portia rose between us, batting pasta around into little piles with a silver fork. I wanted to be her, and I wanted to be the opposite of her.

I took a tiny bite and got a burst of garlic.

"Sensing my discomfort, he changed the subject, "What was your French family like?"

The question caught me off guard.

"They were great. My cousin Solange taught preschool and she was really energetic. And Jacques always made these corny jokes about how everyone in the world was really a Balzac character from *The Human Comedy*. He was a teacher too, a literature teacher in a lycée. And they had this wild son, Étienne, who I had this love-hate relationship with. They were lovely. I mean, they *are* lovely."

"But you haven't seen them yet? Not since you've been here this time?"

"How did you know?"

He smiled indulgently, tossed back a curl. "I know something about moving on. You'll look back eventually."

"There's something kind of martyr-like about them that makes me sad. Maybe because they are so pure. Solange has these firm, busy arms, always in motion like the kids she taught. And Jacques is quieter, with a dark mustache and a slow smile and an absolute certainty that Balzac was the greatest writer in the history of the world. He knows it's funny—he's onto himself—but it does nothing to shake his conviction. They took me in when my dad was sick and made me so much part of the family that I felt kind of guilty for how attached I got to them, disloyal to my own parents."

"But your own parents sent you away."

"They had to," I almost snapped. I stared into the olive oil shining up from my plate. Why had my parents left me in Paris for so long? In a trough between two waves? Learning French? Life had traded me fluency for my father's last touch. Not the bargain I would have chosen. But, as Mom would say, there you have it. Instead of asking so many questions, go make something of your gifts.

"Sorry," Olivier said. "You shouldn't call them until you feel ready."

No, I wanted to protest. Ready or not, I was going to call them later today.

"Although you may not get around to much of anything," he continued, "after Lydia gets here. It's hard to get out of her orbit once you get caught. She and the family can be pretty overwhelming. They can erase everything else."

He told me that I would surely be conscripted to deliver letters between the offices of husband and wife, as they preferred to speak through third parties.

I replied that while Lydia remained mysterious to me, so different from anyone I had ever dealt with, Clarence was quite knowable despite being so erudite. He never appeared shocked by my ignorance. He often liked what I had to say. And he was available to me.

Olivier warned that Clarence could be devious and that I should be careful.

"You're wrong there," I said, refusing to get upset. "But then again he's wrong about you too."

"Oh, so he talks about me, does he?" Olivier grinned, suspending a fork full of penne.

"I'm sure it's complicated," I tried to sound light and knowing. "I mean, you're dating his daughter. Fathers and daughters can be close."

"I'm going to break up with Portia," he declared, putting down his uneaten bite.

I dropped my fork. The wall between us crumbled to lace. "Why are you telling me this?"

"Why do you think, Kate?"

I thought of Portia's voice, so taut and wiry, its oblique mentions of Olivier, never by name, making sure his luggage was in order, managing his shirts, having me go to Hédiard for a gift bag of foie gras and several jars of the jam of a green plum impossible to find Stateside. "Reines Claudes, they're called. It can't be any other kind of jam. And get goose foie gras, not duck. One bloc with truffles and one without. Make sure they put a bow on the bag. A red bow. The color is important. You can leave it on the dressing table in my room."

The dressing table.

"Does Portia know you're breaking up with her?" I asked.

"On some level. She can't not. But you must have noticed that the truth is not exactly an obstacle in this family. Portia has inherited this sort of sad romantic version of her parents spoiledness. She's really not a bad kid, and I care about her. But I can't do it anymore. I can't take the sense of entitlement, the cluelessness, the assumption that her jet-set intellectual parents make her *someone*. She's always saying *someone* in italics to indicate all the people she hangs out with by proxy and all the parents at the New York prep school she went to. And I think she thinks I will be *someone* too by virtue of some inherent prestige. It's all very flattering and pathetic and I want out. Besides," he smiled, "I've met another girl."

In spite of myself, the idea that I might be that girl washed through me, stunningly warm. I took a sip of water, choked, looked away from him.

"Wait. You're not responsible for anything," he said. "Don't get that guilty wrinkle in your forehead."

Was he already familiar with my facial expressions? Of course I was guilty. This conversation was wrong. But I was also elated. These were two feelings that should not exist in the same picture, a travesty. I was out of my depth.

He pressed on. "All I meant was, you opened my eyes that day we walked around together. You're making your own way as your own someone and I'm impressed by that. You're also very, very pretty. You have eyelashes like tarantula legs. And I'd love to spend a little more time with you before I disappear into the mines."

The only release I could find was laughter, which he took as encouragement because he made me promise to meet him in the Marais the following evening at seven. There was a tiny horseshoe-shaped bar he liked, called Le Petit Fer à Cheval.

I said I would be there. I refrained from asking why we couldn't meet tonight. Now that I was on this insane path, I wanted heedlessly to find out where it led. I was scared, and preferred to know the worst rather than be in the dark.

After lunch, he kissed me briefly on the lips.

We walked our separate ways down the rue du Cherche-Midi. I had to get back to my time lines for Lydia. He did not say where he was headed. I turned to look at him a couple of times, his back maneuvering through autumn's trench-coated crowd, shouldering the duffel into which he had packed the clean shirts and the gifts from Portia, which now seemed pathetic rather than intimidating, her desperate stab at buying his waning affections.

Much to Clarence's irritation, I had virtually emptied the "petty cash" drawer to pay for these presents. "Portia asked you to do what?! Poor thing . . ."

ten

Moments after I slipped back into the apartment, the phone rang. Clarence handed me the receiver in the kitchen. "A young man for you," he said.

I was confused. The only young man I knew who had this number was Olivier, and Clarence would surely have recognized Olivier's voice. I supposed my mother would have given the number to my ex, Peter, if he'd asked, but I couldn't think what reason he would find to call me long-distance. He had never shown any urgency toward me. Why now? The mere thought of his indifference made me sure that no boy would ever telephone. There must be some mistake.

It was my cousin Étienne. He seemed to feel none of my trepidation about our cruel past. There was a familiarity in his voice that suggested memories on his part that had nothing to do with mine. He sounded as though we had always bantered playfully and were simply taking up where we had left off. He was, it turned out, a very good actor.

"*Alors, c'est chic ta nouvelle adresse.*"

"*Assez chic, oui.*" My new address was chic enough.

Who was this lady I was working for in such a posh part of town? Was she rich? Did she buy lots of jewelry? Because Étienne was about to start a jewelry line, part precious, part *objets trouvés*.

Very postmodern, I said.

Did he actually want to engage with me? Why was I so afraid? I

55

was no longer the little girl he could tease in a Paris that belonged to him.

He sang the word "postmodern" back to me several times before he declared that he would call his jewelry line "PoMo" and thanked me for the inspiration although he wasn't exactly sure what the term meant (I did not believe him) because he hadn't gone to college (probably true). He hadn't even gotten his high school baccalaureate. Had I heard? His parents were devastated. They had always seen him as a *fonctionnaire,* somewhere deep in the postal system or maybe a *prof de gym.* They hoped he would follow them back to his roots in Orléans, build his own little house down the street from theirs. Here he made himself laugh very loud, and I could see his eleven-year-old neck arched way back, his tongue halfway out and shining.

At ten in the morning, he sounded like he was on speed. I understood why Solange and Jacques were worried.

"I'm just home from a big night," he said. "Hey, we should go clubbing together sometime."

"With pleasure."

So, he was going to court *me* now. How odd.

"Yes," he said, "you've always been eager to please."

Was it that simple? I winced.

This was the slender and harsh boy with the pitch-dark lashes who had made it clear that he did not want to know me in the schoolyard, me, the milk-fed American cousin who did not know the *élastique* routines of the other girls and had visible knots in her hair and who studied so hard that his parents never stopped asking why he couldn't be more like me. They pointed to the big books I read and my promising drawings. He was forced to be polite to me because I was a *pauvre fille,* a poor girl who was losing her father. Didn't he know how lucky he was, they whispered, not to be abandoned? *Mais elle me barbe*, he said. She bores me.

Did he remember that I had gotten lice and he had called me *dégueulasse?* Did he recall that I would do anything for a chocolate éclair, even slip him the answers to a math test or hold hands for ten seconds with the dirty old man on the bench outside the hardware store while his friends watched? Did he know now that it wasn't for the éclair but for love of him that I had been willing to prove so brave? I had simply been more mortified by my love than by the base act of accepting a pastry for my favors. Shame is good cover.

Now, though, over this phone eleven years later, *he* wanted to know *me*.

What was I doing this weekend?

He was having *un petit dîner chez lui* on Friday night. Would I come?

Two nights from now. I took a deep breath and asked what I could bring.

He said he loved champagne and that it would be great to see me after all this time. He hoped I was still cute. He gave me an address. The closest Métro was Bastille. And by the way, did the woman I worked for shoot *publicités*?

Absolutely not, I said. She's not that kind of photographer. Then I told him I loved champagne too, although I'd only had the real kind once or twice. Maybe we would discover some affinities after all.

Once I had seen him, I would call his parents and make a plan to visit them in Orléans.

eleven

That evening, Clarence sent Claudia and me to a Pasolini movie about Christ's life, scored with Bach's *St. Matthew Passion*. He said it was heartbreakingly beautiful. He wanted to know how we would react.

As the movie played, black and white, lyrical, unstudied, cast with ordinary Italians playing peasants who were at once beatific and disillusioned, I recounted it to Olivier in my head. I saw his eyes react, his chin cocked in its listening pose. I had never been so focused—or so distracted.

Several times, the heat of Claudia's gaze lit my face, and I swiveled to see her expression like that of the people on the screen watching Jesus suffer. Their eyes deepened to the swell of the gorgeous choruses, so that they looked both infinitely wise and clueless. Claudia's pupils burned me with the same idiot understanding, blessed somehow, but also brutally judgmental.

I squirmed. Yet I was touched by her attention. I knew she could sense an obsession under my skin. I wanted to describe it to her, to tell her about Olivier, to begin to forge a real bond. And even though I couldn't talk to her, her growing friendship was a comfort.

"What did you think of the film?" Claudia asked at a traffic light on the way home.

"Clarence was right. It was beautiful. The music and the faces were so full."

She kept staring at me, waiting for me to break through my own babble.

"It seemed so innocent that I feel like it was kind of deceptive," I blurted.

"Is it bad to be deceptive?" She was pushing me to confess whatever my secret was. I wanted to believe it was out of a growing intimacy, but I couldn't be sure.

"It's hard not to be a little deceptive," I owned. "I'm not talking about lying really. Just that you can't always bare your feelings like the people in that movie. You can't be moved all the time. For me, it would be like I was always drawing, having this intense scruple about getting it exactly right. With no blurs. I'd go crazy. Life isn't like that."

"Ah, but you also go crazy in life with too much hiding. I think you will learn to be more relaxed as you get older, Katie."

"I'm trying." By this point, I had little idea what we were talking about, only the conviction that she was boring into my soul, and that, no matter how well-meaning she was, and how much I enjoyed her companionship, I wanted my soul to myself for the time being.

"I know you are trying," she said gently.

Deciding perhaps that she had gone far enough for one evening, she let me be the rest of the way home.

Grateful for the simple sounds of traffic and footfall along the boulevard Raspail, I returned to my inner arguments about Olivier.

It wasn't as if by going to the Fer à Cheval tomorrow, I might betray a friend. Portia was not my friend. She was a thin and imperious telephone voice with high boots, a blond face in an expensive frame in a house in New York City that had nothing to do with me. And Olivier did not love her. He'd made that very clear.

I told myself that seeing Olivier wasn't wrong. It was my own business. If I were to give in to the temptation to confide in Claudia right now, she would tell Clarence, and I had a strong feeling that no matter how much he liked me he would not be sympathetic to my falling into the arms of his daughter's ex-boyfriend.

59

Clarence and Claudia seemed the types to condone a romantic secret. Only not my particular one.

When Claudia and I arrived at the apartment, she made a lamb couscous, with raisins and chickpeas, while I clipped and read articles on Germany. I was familiar now with the names of the players, with Kohl and Honecker.

What had we thought of the Pasolini? asked Clarence as we ate. Did we like *cinéma vérité?* Did it make us feel truthful?

I said that there was something infuriating about the gorgeous actors: they were totally innocent and yet they had an almost creepy all-knowing quality, kind of like children in a horror movie.

Again, Claudia's gaze seared me with suspicious concern.

Clarence laughed. "Horror, you say? Not bad. And Claudia," he turned to her as to the next pupil, "what did you think?" His tone with her was no different from with me. We were his little girls.

"I think what's interesting is the way the power of chance plays such a strong role in Christ's destiny. He doesn't have our modern egotistical notion of self-determination. He follows a path."

Happenstance and fate, I was learning, were among Clarence's favorite themes. He expressed annoyance at the common assumption that we do everything for a reason, however conscious, that we are actually capable of guiding ourselves through life and therefore have most of the responsibility for our situations.

He thought that way too much power was attributed these days to psychology. As he experienced more and more of life—he was in his fifties now—he felt a growing respect for the random as well as for Greek tragedy. So much, indeed most, of what happens is beyond our control, he argued. And it is both self-aggrandizing and self-flagellating to maintain otherwise.

I agreed with him and gave an example straight from the mouth of my cousin Jacques: "Madame Bovary was *such* a victim of circumstance. She only committed adultery because of the limits of her situation. How can you blame her?"

"Precisely!" There was a happy camaraderie in his voice, the professor letting the student in.

"Of course," he continued, "I'm not advocating passivity, per se. That would be preposterous. No, not passivity, but there is a wisdom to acknowledge fate, and the modern world is losing sight of it, don't you agree? Claudia, you're awfully quiet."

"You know what I think," she sighed with mock mystery. "Or at least you should."

I told them I had never had a couscous before, that it hadn't been in Solange's repertoire and that it was delicious.

"I'll teach you how to make it," said Claudia.

The phone rang. Clarence picked up, grinned, then frowned. "No, my dear, I didn't have the pleasure of seeing Olivier off for good, but his things are gone and he's left the keys, thank God. I believe he's in a hotel for a couple of days before he flies to New York, but I'm not privy to his schedule, nor do I wish to be." His frown deepened as he listened. I could hear the higher tones of Portia's voice. "No, Portia. I have no idea what he said. Would you like to speak to Katie? She handled it, I believe. Or else Madame Fidelio dealt with him. As I say, I wasn't here." He rolled his eyes in Claudia's and my direction. The notes trickling from the receiver grew shriller. "Listen, Portia, I love and admire you and I have to tell you that boy is an idiot and you are better off without him."

Had Olivier done it already? Had he told Portia goodbye over the phone?

Clarence grimaced. "I tell you I don't know. Here, I'll pass you to Katie."

I braced myself but was saved by Portia's shriek of "Don't you dare!" sailing out into the kitchen.

I understood her. Why would she want to share her heartbreak and humiliation with a total stranger?

When Clarence hung up, he clucked, shook his head, sat down to his couscous. "Portia says," he chuckled sadly, "that she senses Olivier pulling away." He popped a chickpea into his mouth. "Rubbish, I say. Rubbish, Portia."

"Don't you think you should be sympathetic to your daughter if she is in pain?" asked Claudia.

"Yeah," I echoed lamely.

"I suppose I should try," he answered. "But it's hard when I know the pain will seem absurd in a matter of weeks."

Sighing, Claudia reached for his hand, which he whipped away with a significant glance at me. A tiny suspicion peaked, but I let it flow away.

"Is everyone excited to see Lydia?" I asked cheerfully, realizing as I spoke that I was testing the waters to see whether or not Claudia would stick around when Lydia finally arrived day after tomorrow.

"You're going to be rather busy, my dear Katie," quipped Clarence. "Lydia can be a bloody slave driver when she's working. You ought to rest up tomorrow night."

I reddened. I had other plans.

"I will clean up all of my papers and my affairs." Claudia's voice was a hiss of escaping steam.

"Perhaps you should, dear. Lydia's a bit of a stickler for tidiness."

As he began to hum the opening theme of the *St. Matthew Passion*, she rose impatiently from the table.

Once Claudia had left for Montparnasse, I teased Clarence gently that she had a schoolgirl crush on him. "She's even worried that Lydia doesn't appreciate you enough because she's too American to get you. It's classic, right? Oedipal? She's fascinated with you." Possessed by my own impossible infatuation, it was a relief to talk about someone else's.

"You're both very imaginative young women," he said, smiling his dough-lipped smile and drumming his fingers on his wineglass.

twelve

I reached the little horseshoe bar at dusk. Olivier was there already, sipping something brown that I guessed was whiskey. As I caught his eye, I could feel my face a confusion of deep blush and the pink chill of the first really cool day of fall. The only coat I had that didn't embarrass me was too thin for this weather. I had walked fast to stay warm. My whole body was pumping.

There were half a dozen people sprinkled around the old wooden U-shaped bar. When Olivier pulled me in for a kiss in front of all of them, I was stunned. He introduced me to the bartender, Michel, dark and foxishly thin. He said that since it might be tricky for me to get mail from him at the house, he would write to me in care of Michel. He untied the old black and white plaid scarf that had been Daddy's. Mom had given it to me when I headed to college on the East Coast, saying she had saved it all these years because she always knew it would come in handy.

"I love this," Olivier said, rubbing it to his cheek. "It's so soft."

"Thanks. It was my dad's."

"It *is* your dad's."

Michel asked me what I would like to drink and all I could think of was a Kir.

From the bar, Olivier walked me to the Place des Vosges, the sixteenth-century red brick square with geometric grass and black iron benches. Victor Hugo had lived here. It was Olivier's favorite square in all of Paris. He took me to a bench under a chestnut tree where he made me promise to sit and read his letters. He wanted to picture me there.

He felt me shiver and draped his coat over mine. Then he gave me his hand. He began to massage my palm so that his *chevalière* pressed and rose, rose and pressed.

"Your ring is like a hint of lost treasure," I laughed, "like the one thing that was saved from the shipwreck."

He laughed too. "It's all very tragicomic, isn't it? I could have had this whole other life like you could have had a completely different childhood with your dad being some kick-ass movie director. We can't take anything for granted, can we?"

"And Portia can?" I ventured.

"I told you she's spoiled. She thinks she has desires, but they're all just about acquiring more to pile on to what she already has. There's nothing burning."

"At least she has good taste."

"There's that."

"Have you actually told her you're breaking up with her?"

"She's not stupid. She knows."

When he kissed me, he whispered, "This is true. We understand one another. *On se comprend.*"

But I didn't understand anything except what I felt like doing there and then. Which was so obviously what he felt like doing too.

The old family crest pressed softly into my ear and then into my back, my legs. His hands were running through my hair.

I pulled away so that he could look at me. "Olivier, what are we doing? What about Portia? Are we doing something terrible to her?"

"People are meant to follow their hearts. There's nothing else." He gave me another whiskey-sugared kiss.

I succumbed to the magic of selfishness and went with him

back to his quirky room on the third floor of his *hôtel de charme,* steps away from the Picasso Museum.

At six the following morning, after a last kiss and a whispered "See you again tonight? Promise?" I padded down the hotel's narrow red-carpeted stairs, past the darkened reception desk and out into the cold rose-tinged city. I decided to walk home.

I wound through the Marais back to the Place des Vosges, ran my fingers briefly over our dewy bench, and resolved, as I buried my hands in my coat pocket, to treat myself to a pair of gloves the next time I was paid. I went through the brick archway leading out onto the rue de Rivoli and headed for the small bridge to the Île St-Louis.

While crossing the river, I formed a perverse desire to come clean with Lydia. What better time than today, when she was finally to arrive in Paris? After all, she was a mother and mothers forgave and she obviously didn't think Olivier was right for Portia and maybe she would be grateful to me for taking him away, or at least understand. I had already lied about having the money to afford this job, and about knowing her work my whole life. Yet there was still time to explain. I did not want to lie any more. You could only do so much to please people. When I saw her, I would tell the truth.

But the shuttered shops and cafés of the tiny island, with the hidden worlds and lives they suggested, filled me with a very different idea: to keep my own life private, to carve out a space for myself in this new Paris I was inhabiting. I was going to see Olivier one more time, tonight. And it would be *our* time.

Mom's voice floated to mind. "Separate the personal from the professional, Katie. It's one of the fundamentals of a healthy life. Never mix. Keeps you straight."

As I reached the tip of the Île St-Louis, the Île de la Cité came into view. The flying buttresses of Notre-Dame, so imposing in their silence, offered a fresh perspective, the beauty of Olivier's sleeping face, the perfect stonework of his chest. On principal, I had never drawn from memory, but I thought for the first time I might be able to.

At the cathedral, I faced off with a gargoyle and was struck by the potential ugliness of my actions. But then I heard Olivier: "Please, Kate, I know you would never want to hurt anyone. Believe me that it's over between Portia and me. I've been trying to tell her for months, but she won't hear it. She's never not gotten her way, and it's a shock to her. She's a casualty of privilege. They're all casualties, Lydia, Clarence, Josh. It'll be a shock to all of them for Portia to be left. It might take a little time to sink in. Portia's unstable. But she's not your responsibility."

"I suppose not."

"I can do this," he had said across an inch of pillow. "I can get out of this situation. This family is a vortex. But we can't let them rule our lives. Not after I just spent weeks in Italy thinking about you." Another kiss. "This is *our* twist of fate."

I smiled at the gargoyle and continued on my way toward the Left Bank.

At the base of the boulevard St-Michel, I looked at the sleeping giant, Gibert Jeune, the enormous yellow-awninged bookstore I was coming to love. Like the novels it housed, it filled me with a sense of hope all tangled up with impending tragedy. My chest tightened at the memory of Olivier's finger scrolling across my breasts.

What if all that playful scribbling on my body vanished, along with our magic spot? What if there were no letters? Or the letters were not warm? Or he went home and found he was in love with Portia after all? What if he tasted the Hédiard goose liver while contemplating one of his perfectly pressed shirts and slipped back into the life he deserved?

A drunk resting against a thick tree told me it couldn't be that bad. "*Allez, mademoiselle!*" he grunted. "Give us a smile."

As soon as his voice had broken the morning silence, I began to hear other noises, small cars coughing into the fog, the rustle of falling leaves, various footsteps. All the way home, the day grew in my ears so that I had to struggle to keep a pocket of silence hidden inside me, a place to return to later on my own.

As I became fully aware of the action of the sky, cloudy and dramatic, I finally came to terms with the fact that Lydia was coming home from Germany today. This was no time to brood.

thirteen

A few hours later, I set out for the Luxembourg with the ever-sympathetic Orlando. I was afraid. I realized that the paint colors in the house, which had been congealing all around me as in a dream, might be very wrong. Lydia was going to hate the entryway. She was going to say the living room was too pale and the dining room was depressing. She was going to ask why anyone would paint a bedroom pea green. Why hadn't I been more vigilant? But what could I have done? Maybe I felt guilty because I liked the Moroccan painters so much, loved their music and the way that Claudia spoke Arabic to them, but I knew they probably weren't up to Lydia's standards. "Who are those people Clarence has found? Not professionals?"

Would this disaster turn out to be my fault? I had never done the apartment walk-through with Clarence that Lydia had asked for, comparing his vision of the wall colors to mine, giving her a report. But she had mentioned the idea only once and I hadn't thought it was my place to bring it up again.

I pulled Orlando down chestnut-lined *allées*, dragged him brutally fast to judge by the cross looks I drew.

Shit, were my German time lines all wrong? Had I hidden the Rushdie photos well enough? Lydia didn't want Clarence to see them at this juncture, and Clarence, she warned, was always snooping. And what about the envelope of proof sheets, the one labeled "Book Burning in Bradford, January 14, 1989?" with the close-ups

68

of the word "Satanic" as the flames were beginning to lick it, right before it was engulfed? Had I buried those proofs in the right drawer?

Was Marine, the snotty black and white printer, going to tell Lydia that I was a ditz when it came to photography? Would she say that my look was blank when she mentioned Magnum? That I did not know that Picto was the *only* photo lab in France? That I had no lay of the land? And would Lydia defend me while secretly wishing she had hired someone more with it? Or would she fire me on the spot?

Orlando was miserable. He didn't like to run. "Your dog is dying of thirst!" snapped a passing businessman.

I stopped. Orlando's tongue was hanging low and puckered. There was white phlegm webbing the corners of his mouth. Of course he was thirsty. How could I be so blind? I lead him to the closest puddle, which the poor dog began to lap furiously, and where I immediately drew more indignation. *"C'est dégoûtant!"* *"Pauvre bête."* I burrowed my hands into my jacket pocket and fidgeted stupidly with the red note that Olivier had left under my door.

"Hey, you went to Yale, didn't you?" It was a jogger.

Before I could answer, I realized with blinding certainty that I had to destroy Olivier's letter before anyone saw it. I started to crumple the paper. I thought I looked like I desperately had to go to the bathroom because a shadow of disgust crossed the jogger's face. But I quickly saw that she was not watching me squirm but focusing on the passersby.

"The people here can be so rude. That's nothing but rainwater he's drinking. It's fine for a dog."

I wanted to hug her.

"I totally recognize you," I said. "You were in Branford, right? I'm Katie."

"Christie."

It turned out she was here doing the sort of paralegal job Mom wished I had. And she seemed so cheerful and blond and unconfused that I thought maybe Mom was right. Here Christie was jogging in the park before a normal day's work, while I was subjecting a panting sheep dog to one of my anxiety attacks.

She and I had surely passed one another thousands of times in college, with no flicker of conscious recognition. To say she was a pressed and pretty WASP from prep school, and that I was a mutt who still could not place Groton and Choate, was too reductive. There had been more blending of worlds than that at Yale. But perhaps not so much that she would have felt this friendly, immediately locking me into a drink date at Les Deux Magots two Fridays from now, were we not the only ones of our species in the Luxembourg this morning. As I took in the pert ponytail and perfectly open smile, the INXS lyrics "You're one of my kind" unfurled inside me. I remembered a passage from Proust where the narrator goes to a seaside resort for the summer and realizes that people from classes that would never interact in the city are delighting in one another's company in a foreign atmosphere. The Proust, the INXS, the beautiful girl who wanted to know me, the river of Parisians going by, I suddenly saw it all in a Baroque X-ray.

As I fumbled in my bag for a pen to write down Christie's number, I felt for the fifty-franc note that Clarence had given me to buy lunch on the way home. It wasn't there! I felt again, found it, recalled my shock of shame at the tremble in Clarence's voice as he had gone over what to buy with me.

"Get a poulet rôti, well done, and some céleri rémoulade. She likes jambon cru, but for goodness sakes don't get any regular cooked ham. She can't abide the stuff. Says it's watery. You might pick up some of those puff pastry things with the béchamel and the chicken. She loves those when she's not dieting." No ham, nothing with mushrooms. No eggplant or peppers. No egg.

The man was terrified, reduced. He would have no time today for my musings about the Luxembourg as art, and neither should I. We were both in grave danger of fucking up.

I told Christie I would call her to confirm that I was free as the evening of our drink approached. I wasn't my own master, I explained. "Well, I'm off at six every day," she said with sweet certainty. "So great to run into you." And she jogged away.

I pulled the crumpled money from my pocket. I walked to a *poubelle* with every intention of throwing away Olivier's note, but buried it in the pocket of my jeans instead.

Then I led Orlando out of the park toward the food shops on our list. One by one, we hit them.

The baker slipped him one of yesterday's croissants. The *traiteur* had a sliver of pâté for him, but none for me.

fourteen

Apparently, I did not err buying lunch because Lydia ate with pleasure, chattering about how each taste brought Paris back to her, how good it was to be here.

She did not mention the paint colors. She talked instead about the perfect crisp weather and how telling it was that Orlando liked me because he was such a good judge of character and would I mind spending a couple of hours with her in the office after lunch? She had some letters to dictate.

She was framing the day to make it pleasant, getting Clarence and me to smile. We agreed with her that the poulet rôti from the rue du Cherche-Midi was indeed the best and the most evocative of our little corner of Paris. Where in the States could you find a chicken like this?

"Have you explained the office system to her yet?" Lydia asked Clarence.

"I wouldn't call it a system, exactly, my dear. 'System' is a trifle too serious, don't you think?"

"Call it what you like," she turned to me, "but Clarence and I are very private about our workspaces. He doesn't come into mine, and I don't go into his. It's respectful, if you will. But it does mean that you, Katherine, as a neutral party, will have to carry messages from time to time."

I almost said, "I know. Olivier prepared me for this." And the deliverance I felt at not having slipped made me fear I could never come clean.

"So," Lydia looked at me mischievously as we sat down in her office after lunch, she at her desk, I in a nearby chair, "I'm going to do something simply awful and I hope you won't mind."

I couldn't think of anything funny to say back.

She gestured to a pile of envelopes. "I'm sinfully late answering some of these people. I've missed about ten invitations this past month, given no word, no sign of life. With Germany and Rushdie side by side, my social life is starting to look like Beirut. So, here's where you come in. I'd like to blame some of this on you. Our line will be something like, 'My new assistant is a Deconstructionist from Yale. She doesn't do the date and time thing very well yet, but she's a quick learner and we have high hopes for the future. So sorry your invitation had to be a casualty of literary theory,' something like that. You can refine it. I'm sure you're a better writer than I am. Is this terrible? Do you mind? I mean you don't know these people. You don't begrudge me a little scapegoating for a good cause?"

"Are you kidding? Blame me for anything!"

We had a hilarious afternoon going through her pile of neglected correspondence, pretending I'd misplaced letters and inverted dates. As I scribbled her responses on a legal pad to type up later, she painted me as a distracted intellect. It was flattering in a back-handed sort of way. With each completed reply, each fresh easing of her conscience, she grew more buoyant and more brazen in the lines she dictated until finally I had used some poor woman's invitation to a chamber music concert as a bookmark in my Foucault and forgotten all about it.

With the opening of every envelope she gave me a quick portrait of the sender so that I would be able to recognize him or her *when* we did meet. The cast of characters sounded fascinating. And the events we had missed were fabulous. There was a *soirée* where we almost definitely would have seen "Sam" Beckett. There was a note

73

from Salman Rushdie's French publisher. We had to answer that one carefully. There were art openings and wine tastings, some in New York, some in Paris, a hunting party in England, a cocktail party for the *New Yorker* in Rome. It all blended into an enticing swirl of missed faces and events gone by, the stuff of future dreams.

"Thank you, Katherine. I could never have faced all that alone," said Lydia as the sky through her office window started to darken. "Now, I think we've earned a peach Kir, don't you?"

I dared to look at my watch to see how much time stood between me and Olivier. It was almost five o'clock. Three hours. I would have a drink with Lydia, excuse myself around six, spend half an hour showering and dressing, head back to the Marais and our horseshoe bar.

"Absolutely, it's time for a Kir. We have earned it," I echoed, flooded with relief at my complicity with Lydia.

"Listen, before we go knock off, I have to mention something. I couldn't help but notice in your notebook some jottings about fashion journalism. I know Clarence is getting you to help out on his book. He's having you transcribe the things he says into that little tape-recorder thing of his, isn't he?"

I nodded.

"Well, I don't mind," she continued. "Really, it's okay. It means he trusts you and I'm happy for him that he has someone he can rely on a little so he doesn't feel so at sea in this whole process. This book is a big deal for him. He *needs* to publish. Nothing has happened in his career in years and it's very, very hard for him. Very hard for a man with his intelligence, especially since I'm so visible. You understand, don't you? This sabbatical is a crucial time for him. And there's a big risk that he's going to lose his focus on the fashion thing, for which he already has a book contract and which is where he needs to be concentrating his energy. He could blow it and start trying to publish articles on the whole Muslim fundamentalist fiasco. He keeps talking about translating his theories about capitalism into some explanation of what's going on. And he's in so far over his head he has no idea. If he tries this he will be a laughingstock, an absolute laughingstock. I love the man, but current events are not his strong suit, and what he needs right now is a critical academic success. So, anything you can do to help him stay on target and in the nineteenth century has my blessing. Does that make sense to you?"

"Absolutely." My alliance had so shifted to my boss that I too saw Clarence in shades of pity.

"And there's no need for him to know we've had this conversation. Obviously, we both want what's best for him."

"Obviously." Line for line, I was reflecting back to her. I couldn't help myself.

"Oh, and, if I'm not too tired, we may have to do a bit more work this evening."

"A bit more?" My inner world shook.

"I doubt I can handle it, but if the force is with me we should begin transcribing some of the interviews of my German subjects. There's a massive amount to do." She dug her eyes into my face. "You look pale. Don't tell me you're afraid of work?"

"No, not at all. It's just that I had plans tonight, but—"

"Oh, I see," she snapped. "Well, never mind then. No work if you have plans."

"Thanks." I found I could still breathe. "I could do it late tomorrow night if that's good. Or any other night or through the weekend."

"You know," she clucked, "we may just have to do tonight. We'll see. We have a deadline tomorrow. But I'll make a call to my editor. You should probably be fine for your plan. And I'm exhausted anyway. Although I feel better now after dealing with that avalanche of mail."

Lamely, I aspired to buoyancy. "Cool." But my voice cracked.

"Well now, it's time for that drink. What do you say?" And she stood up, opened the office door and yelled down the hallway, "Clarence, darling, Katherine and I are ready for our crème de pêche!"

fifteen

After Kirs with Clarence and Lydia, and her joking assurance that he and she were going out in the neighborhood tonight for a proper bourgeois *grande bouffe* to celebrate her arrival, pity I couldn't join them, I went to dress for my final date with Olivier.

I showered and primped. I even dabbed perfume from my free sample collection. Chanel No. 5. Then, after two applications of lotion, I dressed. Black leggings and an off-the-shoulder gray dress in softest sweatshirt material. I put on mascara. I pulled on heels.

I slipped a fresh pair of underwear and some flats into my bag, locked my door, unlocked it to get a lipstick and a book to stare at on the Métro. Then I headed down flight after flight, my heart skipping to the music of the unaccustomed heels.

As I hit the bottom stair and faced the marvelous prospect of the courtyard, the door to Lydia's apartment swung open. It was as though my first step into the night air had triggered a spring. Out popped Lydia in a silk paisley bathrobe.

"Christ, it's freezing," she said. "Come in! Come in! Hurry! The heating bills on this place are killing us."

"I was just heading out actually."

"Yes, I can tell. Nice shoes," she added, ushering me into the foyer. "But you might want to take them off. We have a long night ahead of us, my dear. You have to understand that you did not sign on for a nine-to-five job. No time clocks here. No punching in and out." She gave my face a look that managed to be both cursory and searching. "Of course, if that's not what you want . . ."

"No, no, no. I mean yes."

Although I had no idea what I meant, she took my words as a declaration of my readiness to get down to business. We had to transcribe those German interviews right now. History was marching forward and we couldn't afford not to meet it head-on.

Steadying a tremor as I hung my coat, I asked if I could have a couple of minutes to call and leave a message for the cousin I was supposed to meet. I didn't want him to worry.

This was not, I assured myself, a total lie, as this was the night I had promised Étienne to go to his dinner party. I was breaking two dates.

She said fine, showing no interest. But I felt compelled to add, as we walked down the hallway right past Portia's room, all lavender and perfume bottles, that Étienne had invited me to his apartment near the Bastille tonight, that he was the one whose family I'd lived with as a kid, whose parents had retired back to Orléans, and that he was in Paris now, doing some kind of art.

"Oh, well that makes me feel a hell of a lot less guilty. You can see your cousin anytime if he's local, can't you? Tell him you are standing him up in the name of truth and beauty." She laughed, closing her office door behind us.

I went to the phone book beside the Rolodex to look up the Fer à Cheval, wondering if Portia would be waiting for Olivier tomorrow at the airport in New York, ditching school, holding some expensive bottle of champagne.

There was a knock at the door. Clarence.

"Lydia," he said. "This is ridiculous. This can wait until tomorrow and you know it. The poor girl has plans of her own. She's been working all day."

"Clarence, you have no idea what you're talking about. If you did, you would eat your words. Things are happening too fast in this world for us to pause now. There will be time later. Now leave us be."

77

"But I thought you and I were going out to dinner. I thought you wanted a *grande bouffe* tonight. What happened to the *bouffe*?"

"Look at me, Clarence."

"You look fine."

"I'm wearing my bathrobe. I am obviously not going anywhere, not with you or anyone else. We have plenty of roast chicken left over if we get hungry. The Berlin Wall could come down tonight. Now get out."

I managed to find the number for the bar while, just feet away, Lydia busied herself with contact sheets and notebook pages.

I remained remarkably steady.

"Fer à Cheval, bonsoir!" Background jazz felted over a hum of voices. I wondered if one of them was Olivier's, if he had shown up early to meet me. I looked at my watch. I was supposed to be there in half an hour.

I tried to sound casual. *"Bonsoir*, Michel, this is Kate, the American girl you met on Wednesday night."

"La copine d'Olivier?"

"Yes." A c*opine* could either be a girlfriend or friend who was a girl. There was no way to tell. "He's my cousin," I said meaningfully.

Had Lydia heard Olivier's name through the receiver? If she had, she gave no indication, and I had to assume that she was too consumed with her place in history to bother about my social life.

"Ah, bon? Your cousin?" Michel laughed.

"Yes, just please tell him that Kate cannot make it to the dinner party tonight. I have to stay at work. Something important has come up."

Would I like to speak to him, Michel asked? He was right here.

I looked at the backs of Lydia's ears, bobbing and swaying as she worked. "No," I managed, with a final ebb of hope. "He must be busy in the kitchen. Thank you, Michel, but that is not a good idea. I can't come at all."

A firework exploded in an airless box, I felt my excitement sputter and smoke to nothing. Lydia did not appear to notice my distress.

She kept me in her office until two in the morning, transcribing the escapist fantasies of an East German family bracing for the West. She showed me their portraits.

Around midnight, Clarence brought us a cold supper and a couple of glasses of wine.

sixteen

Over the next two weeks, there was no sign of Claudia. Christie, the jogger, called to push our Deux Magots date to the following Friday because she had been invited to Deauville for the weekend. Whenever I could, I went to museums to sketch, finding an accustomed solace. But I didn't have much time. Lydia and Clarence were quite demanding. I grew familiar with the themes of their arguments, the aesthetics, the politics, the climate of suspicion. I found it all maniacally entertaining. Until the day it became too much.

We were having tea in the kitchen.

"Clarence, how can you possibly say that Britain isn't a racist country? What a ridiculous thing to say. Don't you agree, Katherine?"

They both widened their eyes over me, clam shells parting to take in water.

Then Lydia continued at Clarence. "I've heard you, yourself, use the word 'Paki.' Don't deny it."

"Utter fantasy on your part, but that's beside the point. The term 'Paki' will be reclaimed, like the term 'Black' in America. Someday it will be turned on its head and seem to be made powerful."

"Seem to be made? Will it be powerful or won't it? Say something, Clarence, that actually means something, please."

"My point, and don't pretend you can't fathom my point, is that it's not in the interests of capitalism to be racist because capitalism is not about your nature or who you are. It's antimaterialist. It dissolves differences. It wants everyone to be a consumer regardless of race or religion. The whole danger of capitalism is this."

"The whole danger of capitalism is that it isn't racist! Good one! Put that in your book." Lydia turned from him to give me a big satisfied smile. She was stirring one of her papaya pills into a tall glass of water. "I need a longer spoon. Clarence, have you seen the long spoons?"

"Not lately. Maybe that Olivier bloody bastard sold them at the flea market to buy a Birkin bag for his mother."

"You've got to love a man who knows his handbags." Lydia was talking directly to me now.

Clarence winked at me as he addressed his wife. "Lydia, all I'm saying is that your approach to the Muslim problem in England is all wrong and it's going to be bad for your career. People are accusing you of missing the point, the point not being Mr. Rushdie, the paranoid publicity hound. The point—"

"The paranoid publicity hound who is much more famous than you will ever be and—"

"Whose books are unreadable."

"I liked *The Satanic Verses*. Katherine liked it too—right, Katherine?"

"It's funny," I said.

"That's neither here nor there, my friends." Clarence heaped a spoonful of Olivier's honey into his tea. "The point is that capitalism is pluralistic. Like fashion."

"I have an idea!" Lydia cried. "Why don't you stay here and write about fashion not being racist and I'll go to England to take racist pictures."

"Don't think I didn't see you jump outside Bon Marché yesterday when that Arab kid got too close. When you're not working, when you're a private citizen, you're as racist as the next person."

"First of all, you're lying. I did not jump at all. Second of all, we're not talking about me as a private citizen. We're talking about my work, which you have no right whatsoever to control. I'm going to England to photograph an identity crisis."

81

"What did Susan say about photojournalism, that it's sublimated looting?"

"Susan loves my work." She turned to me. "That's Sontag, by the way."

"Don't patronize Katie. She knows perfectly well who Susan is."

"*You* are calling *me* patronizing. I give up."

"It would be one thing if you were going to England to see the *people*, but you're going to go take portraits of that rubbish writer in his overpriced, overhyped isolation."

"The man's life is in danger."

"He's a symbol. I can't believe this! You're complicit, Lydia! Rushdie is becoming a symbol and you are complicit!"

"He's not a symbol. He's a man, actually, and I believe you're jealous."

"No, I'm not remotely jealous, you preposterous woman. I'm simply worried about a crisis in your career. People are saying you've abandoned your photographer's impulse and are becoming a sycophant. They are saying—"

"What people? Your quote, unquote housepainters? Your graduate students?"

"They are beginning to think that you are becoming an illustrator. You used to be the one who was shooting from within the crowd and not focusing on the pageantry."

And on they went, the two wings of a cornered moth, beating furiously while I rinsed the dishes.

Finally, Clarence broke from the argument and told me he loved the honey I had bought.

"It's from the farmers' market on Raspail," I said.

"I thought so. Best market in town."

In the wake of his cheerful comment, I began to tremble. I was guilty, and not only of letting him believe that I had bought the honey when Olivier had. I was guilty, like capitalism itself, of not being solid, of transgression, of dissolving into version after version of a person depending on what was before my eyes. I was living proof of why aesthetics are more important than morals in the modern age, why they are the major component, according to *both* Clarence and Lydia if only I could get them to listen to one another, of the truth as we now know it. I was diaphanous and I was nervous and if I wasn't careful, I was going to break a precious teacup right here in the sink.

"I'll be right back," I said.

I left the apartment, and flew up the five flights of the *escalier de service*. Only as I slid my skeleton key into its hole did my hand and arm begin to solidify. The rest of me followed until the weight sunk back into my shoes. I was a person, a distinct one, a person loved by a boy named Olivier. And in order to celebrate this being, not to pierce her new skin, I moved, with slow and comic delicacy, toward the secret place that was my sock and underwear drawer. There, buried at the very back, tied with a ribbon, were three letters. The first was the note in the red envelope that I had not been able to throw away. The second, Olivier had left for me at the Petit Fer à Cheval the morning of his departure. He had written it while he was waiting for me to show up. "Where are you, Kate?" The third letter he had mailed from the airport, also to the Fer à Cheval.

I melted into my futon to reread.

Olivier's letters covered the time we ought to have spent together, his last night and morning in Paris before returning to the States and working life.

While his handwriting was beautiful, the actual contents of the pages were not what I might have expected had it been a good idea to expect anything in particular. The letters gave me virtually no information about the promised breakup with Portia and suggested no plans for us to meet again, but they were affectionate. The last one was my favorite because it ended with a pastel rendition of an elongated me, flawless as an ad, reading a letter on a bench under a tree with the red brick and black iron detailing of the Place des Vosges in the background. *"J'imagine Kate"* was penned below. It wasn't a real drawing but a pastiche of symbolic shortcuts, the sort of thing I would never dare to do but that I admired the way nerds admire hip kids, with grudging confusion. Where did he find such ease?

In his image, I was groomed to a sheen, reading his words in the most picturesque square in all of Paris, wearing a long fitted dress that washed over the edge of the bench. My hair was down. The toenails resting in my delicate sandals were painted a soft pink. If this was how he saw me, then maybe I *would* be perfect someday.

"A bientôt, ma beauté."

Ma beauté folded her letters back into their envelopes, retied the ribbon, arranged undergarments and closed the drawer.

What the hell was I doing?

Although I was beginning to understand that Lydia and Clarence could be unkind, that they often fed on a desire to humiliate each other, I still hoped they would love me. I felt myself on the verge of folding into Lydia's rich and textured family, so different from my own white-walled mother-daughter starkness. And this feeling gave me moments of utter security that it seemed crazy to risk on a boy.

I picked up the snapshot of my parents and heard my mom from years ago. "I can't handle both of you. It's for the best. You will be better off in the long run with your cousins. And won't it be wonderful for you to learn French? Daddy never really learned, you know, and he's always wished he had."

"Yes, French." My dad's voice was not strong. "A big regret. Why the hell your grandfather never spoke it to me will always be a mystery. It's a good thing Jacques was a patient kid, best cousin a guy could dream up. Spent two of the greatest summers of my life horsing around with him, each one trying to speak the other's language. You'll see, he's a lovely man. And he will teach you to talk like a novel. I'm so proud of my little girl . . . French. It's the one that got away."

I had gotten the language quickly, and I had had more time to practice than anyone anticipated because my father outlived the doctors' predictions.

I remember Étienne saying to me, over his shoulder as he

passed me on a bicycle, that I was hanging around longer than I was supposed to. I'd been with his family almost a year. "They told us you'd only be here for a few months. *Tu traines.*" Literally, you're dragging. You little beggar.

We were riding rented bicycles in the gardens of Versailles. His parents had thought it would be a nice cultural outing.

There were daffodils everywhere, but it was still cool, and the long formal lines of poplars rippled in a May wind. The enormous château, reflected in water everywhere, looked like a gilt prison we had somehow escaped to race along these sandy paths past ornate statues, secret flower patches and temples of delight in marble and sandstone. Étienne's parents had said they would meet us at one o'clock for a picnic in front of the Petit Hameau, Marie-Antoinette's "rustic retreat" where she once played at raising sheep. There they promised to explain to me why this place demonstrated the absolute historical necessity of the French Revolution.

Perhaps Étienne was annoyed at having to spend an afternoon *en touriste* with his earnest American cousin instead of prowling the streets with his friends, and that is why he would not wait for me when I stopped to tie my shoe. "You're dragging again."

All I wanted was to belong with somebody, to feel a presence at my side in that spring chill. Instead, I got lost in a green maze trying to get to Marie Antoinette's farm. When I finally did find "my family" behind a mound of lavender—Solange, kneeling on a small picnic blanket, buttering baguettes for sandwiches, Jacques buried in a paperback of *La Cousine Bette*—I was crying.

Solange began unpacking sliced ham and cheese. "Katie, there you are! *Te voilá!* We thought you had decided to try a different restaurant."

Marie Antoinette's village and model farm were kept weirdly clean and charming. The sheep looked overfluffed. It was creepy, I thought, to be picnicking in the shadow of the toy farm of a beheaded queen. No matter how *charmant* it was.

Étienne was sprawled in the grass beside his bike, looking not proud. I dared to suspect he felt sorry for me.

I felt utterly rejected. I hated my parents for sending me to France. I hated Versailles, full of ghosts. I hated this cold air. I hated these ham sandwiches. Too much bread and yellow butter and not enough meat because Solange and Jacques were saving for their retirement house. Always saving. I wanted to go home.

But, when I called that night, Mom reminded me that she and Dad had talked it over many times and it was for the best that I stay in France.

When she passed the receiver to Dad, he said, "I'm delighted to think of you making your way in Europe. Very proud. They tell me your accent is perfect. What I wouldn't give . . ." For as long as he could still speak, he repeated those exact words in every phone call. "They tell me your accent is perfect."

seventeen

With farcical timing, Christie, the Luxembourg jogger, and I both arrived at Les Deux Magots at precisely 6:30.

Agreeing that it was warm enough this evening to drink outside, we sat beneath the evergreen awning, each with one eye across the *place* to the Gothic entrance of St-Germain-des-Prés and the other on our fellow consumers.

"*Je vous écoute,*" said the waiter.

Christie ordered a *coupe de champagne* and so did I, wincing at the price on the menu, promising myself to have oatmeal for dinner that night. Frenchwomen, Christie remarked, don't sip wine before meals, especially among themselves, but you often see them drinking champagne.

What about Kirs, I asked?

Déclassé! She laughed a "get whatever you want but not really" laugh. Her ponytail was smoothed back and low. She wore a cropped and fitted blazer over a camisole, tapered pants, and suede loafers. She even had lipstick on. She could be a *Parisienne* if she weren't so tall and broad-shouldered. People probably thought she was a Scandinavian model.

It was too much for me to aspire to, so I fell into a state of admiration, stunned that she took such an interest in me. I lived in the greatest neighborhood. My legs looked so hot in my miniskirt. She loved my cowboy boots. And it was cool to have another attractive girl to hang out with in Paris. She'd have to introduce me to the *bande* of boys she had met through work.

The boys were *BCBG,* "You know, *bon chic bon genre.*"

I nodded. Because *BCBG* implied breezy entitlement, the closest English classification was "preppy," but "preppy" suggested a ruggedness that was nowhere to be found in cinched and pressed jeans, impeccable shoes, heavy cologne and perfect knowledge of a codified set of twirling dance steps called *le rock.*

These boys were a lot of fun, said Christie, and you never had to pay for anything with them. It was a cardinal rule. Not even the candy that the *dame pipi* sold in the bathrooms at Les Bains Douches, a club in an old bathhouse. I was going to love it. "So how *did* you get such a fabulous job? I'm jealous. You must be totally connected."

"No, no, it was random. Just had a roommate who knew Lydia's daughter, and happened to write a letter at the right time. I know no one, I swear. And the job's not as fantastic as it sounds. I run a lot of errands. It's hard to figure out what the substance of it really is, if it's about German reunification or walking the dog. I get really anxious about my priorities. And I had to pretend I had money to get it because it pays nothing. When I don't eat with the Schells, I live on cereal."

"Don't tell me about exploitation and errands. Or sexual harassment, which isn't even a term here. They call it appreciation, and, to be honest, I don't mind being appreciated up to a point. You have to be comfortable in your skin to function in France as a woman. You can be uptight about your femininity, but only about preserving it. And I can't get bent out of shape because I can't afford not to work."

"Really?"

"Believe me. I only look like this because I played all the preppy sports at Yale and I have a good eye. I've stopped trying to tell the *BCBG* boys that I'm not rich, because they don't believe anything that doesn't make sense to them, which is part of their charm obviously. They think I live near Pigalle because I want to make some

kind of statement and rebel against my parents. Most of them still
live at home. You'll see. You'll meet them. I already have one picked
out for you. His name is Sébastien, but we all call him Bastien.
He's a count."

I wondered what Bastien looked like, felt a pang of disloyalty to
my beautiful and faintly tragic Olivier.

Our champagne came and we *tchin-tchinned*. I had to look her
in the eye, she said, twinkling, otherwise the Parisians would think
I was a *porc*.

"Thanks for saving me from myself!" I glanced around the cobblestone square, framed by the church, the boulevard St-Germain,
and a host of tiny streets. The champagne flooded me with a sense
that no avenues were closed to me yet. I was young. Any of the
people whose eyes I was catching in the café, any of the *petites rues*
or *grands boulevards* could take me someplace.

My gaze rested on a nearby table, where two pert young women
were working their neat way through triangles of raspberry tart.
Their hands had swirling energy as they talked and chewed. The
raspberries took leap after balletic leap into their small mouths.
"C'est pas possible!" one was saying as the other lifted a beautiful,
even forkful of pâte sablée and crème pâtissière and framboises.

"You're wondering how they do it, right?"

I hadn't been wondering anything, just taking it all in, but I
nodded. "How *do* they?" How do they what, exactly?

"Mainly this stuff called bio-lite. They'll spend two or three
days a week drinking nothing but this disgusting dissolved powder
that totally cleans you out. I tried it once. I thought I was going to
die. And they do things like chew up nuts at cocktail parties and
spit them into napkins. They're not opposed to bulimia, but controlled bulimia, not the binging kind."

"Really? They don't look that messed up to me."

"It's not considered messed up here. That's the difference.
What we would call a pathology in the U.S., they consider part of
their hygiene, part of making sure you stay attractive, part of your
duty to yourself. In the U.S., we turn everything into a medical

condition. Like pregnancy. You're pregnant in the U.S., they treat you like a sick person. Here, you're a woman who's had sex. It's a whole different take. We think extreme dieting is gross. I even do. I can't help it. It's cultural. They just don't see it that way."

I was so impressed with this absolute explanation that it didn't occur to me that eating disorders and pregnancy might not be equivalent. "I see what you mean," I said. "That's so interesting."

The young women had finished their pretty tarts and looked blissfully undisturbed by the three days of bio-lite fasting ahead of them. They were lighting cigarettes.

"It kind of turns our notions of empowerment on their heads." Christie finished her champagne. "What are you doing later tonight? Do you want to go out? You look fine in those clothes, and I can do your makeup *chez moi*. But you have to promise to let me pluck your eyebrows. Brooke Shields is no longer the French ideal. We're meeting for drinks at Bastien's in the Seventeenth around eight-thirty or nine, then we'll be whisked to dinner somewhere. Come on."

At Pigalle, Paris starts to go uphill toward Montmartre. Christie lived right off the busy red-light square on a tiny steeply angled street. To get there, we passed an old strip club called La Nouvelle Eve. The crêpe-vending booth outside had smudged glass, industrial-sized vats of Nutella and cheap jam, and a ready-made stack of crêpes. "Tourist crêpes," she whispered as we passed. "No self-respecting *travelo* would touch one."

In my childhood memory, Pigalle was sparkling with transvestites, gaily begging the question, "but who am I really?" Now they all looked exhausted to me, much older and calcified in their roles, like listless extras playing footmen in a period film. They had no energy for questions.

The sex shops looked fake. The men mumbling *"salopes"* as we walked by sounded bored. Colors were faded everywhere and the trash looked ancient. Tourists were asking each other if they knew how to find the *Moulin Rouge* up the hill. A few thin and shedding trees were surrounded at the base by circular iron grids, metal doilies full of decaying leaves and yellow Métro tickets and cigarette butts.

"They're going to tear all this down soon," Christie said knowingly. "Developers."

But as soon as we turned past the clouded crêpe booth and faced up the narrow street, things came alive, *petits commerces,* a horse butcher, a *crèmerie.* Clay chimneys piped up and down. The cobblestones were shit-smudged, and there was a peeling poster for a "live sex" show on the wall by Christie's door.

Christie did not have an electric keypad on which to type a code that would let her into a *cour intérieure.* She had a lot of heavy keys.

Her apartment was dark and small, but she lit it dramatically with colored bulbs. The accents here were exotic. "I'm shedding the preppy thing." A flood of pink light over the dressing table illuminated all sorts of cosmetics nestled in silk-lined baskets or hung on ribbons by the mirror. There was an overflowing hat tree and a spangled Indian bedspread, a bursting gold-lit closet. It took a few moments to understand that behind the silver curtain in the corner was a shower.

This place was so different from anything I would have pictured when I encountered the jogger in the Luxembourg that I wished I could draw it, not, as I usually did, to faithfully record some line of beauty, but to remind myself that things weren't always what they seemed.

From a silk pouch, Christie produced a pair of tweezers. "Eyebrows. We're going to make them even more beautiful. Sit down on the stool."

The *bande* was certainly nice enough, assured and well mannered. The count, Bastien, had a handsome fleshy face and a smile that crinkled his eyes into deep-set stars. His hair was short and dark, his jeans tightly belted in snakeskin, or maybe alligator, with a buckle in the shape of an H that I would later identify as Hermès.

I assumed Christie had told him about me because there seemed to be no question but that he was my escort for the evening. And he fit so effortlessly and solicitously into the role, making me feel that whatever I said and did was worthy of his leathery smile, that I felt I had stepped into a ballet to which I miraculously knew all the steps.

It was true that we women didn't pay for anything. *"Tu plaisantes,"* laughed Bastien when I tried to buy him a drink. "You're joking?" We were at an overpriced and mediocre Italian restaurant where the members of the *bande* were well known and where the waiters looked from the women to the men and winked. I learned over dinner that socialists were idiots, *"débiles mentaux,"* and that Americans were puritanical but that I was obviously an exception because my French was so good that I could pass, they said. *"C'est rare!" "C'est exceptionnel!"*

After dinner, we careened in a black Mercedes and a silver Citroën of the armored crustacean variety to the Bains Douches nightclub. There was a dense crowd outside, but we pushed through and the velvet rope broke for us like water.

Although it was past midnight, I did not feel tired, only ghostly. Inside, several of the boys had bottles of vodka and whiskey with their names on them in a glass case. These cost a fortune and explained the miracle of our seamless entry.

Bastien kept my glass full, but not too insistently because I did not look like the kind of American who could swig her alcohol, which was not a bad thing, he whispered with a gently ironic glance at Christie doing shots with his best friend Christian, a tall, thin doe-eyed creature whose lashes kissed when he blinked in the strobing dance lights.

There was a Stéphane and a Georges and a Charles and a Pierre-Louis, appearing to me as a gyrating mass of signet rings and starched jeans and sweaty temples. At one point, Pierre-Louis invited me to dance to a Psychedelic Furs song and began to twirl me in and out in the preordained fashion that had always baffled me. I burst out laughing. So did he. "She does not know how to dance *le rock!*" the boys chorused to one another, not so much mocking as astonished to discover my exoticism when I had given off so many signs that I could be one of them. They proceeded to take turns trying to teach me their moves. Christie doubled over.

We stayed until sunrise, ending up in a shallow tiled pool by one of the dance floors, plunging, then standing to sway in knee-deep water. It was hard for me to believe that I was inside this scene, arm in arm with strangers in wild celebration while my heart wished to be with someone else. But I was having a good time.

After the club, somebody knew where there was a twenty-four-hour bakery and we drove very fast to pick up croissants to take back to Bastien's. His parents were away in Deauville.

I sunk with a cup of coffee into a caramel-colored leather sofa, looking at a terrible Georgia O'Keeffe rip-off of an electric blue orchid. There was a stack of *Madame Figaro* magazines on a side table, a scattering of Venetian ashtrays, a white baby grand piano and wall-to-wall carpeting.

I started to compare this tasteless comfort to the eclecticism at Lydia's and these soft and careless philistine boys to my complicated Olivier. Despite their astronomical bottles of alcohol and their vulgar furniture, I had responded to the ways of Christie's *bande* without thinking, the way you respond to a pop song, and I was now vaguely ashamed.

Olivier's image began to haunt me. I felt the shadow of the Marais hotel sheets over our two faces. I basked in the sympathy of his gaze at my description of waiting in the Nineteenth Arrondissement for my father to die. I had explained that as the time dragged out into one year and then another, Paris came alive with signs that he might be going to survive after all, that Mom was nursing him to health. They simply didn't want me to come home until they were sure everything was perfectly fine. They were responsible that way.

I read proof of my father's miraculous recovery in everything, the ink marks on used Métro tickets, the arrangements of the crocuses and tulips at the park, the number of *deux-chevaux* cars that

I passed on the walk to school, the looks my cousins gave me, the pattern of my salad leaves.

"I know what you mean," Olivier had whispered through my tears. "Our lives have not been easy." And then, with a few strokes of his body, he had transformed all my anxiety into a predawn orgasm.

Why did Olivier have to work so hard and so far away while these *garçons* enjoyed life in Paris in their parents' plush apartments? Why had he lost everything that they so blithely had? Olivier was a disinherited prince, working his way to what others came by effortlessly. Although we were from very different worlds, he too had to create his own luck.

Suddenly, I heard the first few notes of a Chopin nocturne coming from the baby grand. It was Count Bastien himself at the keyboard. The Chupa Chups lollipops from the *dame pipi,* who sold them in the club's bathroom along with lip gloss and tissue packs and perfume spritzes, bounced in his blazer pocket as he played. And he played beautifully. Any hardness to him that I had been nurturing dripped away on the notes. His eyes were bright with concentration.

I wondered if I understood anything at all.

eighteen

"This is unacceptable!" Lydia was pointing to a puddle of dog pee dangerously close to her Rococo clock, which was still on the floor because she had fired Clarence's painters and the apartment walls were in limbo. "I can't live like this!"

"I'm sorry, I didn't know I was supposed to walk Orlando on weekends. I thought Clarence usually did it."

"Well, Clarence overslept today and obviously you did too and the ultimate responsibility has to be yours. Or the two of you have to come to an agreement because I have too much work to do for things to fall apart around me."

It was Saturday at noon. I had gone to bed at nine that morning, after the night at the Bains Douches, not drunk but not unpoisoned. While Lydia was yelling, I heard an alternation of techno music and Chopin, but could not keep both in my head at once, the way you can't see a duck and a rabbit simultaneously in that famous Wittgenstein drawing we studied in freshman philosophy.

"Listen, I've got England, I've got Germany, I've got people coming over tonight. On top of everything I've got to entertain, and I cannot have this!" She gestured to the wet floor, her eyes rounder and more reflective than ever so that they shone with all the colors of the compromised living room, the rich cushions, the bronze of the clock, the gleam of urine, the glare of windows. I thought I was seeing a Cubist painting when suddenly her eyes were on me, and there I was in bright shards.

95

"No, I cannot have this!" She ripped her gaze away from me and left the room.

I went to the kitchen to find a rag and some soap, and there I saw the empty honey jar, which was what I had come down for in the first place—a spoonful of honey to put into the tea I had planned to carry back up to my *chambre de bonne* for a leisurely and reflective weekend morning.

Fine, I'll buy my own honey, I thought while I was cleaning up Orlando's pee, careful not to touch the goddamned clock. The poor bronze fairy looked put-upon caressing the snake above the clock face. It was quarter past twelve. Hell, from now on, I can buy all my own food. She's not my mother.

I scrubbed the floor thoroughly, with creeping bitterness, checking and rechecking my work.

When I came out of the living room, and into the hallway, rag in a soapy bucket, Lydia was walking toward me as if by coincidence.

She had softened. "Listen," she said, "I'm very tense right now. I can't tell you too much, but I'm worried about Salman and I need to go see him. And I've got to go back to Germany soon too. I have a lot on my mind. So, why don't you talk to Clarence about the dog and figure it out between the two of you? After all, he's on sabbatical and his book has nothing timely about it. Although I guess you could argue that fashion theory is going to go out of fashion pretty soon." She laughed and I found myself joining her in nervous relief. "So, he can take some responsibility for the household and I'm sure he'd be delighted to coordinate with you. He adores you, you know. I mean, if you ever want to go away for a weekend, simply clear it with him and make sure he knows he's on duty for Orlando. I'm afraid I absolutely can't be counted on right now for this sort of thing."

She avoided looking at the bucket in my hands. The actual fact of the dog pee was being retouched so convincingly that I began to feel better and like it wouldn't be so terrible to keep drinking her tea.

"Listen, one of my old editors from *Look* back in the sixties before you were even a twinkle in your mother's eye, one of my oldest friends, the guy who published my first Vietnam shots, is coming for drinks and dinner tonight. His name is Hugo DeLeon. He's Franco-American, like you. Now he's at *Paris Match*. I think they are going to do something big on Germany at *Match*. So, it's an important evening for me. I can't stand his wife but that's another story. And maybe the editor of the *New Yorker*. I know he's passing through town and I have my sights on the *New Yorker*. I think it's a new frontier."

"But they don't publish photographs, do they?" I was disproportionately proud of knowing this fact.

"Ah, but the times they may be a-changin'." I think she winked at me. "And do you know Harry Mathews?"

I shook my head. "I don't think so."

"The novelist? *Cigarettes*? Oh, you'd know if you did. You've got to know Harry. It's impossible to get along in Paris without him. And we may get Umberto Eco. He's in town too. You know, I was one of the sources for that piece he did in 1986, 'A Photograph' in *Travels in Hyperreality*."

I nodded.

"And let's invite Henri, if we can get him in such a big group. And this horrible fashion writer I have to be nice to, Sally Meeks. Every time I tell her I'm depressed about my weight she buys me chocolate to cheer me up because she knows I can't throw it away. But that's neither here nor there. So, we're going to have drinks here and then go to La Truite Dorée. I was wondering if you could call and make a reservation with your beautiful accent. Maybe for nine o'clock? What do you think?"

Was I invited or was I the secretary? The flutter between joy and hurt was faster than my heart.

I stuttered, "Nine o'clock is a good time."

"*Parfait*! So, we will be how many?"

While Lydia was counting on her fingers and moving her lips, I recalled Clarence opining about the Truite Dorée around the corner, and about two exquisite items in particular. One was an artichoke heart, a fresh one, not from a can ("Imagine cooking the whole artichoke simply for the heart and tossing away the leaves! The wastefulness is positively aristocratic!") topped with crème fraîche and the slenderest haricots verts. (Claudia shook her head and laughed at this description. "I despise that wasteful, buttery, bourgeois cuisine of yours. Please, Clarence, please stop talking!") The other item was a clementine sorbet inside pistachio meringue ("The ultimate in palette cleansers"), which I had spun into something fantastic in my mind, one of Albertine's elaborate ice-cream constructions in *La Prisonnière* that I had been coveting ever since reading Proust the summer between sophomore and junior year, on Jacques's suggestion. We wrote back and forth about it for months.

"Go through this with me, will you?" said Lydia. "We have Hugo and his sorceress, Bob, Harry, Henri, Sally, Clarence, you and me. That's nine. Did I forget anyone?"

"You forgot Umberto Eco!"

"What would I do without you?"

"Is the number for La Truite Dorée in your Rolodex?"

"Should be. Listen, go make the call and then get out of here and enjoy the day. It's Saturday after all, and you're young and in Paris. Go paint something. And make sure you're here by seven for drinks."

I turned to take my bucket of dog pee back to the kitchen, but she called me back softly. "One more thing."

"Sure."

"Have you ever seen this Claudia person who hangs around Clarence when I'm not here? Clarence says she's stark raving mad. Is that true? I trust your character judgment, you know."

"Are you talking about Claudia, the grad student? You've not met her?"

I knew perfectly well that Lydia and Claudia had never seen one another, but I did not think this should be true. It left too much room for suspicion and misconception where I persisted in wanting familial understanding.

"No, why? Does she talk about me?"

"I figured you had to know her or have crossed paths or something. But Clarence talks about you so much to Claudia that it probably seems like the two of you are in the same room."

"So is she crazy?"

"She's expansive is what she is."

"And strange-looking. Clarence said she was a strange-looking sort of dwarf."

"Claudia?"

"Is she a crazy dwarf?"

"Well, she's pretty small and she's definitely not ordinary. I get the feeling she looks up to Clarence intellectually and in a very daughterly way, but I couldn't say if she's clinically crazy."

"Well, Clarence already has a daughter. He doesn't need to drag in raving diminutive grad students. Not into this house."

"No, I suppose he doesn't."

I sloshed the rag in the bucket a couple of times. She crinkled her nose.

"Anyway." She smiled. "Neither here nor there, is it? Let's have fun tonight."

"Drinks at seven?"

"Drinks at seven."

"Is there anything I can do to help get ready?"

"Aren't you a dear? You know there is one thing. You wouldn't mind picking up some petits fours at Hédiard, some of those lethally delicious pâte feuilletée things? You know the ones I mean? Get two dozen. And maybe a few hundred grams of their fabulous pistachios. If you could have it all here by, say, six-thirty. I've got Madame Fidelio coming to help me set up. Don't forget to keep the receipt."

nineteen

That afternoon, I went to see Étienne for the first time in ten years. When I had finally called him to say I was sorry to have missed his dinner party, that it wasn't my fault because Lydia had made me work all night, which was technically true, he had asked me to meet him at the Edvard Munch show at the Pompidou Center.

I spotted him first. He was the city of Paris in human form, quite transformed over the past decade, but unmistakable. Still slight and long-lashed, although his hair was much curlier and his jaw had thickened, he was standing in front of a painting called *The Dance of Life* looking behind the scene of ethereal couples, waltzing on dark grass at the seashore, through to what appeared to be an orange pillar with an orange ball floating on top, somewhere out on the ocean.

He wore a metallic t-shirt with shoulder pads and tapered black jeans tucked into combat boots. I could tell from the fixity of his gaze that he had seen me but didn't want to waver until I recognized him. After all these years, he was still pretending to ignore me. And, although I was no longer hurt, the knowledge of how hurt I once would have been was acute, and I had to hold myself back from crying out.

When he had asked me to the Pompidou Center, he'd said he would be wandering through between two and three and that I should see if I could spot him. He had changed *un peu*, he told me. His ass was even better now.

There was a familiar current of love and embarrassment, while I feigned hesitation and he total absorption in the painting. But what swirled between us was only the dust of our past, catching light here and there to make us remember that we had changed. He no longer wielded the power of rejection. I couldn't believe I had been so wary of seeing him again.

I touched his arm. "He was depressed, Munch, wasn't he?"

"*Un malade mental.*" He embraced me warmly. "*T'es belle,*" he said. "I'm so happy to see you. I was annoyed, you know, that you waited for so long to call me after missing my dinner. Not very well brought up, are you? But now that I see you, I'm not angry anymore. I'm cool. Are you cool?"

"I think so. You look the same, except for your hair."

"And my ass, my Mick Jagger ass? It's something, no?"

"I'd have to see you in leather."

He linked arms with me and we walked around the show, agreeing that we were much happier now that we weren't such inhibited children. It turned out the shapes he had been staring at, the pillar and the ball, were a moonbeam and a moon. They were everywhere in Munch's paintings. The bases of the columns pooled as their light dissolved into the ocean. Couldn't I see? Étienne wanted to incorporate these "tragic" moonbeams into his jewelry line. He was going to chain round moons to cylinders and make pendants out of them. And could I guess what *matière* he was going to use?

I shook my head. We were in front of a painting called *Self-Portrait in Hell*, in which the naked painter's own shadow appeared huge and murderous behind him.

"I'm going to use chunks of the Berlin Wall. They are starting to chip away at it already, but soon there will be mountains to take. The colors are going to be fantastic. Can you imagine all that graffiti? I have a contact in Berlin. He's going to bring me the best pieces. I wish I could go. It's going to be an incredible party. But at least I will have the souvenirs. I can't wait. I can't focus on anything else. Do you think your photographer will be interested?"

"Interested how?"

"In shooting my jewelry? It's so American of me to make something exploitative and market it. Don't you think she'll be interested? It's so capitalist, the art from the rubble. It's fantastic!"

"She doesn't do still lifes."

"Then we'll have a party for her to shoot us wearing my jewelry. She'll love it, as an American, because it's disposable."

"Why would you want to make something disposable? What's the point?"

"*C'est la sagesse, ma belle.* Wisdom. Life is disposable."

"Aren't we the Zen master?"

There was a glimmer of pain in his eyes.

"Well, it's going to be unbelievable, my jewelry," he said quietly.

"I'm sure it will."

It was wonderful to see him, like coming home, but he also unnerved me. A layer had fallen away from him, like the chippings around a sculpture as it takes final form. His new shape was at once familiar and perplexing. I was going to have to look long and hard in order to make it out.

I wondered what he made of me.

"Tell me something about your photographer," he said.

"I don't feel like talking about Lydia right now. She's been horrible lately. *Une salope.*" I started backward at my own words as though they had been fired from a hidden gun. Stunned, I looked at my cousin. But he had not said anything. They were my words, all mine. I simply hadn't admitted I harbored them until now.

"Tell me." Étienne's eyes were anything but hollow. Because his face was too thin, they were even more startling than before, like roasting chestnuts right before they burn. "*C'est une vraie salope, alors?*"

I nodded. Yes, a bitch. Already the term was a bit less shocking in my mouth. I told him about the dog pee freak-out and about how afterward Lydia had sent me out to buy us papayas for lunch, because we had been eating like pigs and we had a *grande bouffe* tonight. I reminded her that I loved papayas. We didn't have to think of it as punishment.

We had eaten the papayas in morbid silence because they had cost twenty francs each and I should have better judgment than to spend something so obscene on lunch. How could I sabotage her like this? Things were going to have to change. People around here were going to have to take responsibility.

I had no idea where I stood with her, and all because I had overpaid for the papayas I thought I was supposed to buy so that I could keep her company on her doomed diet. *"C'est insupportable,"* I said. There was a whole new region of hostility in me. "But until talking to you, Étienne, I had no idea that I could get this angry."

Étienne appeared to be listening so deeply that I thought he was going to solve the mystery of Lydia's personality for me. But instead he asked, *"Alors c'est vraiment une grosse bonne femme?"*

"Merde, Étienne, no! She's not obese. She's completely normal-looking. She's even kind of great-looking, not teeny like a French-woman, but stylish. These potions and papayas and pills are ridiculous. Especially since if you saw her work . . ."

"Well, but maybe she wants to be delicate like a real *Parisienne. C'est logique."*

Then we went to a café for an espresso, looking out on a fountain of bright kinetic sculptures.

Étienne said it was ironic that we were so cold to one another as kids.

But I wasn't cold, I said, I was shy and scared. You were cold.

Was not. Was confused. Was figuring out I was gay.

I almost yelled that I was an idiot. Of course. That's why he'd rejected me. I'd made him uncomfortable with my hopeless crush. So much was becoming clear. But I tried to act like I had always known he was gay so as not to appear naïve. I put on a game face while he ordered a fondant au chocolat and ate it fast and furtively.

"C'est bon?" I asked.

"Almost as *bon* as *chez Hédiard."* Did I remember his mother's old joke?

Of course I did. I walked by Hédiard all the time now.

"*Maman* and *papa,* they are ensconced like mollusks in the plastic house they've built. All those years of not living so they could plan to be old, cooking the same righteous boeuf bourguignon and rereading *La Comédie humaine,* always *La Comédie humaine*! Papa says he never needs to see Paris again because he can go there with his volumes, in his armchair, in his slippers."

"But your parents are healthy?"

"Of course they are! Healthily ashamed that their son is *au chômage.* Their only child on the dole. They always dreamed I'd be gifted enough to have some prominent post in our great bureaucracy. They think I've wasted my life. I'm sure they've told you, they think I'm irregular. You know what that's code for, don't you?"

I nodded. It was already impossible to imagine him heterosexual.

"But you're making jewelry. Isn't that the beauty of the French system, that it supports struggling artists? It's great that someone like you can collect unemployment while you need to, right? Aren't your parents socialists? Don't they believe in that kind of thing?"

"They believe in the idea of that kind of thing. The practice is different. They are socialists who have sacrificed everything for a little piece of property and who think homosexuality isn't conducive to family dinners." He scraped up the last of his crème anglaise, sucked dreamily on the spoon.

"Well," I told him, "I think of your mom's '*chez* Hédiard' line almost every day. In fact, that's where I got Lydia's stupid papayas. It was the only place I could find them. It wasn't my fault they cost so much."

"*Calme-toi.* Tell me why this Lydia is working in Paris? Why France and not America?"

I explained that TV was replacing photojournalism as a way of giving the news. So, photojournalism had to reinvent itself. When *Life* folded in 1972, that was a moment of death for photojournalism in the States, not total death, but a kind of defeat. And at the same time all these photo agencies were starting in Paris that were more sophisticated. They knew that the photographer couldn't pretend to be a fly on the wall because she couldn't compete with the fly of TV. Instead, she had to show she knew she was part of the scene. That was Lydia's genius. Anyway, these Paris agencies made it so that photographers could freelance instead of working for one magazine. Some of the best of them set up bases here. Lydia had had her apartment in the Sixth since 1974. She worked for Magnum and Agence VU and one called Editing and another called Métis . . . "And did you know that the Magnum agency is named after a magnum of champagne because all that Robert Capa drank—he was the founder—was champagne?"

As I spoke, I felt myself synthesizing the lore of the Schell household. I had been listening to Lydia more carefully than I knew.

"*Sympa.* You understand so much."

"It sounds like I do, but it's only little facts that I've picked up and I've made a story out of them. There's tons I've left out." I underplayed the pleasure I got from rendering Lydia's history in such vivid detail. It was like drawing, only more complicated.

When Étienne asked me if I'd been going out at all, I told him about Christie and the *BCBG* boys and our night at the Bains Douches. My tone was deprecating because I guessed that this was not his scene and he would disapprove of a kind of snobbery that was not his own. But, when he simply nodded, I added the detail of the surprise Chopin at sunrise. "So they weren't complete philistines." Still no reaction beyond a lowering of lashes toward the empty cup and sugar packets.

He asked for *l'addition,* and when it came, he pulled it to his bird breast. "*Je t'invite,*" he said.

Christie had told me that, in France, friends of the same class took each other out. It was one of the more graceful aspects of the culture. "You hear it all around, '*je t'invite*' '*je t'invite.*' 'I invite you!' The implication is that you'll meet again and again and keep inviting each other in turn. It's never a done deal. '*Je t'invite.*' It has such a nice ring, don't you think?"

This was the first time the little phrase had been directed at me, and it felt like a sacrament. "*Merci, Étienne.* Next time, it's me."

105

"I was worried about seeing you," he said. "Because you knew me before."

"That's exactly why I was worried too. You know where I come from. I thought you might still make fun of me for having messy hair and being a nerd and a hanger-on."

"No, I don't want to make fun of you anymore. I want to relax with you."

I began to tear at the loveliness of his words. "You have no idea how badly I need to relax."

"I think I do." He smiled.

I pulled on a gray tweed pea coat, bought used in college like my trench, its lining much too thin for the day. I hadn't wanted to wear my stupid down jacket to meet Étienne.

"*T'es cool, toi.*" He did my top button. "Well, I can't get you into Les Bains Douches," he said. "But I can get you into Queen sometime."

twenty

Leaving Étienne, I went to the library to find out what I could about the crowd I was to meet that evening at the Truite Dorée.

Hello, my Olivier, from the library at the Pompidou Center. I've ridden the glass tube escalators you told me you hate. Sorry to offend your aesthetic sensibilities, but you probably know this is the only open-stack library in Paris and I'm frantically doing research on dinner companions for tonight. Umberto Eco is coming! I wish I could talk to you and find out what he's like because you've probably met him. All I know is that he thinks Portia is exquisitely beautiful (Clarence) and that he loves Lydia's work (ahem). I've found a book of his essays and am about to start, but chatting to you is much more compelling than the theories of some old Italian genius. (And you're cuter, a lot cuter, than his jacket photo.) But back to dinner—there's going to be a writer named Harry Mathews. Clarence says he's in the CIA. Lydia says that's ridiculous. I wish I knew what you thought, although I imagine you agree with Lydia on this one. It's funny, but I carry such a vivid version of you in my head that I often feel like I know what you would say in a given situation, which is strange considering how little physical time we've had. Not to be morbid or anything, but I feel like I've known you my whole life and you've suddenly died and I'm the repository of your memory . . .

Sorry to sound nuts, but I have to admit that I'm a teeny bit hungover still. Remember I wrote to you about that Yale girl I bumped into in the park? She and I went out together last night and it was wonderful. I simply assumed because of her look (smooth blond hair in perfect ponytail, lovely square shoulders, beatific expression) that she was some rich preppy girl. And in college we never said two words to each other because we were in such different orbits. But it turns out she's having to make her way here too, although from a different angle. She lives in Pigalle and works in a law firm. She's headed to law school in the fall. Anyway, she's cool and we had a good time, but we overdid the wine.

I saw my cousin Étienne today. I was nervous because I thought it might make me sad or embarrassed, but it was great. Felt a real connection to my past but also like I may not be stuck in it. Turns out he's gay, which was probably obvious all along. I think we are going to be good friends.

The weather is changing. Yesterday was warm but today is freezing. I got my mom to send me the down jacket that I tried not to bring because I thought it wouldn't look right in Paris. So much for pride! But even in the cold, the city is beautiful, and I feel a bit guilty getting to wander around in all this loveliness while you are stuck in an office. If I were you, I would complain about the takeout food and working for people who only use sports analogies and about never seeing the light of day, but, then, that's my stereotype. You obviously have a much healthier attitude toward doing what needs to be done.

Lydia has asked me to help her to archive some old photos she has in a couple of file drawers that she knows are full of treasure but hasn't been able to deal with, stuff that she has kept over the years for various reasons and now she wants to make sense of it. But I'm not sure she can go through with it. She says she's too busy to tackle any kind of organization but that in my spare time she'd love it if I would bring some kind of order to this cabinet.

*What she does, I've discovered, when she gets antsy, is
open her drawers and pull something out at random and
kind of brood over it and then shove it back in. It's a form of
procrastination, like she wants to remember the time from the
picture she's looking at, but not fully remember it because it
might make her sad about the time she's in now. I don't know.
She's so complicated.*

*Yesterday morning I came into her office to see what she
wanted me to do for the day, and she was crying over a print,
rubbing a white border between her thumb and forefinger.
She didn't seem to mind that I saw her crying. It was this
black and white picture of a Vietnamese family crossing a
river to escape the Americans. They were up to their necks in
muddy water. I wondered if something terrible had happened
to them right after she took the picture, like when Gandhi got
assassinated a few hours after Cartier-Bresson did his portrait.*

*I asked her if the family made it across. There were four
children, and the parents looked like they wouldn't be able to
hold them up much longer. There were these bamboo leaves
in the foreground that you wanted to push aside to see better.*

*It turned out Lydia wasn't crying for the people in the
picture but for a photographer friend of hers, her best friend
at the time, she said, the first woman photojournalist to be
killed in Vietnam—"to die in action" was how she put it.
Apparently this woman was young and naïve and came into
Vietnam as a kind of official photographer who was supposed
to toe the U.S. party line, but once she was there and saw
how horrible it was, she started taking pictures that showed
the truth and they tried to censor her and she learned how
to stand up for herself. She took some of the best photos,
the ones that turned the tide of the war. Then she died in a
helicopter crash, "in '72," Lydia said, sounding all scratchy
and distorted like her voice was coming through some vast
distance in time. She seemed a little crazy. She started talking
about riding the transition from black and white to color and*

how all these changes can make you very, very tired and about
when Life *magazine* folded, that was some defining tragedy
in her life. I think she said, "Our mission used to be so clear."
Then she asked me to go make her some tea, and by the time I
got back, it was like the whole thing about missing her friend
was sealed and forgotten and we had this incredibly busy day
ahead of us and chop-chop!

Well, you can't exactly picture me right now on your
lovely bench in the Place des Vosges, but I am looking
pretty languid sprawled out across a table in the fluorescent
library light, surrounded by high-school kids scoping each
other out. I can see through the glass and steel walls to the
square below with the jugglers and the fire-swallowing guy
entertaining small crowds. It's kind of medieval down there.
Talk about time warps.

Anyway, I miss you.

Love,
Kate

twenty-one

The artichoke hearts were as Clarence had described them, only more perfect. There were two of them in the center of my large gold-rimmed plate. Each heart was mounded with cream, latticed with green beans and sparkled over with a bright dice of tomatoes.

I was sitting at a big round table between Clarence and the photo editor from *Paris Match*, Hugo DeLeon. Next to Hugo was Harry Mathews, a great-looking older man who had taken my elbow on the walk over and said, as though delivering inside information, "The thing you'll learn about Paris: carry an umbrella with you at all times." Maybe he *was* in the CIA. Next to Mathews was Hugo's wife, who was quiet and not especially sorceress-like despite Lydia's earlier description. Then there was Umberto Eco, oracular in the mist of his cigarette smoke. Then Lydia. Then the *New Yorker* editor, who had known Lydia for years and had asked me with kind concern if I was "okay" over drinks back in the living room. Beside him, Sally Meeks, the fashion writer with whom Lydia seemed to be in some kind of sibling rivalry ("See, the skirt's too tight. She's always taking advantage of these free sample clothes that don't fit her"). And it was back to Clarence, and then me.

Hugo was telling me how lucky I was to work with Lydia because she was a great artist *and* a popular storyteller. Her images were epoch-making. They transcended the facts.

"You know, you should be careful," Clarence interrupted him. "Photography out of context is dangerous, very dangerous."

I wanted to give him my attention, and tilted my chin in his direction although I was dying to taste my food and my eyes kept drifting to Umberto Eco.

"Without context," Clarence went on, "it's all about the desire to be entertained, not the desire to know."

"What's the sin in entertainment?" asked Hugo.

"Who mentioned sin?" Clarence quipped. He and Hugo began a friendly argument, trying to resist the pull of Umberto Eco's fame, but they could barely concentrate on their own thoughts and the discussion went nowhere.

None of the conversations around me were sustained because everyone was half-listening to the famous writer. Although we were only beginning our appetizers, the table had fallen silent several times already as he spoke, a situation he accepted quite naturally by opening his gaze to include not only Lydia, with whom he was ostensibly talking, but all of us. His thick beard swirling in smoke suggested unknowable depths. His glasses magnified the candle-light into flames that engulfed us all.

I could not tell if it was with pleasure or with resignation that he said, "Yes, they do say that, with the Vatican's condemnation, I am the Italian Salman Rushdie, but I think it's a grotesque exaggeration. Besides," here he laughed, "Rushdie hated *Foucault's Pendulum*. He thought it was boring and overstuffed and that most of the people who bought it were never going to read it. They wanted it for their coffee tables so that they could appear learned."

"Do you think that's true?" Lydia asked him, her voice rising to fill our expectant ears.

"Listen, if people buy my books for vanity, I consider it a tax on idiocy."

As he put out his cigarette and lifted his fork, I tasted my first bite of coeur d'artichaut. It was the most delicious thing ever. I thought with an inward smile of a trip to the supermarket with Mom when I was about fourteen. I had seen so many artichokes in still lifes that I was curious and slipped a couple into our cart. Mom caught my wrist. "Artichokes," she had said, "are a special-occasion food. Now put those back."

I took another bite, a small one because these were not big hearts, and I tried to distinguish the different textures in the dish, the cream, the firm tomatoes and beans, the soft flesh. Maybe Christie was misguided about the women here being thin only because they were drastic. Maybe it was actually because things were so thoughtful and structured that they did not need to be large for you to experience them. With apologies to Claudia, I loved bourgeois food.

I had walked by this neighborhood restaurant several times a day for weeks so that I had a deep passing knowledge of it the way you know the spine of a book that has been sitting on your shelf. Inside now, I had been introduced to the *patronne* (*"une vieille amie du quartier,"* Lydia called her). I had discovered the rustic décor and the *cheminée* and the red and yellow Provençal upholstery on the chairs. There was a wrought iron chandelier over our table that held real honey-colored candles. I knew I was supposed to order the artichokes and the bar au sel, which was not necessarily salty, Clarence explained, but baked in a salt crust to keep the fish especially moist.

Clarence was shaking his head with pleasure as he chewed.

"It's ironic," Umberto Eco was saying, "all the honorary degrees that have come to me *since* the popular novels. The universities are all in the sway of fashion. But I understand them. This fame of mine, it acts like a filter. People trust it. People put inordinate trust in me and my opinions. I find it very perplexing. They expect me to save them from all that is irrelevant, to decimate the white noise, if you will."

Again, the table quieted around him. I knew that, long ago, his father had wanted him to be a lawyer too.

"Not your theory of decimation again!" Lydia was flirting. "I'll never forget that from our first interview." And she raised her voice in my direction to explain. "Katherine, I told you Umberto and I worked together on a piece about photography years ago."

"No," Clarence interjected. "No, if you will only choose to re-member correctly, *we* discussed the need for cultural filters in an age of information overload, my dear. Umberto and *I* discussed how the illusion of democracy at the bookstore is like the illusion of democracy in the appreciation of images. The same concept goes for prêt-à-porter, by the way. Precisely b*ecause* there is so much access, only the informed have a clue as to what to read or see or wear."

"Darling, we're not talking about your manuscript. We're talking about—"

"Listen, I understand decimation. I have given decimation a lot of critical thought and you think it's a joke, Lydia." He speared the last of his artichoke as his plate was cleared and began a more gen-eral address. "She has no idea what the theory of decimation could possibly mean. She's just an artist. *I* am the critic in the house." His smile froze in triumph. He turned decisively to me and Hugo and whispered, "Did you notice that Mathews drank nothing but Perrier back at the house?"

"And that proves to you that he's CIA?" Hugo chuckled.

"It's not insignificant."

"You know it's a practical joke Mathews is playing on you con-spiracy theorists. You know that, Clarence?"

"Ah, Hugo, you say he's pretending. But, remember, how quickly we become what we pretend to be."

On a silver platter came the fish, steaming from the crack in its massive salt crust. Once we had glimpsed it, it was whisked off, filleted and returned to us on beds of julienned vegetables. So, this was civilization.

La patronne knew that Lydia liked the glow of a fire from the small stone *cheminée*, especially on a chilly night. I overheard her saying that she would have the *maître d'hôtel* light it for her since there was a *courant d'air* tonight, wasn't there?

"*Merveilleux, madame. Merci!*" Lydia raised her voice slightly, in delicate advertisement of their intimacy.

La patronne stayed on a beat, her eyes tracking the waiter kneeling by the fireplace, watching him strike a very long match and put it to the kindling. "Madame, how is Monsieur Olivier? Has he gone back to America?"

"He has left us for the world of finance. It's terrible, isn't it?"

Terror. I felt terror. They must have come here often over the summer, Lydia and Olivier, when there was no one else around. *La patronne* was familiar with Olivier. She liked him. Had she seen us strolling together through the neighborhood? Would she mention it in order to prolong this illusion of friendship she was sharing with Lydia? Was some throwaway line about Olivier about to ruin my life?

The back of my neck burned. The shame of getting caught was unimaginable. Why was I living so dangerously? Was it a form of jealousy? Did I want to be Portia? Perhaps on some level I did. But it wasn't only that. There was a deeper reason I was risking everything for a guy who wrote bad letters: I could write back and know that he had been here too, at this very table, and could share with me more closely than anyone the life that was Lydia and Clarence's.

With no more mention of Olivier, the *patronne* went to get the *carte des desserts* and Lydia turned back to Umberto Eco.

"Now," she said. "I want to talk to *you* about the Berlin Wall."

He winked at her.

I took a sip of Burgundy. My fear of unmasking began to flame out like one of the twigs in that beautiful old *cheminée* over there. Olivier's name was forgotten for the evening. Quietly, I breathed.

I wondered aloud what to have for dessert. The clementine sorbet in the pistachio meringue or the chocolate soufflé?

Clarence argued for me to taste the former.

Hugo pushed the latter. "It's the best soufflé in town. Better than Lucas Carton. Better than La Tour d'Argent. You cannot forgo it! Don't listen to Clarence about the sorbet. Sorbet is pathetic."

Not wanting to take sides, I chose profiteroles with chestnut ice cream.

• • •

Lydia and I had our stockinged feet tucked under us on the living room couch.

"Wasn't that funny at coffee?" She chuckled. "Umberto was pretending to be facetious and Harry was pretending to be grave, when they are both such lighthearted beings."

"It was nice," I ventured, "the way Umberto kept including Harry in his statements about the life of a famous writer, as though Harry were as famous as he was. It was gracious."

"How could neither of you have picked up on the strain in their amiability?" The tremble in Clarence's lips was exaggerated by drinking. "Umberto and Harry were circling each other like territorial dogs."

"Stop suspecting everyone's motives all the time. It's unbecoming. Katherine is right, Umberto was being nice." Lydia sipped Armagnac from crystal she had smuggled from Prague.

"Your statements make scoops as do your silences," I said in a low oracular voice, stroking an imaginary beard and pretending to blow smoke. "He was looking straight at Harry when he said that. It *was* nice, Clarence." I had had way too much wine, but Lydia and Clarence wouldn't let me go to bed without Armagnac and a postmortem.

"Men," laughed Lydia, raising her little stolen glass to me.

Clarence glared at her. "Who would Eco be if Sean Connery hadn't starred in *The Name of the Rose*? The most famous man in the literature department in Bologna?"

"Clarence, we all know you're jealous."

"Jealous? The man's a bleeding egomaniac."

"Enough!" said Lydia. "I'm sick of talking about all these men. I want to talk about who had the worst outfit, Sally in her pilfered Sonia Rykiel or the sorceress, Madame DeLeon? What is Hugo doing with her besides cheating? What was that blouse? Was it actually crocheted? Care to weigh in, Katherine?"

Clarence came to my rescue. "That's not the real question, my dear. The real question is how damned good were those artichoke hearts?"

116

"You know Lydia," I raised my glass, "I have to agree with him. The artichokes were the heart of the matter."

Silently she assented and we clinked our Armagnacs together with a round of *tchins-tchins*.

Clarence tried to give Lydia a hard time about her sudden departure for England tomorrow, announced during the dinner conversation about Rushdie, but she would have none of it. She could manage her own career, thank you very much. There was something she needed to shoot. Something imminent. It wasn't her fault that the world was changing so fast on so many fronts. But it *was* her job to keep up. She would spend a day in England, then head straight back to Germany and stay until "it" happened.

I thought, with a guilty spread of happiness, that her leaving meant Claudia would probably return to the house. I looked at Clarence as he shrugged at his inability to have "any say whatsoever in anything." His shy smile told me he might be thinking what I was.

As I finally started up to bed, Lydia took my hand and asked for one more confirmation that Hugo DeLeon had said "good things" about her. Had he mentioned the *Match* retrospective on Germany? The photo she hoped he would include?

"All I can tell you, Lydia, is that he thinks you're fantastic and that my working for you is the job of a lifetime. At dinner, he kept telling me how lucky I was. He said you were epoch-making."

"He did, did he?"

"He did."

twenty-two

Of my dad's stories, the one I pictured most vividly, even though very little happened, was about the Berlin Wall. A few years before I was born, he was in West Berlin, at the film festival, with the first movie he had directed in his own right. He decided to go to the opera in East Berlin and drove back and forth through Checkpoint Charlie, on what I envisioned as a cold and moonless night, by himself in a rental car. The opera was *Don Giovanni*. Nothing in particular took place, but he spoke with such awe of the night crossing, the barbed wire and the mysterious guards shining flashlights on his passport, that I got the sense he narrowly avoided being swallowed into the void of East Berlin for love of music. The Wall he described was a geographical fixture, like the Grand Canyon.

On November 9, 1989, it came down in a riotous celebration. At first, all I could think about was how astonished Daddy would be.

Lydia was in Berlin. After reading and clipping the newspapers for her, I made a drawing in my sketchbook of a tiny section of Lydia's desk, my coffee cup, a pair of scissors, a pencil and a pen. It took me almost three hours. Then I did something I had never done before. I titled my work: *The Berlin Wall Falls.* Up until now, all my pictures had been exactly what they were, *Potted Ficus, New Haven, April 10, 1988; Peter's Foot, New Haven, January 1989.*

There was nothing suggestive about them. Even though this was still the classical drawing that my teachers had assured me I would grow out of, it began to be personal.

Tingling with satisfaction, I got up to walk Orlando. On my way out the door, I was joined by Claudia, back on the scene with Lydia away. I had guessed correctly.

As we approached the Luxembourg, I asked her why she refused to come to the house when Lydia was home. I knew that she was infatuated with Clarence, but I didn't have a handle on the true parameters of her feelings, or how realistic they might be. I thought maybe I could fold her into the family.

"I do not want to bathe in the same atmosphere with that woman," Claudia said.

"But you might actually like each other. She asks about you. Maybe you should come for Thanksgiving?"

I realized as I extended this invitation that it was not mine to make free with, that I was not quite a daughter of the house. And I was relieved to feel sure that Claudia would not accept.

Indeed, she declared that the ambience at "that dinner" was sure to be sulfurous.

"Is that woman genuinely interested in other people?" She knelt to pet Orlando, whose eyes had a faraway golden look in the autumn fog. She was wearing hand-knit gloves with a different color for every finger.

"When she focuses, she's interested," I said. "When she doesn't, you become invisible."

"Do you mean to say she has that kind of light that shines and then vanishes?"

"I guess so. And right now she's shining it like crazy on Berlin."

A gust of wind broke off a couple of straggling leaves from their branches. The barren trees allowed us to see through to the park's patterns, to notice how perfectly symmetrical the quadrangles were, how precise the flowerbeds.

When we had completed our loop and Orlando was tugging on

his leash toward our usual gate of exit, Claudia reminded me that we had to get back as Henri was coming to lunch.

Henri Cartier-Bresson cut into our bread with his pearl-handled pocket knife, squirted hot sauce from a tube he carried everywhere onto our dry sausage and tabouleh and hard-boiled eggs, quietly deploring *nouvelle cuisine* as the latest travesty of the bourgeois social order while Claudia looked victoriously at Clarence and I wondered if those artichoke hearts and chestnut profiteroles had actually been all they were cracked up to be.

Here was an artist who *wanted* our company, Clarence joked, not like Lydia's preposterous "housepainters" (as in "Hitler was one"), the crew she had hired to replace our beloved Moroccans, and who treated the three of us like Madame's unruly children. Henri actually liked being with Clarence, Claudia and me, got a kick out of what he called our *géométrie.*

Henri's movements were weightless despite broad shoulders, height and the aura of his many years. His eyes were blue and unfaded. While his face was agile, he chose to keep it mostly at rest. There was almost always some expression, though, softly crouching inside him, waiting for its moment to beam. If there were such a thing as a natural athlete, he would embody it.

"Ah, saucisson sec, why does one need anything else?" He cut himself a generous slice, flashed a smile, then carefully laid down his knife.

"Henri, why do you keep trying to pass for a simple man with that knapsack and those shoes? Everybody knows you are the scion of a *grande famille.*"

"That's anecdotal," Henri said.

"Henri believes," explained Clarence, "that the anecdote is the enemy of art, especially photography."

Henri squirted a red line of hot sauce along the center of a celery stalk.

Claudia swung all her hair to pour over her left shoulder. "Would you say then that what you feel for the downtrodden is

120

interest, visual interest, and not sympathy? Might you be a colonizer, Henri?" She was practically purring so that only the meaning of her words was hostile.

"You're missing his point," said Clarence, as Henri bit neatly into his celery, looking from one to the other of us and at our four plates. "Henri doesn't set out to tell stories. He discovers visual order and the drama takes care of itself. It's the old surrealist mantra, right, about the hidden power of coincidence? How does it go? 'Put oneself in a state of grace with chance?'"

Henri finished his celery and cleaned his plate of tabouleh with fresh mint and cucumbers, dabbing up the last of his hot sauce with a crust of peasant bread, which he fed to Orlando under the table.

"Well," I ventured, "even if it is all about chance, you can't help but feel some warmth and concern for the people you photograph, can you?"

Although he did not answer, he smiled and I felt his focus. Regardless of my status, I was an important part of the composition here at this lunch table. Like the bars on a grate or the shadow on a face or the light on a wall, I might prove to be the nonnarrative secret to this picture's success. You never knew.

Claudia asked Henri if he wished he were in Berlin today. Surely the breaking down of the Berlin Wall was a decisive moment.

I thought the question could be construed as a cruel reference to his age or a hint that he might no longer be pertinent. But he did not appear to take it so. "The decisive moment is when time is stopped by the camera. Or by the drawing pencil. It is framed later by the flow of history. So, I am working in Paris today," he said cheerfully, rising to carry his plate to the sink. "Just like Kate."

Clarence stood too. "I love this about you, Henri, that you are quintessentially French in the best way."

Claudia, Henri and I all looked confused.

Clarence was delighted to enlighten us. "He's French in that he allows that everyone can assimilate, immigrants and artists. They can all become the citizens of their current country or the actors in their current dream. Don't you see? This implies that anyone who wants to badly enough can become an artist. You, Katie. You, Claudia. Even yours truly. It's wonderful. And generous."

Claudia looked at both men adoringly.

"What are you doing these days, Kate?" Henri asked. "I'm curious to know if you have started on portraits."

"I don't really draw people I know, except to make a study maybe of a body part. I do models, but I don't think you could call them portraits."

"Why?" Claudia turned to me.

"I guess I don't want interference," I said. "I don't want symbols or, or"—I smiled at Henry, "anecdotes to get in the way of drawing."

"You are still trying to avoid a style," Claudia said. "It's quite impossible to do, you know, to avoid a style."

Claudia was sipping red wine. I tried to make the shape of her glass abstract, simply a shape, but I couldn't help seeing beyond the form to the fact that the drum of her fingers on the stem was sensual and that the liquid inside was making her shoulders sway to invisible songs. This was too much information for me to work with. My hands were unsteady, my work clouded. When I got to her amazing hair, I wanted to be done with it and began to rush. I practically scribbled a crawling, hazy mess.

"I look like I have lice!" She said when I let her see over my shoulder. "I had a horrible case of lice once as a little girl and they made so much fun of me in school. They said I had bugs in my pubic hair, which of course I believed." She stared hard into my terrible picture.

"I had lice once too," I said by way of distraction. "When I lived here, in Paris, a long time ago. And I was in love with my French cousin Étienne, who teased me along with all the other kids in the schoolyard."

"Did they say you were dirty?"

"Of course. And now look at us both with our long thick, shiny hair. We've shown them, haven't we, Claudia?"

"How is your cousin now?"

"He's gotten nicer. And he's gay. I mean, he probably always was, but now that it's out in the open it's easier for us to get along."

"Is it nice for you to have a common history?"

I nodded vaguely.

"What about his parents? Have you seen them much?"

"Not yet. They live in Orléans."

She shot me a look of concerned suspicion. "Orléans is not far away. But you have spoken to them?"

"Not yet."

"Why? Aren't you worried they will think all this—" she gave an opulent wave around the room—"this high life in the *Sixième* has made you want to forget them?"

"They could never think such a thing," I said unsteadily. "I'm not like that." I took a sip of Burgundy from a gorgeous bell-shaped glass. So, what was I like?

"I was planning on calling them soon," I said.

"But they must be like parents to you."

"Yes, they are. Very much, but not exactly."

"You feel guilty about how much you loved them?"

"What do you mean?"

"I know all about dreams, remember? You dream that if you had not loved them so much, perhaps you would not have let them replace your father?"

"Claudia, no offense but that's a little far-fetched." I snapped my sketchbook closed. "We're not that complicated in my family."

"Perhaps, but you will admit that you don't want to remember what it was like when your father was dying, even though you have tenderness for your cousins?"

Despite my resistance, her approach was hypnotic.

"Maybe," I owned, suddenly wildly sad.

"It will be fine once you call them. They will be glad, and so will you. Shall we start on the couscous?"

We went to the kitchen together. We had soaked chickpeas overnight. She showed me how to brown lamb with onions, ginger and tumeric, to simmer raisins with the chickpeas and with cinnamon, to add a touch of honey toward the end. The slow method of it all helped me recover my mood, but I was now aware that I floated over a pool of regret.

Once the lamb was finished, we put the couscous grains, which you had to moisten first—very important—in the steamer. Then we sat down to another glass of wine. "Katie?"

"Claudia?"

"Does Clarence ever talk to you about his son?"

"Not much."

"Not even to you, then? That poor boy is the *non-dit* in this family. The unmentioned."

"He was in the house when I met Lydia in New York, but he never came downstairs. She kept trying to engage him, but he wouldn't bite. She even offered him my spring rolls," I smirked.

"So, you have never seen him."

I shook my head. "Only pictures. He's not as good-looking as Portia, but he seems like a pretty normal kid in his Deadhead phase. I doubt there's anything to worry about."

"But what if all this hatred toward the boyfriend of Portia's, this venom of Clarence's for this Olivier person, what if it is in truth for the son?"

"Wow. I never thought of that. I'd sort of forgotten about Joshua."

"Everyone has. Poor child must feel like a ghost in this household."

"Maybe he prefers it that way. Wouldn't you?"

She began to laugh and I joined her.

"What," Clarence came jovially into the room, "are you two cheeky things giggling about now? It smells fantastic in here!"

Soon after dinner, instead of pouring drinks in the living room, Clarence looked at his watch. "It's late, you know. Claudia, you should be getting home or no one will get any work done tomorrow."

Dropping eye contact with us, Claudia began slowly to gather her things.

"Katie," said Clarence, moving down the hall, "can you help me out with something? In here."

I followed him down the hallway into Portia's bedroom, where I had come to know three perfume bottles in particular, with gold labels tied around by golden threads, all by a *Parisienne,* a family friend, named Annick Goutal. Gardenia Passion, Eau de Charlotte, and Petite Chérie. There was one wicker basket of lipsticks and glosses, another of matchbooks from restaurants all over the world. Snapshots and postcards were stuck along the sides of the gilt mirror, two featuring Olivier in what looked like New York, some water lilies from the Marmottan, a black and white view of the Place des Vosges.

Clarence was pacing with pale purple paint swatches in his right hand, looking desperately up at the molding.

"Lydia says she's trusting me with this one and I honestly have no idea how to proceed. She thinks Portia's depressed over this idiot boy who says he is leaving her, thank God, and she thinks somehow that having her Paris room spruced up for Thanksgiving will help, or at least make her think her mother cares . . . You're artistic, Katie. Which one of these shades will work with the fabric?"

Squinting thoughtfully at the ceiling, I pretended to be in Portia's skin and wanted to cry because I did not have a father to fret about the color of my room or the state of my love life.

"That one. The palest one. The lilac, I think it is." I stared harder at the molding, bit my lip.

"Thank you." He flopped onto the bed. "This whole process is so bloody symbolic for Lydia. You know we make fun of her for it, but these are the kinds of rituals she has to go through, these neurotic rites, to give her a sense of a grasp on life so that she can work. Her whole career is about outrunning irrelevancy, you know, reinventing herself in the face of constant advances. It produces untold anxiety. We can't possibly know what that's like. She's quite an amazing woman."

"Yes, she is."

Claudia called out goodnight to us without coming in. We heard the front door of the apartment close.

"You know she's in a hotel room in Berlin right now, calling her lab every five minutes to check progress. She has to get her pictures on the wire first thing in the morning. It's her whole life. She won't go to bed on a night like tonight."

I detected nostalgia in his voice for a time when he might have been sleepless in that hotel room beside her, and the notion of physical love between them became conceivable to me.

"So, what about Joshua's room?" I asked. "Isn't he going to come for Thanksgiving too?"

"Ah, there's the rub. Do we try to do something nice so that he can mock us or do we neglect to do something nice so that he can point it out? We have no idea how to handle Joshua, you know. He smokes pot all day in that ridiculous boarding school of his. He thinks he hates us. Perhaps we could try to do something psychedelic? Can you imagine the expressions of those brutish housepainters if we asked them to do paisley and glitter? *Monsieur, êtes-vous certain? Que dirait Madame?* But seriously, there is no solution."

"What about an Indian bedspread from that shop by the Luxembourg and some groovy pillows?"

His eyes moistened. He leaned deeper into Portia's bed. "That just might work."

"Maybe you could do the moldings dark, like magenta or something?"

"You think? You think magenta would give the right message? Lydia thought maybe even black. A touch of black. Not too much. But magenta? Katie, we rely on you. What do you think? Honestly?"

So they *had* been discussing Joshua's room.

126

"Magenta or black? Let's concentrate for a minute," he said.

But I couldn't concentrate. Or at least not on colors for the bedrooms of other children. Because what all this desperate painting and nest-feathering really meant was that Joshua and Portia would be here for Thanksgiving in less than two weeks.

twenty-three

"I don't buy this, Katie. You *have* to be able to explain what's wrong."

"Nothing's wrong. Bastien is perfectly nice. He might be fun to kiss at some point, but I'm just not attracted."

"But he has all the elements for a Parisian fling! He's good-looking, he's nice, he's festive, he even plays the piano, and he's a count with a château and everything! Don't you want to check out the château? In champagne country? Or the giant house in Deauville? What a hoot is that? *And* he doesn't take the whole *noblesse* thing too seriously or call his parents *'vous'* or anything absurd. He treats it as sort of a lark."

"Well, he can afford to laugh."

"You've said that before, and you know what it makes me think? It makes me think there's some other boy who *can't* afford to laugh, and I can't believe you're keeping it from me. *C'est pas sympa, ma belle!*"

I fiddled with a pair of vivid pink underpants drying on a string. There were two pink pairs, two skin-colored, a black, and a lime green bra that I loved, all clothespinned in front of my electric space heater.

"You're hurting my feelings," said Christie.

"You swear you won't tell anyone?"

"Who would I tell?"

"Just promise."

"Okay."

I looked around my garret. There was no spot anyone could possibly be hiding to listen in. Besides, no one was interested in this place. When I gave Lydia my monthly rent envelope (cash, please), she barely acknowledged it because we didn't need to speak of such things. I simply appeared downstairs every morning. My room was unmentioned, left entirely to me. I had decorated it with scraps from my recent past, tacked up postcards of waterlilies and of a sculpture of a car that looked like a monkey from the Picasso Museum and a Polaroid of *la bande* splashing in the tiled pool at Les Bains Douches in which I looked flushed and happy.

Since I had no closet, virtually all of my clothes were on display on plank and cinder-block shelves or hanging on the metal bar. I had about a dozen books and a box of oatmeal by the pan on my burner, a couple of bananas, some raisins, some tea. With a glance, I could take stock. Only the old dresser held my dubious lot of treasure. It was safe to talk here.

"I'll tell you everything," I said, "but I need to ask a favor first. If I go away one of these weekends and Lydia and Clarence are out of town, can you walk Orlando for me?"

"Of course. Are you kidding? For a look inside that apartment? Now, come on, who is it?" She folded herself into a locust on my futon. I had splurged on one of the Indian bedspreads I had told Clarence about for Joshua. It was embroidered with elephants and chaotic swirls of tiny mirrors that spiraled from Christie's lanky body.

"I've told you the Schells have kids, right? Well, when I first got here, their daughter—her name is Portia and I've never met her, just talked on the phone and she sounds horrible—her boyfriend, Olivier, was staying in the apartment because he was traveling around Europe for the last time before he started an intense banking job and wouldn't be truly free again for years. And he was going to show me the alarm and the washing machine and the way up to my room, and we sort of fell in love, but obviously couldn't fall openly in love, and then he came back to Paris one more time and we saw each other again and he told me he was leaving her."

"Did you sleep with him?"

"Yep."

"Oh my God."

"It's not like that. It's not some scandal. We have this amazing connection. We've been planning to meet somewhere for a weekend. Not in Paris. Paris would be too dangerous. Portia is really upset about the breakup apparently. But maybe London."

"Honey, you barely know him. From what you're saying, you have a couple of nights' worth of memories. Am I wrong?"

"Great memories."

"Do you really believe you're in love?"

"Um, yeah. I mean, sometimes I worry in the short term that the future is muddled and I can't picture how it will all end. Things work out, though. That's something I know in my bones. Maybe that's why I can calm all these high-maintenance people down."

"I doubt that. I think you calm crazy people down because you're so eager to please that you never make them feel bad."

"I do please people." My voice cracked. She had struck a chord. "I guess it makes me seem stupider than I am. But I have this feeling, Christie, that being an idiot isn't necessarily stupid. I mean I know just enough to know how little I know. Everyone I talk to is smarter than I am. Or at least they are in the moment. I want them to know how smart they are, and I want them to be happy. Does that make any sense?"

"Not much." She looked at me as into a muddy puddle, and I felt all the emotional murk of my argument, but her voice had grown sympathetic. "I want to hear more about this Olivier. Has he broken up with the daughter-girlfriend yet?"

"Yes. According to Clarence, she's taking it hard. That's going to be weird. She's coming for Thanksgiving and everyone expects me to be nice and cheer her up. I'm so nervous. Once I see her face, I'm going to feel terrible."

"Wait a second. I have to point something else out to you as a friend, Katie. This all seems pretty incestuous to me. I mean, that's how it looks from the outside. You're wanting to be part of this family, but you stole this girl's boyfriend."

"I didn't steal anyone! You can't steal a person. This is *our* twist of fate." I blurted. "A person does what a person wants," I added lamely.

"Up to a point, and then a person becomes an asshole."

I pushed down the thought that she might be talking about me. *"Olivier's* not an asshole. He's disentangling himself from Portia and her family. It may not be easy because she's so spoiled, but I trust him."

"You don't feel guilty?"

Maybe if you are dying to please, I began to think, the things you end up doing for yourself can only turn out devious. But if you do nothing for yourself, then who are you?

"Do you want to know what Portia made me do today?" My voice strained with the effort at conviction. "She called with this skinny efficient voice of hers and told me I had to go to the pharmacy to pick up a prescription for her from some fancy doctor friend of her mother's. She said that her mother had told her to call me. She always blames it on Lydia. Only Portia made sure I understood that whatever I was getting was for *her* because she 'really needed it with everything that's going on.' But the way she said it wasn't like she was letting me in at all, more like she's showing me how important her emotional state is, how I need to drop everything and run to the pharmacy. She thinks she can interrupt my whole day to send me to stand in line for a shitload of Valium and then have the pharmacist tell me to *'ne pas en abuser, mademoiselle.'* I mean, go pick up your own Valium. I'm not the—"

"You *are* the assistant."

"I'm Lydia's. I'm Lydia's research assistant. I don't need to know about Portia's meds."

"So Portia's an exhibitionist. That doesn't make you right."

"Okay, but, if Olivier loved her, he wouldn't have been spending the summer without her, right? Don't you think she should have figured that out and taken the hint?"

"Okay. From one perspective, your adventure is all totally normal and hormones in the wind and utterly romantic. But from another perspective, it's kind of fucked up. I mean, Portia is your boss's daughter and you work in your boss's house."

131

"I know it sounds fucked up, but I've never seen her before in my life. Am I supposed to quit my job because I fell in love? People fall in love all the time." I was hugging myself into a ball, the larva to her insect.

"You *will* know her, is all I'm saying. There has to be more to her than phone orders. And it won't be easy. This is heavy, Katie." Her tone shifted into a more pragmatic register. "If they find out, you're going to be scapegoated to high hell. They will no longer think you are remotely great. We have to watch your back. Tell me, where is Olivier now?"

Later that afternoon, in a phone booth on the Place St-Sulpice, I called Morgan Stanley collect.

"Morgan!"

The international operator had a collect call from Paris for a Mr. Olivier de Branche Craft.

"Yes, of course, I accept."

"Hi."

"Hi. It's so, so good to hear your voice. Like a ray of sunshine. I miss you."

"I miss you too. It's not sunny here at all, though. It's raining."

My breath, heavy from my attempt to outrun the storm, was misting up the booth. The shapes of the square outside, the stone slabs and the arches of the doors, the curved green news kiosks, all appeared to float. The passersby swam through my head. But, at the sound of Olivier's voice, I felt anchored.

"I'd love to see the rain in Paris. Where are you?"

"Near St-Sulpice. By a café, the Café de la Mairie. And it's pouring and gray and I'm wearing this horrible down jacket that I hate. I look ridiculous."

"You couldn't look ridiculous. I have no memory of anything ridiculous about you. I'm sure everyone passing your phone booth is falling madly in love with you and I hate that I'm not there to fend them off."

I laughed. The people going by were either smoking under

umbrellas or running with newspapers over their heads. "So, about the weekend in London? I have someone who could walk the dog. My friend Christie."

"You have no idea how badly I want to see you, but there's a chance that if we plan something I'll get hammered at the office and have to cancel."

"Well, it's not like I have a zillion plans. So if you have to push it back, that's okay."

He took the kind of deep breath you might begin an acting class with. "You know what? You're on. Four weekends from now. I'm looking at my calendar. The second weekend in December. You, me, London."

"So, should I buy a plane ticket?"

"I'll take care of all that."

By the time we hung up, the glass of the phone booth was a film over my eyes. No matter where I went from here on out, I would see the world through this film because Olivier and I had a plan. In a month we would be together in London.

I went to the Café de la Mairie and spent a week's food money on a mushroom omelet and a glass of Burgundy.

twenty-four

Suddenly, Claudia was leaving Paris. I came down from my *chambre de bonne* on a bright, cold morning, ready for tea, bread and honey with Clarence and Claudia around our table, but no one was there and the kettle was not on.

I found Claudia in the dining room. With Lydia away, Claudia had been spreading her materials over the big table again. We followed our routine of meals and work and talking into the evening until it was time for me to go upstairs and her to return to her studio in Montparnasse. Most mornings, she appeared in time for breakfast.

Claudia had taught me another couscous recipe, more elaborate than the lamb, with seafood and chicken. Things had become almost as gay as they had been back in September.

But now Claudia was unsmiling. She was sliding her piled notes and her printouts into manila folders, one for each of her Moroccan dissertation dreams, numbered and titled, and layering these folders into a dark red carry-on case. She was rolling up the sweaters and shawls she had strewn around the apartment and burying them in a large duffel bag by the front door.

She said that her thesis committee at Berkeley absolutely had to see her now. There was a problem with her adviser. She was going to have to finish writing in California.

But wasn't her thesis adviser a cretin? Wasn't Clarence her real guiding light? Where was Clarence anyway?

"Sleeping, I assume."

Clarence never slept in.

Well, then perhaps he didn't feel well, she said. In any case, she hadn't seen him yet today, but she might have to leave without saying goodbye because her plane took off at noon and she wanted to go by RER train to the airport. Would I walk her to the Métro station at St-Michel?

Of course I would.

I stayed on her manic but methodical trail up and down the hallway, from dining room table to kitchen to living room, back and forth between the suitcases, as though I were trying to follow the logic of one of her dreams. But although I could shadow her movements, even hand her a notebook or a gold-embroidered wrap from the back of a chair, see the progressive layering of her dissertation and colorful clothes as she packed, I could not quite understand why she was leaving. It was clear that she was tired and nervous and that she was performing her own Baroque departure ritual. But it did not make sense. So, I tried asking questions.

"Did something happen in the last few hours? You didn't know you were leaving last night, did you? You didn't say anything."

"Yes, I had some phone calls once I got back to my place."

"But how can it be such an emergency for you to see your committee right now?"

"There is a deadline for my defense, and I did not understand how important it is. My work may not be accepted if I do not go to Berkeley now. Trust me, I have to find my adviser." For the first time this morning, she looked directly at me and saw that I was sad. "And I also have my best friend in Berkeley who is very sick, so it is a terrible coincidence. I must see him also."

"I'm sorry." I did not know she had a best friend. "Did you have a phone call about that too?"

She stood still. "He has AIDS."

"I'm so sorry. When did you find out?"

"I have known for a time. But now suddenly he feels very bad and I have to go home anyway for my work. So, the urgency is clear for me."

135

Clarence appeared in the dining room in a brown bathrobe. His graying chest hair was matted. He rolled clouded eyes over the table, so alive only yesterday with evidence of Claudia's work. He squinted at its bare surface. He did not see well without his glasses.

"Good morning," he said.

We mumbled greetings.

"Cheer up, you two," he yawned. "This seems like a sudden bloody nuisance for Claudia, but in truth it's the best thing that could have happened to her, her committee threatening to pull the plug, as they say. She's basically finished, you know, and her committee knows it. We all do. It's now a question of doing the conclusion and formalizing some odds and ends. Then, she will have her degree and get on with her life."

"Yes, I will get on with my life, won't I, Clarence?" She shoved the last folder into her carry-on. "I have also told Katie about Francesco being sick."

"Yes, but that's not the reason you're going." His composure slipped. He sounded irritable. "No, the important thing is that you have been given an ultimatum, which is crucial to your career, my dear Claudia."

"Yes, I suppose that is the true version of events."

"It's not a bloody version! It is the thing that is happening. Paris is nothing but procrastination for you. We've been over this."

I had never heard Clarence bicker with Claudia before. Their arguments had always been playful and theoretical. Perhaps he realized this too because he apologized.

"I'm very sorry, you two," he said. "I've had an awful bout with insomnia and I'm afraid I'm going to have to go back to bed. This happens to me from time to time. So, I'm not 'in my plate today,' as the frogs say. You'll have to excuse me. And I can't find my glasses. Claudia, you haven't seen my glasses?"

"Why would I have seen them?" Claudia hissed. "Why don't you look in your own bedroom?"

"Right, I'll just go lie down now."

Claudia went to the bathroom.

Instead of going back to bed, Clarence motioned me into the kitchen, put the kettle on, and told me that I should know that Claudia was quite unstable, if brilliant, and that in order for her to have a career, which she richly deserved, she would have to have her energies channeled by forces far stronger than ours. He was not up to the task, and he was not her official adviser. It was crucial that she build the kind of academic alliances she was going to need in the States. We couldn't care for her forever. No, the time was right. Besides, he was on sabbatical to finish his own book. He had deadlines. He couldn't afford to be distracted like this anymore.

"Well, I'll miss her," I said.

"She'll miss you too. In fact, I hope you will help her to the Métro station. I would, but I feel awful, and Lydia's on her way home so I have to pull myself together somehow."

"Lydia's coming today?"

"Yes, she called. She's decided to descend on us early. She needs to start processing all her German photos. The nightmare resumes this evening." He laughed.

"Oh." It would be bad form to laugh with him, but I managed half a smile before I changed the subject. "It's so horrible about Claudia's friend with AIDS."

"Oh, that. She's conflating things, as usual. She has mentioned the sick friend once or twice, but, in all honesty, he may be made-up. Her grasp on reality is hardly firm, you realize. The AIDS story is simply heightening the drama of it all. Claudia is a bit crazy, you know, a bit touched."

I wanted to shake him. Until this morning, I had assumed Claudia was one of us. But today she was a crazy distraction and we wanted to get rid of her and good riddance. Had she been a burden this whole time? Had Clarence been desperate all the while for her to leave so that he could concentrate? In my fantasy that she was in love with him and perhaps he a little bit with her, had I completely missed the point?

Claudia was out of the bathroom. She was ready to go. She

strapped her duffel bag to a set of traveling wheels and slung her carry-on over her shoulder. She and Clarence had a stiff hug by the door.

As she and I set off across the courtyard, Madame Fidelio, clutching an armful of newspapers, watched us from her doorway.

At the top of the stairs of the St-Michel Métro station, Claudia took off her multicolored gloves to open her wallet for a ticket. I kept my hands in my pockets. It was freezing.

"Listen," she said, quick and conspiratorial. "We finally have a few moments to speak. I am very sorry to leave you so suddenly. And there is something I must tell you. Clarence said to me last night that you are like the beautiful sky, serene over a battle."

I shook my head. More proof of my role as a sanctioning observer.

"But you are not a placid sky. You cannot let him think that. It is very important that you start expressing your own opinions, giving them a voice. Like when you draw, you make choices, no?"

"Not really. I draw as purely as I can."

"That's not true. You make choice after choice, my dear."

I wanted to tell her she was mistaken, but suddenly I wasn't sure.

"I know you are very strong," she went on, "not too high above the world at all. No, Clarence is wrong. He does not understand the way the real world is working."

She embraced me less warmly than I would have liked and hurried into the station. The wintry air rippled around her disappearance, settling again within seconds.

I looked up at the leafless branches above St-Michel. I had been in Paris nearly three months. It was time to call Jacques and Solange.

twenty-five

Jacques answered the phone. There was no accusation to modulate the delight in his voice at the sound of mine.

"How is my little Rastignac? You are seducing all of Paris, no? Your mother tells us you are a rising star in the world of the arts."

His words unleashed an olfactory memory of the tiny kitchen in the Nineteenth, a blend of bouillons and coffee grinds, slow-cooking garlic and browning crêpes. It was a historic smell, old and textured despite the soulless concrete walls of the apartment bloc that encased it. Since the kitchen was the warmest room in the house, I did my homework there, on a laminated table cloth with an orchard theme. Jacques would slip dark chocolate into my pencil case, for inspiration.

"Rastignac?" I laughed. "You're still impossible!" Instantly we were back in our age-old joke where I was Balzac's Provençal hero, decoding the capital, and, after a few disastrous mistakes, taking it by storm. "How are you? How is Solange?"

"Solange is cooking bolets in case you decide to come to Orléans for dinner. You should see the beautiful kitchen we have here. She is like a fish in water."

Bolets were my favorite mushrooms. We used to drive out to the country to gather them in the fall, then take them to our local pharmacy to be checked because it was the job of every *pharmacien* to recognize poison mushrooms that might have masqueraded as edible. Afterward there was a flurry of omelettes aux bolets, chickens in their earthy fricassée, even the occasional veal dish to celebrate our harvest in style. At the end of each meal, Étienne would pretend to be poisoned and stage a gasping death over dessert, until one day he stopped. His parents must have told him that making light of death was insensitive to my situation.

When Jacques put Solange on, she asked if I was eating enough in Paris, if the lady I worked for knew how to cook or had *domestiques* to do everything for her, if my work was interesting, if I would like to come and spend Christmas with them.

I said I would love to come. Would she please make rabbit with prunes? I thought I could picture their Orléans interior, comfortable and cluttered, with the collection of Limoges china pillboxes displayed in a glass cabinet in the *salon*.

"*Lapin aux pruneaux, mais bien sûr, ma cocotte!*"

Then her tone changed to pleading. Had I seen Étienne?

Yes, I had seen him several times. I loved seeing him.

How was he doing? He was living such an irregular life that they were worried about his health.

I could hear Jacques breathing in Solange's ear, "Do not worry Katie so about Étienne. Do not perturb *la petite*," as though I were still a little girl in need of shelter from bad news.

I assured them that he was full of energy, that his rent-stabilized apartment near the Bastille was big and decent. He had managed to take over a lease from a friend who had moved away. This was only a little illegal. Besides, artists had their own moral code, no, apart from the rest?

"He's invited me to move in with him instead of paying rent to my boss. But I can't. It's part of my contract that I live on site. I'd love to stay with Étienne though. You should see how clean his place his. He's a maniac about cleaning." I laughed. "But you must know that." I didn't mention his passion for shoplifting household products—bleaches, brooms, even an iron once.

"And does he cook for himself?"

"He's an elegant cook. Everything he makes is pretty. And interesting. He makes very colorful salads."

"Yes, but are they nourishing?"

"I wouldn't go that far," I said as lightly as I could. *"Il surveille sa ligne."*

"Sa ligne?" She sounded terrified.

"He looks wonderful, Solange. And happy."

"Maybe he will come for Christmas too?"

twenty-six

Gingerly, I held a photograph of one of the very first breaks in the Berlin Wall. It was taken in the morning, from the west. I saw a line of movement, framed on either side by gray concrete scrawled with black graffiti. The gray was the standing Wall, probably rubble by now but here still imposing. The section of light in the middle, the break, was only bright by comparison. It was not a dazzling morning at all, and still the daylight was a relief.

From behind, there was a row of raised arms, waving bunches of flowers, reaching through the fresh gap toward a row of police officers on the other side. From the thrust of their bouquets, I guessed that the West Germans were singing or chanting. The East German soldiers, in olive hats, were looking through the hole in the concrete, out over the flowering hands, toward the other Berlin.

Paris Match was preparing its special issue dedicated to the history of the Wall. It would include this shot of Lydia's in my hands. The space in the concrete, a slice of light and of movement, was a strip of hope, Lydia said, right before everything was leveled.

The doorbell rang and I excused myself to go answer.

It was Madame Fidelio with a package for *la jolie petite,* who was coming tomorrow with the brother. Madame Lydia must be very happy, *non?* And all the painting in the apartment was finished? She stepped through the foyer doors into the hallway, peered into the living room where two workmen were finally hanging the brass clock up over the mantel where it belonged. The living room walls were now a few shades lighter than a papaya. You might call them apricot.

Madame Fidelio turned to me and clucked.

"Katherine!" Lydia called me back into her office. "I need you *now*."

I felt a surge of anxiety about an amorphous task she had set me a few days back, Research on the Muslim religion that I hadn't started for lack of a clear idea how. Was she going to call me on it already?

The mock-up of the upcoming *Match* was on her desk. The cover was going to be a wide shot of a huge mixed crowd, hanging out under what I now easily recognized as the Brandenburg Gate.

Just above the Brandenburg Gate photo was a half-eaten container of the spring rolls from the great Vietnamese takeout place on the rue du Bac. She had made me promise not to let her have those anymore. Who could have picked them up?

"Lydia," I said, hoping to preempt disaster with an earnest question, "I don't understand what exactly I'm supposed to do about the Koran scholars in England. I'm not sure where to begin." She had told me to summarize the thoughts of a few modern Muslim scholars, but hadn't told me why or which ones. "I mean, do you want me to go back in history or just stay in the present? What is this for?"

"You're smart. You're well educated and resourceful. And *verbal*. It's all a question of words. I know you'll figure it out."

So much trust was staggering. I wanted direction. I wanted to do a good job. To be taken on faith, with no guidelines, made me deeply nervous. I began to formulate another question, but she interrupted me.

"All right," she sighed. "We have two days to pull Thanksgiving together. In theory, Portia is smuggling in the cranberries from the States. We'll see if she remembers. We have the turkey ordered and the sausage for the *farce* from that wonderful *charcutier* right off of Montparnasse. I like to do a hazelnut and prune stuffing. We can get the fruit and nuts at Hédiard. And for the rest, the vegetables and what have you, we'll go to Bon Marché and have a big *livraison*. Is it terrible if I don't bake pies? Maybe you can stop by Mulot and order one of those chestnut Mont Blanc fluffy cake things. Portia loves a Mont Blanc and you can't get them in New York. But for the apple tart, go to Poilâne."

"Where's Poilâne?"

"On the rue du Cherche-Midi, right around the corner from that awful Futurist sculpture of the soldier on the horse."

"I'll find it."

"Of course you will. You find everything, don't you? Do you think we need a soup to start? Does your mother do a soup? How does your mother do Thanksgiving?"

The way Mom "did" Thanksgiving was so foreign to all this that I felt a sad sense of righteousness and was relieved when Lydia did not wait for an answer and segued straight into her wine anxiety.

"I'm going to send Sally into the *cave* even though I'm loathe to. But she's a terrible wine snob and I have to trust her because we may have Rushdie's French publishers at the table. They've had bomb threats, you know, poor souls, and they may leave the country. But if they're still here on Thursday, then we can't have anything less than a Margaux, and I don't trust Clarence further than I can throw him with Bordeaux. He can work his way around Burgundies and Rhônes, but he's hopeless with the Bordeaux. He has this ridiculous notion that they're overvalued, so he refuses to pay attention to them. You'll see, when he sees we're drinking Margaux for Thanksgiving, he'll sulk all night . . . Or maybe I'll send Harry down to the *cave*. What do you think? Harry's even better than Sally for this sort of thing." She handed me a legal pad. "Let's make a list. Then maybe you'll take it to Clarence—he's been locked in his study all day, working, we hope—to see if he thinks we've forgotten anything."

As I took Lydia's dictation, black felt on yellow paper, the fact of Thanksgiving, which was really the fact of Portia, became inevitable. So much of this fuss was for her. She *was* the occasion.

"As I say, Portia loves chestnuts. Let's put some in the Brussels sprouts. You can get them already roasted at the *épicerie* in the Bon Marché. Add chestnuts to your list for our long-suffering Portia."

As I wrote the word "chestnuts," a dam burst inside me. A long slow buildup of guilt and fear, come to its tipping point, flooded my conscience. I looked down at my shaking hands and couldn't believe they still held their shape.

I could argue all I wanted that my meeting Olivier had been an amazing coincidence, that I had put myself in the way of chance, that he would have left her anyway. But try telling that to Portia, who had asked me to count the pills in her Valium pack and report the number back to her before leaving them in the drawer of her dressing table. The top right drawer please.

Portia was coming tomorrow, for real. Everything was about to change. The wall between us was coming down.

twenty-seven

Portia was impossibly thin, short but willowy, otherworldly as a surrealist watercolor. The explanation for her great delicacy did not remain a secret very long.

"Heartbreak," she said when she saw my eyes drop to her sagging suede pants the first time we were alone. "I don't usually look like this. I can barely stand to eat." There was accusation in her voice.

I stiffened. Was she waiting to pounce on me? Was it conceivable that Olivier had told her? Or that Madame Fidelio had seen the two of us wandering in and out of the courtyard that first day, guessed, and taken Portia aside to say that this assistant was even more of a slut than the last one?

Although Portia's blond hair and blue eyes were recognizable from her pictures, I could not match her expression to the voice on the phone. She didn't look officious. She looked dramatically sad.

"Your mom told me you've been pretty upset." My instinct was to be nice, but being nice made me queasy. This moment of meeting her was the moment I became a liar. Passing through it, seemingly unscathed, was bizarre. It was the abruptest change of season I had ever been through, like getting off a plane in the Caribbean in February, which I'd never actually done, but I bet she had.

A surge of jealously steeled me. "Your mom says you're having a hard time getting over your ex-boyfriend."

"Really?" The roll of her eyes was suspicious, but I could not tell whether she suspected me, suspected her mother, or was

146

simply in the habit of mistrust. "What exactly did my mother tell you?"

In a flailing attempt to hide my fear, I clung to the rules of conversation and answered her as normally as I could.

"Well, she told me that she's worried about you, about your breakup and how hard it's been. I think she's worried you don't feel like you can talk to her. Typical mom stuff. She wants you to feel better."

"I wish it were typical mom stuff. I wish she were truly worried about me. I wish she could be." Her words were as airy as she was, but her eyes were solid, big globes shining at me with what might be the beginnings of gratitude. They bulged like Lydia's, but they were deeper set and in such contrast to her fairness that they leant a shadowy quality to her beauty.

Clarence had described Portia as pure and ethereal, a Raphael. No, Claudia had disagreed, from her photographs Portia was a Caravaggio, but no man could say that about his own daughter. Because Caravaggio's models were prostitutes.

In any case, I began to think that she was a work of art, with all of art's signifying power, and that right now that power was concentrated in those big strange eyes, which seemed to say, "Thank you for letting me know that my mother has asked you to spy on me. I understand you're going through the motions of your job, but I also get that I can trust you, right?"

I felt a perverse compunction to stop the bleeding from my own misfired gun. This was not at all what I expected.

But just as I was beginning to think I might like her, Portia pulled herself together and asked how I was enjoying Paris. "Isn't the shopping out of this world?"

The shopping? On six hundred dollars a month minus four hundred for rent? Did she know she was being deeply rude? Was she clueless or was she trying to show me who was on top?

No, it was none of those things. She was simply attempting to place me. And I felt so unplaceable that her appraising glance did not so much offend as depress me.

What could she see? A brown-haired girl with pretty eyes and apple cheeks, broad healthy shoulders and long legs. I had a high bouncy ponytail. I probably looked like a nice, sympathetic person. I wore a short denim skirt with leggings and leg warmers and an asymmetrical sweater several years out of style. I had on shoes that Christie had bought in the last round of Parisian sales which had proved too small for her. They were two-toned olive and red. I did not look like an idiot. I did not look threatening either.

"The Parisian women certainly are out of this world." I let out a lame giggle. "They're so put together compared to us Americans, or compared to me I mean."

I sat down on the couch and began to knead a cushion.

Portia smoothed the buttery seat of her floating pants and joined me. From the hallway, smells of fennel sausage and onions curling in underneath the door began, softly, to knot us together. Lydia was working on the stuffing for Thanksgiving dinner tomorrow.

The living room, like Portia's bedroom, was in a perfect state of readiness for her arrival. She knew nothing of the messy preproduction that the rest of us had endured.

"I haven't had time to shop much," I added. "There's been a lot going on here. It's been interesting though."

"It's a madhouse. Still, I can see why it might be interesting from your perspective. Dad says you have a great attitude."

"Your dad's sweet."

She filled her face with meaning. "Listen, did my mom happen to mention, when she was telling you how worried she is about poor me, that she's still close with Olivier?"

I dug my nails into the couch. "Well, no, not so much. I mean she did say that it might be your perception that she's close with him because she and he used to get along. She may have thought he was charming while it lasted, but, but, but *really* she is *your* mother. So I can't imagine she's too worried about staying friends with an ex-boyfriend of yours."

"Of course you would assume that, wouldn't you? Any normal person would. Mothers are supposed to be loyal to their daughters, right?" She was tearing. "Olivier was here, you know, spending time with her, right before you came, going to restaurants with her and drinking wine. They were talking about me together in my own house, concerned about me like I was some child. It's her fault he can't take me seriously. She has no boundaries."

I turned my face downward to the pathetic, but lovely, suede pants. "I'm so sorry," I said.

No, this was not how I expected to feel.

The living room door opened and in popped Lydia. She was wearing a yellow Provençal apron. Her voice rolled gravelly and flirtatious. "My girls, you have to come taste this. We may have to send Clarence out for more tarragon and more sage. It might be a little bland. But you'll tell me. Come, come."

We followed her into the kitchen, where a bowl of cranberry sauce was cooling in the center of the table.

The lovely smells were coming from two blue Dutch ovens, one large, one small. Lydia danced in their steam. She did not want us looking so perturbed in her festive kitchen. "You girls are much too serious. Portia, you look like death warmed over. When was the last time you ate?"

"I eat ice cream every night, Mother."

Lydia sighed at me. "Her roommate spoons it into her mouth. A few bites of ice cream, and that's it. How do you study on that?"

"It's the only thing I can stand to swallow right now."

"I wish I had that problem!" Lydia dipped two teaspoons into her stuffing, blew on them long and loudly, then held them to our mouths. "Tell me! Tell me!"

As we tasted the stuffing, I saw a flicker of pleasure in Portia's face. It was over as soon as it began, but it was enough to show me that she could stand to eat, and that maybe there was hope for her.

"It's great, Lydia," I said.

"More herbs? More port? Speak now."

"No, it's perfect."

Portia looked at the smaller pot. "What's in that one?"

"Your brother's stuffing."

149

"He can't eat our stuffing?"

"He's announced he's a vegan. And I can't have my son with no stuffing on Thanksgiving. What kind of *mère indigne* would I be?"

"Unbelievable!" Portia fluttered on a gust of anger. Her voice grew bigger than she was. "I cannot believe you are catering to his every whim, always catering to him. You're creating a monster! Besides, vegans don't eat turkey."

"I know that. I'm going to stuff him a pumpkin and I'm happy to stuff one for you, too, darling if you're feeling left out. Would you like one too? A pumpkin for my pumpkin?"

"I can't fathom this!"

"How did you make Joshua's stuffing?" I asked cheerfully.

"I'm glad somebody's interested. I used bread cubes and lots of celery and nuts, some vegetable stock. It's not half-bad. Would you like to taste?" And she took back my spoon and dipped it into the smaller pot.

"Mother, stop!" But it was too late. "Mother, how can you be so completely disrespectful? He's a vegan for Christ's sake! You can't plunge a sausage-covered spoon into his stuffing!"

A spasm coiled through Lydia, halting in a crazy electric smile. "He'll never know, will he?"

"It's all for show with you, isn't it?" Portia left. Seconds later, we heard the door to her room slam shut.

I took the spoon from Lydia and tried the vegan stuffing. "This one's good too," I said. I still had not met Joshua. He had vanished to his room immediately on arriving. So far, this celery and nut mixture was all I had to go on. I began to picture someone squirrely.

"Of course it's good." She shook her head to relax her mouth. "It's good because I made it for my son. You don't think she'll tell him about the spoon, do you?"

"Oh no, she wouldn't," I said. "She wouldn't say anything." Portia's forgotten all about it. I was fairly certain that her brother's potential offense was simply one more path back to her own sorrow.

"How do you think she's doing?" asked Lydia. "Has Oliver been just terrible to her? Maybe you'll be able to give her some

150

perspective, engage with her about Paris, do museums, do some shopping, go out. I can tell she likes you."

"Of course. I'd love to." The fact that I *had* to be nice to Portia would save me from total hypocrisy, wouldn't it? It was part of my job to be polite even though she made me feel awful about the way I dressed and the fact that I could not afford to be like the magical women here in Paris any more than I could afford to fly home to my own mom for Thanksgiving. I needed to smile at her, no matter that she would consider me her worst enemy if she knew where I stood with Olivier, because my desire to be loved was stronger than my guilt. And because, despite her irritating qualities, I was already drawn to her. "I'll try my best to cheer her up."

"Tell me, Katherine, does she blame Olivier?"

"No," I said in a horrible rush of relief, "I don't think she can blame him yet." She blames you, Lydia, ridiculous as it seems, you and you alone.

I excused myself, ran up the five flights to my room.

From the family photo on my packing chest, I felt the enduring light of my father's approval. His eyes were beaming. The set of his mouth was gentle.

During our weekly phone calls from Jacques and Solange's house, his voice had grown progressively more positive and all-forgiving, as though he were realizing that time was too short for criticism, that the only thing worthy of passing on was unconditional love.

It was a love I returned every day of my life. But was I proving worthy of it?

As he died, Dad also grew more nostalgic for the myth of his French origins. He referred with outsized intensity to the two summers he had spent with Jacques camping in the South of France. He said that if he had to miss me, he loved knowing that I was getting back to our roots.

twenty-eight

Late in the afternoon of Thanksgiving day, Christie called me at Lydia's to say that Bastien's parents had told him, out of the blue, that they were getting divorced. "Bastien's devastated. His father is almost definitely having an affair. But that's usually not enough to break up a marriage in this country. The affair isn't what Bastien's upset about. He thinks they should stay together for him, which makes some sense until you realize that he's twenty-five."

"That's terrible." I wanted to get off the phone. Clarence was getting ready to serve *l'apéritif* in the living room and I felt sure that Joshua would finally make an appearance. The guests would be arriving soon.

Madame Fidelio was helping Lydia in the kitchen. There were rich smells and much clanging of dishes. A big flower delivery had arrived, masses of roses from Salman Rushdie's French publishers filling the kitchen sink. Well-brought-up people apparently sent flowers ahead of time rather than foisting last-minute bouquets on their hosts. ("*Savoir vivre* is so refreshing, isn't it? Doesn't it drive your mother crazy, when people show up and throw loose flowers at her in the middle of a party?") I might be expected to arrange the roses. I wanted a drink. This was not a good time to talk.

"Christie, I should probably go. Can I call you back later tonight?"

"Sure, but let me tell you what the upshot is."

"The upshot?" I have to go.

152

"Bastien is so upset. He honestly had no idea about his parents. He thought they were in love. He keeps crying and playing the same piano piece over and over."

As she started to hum a bit of the *Moonlight* Sonata, Bastien's sorrow, no matter how silly his life might seem, became flesh for me. I had seen his mother once. She had hair like cotton candy, but he adored her. I began to picture him in his vulgar beige *salon* crying at his piano beneath the orchid painting. It was terrible.

Portia's voice from the kitchen yanked me back into the Schell orbit.

"Mother, why are all these flowers just sitting in the sink? They look so depressing."

"Don't ask me. I have no idea where people have put my vases. Is your father opening the Sancerre yet? Do we need to send him a note? Where's Katherine?"

Christie was still humming into the receiver.

"So, what *is* the upshot, Christie? I'm sorry but I should hang up. Things are heating up around here."

"He's so upset that he's blowing off both his parents for Christmas and he wants us to go to his house in Deauville with him for a *Noël de réfugiés*. He says the casino will be open and that winter is the best time for oysters."

To be a refugee in Deauville at Christmastime. I certainly didn't have the money to go back to the States, and Lydia and Clarence planned to be in New York, where they "did" Christmas better. Paris was somewhat depressing over the holidays, Lydia said. Deauville was tempting. But I had promised Jacques and Solange.

"I was going to spend Christmas in Orléans with my cousins."

Christmas Eve was the one night of the year when Solange splurged on scallops. She arranged them in a buttery tarragon sauce in their giant shells. It was a big deal. But if Bastien was really suffering, and I could somehow help, and have oysters and champagne in a seaside casino, maybe this was the moment to choose the new over the old. I couldn't turn my back on either picture.

"I'll have to think about it, Christie."

As I came into the living room, Clarence handed me a glass of peach-blushed wine.

None of the guests had arrived yet. We were *en famille*.

Joshua, sitting on the ottoman, had what looked like an old magazine open in his lap. He was bent over a picture of a pair of scissors. There were pimples on the back of his neck and a premature slackness to his shoulders. He squirmed in his button-down collar and burrowed his gaze into the pages.

Clarence walked behind him, peering into the magazine. "A revolutionary invention, the scissor."

"Clarence," said Lydia with high-pitched weariness, "must you go slapping down interpretations all over the place?"

"I thought I was making conversation with my son, my dear."

Joshua flipped slowly to a photograph of a wrench, then blinked up at me. He was stoned.

"Hi, I'm Joshua," he said, holding out his hand for me to reach. When he failed to stand up, I was faintly disgusted. It seemed the manners of the French *BCBG* boys were leaving their impression after all. I was beginning to expect certain things.

Joshua had his father's full lips and generally overripe features, so that Portia, in a silk shirt dress, high heels, red lipstick and blush with pale powder foundation, looked chiseled beside him. They were both strangely old, but she wore it better.

Madame Fidelio came in with a vase of red roses, tightly arranged. She shot an irritated glance at my wineglass, then turned to Lydia. *"Ça vous plait, madame?"*

"C'est magnifique, Madame Fidelio. Put them right here, on the *table basse."*

Madame Fidelio obliged, putting the flowers on the coffee table, then rushed off, muttering insinuations in my direction about how many more flowers were still in the kitchen sink waiting to be arranged.

I gulped my Kir.

"Portia," said Joshua, "what's with the lipstick? You don't

need that shit. Does Olivier make you feel like you need that shit?"

"You've all misjudged him!" Tears appeared, gathering powder as they streaked down Portia's face, swelling into pearls. "He doesn't take everything for granted like we all do. He has to work and think so hard. He understands how much work it takes to make something beautiful. He's so pure that way, so honest."

"Like an artist," I said helpfully.

"Like an asshole," said Joshua, staring at me as though he couldn't believe I could be so disconnected from reality.

"Please, Joshua," said Lydia.

"No, Lydia, let him talk," said Clarence. "He's only voicing his concern. It's his way of telling his sister she's beautiful, naturally so, and that she doesn't need all this rubbish on her face."

"Yeah," said Joshua, and flipped his bloodshot gaze back to the magazine, which I saw was the *Fortune* from 1955 that Lydia had recently bought at an auction. It had a famous photo essay in it by Walker Evans called "Beauties of the Common Tool." I supposed she had put it out today for the Thanksgiving guests to admire.

Portia did not stop crying. I went to get her a tissue, for which she looked disproportionately grateful. I finished my drink. I said the flowers were beautiful and everyone agreed except Joshua, who was tracing the wrench on the page with his index finger.

"Joshua darling, be careful of that Walker Evans. It's a treasure," said Lydia. "And it wasn't cheap."

"Don't you want your peach Kir?" Clarence motioned to Joshua's untouched glass.

Joshua looked up from "Beauties of the Common Tool." "You're right, Mom, this is a very nice essay. You should do something like this. Let's see, what would your common tools be? Fax machine. Credit card. Diet pills. Different-color diet pills. Papaya diet powders. Straws. I can see it now, all elegance and purity."

Clarence picked up Joshua's glass and thrust it outward, sloshing pink wine all over his hand. "Please let's not start off this way. Your mother's been cooking for two days. Have your drink, Joshua."

Joshua waved his father away. "Can I at least have a real drink?"

Trembling now, Clarence turned the bronze key in the red lacquer cabinet full of bottles and glasses. I recognized the Armagnac and the lead crystal from Prague. "Be my guest, son."

"Got any scotch?" Joshua stood and went to look. I saw his eyes skid along the shelves and recognized his confusion. He wasn't sure what he was looking for. He didn't know his stuff.

Clarence, as if to give him privacy in his embarrassment, turned his back to Joshua and blocked him from our view.

"Lydia, don't take it wrong. He's merely showing his appreciation for what you can achieve when you're true to yourself as an artist."

"Well, this is no fun." Lydia grabbed her glass and went to the door. "I'm going to baste the turkey if no one here needs me. Clarence, give Joshua the single malt that Harry Mathews brought over last month. Harry always knows what he's doing."

"Enabler," Portia muttered. "You're always getting Joshua drunk. It's so irresponsible."

"Listen, you." Lydia put her hands on her hips. "I know a lot more than any of you about responsibility. I helped end the Vietnam War and I will not be called irresponsible in my own house."

Joshua gulped his scotch and addressed me. "Mom just missed being World Press Photo of the Year in 1968. She was there when that guy took that *really* famous shot of the soldier shooting the prisoner, the one that *was* photo of the year."

Lydia went out and slammed the door.

"Joshua, that was perfectly beastly of you." Clarence motioned us to sit down. "Don't worry though. She won't disappear. She might have"—he shook a scolding finger at his son—"were it not for the guests. She'll pull herself together for them. But let's talk about something else, shall we?"

Joshua poured himself a second scotch. "Okay, let's. Let's talk about Muslim fundamentalists."

"Oh, please," Clarence moaned.

"No," Portia sniffled, "this is interesting. I want to hear what my brother has to say."

"All I have to say is there's some weird shit going down and Mom's back in the old fatigues."

"Your mother gave up war photography when she had you two. That was our pact."

"Some pact," Joshua laughed. "She's headed to England on Saturday for some big 'Death to Rushdie' demonstration."

"Nonsense. There's no war in England, and your mother isn't going anywhere."

"Oh yes she is. She's leaving before our vacation is over, leaving us here in Paris with you to try to get herself a photo-op. Fuck that, right?"

"Don't be disrespectful of your mother's career. And she's not going to England on Saturday."

"Fuck she isn't. And fuck her dinner." Carrying his drink, he stormed out of the room.

In his wake, pale Portia looked positively angelic.

twenty-nine

I woke up with a headache. Lydia had sent Harry Mathews, and not Sally Meeks, into the cellar to pick a Margaux worthy of the Rushdie publishers, who turned out to be as pretty and as overwhelming as their flowers. They had not spoken a word to me all night. Harry, though, kept saying he promised to look out for me in this crowd if I swore I would buy an umbrella soon, reminding me of the promise he had exacted the night of dinner with Umberto Eco. He also kept refilling my glass because this Margaux wasn't the kind of stuff you came across often. This morning, I was suffering from his generosity.

Hangovers were suffused with shame for me, which I attributed to the sense, lingering from college, that I was wasting Mom's hard-earned money by killing brain cells with alcohol and lying around uselessly for hours, eating toast and not going to class. So, I was sheepish when I came into Lydia's office at ten o'clock, and I thought she was too.

"Listen," she said. "Why don't you have the day off today. I'm going to take Portia shopping with Sally and her discount. Journalists can get thirty percent off almost everything here and of course Sally milks it.

"But poor Portia could use some cheering up. So, I don't feel too guilty cheating the French government. She's still wearing that awful makeup that she thinks Olivier likes, because it reminds him of his perfect mother somehow, and I heard her sobbing in

158

her room last night. I think it would mean a lot to her if I had a day with her, shopping and lunch, a real mother-daughter day. You understand."

"Of course." What was all this about Olivier and the awful makeup? Was the girl in his sketch reading his letters on the Place des Vosges wearing foundation and blush along with her pink toenail polish? I would have to take it out tonight and look more closely.

"Has she said anything else to you about Olivier? She won't talk to me, you know. I can't understand why, but I have to assume it's developmental."

"She's said she's heartbroken."

"Poor girl. This is terrible. Why is he doing this to her? He should love her, don't you think? You'll see when you're a mother. Nothing is more upsetting than seeing your child suffer. Who on Earth is he to reject her?"

I stiffened inside. Olivier was not simply someone who had rejected Lydia Schell's daughter, he was my fantasy. How dare she? But, then again, how dare I?

When I moved to escape, she called me back. I braced myself for a new errand.

"Katherine, I saw you with a sketchbook the other day. It got me thinking that I never hear about your drawing or painting or whatever it is you do. It's fine if you want to be quiet about it, but make sure you make some progress. Time flies, even at your age. You'd be surprised. And if you ever want to show me anything, of any kind, I don't have such a bad eye, you know. I'd be interested. Don't feel embarrassed."

"You have time?" Her curiosity was too thrilling to process. I could only blush.

"Of course I have time," she said. "Well, maybe not before I leave on Saturday. But after this England trip I'll have some time."

"Thanks."

She looked at me sideways. "Katherine, if you want to do something creative, life won't wait."

"I'm going to do some sketching in the city this afternoon."

"That's wonderful, but before you go, take this to Clarence in his study, will you?" She handed me a folded note. "It's something about dinner tonight. Oh and you don't mind taking Orlando with you, do you? The poor beast could use some exercise and we're all awfully tied up around here."

Bristling, I said that of course I would take Orlando. Was that the price I had to pay for the glimmer of interest she had just bestowed on my artistic development?

I smiled a crushing smile, buried my defiance, gathered the note, the leash, and a new sketchbook, which had been a present from Claudia after my disastrous portrait attempt. It was the expensive, marbled Italian kind. She had said that she wanted me to use it to start copying the Old Masters and at the same time sketching the people I met and the things I saw. She said I should also take notes.

"Alternate these things and you will see all kinds of hazarded connections. You don't have to show me. Although I would be very interested. And I admit that I would be curious to see how you draw Clarence's family, if you ever decide to draw them. I will want to ask about them, but I should not. I hate the term 'self-control,' and I despise the term 'exercise.'" She laughed. "But, I will exercise self-control and ask you no questions. And seriously, it is time for you to begin your own work, not just doing studies to calm yourself. You must start admitting that you make your own art. Otherwise, you will drown in that house."

Leaving Lydia now, I recalled the sketchbook in Claudia's small hands, those colorful gloves. I couldn't quite believe she was gone for good. It would have been right for her and Lydia to have known one another. I had a powerless urge to bring them together.

On my way to Clarence's office with the note, I bumped into Joshua with a bag of croissants, chewing loudly down the hallway. The sweet odor of yeast mingled with patchouli.

"Hey, thanks for picking out my Indian bedspread. Dad told me it was your idea. It's cool."

"Sure."

"So, how was dinner? Unbearable?"

"Oh, it was fine. Really, everyone had a good time. Your mom's an incredible cook when she puts her mind to it. How was your pumpkin?"

After the blowup last evening, Lydia had asked me to knock on his bedroom door with a plate because she hadn't slaved over his special stuffing for nothing and he was always hungry what with growing so fast and all the dope he smoked, and he wouldn't dare slam the door in your face, Katherine.

"The pumpkin was all right."

"Cool."

I knocked on Clarence's study door. I said I had a note from Lydia.

He was right in the middle of something. Could I slip it under?

I did. I turned to go. He called me back, opened the door a crack and returned the paper. Could I take this back to Lydia? Across her question, "Cherche-Midi for dinner tonight?" he had scrawled, "Absolutely not. No point in eating Italian in Paris."

I called Étienne, woke him up, asked him to meet me in a couple of hours in the sculpture garden of the Rodin Museum.

Almost free, snug in my down jacket, I ran into Portia in the courtyard. She was walking very slowly, her face strained by the weight of her giant eyes. I wondered if she had taken one of her Valium pills in order to be able to face a day of "bonding" with her mother. She looked long and hard at Orlando and me, as if we were scrambled and she were waiting for our features to fall into place. Then, with strange dips in her voice, she said she would love to take me out for a drink later and did I want to sneak off maybe around five?

thirty

Under an improbably blue sky, I pulled Orlando all the way to the Rodin Museum, where I tied him to a bench from which I had a great angle on the bronze Balzac. Balzac, who, despite the manic upheaval of his own life, always brought to mind Jacques's deep certitude that *Les Illusions perdues* was the most important novel within the most important oeuvre of all time.

I drew, almost forgetting that my hands were cold. As my hangover lifted, I felt a rebirth, my own personal spring at the end of November. Even though it was freezing, it was a beautiful day. My head was nearly mine again and I was finally at some kind of work.

I didn't produce a portrait exactly. My sketch was technically a copy. But it bore the stamp of my fascination for the writer's expression, which I interpreted with an ambiguity I had heretofore guarded against in my drawing. I was gripped by the pointedness of his gaze. Despite a broad fleshy face, he was eagle-sharp. Rodin had captured the contradiction, and I tried to recapture it with my very own shading of eyes and lips.

About noon, Étienne appeared in a tight studded leather jacket carrying two camembert-and-butter baguette sandwiches, and two Comice pears. "I dare you to eat them together," he said. Jacques and Solange used to tease me that fruit in the same bite with cheese was a desecration, but I always liked the combination. "Let's spit on their morals." He laughed. "Let's see your drawing."

I showed him my Balzac.

"Not bad at all. I like how you changed his lips. He looks hungry."

"I didn't change them." I was suddenly defensive. "I don't change things. I see them. I have a talent for seeing. I was just messing around, I guess, with the mouth and eyes. I don' t usually do that."

"Why not?"

"It seems like playing tricks. I like to show the beauty that's really there. It's almost like I'm a machine or a camera when I draw. It feels very methodical, very quiet. Or it has until now. This is not usual for me at all, this fudging."

"So you admit that you did change the lips, even though you don't like to. *Quelle desecration!*"

He made me laugh. "I guess you could say that."

He took a big bite of his pear and a nibble of sandwich. "Ah, cousin, we are beginning to live dangerously, no?"

After lunch, he left to meet his friend from Berlin to collect more pieces of the Wall for his jewelery. I thanked him for feeding me and sat a few minutes longer.

I hadn't been to the sculpture garden since that September afternoon with Olivier. There were no children today, and no one else was sitting on these benches at the back of the garden. But a few couples did walk by, arm in arm, achingly happy. One in particular, sharing a Magnum ice-cream bar despite the cold, caught my fancy.

I untied the dog and headed all the way to the Île St-Louis so that I could buy a two-scoop cone from a *glacier* called Berthillon.

Harry Mathews had told me the night before that the importance of Berthillon ice cream was on a par with that of the umbrella.

I had asked him if this was classified information.

"Not you too? Is there no one who hasn't been contaminated by this viral story about me being in the CIA? It might as well be true for all the people who believe it. But somehow I thought you would escape infection, young Katie. If you're not immune, who is?"

Orlando and I were sitting on the small bridge that connects the Île St-Louis with the Île de la Cité, looking across at the flying buttresses around the knave of Notre-Dame. I was feeding him bits of an empty cone that the lady behind the ice-cream counter had given me, *"pour le pauvre toutou,"* while taking alternate licks of my own fraises des bois and sorbet au cacao noir.

We were not the only ones drawn to Berthillon off-season. The rare lack of gray made the day seem full of possibility, a surprise celebration.

I watched the river, the bookstalls on its banks, the houseboats, the soaring Cathedral of Notre-Dame, the pigeons in the perfect sky, all from the perspective of my spot on the bridge with my ice cream and sheepdog. I took a philosophical lick of chocolate.

Then I saw Claudia.

It had to be her, motionless against the Seine. That could only be her hair.

Orlando saw her too. He choked on his *cornet.*

She stared at us as though it were we who were odd and magical here, we who had appeared out of nowhere. She stood so still that we might have turned her to stone with some mythic power of which we were totally unaware in our innocent *promenade.* Only her hair wisped over her frozen face.

Suddenly, she gripped the side of the bridge, tore her gaze from us and ran away, looking down, trying to cloak herself in that amazing black mane as if it weren't the most blatant thing about her.

We rushed after her down the cobblestone street. She turned. So did we. She broke into a run and we followed.

It was a small island, and eventually she came up against a wall. There was a lot of deep dirty water between her and the Right Bank.

Orlando was deliriously happy.

"Claudia, what are you doing in Paris?" I cried. "Why are you running away from us?"

She took my free hand and looked at me hard. "You are all right? Have you been well?"

"Fine, fine. I'm surprised to see you." It had only been a couple of weeks, but the finality of her departure had made the break seem much longer. "Are you back again for good? Does Clarence know? Did you finish your thesis already?"

"But you are okay? You look it."

I nodded.

She, on the other hand, did not look okay. She looked tired and sad and, up close, her hair was greasy. Her black boots were salt-streaked and scruffy. An orange scarf around her neck, her only touch of color, reminded me of how much more vivid she was before.

Orlando nuzzled her leg. She held on to my hand. "Listen, do not tell Clarence you have seen me. Please."

"Why?"

"This is very, very difficult," she said. Then she raised her face and read something in the atmosphere. "There is nothing more to do, Katie."

"Why can't I tell Clarence?"

"You really want to be implicated?"

"Claudia, what's going on with you? Please?"

"Katie," she sighed, "come."

Orlando and I followed her into the Flore en l'Île, the café overlooking the bridge between the islands where we had originally come with our cones. The dog under the table at our feet, we sat with the beautiful view of Notre-Dame, which she never once seemed to notice.

I ordered a large café au lait. She asked for espresso.

"I'm sorry I acted strangely just now. You were so sweet outside, so happy to see me with your ice-cream cone and your dog. It broke my heart. It makes me feel that some things are still beautiful. I have to tell you, I have been having a terrible, terrible time about lying to you."

"Lying to me?"

"I am in love with Clarence."

"I've always thought you were."

"And he is in love with me."

"Are you sure?"

"Listen, when you took me to the Métro that day, when I said I was going to the airport, I did not leave Paris. I moved into a small apartment here on the Île St-Louis, owned by a friend of Clarence's, a tiny *pied-à-terre*, very small and dark. Clarence was so frightened that you would find out about us, that it would put you in an awkward position with Lydia, that he made me hide from you. I never should have done it. But he is so very scared. He loves me desperately, but he cannot make his mind up to let go of his bourgeois existence. He thinks his children might not understand. But mostly, she has him under her sway. He is terrified of Lydia. But he is about to leave her."

"He is?"

"He comes close to leaving and then he shies away."

"So, you mean *you* are together now, with Clarence? How?"

"He comes to my apartment when he can, but he will not be seen with me anymore. He used to think it was okay for us to look like good friends. But now he's so spooked, you see. So we meet only in my apartment or sometimes in the church of St-Sulpice. And then when he says he must leave, I go to the Café de la Mairie that looks out at the church and I sit there all by myself and he walks away in a different direction. Only sometimes he cannot help himself and he comes to the café too and has a glass of wine at a different table. Does this make you feel strange, because of Lydia?"

"I don't know." I was still trying to untangle the facts. "Wait, so you never left that day when I walked you to the Métro? You went to the Île St-Louis instead of the airport? Is that what you're really saying?"

"We stayed up all the night before, arguing about it. He got scared you were going to come down early some morning and find us together and be shocked. He was having me pretend to leave each night, then sneak back in after you were gone upstairs and go out at six o'clock every morning then pretend to arrive for the day a couple of hours later. I told him I thought you guessed, but he said, no, Katie is in so many ways a little girl. He can be very condescending, you know. And he wants you to respect him.

"He also probably wanted you to think you were telling the truth if Lydia asked you where I was. He wanted you to be able to say I was gone back to America without feeling torn. He did not want to make you lie. He thinks this makes him a better person."

"Well, does he know that you might be telling me the truth now? Did you say what you would do if we bumped into each other?"

"I told him that if you saw me that it would be too ridiculous for him to force me to make up another story. He will be very upset, but I think that this will be good for him to be able to speak to you, to see that once you know he is not perfect you still love him. He needs to be able to talk to somebody besides me. He told me he was finally going to explain the situation to Henri, because he thinks Henri has probably guessed and has an accepting philosophy. That will help, but you will help more.

"I am so lonely here. He is leading the fullest life, and I am in the shadows. But I think it is more difficult for him because he is in a false position all the time. I am very clear that I love him and he loves me. In some ways, even though I'm in hiding, my part is easier."

As the facts crystallized, I loved her for confiding in me. So much began to make sense now. Of course she and Clarence *were* in love. Love had reigned the whole time we three were together. But, now that this was definite, what did it mean for Lydia?

I let my coffee go tepid.

Every once in a while, Claudia asked reflexively if I was uncomfortable, but she went on before I could form a response. She had not had a conversation with anyone besides Clarence in ages, and their time together was fraught and compressed. It was so good to finally talk to another woman.

So, Lydia had suspected, and Clarence had worried that she might ask me about it and it would be too unfair to force me to lie and too horrible to make me tell the truth.

He was protective of me, as of a daughter, Claudia said. But a true daughter, she added, was more intuitive about her parents' happiness than Clarence assumed. Portia would understand.

I was struck by the fact that Clarence had tried to protect me from the complicated truth much like a father. But the childish satisfaction I felt made me suspect that daughters wanted, self-ishly, to be daughters, to be at the center of the world. They were perhaps not as sympathetic to their father's extramarital needs as Claudia was making them out.

Most likely, Portia would not find his situation with Claudia wildly romantic, if problematic and potentially tragic. She would think it was sick.

"So," Claudia continued, "when Clarence first knows that you know about us, he will be feeling scared. But once he sees that nothing terrible materializes, I think it will show him that we can be natural again. I hope this does not make you nervous."

Of course it made me nervous, but I didn't feel there was room in this moment for my qualms.

"Don't worry. You shouldn't be concerned about me. This is not about me at all."

"Ah, but it is about you, Katie. I cannot say how it is going to happen, but your blessing on us, it will mean so much, because this is the moment for him to leave her, and her chintz and her awful clock, and he needs to sense that this is positive. You can help."

"Why now?"

"He has been waiting to make sure she felt good after her German photos. He said he could not do anything until he knew her photos were a success. So, I have been suffering so much while he was going to all these parties and events, going around Paris with her. And now that is over. The excuse is gone.

"But what I worry about is that he will fall again under her sway because she is so very powerful. She has a strong, binding influ-ence, not healthy for him. And I think he is not good to her either. She turns him ugly, you see. He is patronizing about her work. He thinks she might not survive if he leaves. But she will be better too when he is gone. It's simply that they have to be able to imagine the disruption, and that is very, very difficult. It is the thing that seems impossible but is not. That is where you will help."

"I don't see how I can help. It's not my—"

"Believe me, you can help by being yourself and reacting as you react."

I took my first drink of cold coffee.

So, Clarence was going to leave Lydia. The household was going to explode.

"But Lydia's work! Will Lydia still be able to work? I think that for Clarence her work is the most important thing."

"Lydia," Claudia narrowed her eyes on her second espresso, "she is very intelligent. Her photographs tell stories quite lyrically and they are very engaging, but they are also very controlled. First I am taken in, then I am controlled. And I think the problem is this, that she does not have respect for the unconscious urge that is behind photography. She wants to annihilate it with too much work. And this is barbarous."

thirty-one

I rushed home to meet Portia.

As Orlando and I panted into the courtyard, we were greeted by a grinning Madame Fidelio. A *jeune monsieur très bien* had left flowers for me today, she said, handing me a large bouquet of pink and white peonies from Bastien, which I was cradling, incredulous, thinking about how much such out-of-season flowers could possibly cost, hearing Mom rant about the absurdity of South American flowers when there were perfectly good ones in our own backyard, when I bumped into Clarence and Henri.

"Thanks for walking Orlando," said Clarence, obviously for Henri's benefit since I walked Orlando every day. Despite his inherited wealth, Henri had no servants and Clarence didn't like to appear soft.

Henri looked almost timidly at me, as though something had changed between us since last night's turkey dinner, but then he turned to the peonies and gave them a familiar smile.

"I am telling our friend Clarence that I do not believe in guilt." The flowers floated in the blue of his gaze. "Do you believe in guilt, Katie? Do you believe you have any responsibility you don't deeply feel?"

I gave a demented smile and a hesitant head shake.

Clarence must have told him about Claudia, I thought, trying to catch Clarence's attention with a look of significance. But his eyes were scattershot. He took Henri's arm and began to pull him away.

"Christ, not now, Henri. Goodnight, Katie. Excuse us. We're late for the opening of a dear friend. He'll never forgive us."

"But perhaps Katie would like to come to the gallery?"

"Thanks, but I'm having a drink with Portia."

"Lovely," said Clarence in a particularly unlovely voice as he dragged Henri off. After a few paces, though, he stopped, his back stiffened, and he turned around to me. He took his wallet from his pocket and handed me a one-hundred-franc note. "Here. The two of you have a good time."

One hundred francs was an obscene amount of money. He must be atoning for something.

I tried to open the front door quietly so as to have some time to compose myself, into what I did not know, but I did know I was not ready to face Portia.

Ready or not, she heard me and called me into her bedroom to show me the clothes Lydia had bought her with Sally Meeks's journalist discount. The new outfits were laid out on her bed and dressing table, draped over her chair.

"So?" she said brightly. The Valium must have worn off.

"Portia, your father just gave me, gave us, one hundred francs to buy our drinks tonight."

"Oh, he's obviously feeling guilty!" She laughed.

"Guilty for what?"

"My God, Kate, don't be so serious! Mother asked him to come out to dinner with us, and he said he had to go to an opening with Henri, and she tried to make him feel bad."

"Oh. That's all."

"He really is the world's sweetest man, Daddy. I should admire him." Then she laughed again. "I should try to be earnest, like you. Where on Earth did you get those amazing flowers? We have to get you a vase." But she herself made no move to do so, turning instead to contemplate the spread of her purchases.

"Wow, gorgeous," I stammered, splattering my gaze all over her display.

"Check out this Sonia Rykiel dress. Do you think the color will overwhelm me? It's on the dark side, but I had to get it to go with these." And she pulled out a pair of purple and gold Stephane Kélian shoes.

"Of course you did," I said, weirdly recalling that Balzac had died, in debt, from a coffee overdose.

"Aren't they kind of perfect together?"

"Is that agnès b, what you're wearing?" I was realizing how many fashion brands Étienne had made me aware of as a kid. When he was being nice to me, we would flip through magazines together at the newsstand and he would tell me what was important.

"I love that you can recognize agnès b! It's so refreshing. You should see the way people dress at Princeton. Most of the women look like my brother."

"Frivolity is serious business," I said, echoing Clarence.

How bittersweet it was to have escaped Portia's jealous wrath only to envy her shoes.

Pulling open the door, Lydia smiled in on us, unabashedly glad that I was cheering Portia up. "I knew you two would get along," she said. "Didn't Portia and I do well today, Katherine? The clothes are fabulous this fall. Gorgeous peonies, my dear. I hope you didn't pay for those yourself." She winked. "You know where the vases are, don't you?"

Portia was frowning anxiously at her backside in the mirror of her *armoire*.

"Don't worry," I said. "You have no butt."

Remember, Portia has the clothes, but I have the boy. There, I had thought it. Fucked up, as Christie would say. Deeply fucked up.

In order to dodge the feeling, I made a mental return to the sculpture of Balzac from what seemed like an earlier, more innocent time. Balzac once said that a debt was a work of art. Maybe Christie would lend me the money for a nice pair of heels to take to London.

"Mother," said Portia, "Kate and I are going out for a drink. What time is dinner?"

"Our reservation is at eight-thirty. So, take your time. Oh, and here," said Lydia. "Let me treat you girls to an apéro." She handed Portia a fifty-franc note.

"Thank you, Lydia," I said, comparing her cash to Clarence's.

"Thank you, Mother," said Portia so archly that I knew she was doing the same.

Flushed in artificial respite from her pain, Portia pulled on a new pair of high leather boots.

"Those are great," I said.

Portia was a casualty, if not of privilege then of ambition. I found myself feeling sorry for her, clothes and all. Her boyfriend had dumped her. Her father was having an affair. Her mother went on competitive diets with her. Her brother hated her. And the friend she thought she was busy making at this very moment was nothing if not untrue.

But what could I do about it now? Leave? Absurd. Confess? To what, exactly? Push her away? Impossible when Lydia was corralling us. Maybe put up some kind of emotional wall? But where should the boundaries be? Did I actually like Portia, or could I simply not bear the thought of anyone not liking me?

"Hey, Kate," came Joshua's voice through the door. "Your mom's on the phone."

Behind a closed door, I was able to admit to Mom, for the first time, that I had certain doubts about this family.

I tried out an idea on her: "Have you ever thought that, in some way, you always desecrate what you love?"

I plucked a pink petal from one of my flowers and crushed it between my fingers.

"Excuse me? Who's desecrating what over there? Is it time for you to come home, young lady?"

"Mom, it's interesting. I mean, if you saw how marvelous these people could be and then how they treat each other sometimes, you'd wonder, how can people who have so much beauty in their lives be so destructive? And you'd ask yourself if it isn't some form

173

of aristocratic waste. Claudia says there are some moments when Marxist interpretations are still valid."

"I have no idea what you're talking about. I called to find out if you celebrated Thanksgiving."

"Sorry, I meant to call yesterday, but things got hectic."

"Well, I was invited to the Halls. It was delicious. Do they have turkey in Paris?"

I described Lydia's meal. I didn't bother explaining who the people around the table were, but I did tell the story of the vegan stuffing to try to wind my way back to my original point.

"Would you have made me special stuffing if I'd decided to become a vegan a few days before Thanksgiving?"

"I'm not so good at these hypotheticals, dear. We've established that. How's your drawing?"

"You're interested in my drawing?"

Wasn't I supposed to be a lawyer?

"Do you need materials? I will sponsor materials. That I will sponsor. You need something of your own over there."

"Thanks but I've got a sketchbook and pencils. That's all I need for now."

It seemed everyone in my life was pushing me to get to work. I wanted to tell her about Claudia's pep talks and Lydia's promise to look at my stuff soon, about Henri Cartier-Bresson and putting yourself in the way of chance, the decisive moment, Balzac in my sketchbook. I wanted to tell her about Clarence and Claudia's love affair and to ask her how I should behave to Portia. But instead, I cradled the phone, hugged my flowers and let a quick wave of love wash over me.

"Don't let these people make you forget yourself," Mom said.

"Mom, we've been over this. I'm taking away something invaluable from this experience."

"What's that? What are you taking away that's worth so much?"

"It's called *savoir vivre*."

• • •

Once I'd said goodbye to Mom, I called Bastien to thank him for the peonies. His mother answered. I listened for notes of heartbreak in her *"Je vous le passe, mademoiselle."* Was she sad about getting divorced? But her voice was as unruffled as the spun-sugar coiffure I remembered from our one brief encounter in his living room. Christie and I were picking him up for dinner. Madame de Villiers was tapping her cigarette into a white lacquer ashtray. Her greeting was not warm, but it was not stingy either. We were pretty enough for her son, and, as Caucasian-Americans who had been to a good college, we were most likely not issued from the social dregs of our country. We were condoned.

When Bastien came on the line, I told him what a splash his bouquet was making in the Schell household and how approving Madame Fidelio was.

"But do *you* like them?"

"They're beautiful. So kind of you. But I should be sending you flowers. You're the one who is having a hard moment."

He laughed. *"Ça ne se fait pas!"*

Why not? Why wasn't it done? I could send something big and masculine like birds of paradise.

It wasn't possible, he insisted, for a girl to send a boy flowers. But if I wanted to cheer him up, I could come to Deauville at Christmastime with Christie. He had told his parents he didn't want to be with one or the other for the holidays if they weren't together. His father was staying in Paris and his mother was going to St-Tropez, which she preferred off-season. So, would I come?

I would try.

Would I at least be willing to commit to a lunch date tomorrow? He wanted to show me La Coupole. Did I like oysters?

Portia waited until we were framed inside the window of Café Flore to get to the heart of the matter.

She lit a cigarette. "Listen, I know I shouldn't be telling you this because my mom is your boss, but she's sick. These clothes, this fussing over me and calling me too skinny when she used to say

175

you can never be too skinny, it's all guilt because she still talks to Olivier on the phone all the time. And I know she has plans to see him when she gets back to New York for Christmas. She's infatuated with him. He feeds her crazy ego or something. She calls him at night when she's drunk. She's a drunk, you know. I can't be telling you anything you don't know there. She shouldn't call Olivier at night. But she still does it. He's told me. It is sick." She was crying. "And so, so hurtful."

I took a deep breath, tried to evade the crash of my own feelings, let it be all about them. "Well, maybe the person to talk to is Olivier. Tell him you don't like it."

As soon as I was done speaking, I was flooded with something like resolve. This was the moment to tell Portia! The flits of suspicion shadowing across her face as she looked at me, these were my cue. Tell her about Olivier and me. Tell her about her father's affair so that she wouldn't blame her mother for everything. Just let it all out! What was the worst that could happen?

"Portia?"

"Yes?" She was clearly startled by the urgency of my tone.

"I—have you thought that some people just aren't happy? That they are looking for something?"

"Oh, has Daddy been philosophizing to you again?" She gave a deflated laugh.

"I suppose he has." I sighed, giving into an overpowering reticence.

"He's all talk, you know. Sweet Daddy."

I gave a constricted smile which she must have read as empathy because she laughed again and told me I was becoming a friend.

Our champagne arrived. We *tchin-tchinned*. I slipped into a state of catatonic anxiety.

Portia dabbed her tears with the Art Nouveau border of her tiny napkin. She offered me a Gauloise and I accepted.

"Sometimes I wonder if my mom doesn't want to fuck Olivier. Sometimes I even think she might have jumped him already. I wouldn't put it past her."

I had smoked a few times in college, enough not to hack, but I had no skills. I didn't want to mimic her directly, so I glanced all around the room, picking up moves.

The cigarette bought me a minute to think the unthinkable. Lydia and Olivier? What? Of course, the world was perverse and nothing was impossible. This was Europe, after all. But no, Lydia and Olivier could not *actually* have slept together, virtually, maybe, but not actually. Virtually. Actually. Virtually.

"You know," Portia continued, "Mother implies that she knows some dark secret about Olivier. She keeps hinting that there's something he isn't telling me, something that would totally change the way I feel. As if I don't know how I feel! As if I couldn't handle the truth and the two of them have to keep it from me in some sick pact they've formed."

"But, Portia, I mean, what you're saying is that the pact is all in your mom's head, right? It's about the way she makes you feel, not the truth?"

"Like I have any idea what the truth is! All I want is for him to be with me until the summer so I can get through the fucking year at school, and he says he wishes he could, as though there were some mysterious force pushing us apart. Or some fucking person."

Portia was smoking faster and faster, creating a toxic cloud, a Versailles hairdo impossibly balanced on her dainty forehead. The Flore was pulsating to alternating currents of "virtually," "actually," "virtually."

Halfway through my cigarette, I stubbed it out. I had sworn to Mom that I wouldn't take up smoking in France. I had to be true to someone.

And I had to talk to Olivier immediately. To find out what the hell was going on.

thirty-two

Somewhere between midnight and 1 A.M., I crept down my five flights and braved the courtyard. All the shutters in the building were closed around me.

The Schell apartment was sealed behind its heavy "French gray" lids, but who was to say if the sound of my footsteps would rouse its curiosity?

Spooked, I turned back at the threshold and started up the stairs again. I told myself I should wait until tomorrow to call Olivier. One more night wouldn't kill me. Portia and Joshua were leaving tomorrow. The coast would be clearer. And I would have had time to think things through. If I rushed into a confrontation now, I might say something too strong. I might have regrets.

But a faint sound held me back on the second step. The sound, I thought, of Orlando's breathing. Had he smelled me through the heavy front door? Did he hope I was coming to take him for a walk?

No, Orlando, I thought, I'll be back tomorrow to take you out for air. The family will watch me attach your leash and wish us a nice stroll as if we were lucky to go outside together with our joint sense of fun and our limited egos.

The Schells, even Clarence, assumed that my sense of self was no more than a function of them. I was like a courtesan in Balzac's *The Splendors and Miseries of Courtesans,* or at least that's how I translated the title in my head, wondering if the splendors of my job were worth its servility. It was a forceful question, and it pushed me to action. I did not crawl back into my garret after all.

I pivoted on my step and made my way back down into the moonlight, which began to grow feeble in a rising mist, imbuing me with a sudden sense of time running out. If I didn't rush through this night, right now, and say what I had to say to Olivier, then I never would.

Rubber boot soles squeaking across the cobblestones, I made it to the courtyard's outer door. I pulled it open. It creaked in the damp. As I burst into the street, I felt Madame Fidelio's porch light snap on behind me and did not look back.

"Do you still talk to Lydia?" I plunged right in. I knew myself well enough by now to know that if I didn't say what I intended immediately, I wouldn't say it at all. "Are you in touch with her?"

My body was no more versed in confrontation than my mind. It had no idea what to do with itself. My heart was pounding and my phone booth was vertiginous. I held my breath, watched a shady man pass.

"Oh, my Kate," he said, melting with sympathy, "I can't tell you I'm not in touch with Lydia. But there's no harm in it."

"What *can* you tell me?" I tried to stay strong, but felt my anger waning at the sound of his voice.

"She calls me. She wants me to go to things in her place in New York while she's not here. Openings and cocktail parties. Stuff she gets invited to that she imagines I would enjoy. She's a deeply lonely woman, Kate, and I have a mother thing. I can't resist a mother's plea. I'm not saying I'm proud of it."

"So, you have actual conversations with her still?" My breath was fogging the glass. Yellow streetlamps watched me lazily through an incipient drizzle. The occasional coated figure wafted by. St-Sulpice rose in front of me, a high black dream.

Olivier sighed. "It's complicated with Lydia. She's so miserable with Clarence."

My throat clenched with loyalty to Clarence. I took a deep

179

breath. "You probably shouldn't talk to Lydia anymore. It's not fair to Portia."

"You're right," Olivier said solemnly. "But—"

"Don't you think it's a little weird," I persisted, "for Portia, I mean, weird for you to be her mother's outlet? Doesn't that make it harder for her to let go and get on with her life? And for me, Olivier. It's weird for me!"

"I understand. I couldn't empathize more, Kate, but I can't just cut Lydia off after she hosted me for so long in Paris. She was wonderful to me. She took me in. It's delicate."

"Well, you could say, 'Please stop calling me because it hurts your daughter's feelings.'"

"I wish it were that simple. I'm extricating myself gently. I will get away, but it might take some time. Can you believe me?"

"Portia thinks that Lydia essentially told you to break up with her," I said. I had never been quite this straightforward before. It was an out-of-body experience. I was far from sure that I wasn't going to dissolve. But I couldn't stop. "This is going to sound totally messed up, but Portia suspects that you and Lydia are having an affair."

"Okay, that's so crazy I can't even think about it."

"Really?"

"Really."

As my breath steadied, I rested my head on the phone book wired to the wall.

"I guess the Schell paranoia is a little infectious," I ventured at last, surprised that I still had a voice.

"Just a little." He laughed. "Hey, Kate, about London. I'm so sad, but this GE deal is never going to be wrapped up in time for December. Can I buy us tickets for January? Over New Year's? Don't you think New Year's will be festive?"

A whole new month to wait! I had to recalibrate all my hopes.

I tried to sound buoyant. "If I can find someone to walk the dog!"

"What about your friend Christie?"

"I'll have to make sure she's around."

"I could help you hire someone."

I laughed. "Poor Orlando. He's such an unwitting obstacle."

"Speaking of obstacles, I hear there are Frenchmen buzzing all around you like bees in a flower patch."

"What?"

I had the unpleasant notion that he was talking about my peonies from Bastien, that Lydia or Portia had mentioned them.

"Well, can you blame them?" He asked. "I miss you so much," he went on. "I'm the one who's getting paranoid, imagining things. Can you tell me something? Why the hell do we have to feel so guilty all the time? What if we just stopped?"

"I love that idea." I sighed.

The streets leading home felt cavernous. Rain fell in earnest. The moon was gone. I ran in a state of rapture.

Of course I had been sucked into Portia and Lydia's paranoid orbit. Of course there was nothing "going on" between Lydia and Olivier, nothing that time and a little patience wouldn't unravel. It had all become clear, but only because I had found the courage to demand an explanation. Maybe life was simpler than I thought; you actually got what you asked for.

thirty-three

The next morning, Lydia announced that she was delaying her trip to England. She was mysterious about her reasons.

Portia invited me into her bedroom while she packed for her return to the States. She needed an extra suitcase for all of her Paris purchases, but this fact did nothing to cheer her.

"I only bought these clothes for him," she sighed.

I told her that she was smart and beautiful and that she shouldn't base her self-esteem on the actions of one guy. After all, in the fullness of time, all old boyfriends became fond and faraway figments, right? Think about how dire things used to seem in high school. Now high school was funny. Even college. My college boyfriend Peter was hardly a memory and I used to cry myself to sleep at his callousness. Life was perspective.

"I have no perspective," she said. "I love him." And she began to tremble in one of her new outfits, the Jean Paul Gauthier, a tight black skirt and asymmetrical jacket, heels, full makeup.

I looked at her. I decided that our intimacy was one-sided on both counts, as though each of us were gazing at a painting. We had no common view of one another. I thought I could X-ray her unawares; she thought I was her friend.

I could not be disinterested, and yet there was a disinterested voice in me that wanted her to move on for her own sake. There were things to love about her and she was wasting them on the wrong man, who happened to be the very same one I wanted.

When the cab came to pick Portia and Joshua up for the airport, "because," as Joshua put it, "our mother is saving humanity and our father is performing brain surgery in his study, so neither can be interrupted to drive us," I stood between Clarence and Lydia waving goodbye.

Through tinted glass, Portia waved back, sad and formal, as from the slow height of a parade float. Joshua ignored us. The Citroën tires splashed through a puddle as it carried the precious children off, muddying my tights, which I ran to sponge off before meeting Bastien at La Coupole.

I had only had oysters three times in my life, once with my dad as a special treat for dinner right before leaving for France, once with Jacques and Solange on New Year's Eve and once at a house party I was invited to in Newport, Rhode Island, by a college friend. I couldn't so much remember what they tasted like as what they meant.

When I met Bastien, who was waiting for me on a dark red banquette beneath a golden dome, wearing a crisp pink button-down, I launched into an anecdote about my dad telling me, as we watched a seafood platter approach our table at Musso and Frank's on Hollywood Boulevard, that the world was my oyster. I didn't tell Bastien that Hollywood had dropped Daddy like a hot potato once the word got out that he had cancer, that the phone had stopped ringing overnight and the life our family was supposed to have had was relegated to a place of pipe dreams. By saying the world was my oyster as he sent me to Paris, Daddy implied it was no longer his; he had had his fun and now it was time for me to have mine.

"Did you like the oysters?" asked Bastien.

"I liked them as much as he wanted me to."

After ordering a bottle of champagne, Bastien got two dozen fines de claires for us. They were delicious. They burst like little oceans in my mouth. I could have eaten many more, but I thought it might be indelicate to say so.

He told me he thought the shells in the ice were beautiful, and that if I came to Deauville there would be many different kinds.

He would be curious to know what an artist like me would make of their primitive shapes. He pulled out one of his cards. Since he had no profession yet, it showed his name and phone numbers in black script. He turned the card over to its blank side and asked me to do a sketch of an oyster shell for him, as a souvenir of today.

"You're so nostalgic, Bastien."

"I like to preserve certain moments, yes." His fleshy dimples were at once childlike and stubbornly old.

The waiter came to see if we had decided on what to have for our main courses. Without consulting me, Bastien asked for two grilled sole. "It's the only thing to have," he said in answer to my questioning look.

"Very good, monsieur." The waiter was gone.

Now would I draw that shell?

I didn't do party tricks. "I'm not a monkey."

"I never said you were."

I continued my train of thought. "If anything, I'm a weirdly gifted parrot."

He smiled kindly.

I understood that there was an attachment forming in Bastien's mind where in mine there was nothing more than a pleasantness and a fascination with golden-hued restaurants, cologne, family crests that still meant something and shells on shaved ice. He thought we were close. And because I was unworthy of his confidence, I felt compelled to mimic it. I told him I would most likely come to Deauville but that I had to think about my family.

Couldn't I see my family anytime?

Of course I could, but perhaps only Christmas would be symbolic enough to make up for my absence thus far.

When I returned to my garret, loopy from the champagne, I found a plain white envelope slipped under my door.

Could it possibly be from Olivier? Perhaps he had had someone deliver it?

I glanced at Bastien's peonies, which I had taken out of Lydia's vase downstairs and cut to fit in a pair of jam jars on my windowsill.

There was nothing written on the envelope, but I could see through to black ink in florid lines. I tore the seal and recognized the handwriting immediately from the pages Claudia used to spread over the dining room table.

My Dearest Katie,
   I must ask something of you. Something very, very important . . .

thirty-four

Claudia had not told me what it was she wanted, but I had the nervous feeling, as I walked Orlando toward the address she had given me on the Île St-Louis, that she needed me to take some kind of message to Clarence.

Her studio was as small as mine, but much darker and mold-veined, with only a slit of a window above the lumpy velvet couch where she slept. On one of the oldest streets of Paris, the place felt mired in its damp medieval origins.

I felt sorry, seeing her here all alone, her luscious hair matted and pulled back into a rough ponytail, while Clarence and I were roaming around the big freshly painted apartment in the Sixième with different people coming in and out all day and Kirs at five. The injustice made me want to help her.

Pouring me a cup of Moroccan mint tea, she spoke quickly through the steam. "Please, I know it is complicated for you, but you are not a simple person. I see the complexity in you, and so does Clarence. Only now that he knows that you and I have met one another, because I told him right away, he is too frightened to see me. He is in a panic. Katie, I wish you to carry a letter to him. I know he is expecting it, even though he says he is not. He loves me. He needs me. The situation is desperate. He will die soon in that house. Can you do this for us?"

"Take a letter to Clarence?" I swallowed hard. The request went down like a fish bone.

But the idea of saying "No, I can't help you" was so impossible that I blocked out the notion of repercussions. The consequences of my actions loomed vague and foggy, frightening, yes, but peripheral to the current picture. In the here and now my role was to make this wronged woman feel better.

Slowly, Claudia nodded.

"Okay, Claudia."

She took my hands. Her tiny warm fingers swarmed mine in their gratitude. She kissed my forehead.

"Thank you. Thank you. Now, tell me, how is he doing? He seemed so worried about the children when I last saw him. But he said you were very helpful, a balm. He is very happy that you are friendly with Portia. He thinks you will also help her forget about the boyfriend and feel young again. He worries that she is too serious, too old for her years, not natural enough. Is that true?"

"She could loosen up."

"I see," she said hungrily. "What else?"

I didn't want to say anymore, but felt compelled to paint poor Claudia a fuller picture.

"She looks like Clarence," I explained, "but she's so thin it's hard to tell. What stands out about her are her slightly bulging eyes, like Lydia's, that can either be beautiful or strange. The rest of her is kind of pinched."

Once I started talking, I found I couldn't stop. Claudia was starved for intimacy. I had to feed her.

"Or maybe it's that I feel pinched for her," I went on, "because her world is very brittle from her not being able to trust anyone. I think that's why she comes off so unnatural."

"Tell me about Joshua."

"Joshua is becoming even more of an outcast from the family— he's joined the Young Republicans at his prep school to piss them off."

"So tragic."

We sank deeper into the couch beneath her one obstructed window. Orlando slept at our feet.

187

"But," she continued, "can we return for a moment to the idea of Portia not having anyone to trust? You say this is why she is brittle, no? But how can it be that she does not trust her own father? This seems strange to me for her not to trust Clarence."

"She does sometimes, but not all the time, because her mother doesn't trust him and Portia picks up on it. Even if Portia can't stand Lydia, she of course does love her and wishes she were more like a mother and not a selfish artist. Then again, Portia likes having a famous mother because the only other kids she knows all have fancy parents. I guess you could say she's conflicted. Does that make any sense?"

Claudia's eyes were the brightest thing in the room, hot coals in soot. "Tell me. You are a bit jealous of Portia, and you have to be nice to her of course because you are working in that house, but you think she is spoiled, no, insensitive? And she has things you would like?"

"Well, I haven't exactly come out and told her I was poor. I don't think it has occurred to her. I guess because I went to Yale and my mom always tried to educate me so I can talk to her family as somewhat of an equal. But, to anyone who's paying attention, I'm not."

"So you are a bit indignant. This is not a bad thing. I'm relieved to see this, that you are capable of something like anger. But you must not feel inferior to Portia, ever. Clarence says that Portia senses that you are much more at ease than she is. He said she might be jealous of you if she didn't like you so much. But tell me, are she and Clarence close?"

"Well—"

"Closer than she and Lydia?"

"You could say that."

"Do you think Portia understands him?"

"You mean understands what will make him happy? I have no idea." Suddenly, I felt sick. We were being gluttonous with other people's lives. "Claudia, I have to get back. I have a bunch of letters to type before tomorrow. Lydia will be looking for me." With the mention of Lydia, I felt a tinge of panic at what I had just agreed to do.

Claudia handed me the envelope. Like the one she had left for me, it had nothing written on the outside. She stared while I slid it into the pages of the book in my bag.

"Don't worry, Claudia," I said, as much to calm myself down as to soothe her.

I woke Orlando and pulled him back out into the wintery light.

A few paces outside Claudia's building, just beyond the island's interior labyrinth, toward its shore, I wondered if I had actually been in her shadowy studio? The world was teeming with dogs, cigarettes, tourists. It was all so vibrant that Claudia, inside, circling her obsession behind a single window facing a wall, kept alive by the stories I spun from a place she could not enter, seemed impossible. Until I reached into my bag to feel the corners of her envelope stiff in the pages of the Proust I was rereading. Then I knew I hadn't dreamed it.

thirty-five

I found Clarence wandering around the frosty garden in a thick sweater, hat and wool gloves. He was as stony pale as he had been on the morning of Claudia's "departure." A stray hair sprouting from his right ear gave him the air of a grassy ruin.

With my awkward new boldness, I delivered my message in a whispered rush so as not to fall victim to discretion. "Clarence, you know I've seen Claudia and spoken to her. We talked this morning. She gave me a letter for you. It's okay."

"Jesus, not here," he hissed, then stopped dead and stared at the rusting garden furniture. "I'm going to have to repaint the table and chairs, the wrought iron ones. Lydia bought those in Italy years ago. She loves them. And I need to call the gardener. She says the garden looks like Beirut. And the garden is one thing that it's in our power to fix, isn't it, Katie? Well, best get to it!" But he did not move. "You said something about a letter?" he asked, softly apologetic.

"What are you two conspiring about?"

Clarence and I both jumped at the crackle of Lydia's voice.

"Some breathtaking discovery from the world of nineteenth-century fashion? Some *scandale*, pray tell?"

"As a matter of fact, we were talking about painting your garden furniture," Clarence smirked.

"Were you now? What crazy-making color were you contemplating? Tangerine? Chartreuse? Fire-engine red?" Without letting

190

him respond, she turned directly to me. "Katherine, I trust you to talk him down. I think white would be lovely. Or robin's-egg blue. Or even a pale yellow. But what I think is obviously neither here nor there because he will do whatever he damn well pleases to drive me mad, won't he? I'm going to lunch with Sally. Back in a couple of hours. Katherine, I've handwritten two letters for you to type. They're in the green folder by my computer."

And she was off, leaving us at the back of the garden to contemplate the dormant latticework of the climbing rosebush that was Lydia's pride and joy. "So much easier to care for than the children. So much more straightforward."

We stood in silence, beginning to feel the cold, until the front door of the apartment slammed and we knew she was gone.

The letter changed hands. With a brisk nod of gratitude, Clarence burst into speech.

He hit me with a flood of words about Lydia and Claudia existing on separate planes in his mind. Parallel planes. Well, maybe not parallel exactly, but planes that did not intersect. So, even if he were to see Claudia again, he wouldn't be betraying either woman. But it took an overarching mind to see this. He implied that I had such a mind. "As I've said, your father would be proud of you. Your intelligence, and your sympathies, run so deep. He must have instilled that in you."

I nodded.

"What you and I understand better than most," he continued, "is that, contrary to popular belief, we humans have very little control over matters. However, I will try not to talk about Claudia directly with you, Katie, because it puts you in an awkward position. I recognize that. And things should not have been revealed to you this way, by surprise. But then that's fate, isn't it? Fate that Harry Mathews sent you for ice cream to the very spot where Claudia was . . . I would have told you myself eventually, maybe after you had stopped working in Paris. But you were destined to find out on your own."

I startled. Life after Paris had not yet occurred to me.

"And perhaps Claudia was meant to find you. She's been so isolated the past few weeks. I think it's driven her a little crazy. And she doesn't quite grasp the complexity of the situation with my family. It's very black and white with her, which is part of what can make her so bloody wonderful. But, I hope she wasn't too dramatic with you, and that you're not upset."

I couldn't deny that I was uncomfortable, but I didn't know how to admit it either, so I turned the conversation's course. "What's pretty clear is that she's very much in love with you."

He gave a crooked smile. "I know, I know. But let's not discuss it, shall we? It's too unfair to you and to Lydia."

Realizing those should have been my words, that I ought to have been the one to call the situation unfair, I blurted out a lame, "Okay." I looked at the dark branches roping the pale wall and I let myself think of Lydia. It was tempting to imagine her heart as a place of patterned light and shadow, the secret generator of her creative energy. It was easy to think of her as indestructible. As thorny. Until I remembered how delicate the roses would be, how short their season after a hard winter. All our lazy joy in them would be a result of their long absence—and of the labor of a small army of gardeners.

Even if Lydia herself didn't tend to the bush, she anguished about it. She told me that she worried about its flowering year after year. She would look at it from the window of her study and sigh. It was a symbol of wealth and stature, yes, but it was also a symbol of domesticity, the life that would die if untended, the lattice to her art.

Her art *was* human, no matter what Claudia said. When Lydia harangued Clarence about the garden, when she embroiled us all in the redecorating of her drifting children's rooms, it must be because she was, in some part of herself, a wife and a mother. Lydia's reality, although vastly more embroidered than my mother's and mine, was as true as ours. So she had a rosebush and we didn't. So she spoke cruelly to her husband, as we would never speak to anyone. So she had a wine cellar and was selfishly brilliant. But did all this mean she was beyond hurt?

I did not know where to file this question. It had no place in my bizarre idyll with Claudia and Clarence. Yet it was equally real.

I felt the crisscrossing pulls of too many expectations. I told myself the only way to fulfill them all was to keep a level head. The importance of a level head was something Mom had always emphasized, although I doubt she could have envisioned mine in this particular pose. When she grew sentimental, it was often about our shared resistance to what others called stress. "You and I can handle certain pressures. We don't feel the need to exaggerate or indulge in, quote unquote, stress. We're survivors. We have perspective. Remember that."

thirty-six

The following evening, over an aperitif at Les Deux Magots, I ventured the idea to Christie that I was living inside a Picasso, where everyone talked to me about everyone else so that I saw their lives from all angles while they had no idea about mine. I foresaw that things would only get more complicated as time passed. Claudia would ask me for news of Clarence, Lydia would ask me to find out what Portia was thinking, Portia would tell me her mother was crazy, and Clarence would try to find out, without asking directly, how Claudia was doing. All of this would overlay the mutual suspicion between husband and wife, mother and daughter, mistress and lover. Meanwhile, my every conversation with Olivier would recast the entire constellation in fresh light. I was bracing myself for supreme feats of diplomacy. I would have no choice but to take the experience as it came, from all sides.

"This isn't good," Christie said. "Somebody's going to find out something, and they're going to band together and blame you. That's always the way these things turn out."

"But none of it's really my fault."

"That depends on your perspective. Be careful. *Tchin* . . ."

". . . *tchin*. Christie, do you always know how to stand up for yourself?"

"Not always. But I try."

"I'm being cowardly, aren't I? Weirdly brave and sneaky, but, when it boils down to it, spineless."

"Don't be so hard on yourself. You're in a tough situation. But think about what you can do for your sanity."

"That's just it. I have no idea."

The next afternoon, Clarence neglected to tell Lydia he was going to a lecture at the Sorbonne.

"Has anyone seen Clarence? He's vanished again."

"He went to a talk by Julia Kristeva," I said. "It's about the Mallarmé fashion magazine he's so into."

"Kristeva, you say? On fashion?" She laughed almost meanly. "Could it get any better for him?"

Even though Clarence was truly at the university, this fact felt like an alibi, and I a liar because I knew he had been seeing Claudia.

"Clarence is acting even stranger than usual lately," Lydia said.

"Maybe he's worried about something."

"You think it's his work?"

"Could be."

I had visited Claudia early that morning. I had brought her a croissant and she had made me coffee with warm milk. We couldn't meet in the Flore en l'Île because Clarence had told me that Sally Meeks lived on the Île St-Louis, and that we had to be careful because there was "no telling what Sally was capable of." I doubted Sally would recognize me out of context, but I had to respect Clarence's fear; it was so much weightier than my reason.

"But this Sally, she has never met me. Why do we need to hide from her?" Claudia asked me.

"Clarence thinks that if Sally sees me with someone she doesn't know, she's going to wonder about it, and mention it to Lydia. She'll come over to our table and be all friendly and try to figure out exactly who you are. She's all about owning information, he says."

"Does this mean that I am bad news?" She tugged at her hair.

"Of course not. You're wonderful news, Claudia. But I'm not sure how well timed you are."

I had come to her before my workday began, because I felt terrible that it was impossible for her to go to the lecture today, even though Kristeva was a friend of hers, because she was not officially in Paris and Clarence was. Although Clarence had not asked me to, I had come to apologize for him.

"Are you upset about not going to the Sorbonne? I know Clarence feels very conflicted about it, like you have more of a right to be there than he does and it's not fair. I can tell he feels bad because he's acting all sheepish around the house."

"I am not upset about missing this talk," Claudia insisted. "I am upset about the way Clarence looked when he left the church last night. He seems so weak, and his eyes are feverish. He is off balance. I'm frightened."

"So, you're not angry about the lecture?"

"How can I think about myself at a lecture when Clarence could be ill and I cannot see him tonight?"

"He does look a little pale," I said, "but nothing is seriously wrong with Clarence. Don't worry."

"It's that house. It's poisoning him. I sense it. I've loved him for a long time, you know, much longer than he's loved me." She opened her window onto the mossy wall. "I tell you he will die in that house with that woman."

Clarence came home from the Sorbonne with a fever and threw up. Lydia said he was falling apart exactly as his book was coming due, and that this was typical.

From across the Atlantic, Portia worried about him. She called twice in one hour to say he should get checked for cancer. The very fact that he could get sick, Portia reasoned, hinted at the truth that someday he would be taken away from her, and this forced her to imagine the worst.

The next morning, Lydia asked me to take Clarence some chicken broth. "He asked if *you* would bring it up. He says *I* do nothing for his appetite."

Clarence's curls were more silver than ever and flattened with sweat. As I handed him the soup, he gestured to a plastic bowl on his bedside table. "I hope I can hold this down."

"You better hope it doesn't come up black, Clarence."

"Ah, so you think this is a punishment for all the second-rate fashion literature I've been reading? I'm Emma Bovary? Is that it?" He smiled like a gargoyle.

"You got it."

Madame Bovary had died vomiting black from the arsenic she had taken. There was a school of criticism that said she was in fact regurgitating the ink of all the ill-conceived romance novels she read as a schoolgirl, the novels that conditioned her to be disappointed by life and to read its signs all wrong. She was killed by bad literature.

"Tell me again, Katie, what you were saying the other day about how Madame Bovary was a victim of circumstance, that bit about how we don't choose our fate. What was that?"

"Emma Bovary was a good person." I sighed. "My cousin Jacques says her virtues were what led her to her tragic end. She cheated on poor Charles because of her virtues. Virtues, Clarence, not defects, okay? So, don't worry. "

I would have gone on in this placating vein, compulsively try-ing to resurrect this fatherly man, but he was no longer looking at me. He was staring out the window at the garden, so impossibly far away from his sickbed.

"You'll tell her I can't see her?"

"Of course." I wanted to know what exactly I should say to Claudia about his illness, but I got the feeling he wanted my com-munication with her to be out of his hands, my responsibility. He wished to be clean of it.

He thanked me for the soup, said he was tired and sorry, closed his eyes and curled up.

thirty-seven

Portia told me, over the phone, that her mother had mentioned to her that Sally Meeks was heading to Milan to interview Salvatore Ferragamo and scam shoes. So, when I went to the Île St-Louis to let Claudia know that Clarence was sick and wouldn't be in St-Sulpice that evening, the coast was clear of Sally and we were able to meet out in the open rather than in her depressing studio.

The day was gray and mild. I had Orlando with me, and the two of us were on the bridge, me with my Berthillon, he with his free cone, when Claudia came blinking toward us.

No, she did not feel like ice cream, thanks. How was Clarence? I told her.

"I knew it!" She began to pull her hair. "Is Clarence dying? If Clarence is dying, I will come to that house and I will take him away myself."

"Claudia, it's probably the stomach flu. At worst it's mono or something. My god, you're as bad as Portia."

"So, Portia is worried? That is a bad sign. A daughter, she knows when these things are grave. She senses."

Not sure I could continue being nice, I took a lick of sorbet. People whose fathers die young of cancer can be impatient with the flu.

"Katie"—Claudia took me by the shoulders and locked her eyes on mine—"will you do something very important for me? Will you

198

give Clarence another letter? And something else? An amulet I have. It will protect him."

"Claudia, I don't know."

"It is very important he has a sign from me. A charm he can hold. Clarence must feel so alone. He needs to sense me now more than ever."

"It's weird for me, you know."

"Of course, it is a strange, uncomfortable thing, and I would not ask you if I had any other way. It will be the last time." She was crying.

Squirming in the glare of her drama, I'd say anything to get her to stop. "Okay, okay."

Two days passed. Clarence was not getting any better. He barely woke or ate. I promised Portia over the phone that I would make him chocolate mousse. She had a notion that if he had something soft, sweet and delicious, he would come out of his stupor, as she herself sometimes did with spoonfuls of coffee ice cream in bed when she was pining for Olivier.

He was sleeping now in Joshua's room because his "writhing" at night kept Lydia awake. ("This is a horrible thing to say, but he's acting like a character straight out of *The Inferno*. What do you think he's being punished for, poor harmless man? I can't possibly imagine.")

As Clarence grew weaker, I too began to worry. I still refused to indulge in apocalyptic fantasies, but I saw that his misery was real.

After hanging up with Portia for the second time that day, I began to separate eggs, remembering the Christmas when Solange first taught me her technique of pouring the yolk back and forth between the two halves of broken shell while the white slid off into a waiting bowl. "*Comme ça!*"

The egg yolks got whisked with sugar and some kind of liqueur. Then stirred over simmering water so they wouldn't be raw. "A *bain-marie*," Solange whispered from her distant kitchen.

I still had not decided between Orléans and Deauville for Christmas.

Once the yolks and sugar were mixed, I went to the living room liqueur cabinet, fidgeting on my way with the coin-shaped bulge that burned in my back pocket.

I harbored the silver amulet for Clarence, an abstract image strung on a slender leather thread. It came from Morocco. It was a charm to ward off evil, and it was meant to protect him against Lydia. Claudia had told me that until I could get it to him, it could not leave my person. I wanted to be rid of it, to finally be finished as a messenger, but I had not found my moment.

I returned to the kitchen with Grand Marnier, rum and kirsch and called Portia in her dorm room to see which she would like me to use. "You choose," I said.

"I think Daddy likes rum more than fruit flavors. He sort of hates fruit and chocolate."

No, he doesn't, I thought. He eats dark-chocolate-covered orange peels from Hédiard while he works. He stashes them in his bottom desk drawer. He shares them with me sometimes.

"Great," I said aloud. "Let's use rum then."

"Thanks." She sighed. "You'll let me know how he likes it? You'll tell him I helped? That the chocolate mousse was my idea?"

I cooked the egg yolks, sugar and rum, then stirred in melted chocolate, coffee and an obscene amount of butter. Next I beat the egg whites until they formed stiff peaks and folded them into the chocolate mixture. Then I put the mousse to chill in the refrigerator.

A few hours later, once the mousse had set and Clarence was awake, I went to his bedside and we called Portia.

I could hear her try to make him laugh. "Daddy, you're wasting away. Mother's going to get jealous."

When he hung up, I asked him if he wanted to try some mousse.

"You made this by yourself?" he grunted affably.

I almost said, no, I made it with my cousin Solange whom I was supposed to spend Christmas with, only in the hallway just now, looking at nothing in particular, it hit me that I will go to Deauville instead. But I simply nodded and smiled, spooned a bite into his mouth, then took Claudia's amulet from my pocket and pressed it into the damp palm of his hand.

thirty-eight

Clarence did not die. Not even close. After a battery of tests, his diagnosis was a bad case of *la grippe* aggravated by *le stress*. He simply had to wait it out.

By the approach of Christmas, his fever had broken and he was able to accompany Lydia back to New York, leaving me with the problem of the dog if I wanted to go to Deauville with Christie and Bastien, and, more important, to London for New Year's with Olivier.

Were I going to see my cousins instead, I could have brought Orlando. They had a yard with a chestnut tree and a vegetable garden. They loved to walk and would have been happy to take him along on their *promenades*.

But I had decided that Bastien and Christie needed me, and that the experience of a legendary seaside resort was the sort of thing Dad always dreamed of for me. Besides, the thought of returning to Jacques and Solange for Christmas was frightening. All sorts of fantastical and pathetic hopes might be reborn. It might look like I was opting for the luxurious option because I was turning my back on my roots, but that was not the point, I told myself. The point was that my roots were uncomfortably tight and I needed to pull away.

Nonetheless, I felt guilty. So, I went to Hédiard and spent nearly all the money I had on an assortment of chocolates and exotic pâtes de fruits, which Jacques loved. I wrote my cousins a note to say that the *fêtes* had become busy for me in Paris and that I would see them soon, that I thought of them all the time, that Étienne was doing fine and eating well.

By this time, the Schells were long gone, and I was alone in the Sixth.

I had Lydia's special Berlin Wall *Paris Match,* with the Brandenburg Gate on the cover, and a copy of Clarence's best-known book, *Build Me a Ruin: The English Romantics and Artificial Paradise,* on the trunk I called my coffee table, right next to the picture of me with my own parents.

But I was not spending much time among my things. Lydia preferred me to be in the house with Orlando when the family was away. "You might as well take Portia's room."

So I did, although I was careful not to touch her things. I resisted spraying on her perfume or wearing her shawls, even if they were beautiful. "Make yourself at home," Portia said in a friendly phone call, but I did not want to be a creep.

Christie told me it was too late not to be a creep, that I had already completely screwed Portia over, but I tried to argue that every moment had its weight.

It was December 22. If I was to make it to Deauville by the twenty-fourth, I was going to have to figure out what to do with Orlando, and fast.

Before flying off, Clarence and Lydia had discussed my dilemma, but they hadn't solved it for me. Clarence had said I should have my trip. Lydia had agreed but didn't see how it was possible. It wasn't as though I could take Orlando with me, was it?

No, Orlando might not be welcome.

"What about your family in Orléans? Surely you could take him there?"

"I—I don't think that would work either."

"Poor girl is going to have Christmas alone in this apartment. This is absurd. For years, Lydia, I've been trying to get you to hire someone to walk the dog in situations like these. I cannot fathom why you don't do it."

"This is not New York, Clarence. They don't have dog-walkers here."

"How do you know? You're always making these categorical statements. The critics are right. You're getting bourgeois and narrow-minded."

"I'm bourgeois because I won't hire a dog-walker?"

"All I'm saying is that Katie should go to Deauville or to see her family."

"Watch it, Clarence. Katherine is my relationship."

I decided to ask Étienne to help me out.

I called to invite him to go to the Pasolini movie, the one I had seen with Claudia about Jesus, made with the street people as actors. My mind kept returning to its painterly images, and I wanted to know if Étienne would find them as mesmerizing as I did. By way of enticement, I told him the film's young men were gorgeous.

He accused me of using him for his cinema discount. Because he was *au chômage*, on unemployment, he got a *chômeur*'s reduction at the movies. But he said that, even if I was exploiting him, he would love to go. Hadn't Pasolini been killed by young boys in a ritual murder on the beach? He was curious.

Étienne nudged me through the first half. "*C'est chiant*, it's boring, I'm dying." But leading into the crucifixion and through the closing shots of stricken faces and the final chorus of the *St. Matthew Passion,* he kept quiet.

Afterward, we walked automatically back to his apartment in the Bastille, but he would not speak to me, except once in a barely controlled voice. "Why did you make me watch that?"

"I don't know anymore. The first time I saw it, with Claudia, it seemed really important somehow, like this big stage in my development. And I formed these memories that have been haunting me. So I wanted you to see it too, but it fell a bit flat with you there. It didn't seem as natural anymore. And it was more upsetting."

We arrived at Étienne's place. As always, it was immaculate. He used his shoplifted cleaning products aggressively.

In the entry hall was a large junk-shop mirror and a gilt-framed poster of Prince, naked except for a flashing gold cross on his chest and a collage cloak of dried pink rose petals that had taken him *une éternité* to glue on. Usually, he made me stop to admire the even spacing between the petals and the way the cloak cupped beneath Prince's balls, like *chez Bernini*. But today, we walked right by the poster.

His living room was painted coffee brown, with gold accents.

Side by side, we sank into his satin couch. His eyelashes were still fluttering tragically in a prolonged reaction to the movie. I almost started teasing him: "I mean, what would Mick Jagger say if he could see his ass double acting so prissy?"

But I decided a better diversion would be to admire his latest jewelry, rings and pendants made of hot pink-graffitied Wall chips, arranged in two rows on a low lacquer table. True to his original idea, he had dangled cylinders from circles to suggest moonbeams.

"These are lovely," I said. "You found a way to do the moonbeams just like you said you would. You know, maybe I should see if Lydia is interested. What graffiti is the pink from? A word or a picture?"

"Picture."

"Of what?"

"A pink dog."

"Doing what?"

"Peeing."

"Peeing on anything in particular?"

"Another dog. A blue one."

Slowly, I got him talking to me again. I asked him if he was going to see his parents for Christmas.

He didn't know yet. What was I doing?

Well, I had thought of going to see them myself, but I would go after the new year instead. I was maybe heading to Deauville with the *BCBG* friends.

He looked at me funny. He said he supposed if he were me he wouldn't want to spend his holidays in a housing development in outer Orléans either. Was I sure there wasn't a boyfriend involved? Sex?

Not that I knew of yet, I said. I had not told him about Olivier, perhaps because he was so secretive about his own love life, but more likely because I wasn't fully convinced that he wouldn't turn on me again. I still couldn't forget the backward glance over the bicycle as he abandoned me at Versailles. I had to keep something from him.

I said that maybe this Bastien character, who took me out to Lucas Carton for the best meal of my life the other night—by the way, most delicious chocolate soufflé ever—this Bastien might be shaping into a crush. Had Étienne ever been to Lucas Carton? It was a three-star restaurant.

"*Ta gueule!*" Shut up.

Anyway, it didn't matter about Deauville. I probably couldn't go because of Orlando.

"*Le chien?*"

"*Oui, le chien.*"

"You're kidding."

"No, I wish I were."

"You want me to walk the dog for you?"

"I was going to ask you. But you're sure you don't want to go home for Christmas?"

"Yes."

"Your parents won't be sad?"

"I already broke their hearts when I said I wasn't going to be a *fonctionnaire*, remember? They're over me. They don't get sad about things like Christmas. They have their own perspectives. They have their shelves of keepsakes and photos and Balzac volumes and pots and pans to rearrange. And their garden to obsess about. And, besides, if I stay to walk your dog, then I will see the chic apartment of Madame Papaye in the Sixième. And I will *flâne* in the Luxembourg with my big dog. Can't you picture me, shaking my ass up and down the Luxembourg? What a delightful Christmas it will be. *C'est ma fête!*"

"Why don't I take you to the apartment to pick up Orlando? You can look at everything, I swear. You can rifle through every drawer, but you can't steal anything. Promise? Then you can bring the dog here for a couple of days. He's very calm."

"Are you ashamed of me? Of your own flesh and blood?"

"No, I'm ashamed of my concierge. She won't understand you."

He narrowed his eyes until the lashes kissed. "And what am I supposed to do about your dog's hair?" He gestured grandly around the room.

"I'll lend you our vacuum cleaner."

"I have a few of my own, thanks."

"Then it's settled. *Merci beaucoup.*"

"*Pas de problème, ma chère.*"

There was such generosity in his voice that I thought I could venture another mention of the movie. I wanted to understand why it had upset him. I pulled out my sketchbook, where I had been copying a portion of Caravaggio's *Death of the Virgin* in the Louvre, the upper torso and head of the laid-out Mary, her fingers draped with a childish poignancy, as though she were passed out rather than dead, and the woman sitting beside her, probably Mary Magdalene, bent over in sadness with her head sunk into her arms and lap. I had spent hours on the folds of their dresses. But I had also thought about the story they told as much as of the shapes they made. And this was a departure for me.

"Don't you think these could be bodies from the film, sort of rough and heartbreaking? Caravaggio found all of his biblical models in taverns, you know."

"No, I don't know. I have never studied your theories. I'm ignorant, remember."

"Are not."

"But you are becoming more brave as an artist. You are no longer just drawing the perfect lines. You have stopped refusing to see the emotion. You have let your copy be sad."

"Thank you."

"Very sad." Fingering the corners of my book, he looked like he might cry.

I didn't want things to degenerate just when I had saved them, for Paris to be depressing, nothing but a city full of cigarette smoke and unaffordable Christmas presents. So, I suggested we go to Le Studio, his favorite restaurant, and he finally smiled.

"*Super idée.*"

As we were putting on our coats, he took my left hand. With a birdlike tremor, he slid a ring, studded with a roughly-shaped pink rectangle, onto my fourth finger.

"It's beautiful, Étienne! Thank you!"

"It will help you remember me for a while."

I found myself fighting back irrational tears as we put on our coats and headed for the Marais. All the way to Le Studio, I glanced proudly at my Berlin Wall ring. I couldn't wait to show it to Olivier in London.

But if I was going to see Olivier in London, I had to ask Étienne for yet another favor. Christie would be out of town for New Year's. I would need Étienne to take Orlando again. And I would have to tell him what was going on.

Le Studio was a Mexican restaurant off the cobblestone courtyard of a ballet school.

From our table in the *vitrine,* we watched the dancers at their bars through windows on the higher floors.

"*Je t'invite,*" I said. "I'll buy you a taco."

"*Merci, ma belle.*"

He wanted a margarita. I asked for a glass of Côtes du Rhône.

We each took a chip from a bowl. Above us, two men in sweatpants with bare torsos began to work at the barre.

"Aren't they beautiful?" sighed Étienne. "Each one is the shadow of possibility. So many, many possibilities."

I took a deep breath. "Étienne, you're careful, aren't you?"

"You need to be more specific, dear cousin."

"Come on, you know what I mean. You don't take risks?" I hadn't known what I was thinking until I began to speak, but now it was alarmingly clear. I had wanted him to see this movie because

208

I needed to know how he comported himself in a dangerous world.

"You can't say it, can you?"

"Well if you know what I mean, why are you making me say it? Can't you just reassure me?"

He took my hand. "I take care of myself, Katie."

"Promise?"

"I promise I take care of myself."

We both stared at the dancers for a while.

"Étienne, what are you doing over New Year's?"

"I do not plan that far into the future. But for you I will. Would you like me to take Madame Papaye's dog again? I don't mind. But you have to tell me where you are going and what is happening with you because I know you are hiding very much and it gives me pain."

"Oh, Étienne!"

The story of Olivier and Portia and Lydia and Clarence came pouring out of me in all its convolution. At some point, he took my hand across the table.

"*Ma chère,*" he said when I appeared to be finished, "you're engaged in an orgy."

"What do you mean?" Mostly, I didn't want him to let go of my hand.

But he did let go. And he began to laugh so hard his curls shook.

"It's not funny, Étienne. Please don't make fun of me now. Just tell me everything is going to be all right."

"Do you know what an orgy is?"

"What does that have to do with anything?"

He took a bite of his taco, chewed, swallowed, dabbed his lips with a paper napkin. "An orgy is wanting everything on the menu. You, Katie, you want everyone and their father and their brother to love you. Your particular orgy is a kind of *bulimie,* a *bulimie d'affection.*"

"You're right, Étienne. Absolutely right. But, practically, what do

I do now? Do I not see Olivier? Do I tell everyone everything? Or has it gone too far?"

"You're not listening to me, are you, Katie? What to 'do?' Do, do, do. It's too American. You must not try always to 'do.' You must learn to appreciate. To appreciate each thing, each person. You have to be in the moment. You can't appreciate anything if you cannot focus. Certainly not sex. *Pauvre Katie.*"

"What did you call me? That's what your dad used to call me. It was his epithet. Like I was some tragic character in *La Comédie humaine.*"

"We always felt sad for you. Ever since you first came to stay with us when your father was sick and dying. I was angry about you because I hated how sad it all was."

"Really?"

"Really." He clinked his empty margarita glass against my wine. "So, you want this Olivier boy?"

I nodded, twisting my ring. I hadn't touched my plate. My beans were congealing. "I do want Olivier. Yes."

"Then act dignified. Assume your choice. That's the only way. After that, it will either work or it won't. Go to Deauville. Go to London. You will have a sexy time. But not as sexy as me walking my big dog all over town."

thirty-nine

On Christmas Eve, at the casino in Deauville, Bastien kissed me. Using the money he had given Christie and me to play with, I had won a hand of blackjack. As soon as I had collected my chips, he took me in a full embrace, all cologne vapors and soft hands down my neck with Christie beaming on.

The kiss had been building all that day and evening, through sand dunes and long low tides, oysters and fish soup, Christie doing my makeup for the casino, the outsize jewels in the light of old-world chandeliers, the spinning tables, the flush of black and red fans. I had sensed it approaching but had not guessed at its ardor. As a mental affair, Bastien's kiss had been graceful and subdued as the white winter sky. The truth was much less remote.

Gently, I slid away from him to count my winnings. Nearly a hundred francs of free money! I said that our next round of champagne was on me, and for once Bastien allowed himself to be treated.

When he invited me into his bed that night, I refused kindly but unambiguously. I was so suffused with anticipation of seeing Olivier in London in a week's time that my body barely existed in this place. Bastien's seaside mansion in Deauville was already a memory, pale and pleasant.

I spent the night with Christie, who said to be careful not to lead Bastien on, to consider what was going on with his parents, how fragile he felt.

I said that I thought of him as an affectionate friend, and that any romance between us was a fantasy on his part, that he persisted in molding me to some image he had of an exotic American girlfriend, but that I had never encouraged him. I had only been nice. Friendly. Was it my fault if he refused to read my signals?

She insisted that I was fascinated by his manners and his trappings.

Of course, but that didn't mean I had to sleep with him.

Point taken.

Christmas morning, Bastien gave me a Hermès scarf covered in red and orange butterflies. It was the most luxurious thing I had ever owned, but I had no idea how to tie it. Christie did it for me in the perfect neck knot I had been admiring for months. Then she gave me a tortoiseshell headband.

I gave them each a sketch done from the splashing photo of the Bande at les Bains Douches that I had in my room. I had attempted not to break my rule against portraiture and to draw each of us like an unknown model, with no symbolic pollution. But I had to admit that the cragginess of Bastien's face was infused with the melancholy of his freshly broken home, and that Christie glowed in the light of my affection for her. I couldn't make them anonymous.

I didn't fully inhabit a moment until I landed at Heathrow Airport an hour before Olivier's plane was scheduled to come in from New York. It was the thirtieth of December. I wore a Blondie concert t-shirt under my thrift-store coat. I considered this outfit the sign of a decision not to try to pull off something I couldn't. I wanted to be as little like Portia as possible. I wasn't a rich girl whose mother took her shopping for therapy. Still, I could not obliterate her. I was just wise enough to know that you can't make a person disappear by pretending to forget them.

Portia might be back in the States, but she would be back in my life in a couple of months, at spring break.

For days leading up to my journey to London, I had been too

nervous to eat much. Generally, living in Paris made me feel some-what massive, smugly healthy and inadequate by turn. This starving girl at Heathrow was my ghost. Nervously, she scanned the crowd.

The flight from New York had arrived. Face after unfamiliar face filtered out of customs. Maybe I had forgotten what he looked like, he had slipped by me a second ago, and I had missed one of those turning points that can determine a whole life.

With each arriving passenger, my mind darkened. What if Oliv-ier and Portia had reunited and were together right now, laughing at me and my stupid clothes? What if Olivier and Lydia had planned this as a final life lesson for me before she fired me with no sever-ance, no recommendations, nothing? On a practical level, what if I were high and dry in London? I knew no one here. My flight back to Paris was three days away. I had very little money on me.

I saw him. He was smaller than I remembered, with a very short haircut for work which made him look younger and more vulnerable.

My throat clenched. A flush spread outward from the base of my tongue. I couldn't speak. It had been so long that I needed to feel him in order to believe in him.

Touch me so that I can calm down. Prove that you are alive.

The impression of his smallness dissolved as his face came close, blocking out the airport crowd. He kissed me, then pulled back, but not far, still filling my frame of vision, holding my shoul-ders and examining me. I had on no makeup besides the lip gloss, Silver City Pink, that I had been wearing the day we met.

"You're here," he said. "It's you."

"Of course I am."

Barely speaking, Olivier and I rode the tube into London, where he had booked a small hotel called the Basil Street. He said it wasn't far from Harrod's.

The signage in the station was oddly familiar. I hadn't seen bold-face English in months. But the specifics of Cadbury's and "chemists" and "flats to let" were strange to me, almost abstractions.

213

On the train, the English faces were a blur around us. I could feel details escaping me.

Olivier's hands on me trembled. This underground journey was our first foray into our own world. I trembled back.

We came blinking up into unfamiliar streets and sounds, red everywhere on phone booths, buses, cars on the left, roundabouts. There were bulbous black taxis, a billboard for *Cats*.

"This is Knightsbridge," he said, squeezing me with mounting conviction, as though I were growing more real. The name Knights-bridge meant nothing more to me than the pressure of his arm.

The hotel lobby reminded me of Fawlty Towers, crimson carpet, white desk, crisp accents everywhere. The "lift" was operated by a man with a lever. He nodded at our greetings.

Our room was small and patterned. The walls were striped in fading brown velvet. Our bedspread was a bevy of ferns, arranged in concentric pea-green rings. The lamp shades were fringed. I found it all thrillingly old-fashioned.

Immediately we had sex. Then he slept and slept. He had been putting in long hours at the bank, proving himself. He had worked through Christmas. This was his first break since September.

While he slept, I fingered the *chevalière*. I traced the lines of a lost château. I pressed my own Berlin Wall ring into it. A few traces of my pink plaster rubbed off into its golden grooves.

It was past ten at night when he woke up, took me in his arms and said, "London has fantastic Chinese food. I bet you feel like Chinese food. I know a great place that's open late."

"How did you know that Chinese was exactly what I wanted?" It was only as I said it that I realized it couldn't have been truer.

I put on more lip gloss and one of the several Monoprix mini-skirts I had packed.

We sat, thighs touching, on a banquette, rolling slender pancakes of Peking duck and feeding them to one another. He didn't put enough plum sauce on mine, but I let it go. There were only two other couples eating in the sprawling restaurant, and the waiters were probably all dying to go home, but we had a sense of ourselves as charming and welcome here. Who could not be enthralled in our delirium?

They cleared our duck plates. The silence, so tender between us back in the hotel room, began now to ring. Olivier spoke to cover it.

"This wine is abominable, but have some more."

"Thank you."

More silence. Hand squeeze.

I saw some spring rolls on their way to one of the other tables and my throat narrowed. To clear it, I blurted, "Those spring rolls remind me of Lydia!"

Immediately, I wished I could recall the words. I didn't want us sucked into Lydia's sphere. But it was too late.

"She'll never give those things up, will she?" He laughed. "After all this time, she's still hooked. There's something charmingly pathetic about it, right?"

"What do you mean, *still*?" I pulled my hand away. "You're *still* talking to her about spring rolls?"

"I haven't talked to her for weeks, actually. I think she may finally have given up on me." He sighed. Then he looked hard at me, saw my fear and tried to calm it. "Let's not talk about Lydia, okay?"

I nodded gratefully.

But we did talk about Lydia, and Clarence and Portia and Joshua. Despite our fledgling solo voyage, their gravity was central to us. It was our history.

On my third glass of wine, I took another of my unpracticed leaps into full disclosure and told him about Clarence's affair with Claudia.

He couldn't contain his astonishment. "The bastard!"

I told him everything, right down to the chocolate mousse and the amulet. I spoke, though, through a mounting tide of regret. Although he said little while he was listening, I feared that the story of my behavior was taking an ugly shape in his mind. I understood that I was more than a fresh young thing in the winds of other

215

people's passions. I was smarter than that. And I was worse than that. Olivier was my witness.

But, even though we were inches apart, I did not feel his focus on me. His mind's eye was completely on the Schell family. For a while he glared in angry shock, yet by the time I finished, his gaze had smoldered into something like compassion.

"People need such very different things, don't they?" He sighed.

"What do you mean?"

"Well, for example, I feel this need to be successful, and my mother is desperate to get back something of her lost life. So, I guess Clarence needs someone who looks up to him and doesn't make him feel like an idiot. Tenderness. And Lydia has to feel like she can be nurturing. She doesn't want to be a monster. And Portia—" He saw that I didn't want to talk about Portia and caught himself. "They're all needy, but we can't really blame them."

"Do you think Lydia's a monster?"

"Sometimes. No. I don't know . . . But what do you need, Kate? What do you want?"

I took a few beats to contemplate a drunken answer about moving from drawing into painting, about oils being mixed to evoke flesh and portraiture and the decisive moment in the human expression and staying true to classical technique all the while. But before I could attempt to express it, he responded for me.

"You're a bit like me. You feel a compulsion to succeed in order to get back what's been taken from you."

I was confused. "But there's no way to get my dad back."

"That's not what I mean. I'm talking about the life you should have had." He shook his head and I noticed again how short his hair was. Then he changed the subject. "I'm still getting my mind around the fact that Clarence is having an affair. The kids are going to lose it."

"But nobody's going to find out," I insisted.

"You're sure? Lydia has a way of knowing things for a while before she chooses to discover them."

I was at a loss. So, I smiled.

He smiled in return, his attention streaming back to me as from out behind a cloud. "Oh, who the hell cares about Lydia when you're so beautiful." He popped a fortune cookie in my mouth.

The next day was New Year's Eve. We took a walk through Hyde Park, talked about how winding and mysterious it was compared to our geometrical Parisian gardens, how much closer an imitation of the wild. The French, we decided, had no interest in pretending to be natural.

We spoke of Paris, but whenever the conversation drifted toward the Schell family, he sensed my discomfort and guided it away.

At midnight, we drank champagne on our bed in the Basil Street Hotel. We used glasses from the bathroom sink. The velvet wallpaper quivered with the sounds of fireworks and drunken street singing.

His resolution was to work hard and fast to take better care of the people who truly mattered to him.

I didn't have a resolution, not yet anyway. He could tell I was awkward with my lack of direction in the face of his. He didn't press me. He seemed to know that what I wanted right now was not to be called on anything.

"It's 1990, my Kate. A new decade. For you and me."

forty

On my return to my garret, a delightful pile of envelopes was waiting to greet me, one from my cousins, two from my mom, and three from college friends doing their first jobs or internships in various cities. Wrapped in my mirrored blanket, in the orange glow of my space heater, I savored the different handwritings, one after the other and then each over again.

Jacques and Solange thanked me for my extravagant gift and for reassuring them that Étienne was *en pleine forme*. They hoped I would visit soon.

The larger of Mom's two envelopes was a Christmas card wishing me luck in shaping the new decade we were embarking on. There was a note of challenge in it. The second envelope contained a more prosaic letter about how she was spending the holidays with Aunt Sarah, how they would roast a chicken for Christmas because what did two middle-aged ladies want with a turkey? She hoped there was a good reason for my not having seen Jacques and Solange for Christmas and New Year's. If it was a boy, she hoped he wasn't fly-by-night. Jacques and Solange had been wonderful to us when we needed them most. She hoped I remembered. And what, by the way, was *really* going on with Étienne? She ended by saying she loved me very much, which gave me the warm and familiar sense that she was worried.

Dear Mom,

I should start out by telling you that you've guessed right, there is a boy involved in my not seeing our cousins over the holidays. His name is Olivier and he is French-American and he has a promising job in banking in New York. We met earlier this fall while he was in Paris, and he came all the way to Europe to see me just now. Hardly fly-by-night, although I suppose he did fly by night to get here. Hopefully you will meet him someday and approve.

Lydia and Clarence arrive back from the States today and the whirlwind is about to start up again. The break I've had from them over the holidays has given me time to reflect and to understand something: that not all experience is equal, sort of like dishes at a feast. You have to figure out how to sort through it all and eat mostly what you like instead of filling your plate with the same amount of everything. What I mean is that the interesting parts of this job, the chestnuts so to speak, are probably worth some suffering and even some humiliation. How many hours of dog-walking in the rain, how many tantrums over the price of papayas are worth the promise of meeting Salman Rushdie? And my deepening friendship with the Schell family, a friendship that could last and change my whole life, is worth putting up with some craziness, right? But how much? How do you dose it and parse it? If I learn how to do that, my time here will be well spent. But, boy, is it easier said than done, Mom!

It's freezing here. My windows are frosted and the treetops I can see in the Luxembourg are bare and claw-like, blanched against a white sky. I wish you could—"

My chatty comfort was interrupted by a knock at my door. It was Madame Fidelio, breathless from her six-story climb and looking quite concerned. Madame Lydia was home and had to see me for something of great importance right away.

I got dressed quickly in full anticipation of a postholiday papaya mission. I would make sure this time to ask her to set her maximum price before I ventured forth.

"I have to talk to you, very seriously, about you and Clarence and Claudia." Lydia brandished a fistful of handwritten letters.

We were in the living room with Clarence. She was standing in front of the clock, he was sunk into the sofa, I was perched on the edge of the ottoman where she had motioned me to sit with the abrupt passion of an orchestra conductor.

"Did she give you an amulet to protect my husband against me? It says here"—Lydia looked deep into a line of Claudia's writing— 'The amulet will cure you.' It also says that you, Katherine, reassured Claudia that you yourself would place the magic charm in my husband's hand. It says she knows she can trust you. And obviously *she* can."

"I'm sorry," I said softly, stunned that I was still breathing. Shouldn't the world be in flames by now? Shouldn't I have vanished?

"That's it? You're sorry?"

"Lydia," Clarence bleated from his slump on the couch, "give her time to process what you're saying to her. Please."

"Obviously, Clarence should never have dragged you into this. It was the most unfair thing he could possibly have done and he feels terrible about it. But you have to realize two things, Katherine. Actually, you have to realize a lot of things, but two major ones.

"First of all, you have, at least ostensibly, been working for me. Your allegiance should be to me and only to me. And I will never be able to recommend you professionally to anyone in any business because you have no notion of loyalty, and that is the one fault that is unforgivable."

I lifted my eyes to face the next blow, but my gaze was off-kilter. Lydia stood at a strange angle to me, as though I were falling backward while straining to keep her in my line of sight.

Orlando was dozing on the floor. His coat rolled like a muddy sea. I wanted to fall into it and never surface again.

"Do you want to know what the second lesson is?"

I think I nodded.

"What you've done to me is something that women do not do to other women. You've betrayed me not only as a boss but as a member of your sex. You've threatened my family."

I stood up. "I, but I didn't actually do—"

"What you did is unconscionable. Sit down."

I found myself next to Clarence. In a stolen glance, he searched me through the flecked thickness of his glasses. Did he think I might be angry with him? Was I?

Lydia continued. "I can't believe you've had access to my files, my correspondence. I've opened everything to you. I've been completely disarmed by you. I feel so violated."

"Lydia, I'm sorry, but I'm not the one who had an affair."

"Let me finish, Katherine. What you've done is treacherous, but I understand that you may have been getting very confusing messages about where your loyalties should be, and that maybe you were a lot less mature than you seemed, stupider than we thought. I have to believe that this wasn't all malice. I'll try to give you the benefit of the doubt. So, this doesn't have to be catastrophic for you. Not if you're willing to take yourself in hand and think about what you've done. You're not necessarily finished yet. Clarence and I have been talking the situation over, haven't we, Clarence?"

Briefly, he squinted up at her. I could not imagine him doing much talking since Lydia's big discovery. In fact, I could not imagine him ever talking again. What could he possibly say?

"Clarence and I have decided to give you another chance. We've been saying for months that we'd like to keep you on, pay you more and out of our own pocket, let you develop here a little longer. Maybe this is absurd of me, but, without ever truly forgiving you, I could find a way to live with what's happened. It's been a very confusing time for all of us. We could work through this, like a family. As I say, maybe this is absolutely the wrong decision, but I'm making it on instinct."

As she spoke, my waves of shame and anger succeeded one another. Orlando's chest rose and fell with eerie peace.

Had I done something terrible? Or was I nothing but a distraction from the true blame?

I tried to grasp the offer that Lydia was making. And then it hit me: this wasn't an offer. It was a trap. It was sham forgiveness, fake generosity, and I did not need it. No, Lydia, I wasn't that poor.

"I think I should go," I said.

She took a violent step toward me. "Then you're fired!"

"Lydia, please," begged Clarence.

"Clarence, you have absolutely no moral authority here. None whatsoever. Shut up."

To give immediate direction and weight to my decision, I ran up into my room and began to pack. I would leave now. I would go to Christie's. Or to Étienne's.

As I pulled my clothes from their wire hangers, different reactions pierced my consciousness, each as sharp as the next, the points of a blaring star. I was guilty of the inability to distinguish right from wrong. I had sided with emotion over duty. I had been exploited. I had been narcissistic, believing myself so large in the hearts and minds of these people, when in reality I could have been anyone, and there would be a string of Katies after me and I should get over myself. I had acted to defend the romance and true love that Clarence would prove too cowardly to live out.

These people were crass. These people were tragic. These people were ultimately ordinary. Lydia would sacrifice everything for art. She would channel Clarence's affair into her work and never be the worse for it. Lydia was a human being first and foremost. She was traumatized.

I was traumatized. I was humiliated. I was the wiser. Mom would be proud, ashamed, understanding, furious. She would say, make sure you get recommendations for some kind of job because you need a future, get letters of introduction, get something no matter what it takes because otherwise it will all have been for nothing. She would say, learn and move on and take care of yourself.

I was scared. I was strong. Maybe I should stay. What, was I crazy?

My room emptied quickly, most of it fitting into a couple of suitcases, until it was little more than a frame for its own rooftop view with its patch of Luxembourg in the lower right corner.

I took the elephant bedspread from the futon and rolled it into a backpack. I winked at my dad before wrapping his picture in the same tissue paper it had crossed the Atlantic in. I peed in the electric toilet one last time.

I still hadn't figured out exactly where I was going. I supposed I should walk to the pay phone and make sure someone was home to take me in before I embarked with my luggage. I probably needed a cab. But the urge to get my things out of this place was so violent that I pushed the larger of my bags through the door and began to jostle it down the stairs.

After one flight, I heard footsteps rising heavily toward me.

I abandoned the suitcase on a landing and bolted back to my naked room.

I had barely closed the door when there was a knock.

"Who is it?" I asked.

"Katie, it's Clarence. Let me in, please."

Clarence had never once set foot in my room. I assumed that, like Lydia, he didn't quite want to acknowledge how I lived.

His eyes looked inward, taking me in just enough to place me in the cosmology of his own dilemma.

"Katie, you've got to stay. I can't imagine her forgiving anyone the way she's willing to forgive you. She needs you. If you go, the whole thing is too disruptive, too real."

"But it *is* real, Clarence. We can't pretend it isn't real."

"Of course it is. You and I know that. But you and I aren't Lydia. She can recraft this situation if we let her. She's a bloody genius. And we are bloody responsible for her. Please. We really can pay you more if that's an issue," he said, with a quick glance around the maid's room. "You know, you don't only owe it to her to stay on, but to yourself. Your opportunity here is only beginning. You have so much to learn. It's going to all be wonderful again soon."

Clarence smiled, and for a second filled the outline of the father in my heart. I could feel myself bending. But I did not want to.

"What about Claudia?" I asked.

"We will have to cut ourselves off from Claudia, you and I both. And she will cry suicide perhaps but we have to realize it's rubbish. She has to understand."

"Understand what exactly?"

"That there is such a thing as real life."

"I don't know if I can do it, Clarence. I don't know if I can ever be comfortable here again. I feel so terrible now."

"Don't," he squeaked, then looked longingly out into whatever vista he perceived across the expanse of my electric burner. "Please, Katie. Please. I'm sorry. And if you feel sorry too, then the thing to do is stay."

I wanted to hug him, to tell him we would all survive, but instead I fidgeted with the handle of my suitcase and said I needed time to think.

forty-one

No further mention was ever made of my raise.

After I told Lydia I would stay, she was dry and business-like for about a week before drifting into a postapocalyptic détente with me. She did not speak directly of Claudia or my treachery again except to tell me in no uncertain terms that I was not to say anything to Portia. Portia had enough to worry about. Of course, the children had to know eventually, but Lydia herself would tell them, when the time was right. Probably when they were here for spring break, although that was none of my business. My business was to help her to get ready for her upcoming gallery show in March. She had decided to make it openly political. She would include recent work from Germany and England.

I stayed in part because I did not want to miss the flow of history, of Berlin, of Salman Rushdie, of the strange and frightening new rumblings from the far right in the South of France. I still didn't know what any of it meant. To leave now would be like giving up before the end of a novel. And I stayed because Clarence had made me feel I was part of the family, the child who was neither spoiled and ethereal nor spoiled and defiant. Even though I knew with every conscious fiber that I was a servant, I suspended my disbelief in the face of his affection. Our relationship was not dead yet. Neither was his with Lydia. Or Lydia's with me. Or his with Claudia. No matter how unhealthy the view, I was compelled to look on. The story was not over yet.

225

The fact that I had decided to remain meant that I could also decide to leave. And while it was hard to believe I would ever follow through with such a drastic measure, I had shown myself that I could take greater risks than I had ever imagined. No stance was impossible. My drawing was beginning to show evidence of style. Somehow, this gave me courage, made me less timid with Lydia.

By mid-February, buried in preparations for the big show, the surface of life in the Schell household was close to normal, if punctuated with dizzying reminders of recent trauma. Lydia had repainted everything to the point where the original colors were virtually erased. Claudia did not exist. I was Lydia's faithful servant. Clarence was harmless if profoundly annoying.

But there were moments when the old paint would suddenly appear, blood from a fundamental crime seeping through the walls. Even if it vanished as fast as it had come, we all saw. I was reminded in a thousand ways that I still existed in Paris only on the whims of Lydia's grace.

It was strange, this hairlined normalcy, but it was tenable. Lydia was, if anything, more jocular than before. A strident and lordly jocularity. She had won, after all. On all fronts.

Several times, I had tried to call Claudia from my phone booth, but there was no answer. And I didn't have the time these days to stake out her shadowy building on the Île St-Louis. Once when Lydia was out to lunch with Harry Mathews, I dared to ask Clarence if he knew where Claudia was. I hoped she was all right. Perhaps she really had gone to Berkeley this time? Or to Morocco?

He had given me the blankest look I had ever seen.

I had written to Olivier in great detail about the unraveling of events, but his letters in return made no mention of it. I figured the ugliness of the situation was one he would rather not touch.

The invitation to Lydia's opening on the rue du Four in St-Germain was double-sided, with a diptych on either face, one pair of German photos, one pair of British ones. On her desk were the two mock-ups alongside a half-eaten container of the evil spring rolls. She had given me an exemption from my ban on buying them today because we had a lot of stressful material to cover. We had to sign off on the invitation and make the guest list.

"Katherine, your job today is to keep me focused," she said.

"Thanks for finally telling me what my job is."

"Don't be facetious, young lady." Her tone might be light, but her protuberant eyes rolled to see me in a new way. For a moment, they lingered, half-impressed, half-suspicious. I had never been fresh with her before. Then she turned back to the task at hand.

She examined the German side of the invitation. There were photos taken a few days after the one of November 9 for *Paris Match*. They showed the same bunch of bananas, on either side of a wide gap in the rubble of the Berlin Wall. In the left-hand photo, a young man in a biker jacket, with sunglasses and a briefcase, was holding out bananas, smiling. His gesture was luxuriant, full and stretched. In the opposite photo, a man closer to middle age, having accepted the bananas, held them to his chest. His eyes were downcast and apologetic.

The impetus for this exchange, according to Lydia, was an article in *Die Welt* reporting that East Germans had never had access to imported fruit. So, the West Germans thought it was a beautiful gesture to hand out bananas to their suddenly visible neighbors. They drove over the border with carloads.

"My question," said Lydia, "is do I need a title here?"

"What would the title be?" I asked.

"That's the *real* question. I don't have it yet. I need something that captures the symbolism of Berlin. The West Germans are condescending and the East Germans are self-conscious. They feel incompetent and they are on the verge of feeling very bitter about it. So, after that initial moment of unity between the countries, there is this total lack of recognition, right? And in Berlin it's much more potent than anywhere else because there the two peoples are literally face-to-face. These two banana moments are like the last moments of an illusion . . . Can you come up with anything,

Katherine, anything about the power of illusion? The death of illusion? You should know something about trickery by now. Do you want a spring roll?"

"No, thank you."

"Mind if I interrupt?" It was Clarence standing in the doorway. "May I come in for a minute, Lydia? Can we have a moment of mutual recognition in empathy with the Germans, please? Just this once?" He did not wait for an answer, but strode up to her desk. "I couldn't help but overhear you two talking titles, and I have a thought. How about, 'Habits of Deceit'?"

Lydia honored the suggestion with a moment of silence.

"It's rather perfect." Clarence gathered steam. He was hellbent on pretending he hadn't done anything wrong. "If you think about how both sides have lived so long in deception about the war, but each with a deeply different deception."

"Deceit, yes, deceit," Lydia muttered. "Coming from you, that's not bad. In fact, it's downright rich, Clarence."

Either he wasn't going to bite, or he simply wasn't listening, because he went on with undampened enthusiasm. "It gets better! The East Germans think they are about to have the jeans and the televisions and the motorcycles and everything they've ever heard or dreamed about. They are deluded. I think it's unimaginable for us. We three in this room have no idea what it feels like to be an East German. And neither does this guy in West Berlin with his damn bananas. I mean, we're all exactly like him if we're honest with ourselves. We're all clueless and condescending. And we're going to lose patience with our poor relations in about five minutes."

Lydia rolled her eyes. "You don't see the irony in this, do you, you poor man?"

Clarence blushed, but pushed hoarsely on. "So, 'Habits of Deceit' it is. Don't you like it, Katie?"

I looked at Lydia. She was very still, eyes rounded out in concentration. Then I looked away and figured out what I myself thought of Clarence's suggestion.

"I like it," I said.

"Come on, Lydia, don't get mired," said Clarence. "Admit it's a good idea."

"It's not bad. I'm thinking about it."

"That's marvelous, dear. Thank you."

When the two of them began to get along like this, bright threads of hope surfaced in the family fabric. Perhaps the reason Clarence and Lydia could afford to be so mean to each other was that these threads were in fact strong. If they could see that they did love each other, then she would stop calling Olivier when she was drunk and lonely, and Clarence would never cheat on her again. Maybe everything was about to get a whole lot healthier around here.

I hatched a plan to have Clarence write the catalog notes for Lydia's show. It could be their Paris collaboration. Their true *rapprochement*. I could help with the work. The family I might once have helped to ruin could be whole again.

"Can I see that invitation?" asked Clarence.

She handed him the German mock-up.

"These are excellent photos, my dear. What idiocy was going through Georges's mind when he rejected these?"

Georges was one of the heads of Agence France-Presse. He had originally turned down several of the images that were going to appear in the show.

"Georges is trying to turn the whole agency against me. It's disgusting. After all we've done for him. I introduced him to everyone he knows in the States. Everyone. Talk about having no memory. The traitor."

"Bloody traitor. We're not inviting him to the opening, are we?"

"Are you kidding? I've crossed him off the list. First round of cuts."

It struck me that Clarence and Lydia were a united front. They *were* going to stay together. I knew it.

To make the moment tactile, I touched Étienne's ring.

Although I had been wearing the ring for weeks, Lydia chose this moment to notice it in grand style. Her eyes widened over the bright pink chip. "That's not what I think it is, is it?"

"A piece of the wall, yeah. My cousin makes them," I answered proudly. "He's into *objets trouvés*. He's doing rings and chokers and bracelets and pendants. He has a friend who went to Berlin and brought him back some rubble to work with."

"Fascinating," said Clarence. "Instant pillage."

"So you have finally seen your cousins?" Lydia fixed her gaze on me. "I'm glad."

"Not Jacques and Solange in Orléans, not yet, but I see their son Étienne all the time. He has this idea of making jewelry from historical waste products, things that aren't treasures anymore become treasures again."

"Could you get me some samples?"

"Oh, I'm sure he would be thrilled!"

"Any idea what he's asking? I'm feeling flush." She laughed.

Clarence had lost interest in Étienne's ring and was focusing again on Lydia's invitation. "This is vintage Lydia," he sighed, staring into the banana photos.

She snatched the invitation back. "I hate it when you use wine words on me. It makes me feel old."

"It's simply a figure of speech, Lydia."

"Thank you, Clarence. Thank you for clearing that up. A figure of speech, of course. Deceit is also a figure of speech. Very convenient, I'm sure. Now, Katherine and I have work to do here. Please leave us alone."

But, Clarence would not go. As though acting on some fevered resolve to change the state of things, some sleepless promise he had been making to himself to purge bad blood, he stood his ground .

"The Germany work," he said a bit too loudly, "is brilliant. But I will never see the analogy you're trying to make with the Rushdie affair." His eyes glanced over the other page of the invitation, the diptych from England, a shot of a book catching fire, with a DEATH TO RUSHDIE banner half-legible through a smoky haze, next to it a close-up of the writer himself, posed as for a book jacket.

He took the kind of breath you take on a high dive. "If I were you, I would stick to Germany."

"Then it's a good thing you aren't me, Clarence." Lydia did not raise her eyes from her desk. "That's enough from the peanut gallery. Katherine, can you please go back into your time lines and look for title ideas for my show. We'll find one, or one will find us. You know, titles are like sex."

"Like sex?" Clarence and I asked in unison.

"Sometimes titles are instant and amazing. Other times they are a total grind."

I blushed for Clarence. "But I thought we were using Clarence's title. What about 'Habits of —'"

"Listen, we are short on time here. Please go to your time lines and find me something I can actually use!"

Clarence shuffled from the room.

I went to the file cabinet, but before I could retrieve anything, she interrupted me. "Listen, I have to be alone to focus right now. Do me a favor. Read this. A friend of mine at *Granta* in London has published this essay by Rushdie in hiding called 'In Good Faith.' Go read it and see if you can find some ideas for titles for some of the England pictures. There's good stuff about unrest. That's the connection with Germany. Unrest." She looked at me. "That weekend you spent in London over the New Year, what signs did you see there?"

I dug my concrete ring into my thigh. "You know, I spent the whole time I was there inside with my friends. The weather was so terrible."

"Surely you noticed something."

The spring roll crumbs in the takeout container on the desk glistened like the interior of a Chinese restaurant in a fever dream. What if she asked what neighborhood my "friends" lived in? I wasn't sure I knew the name of any residential neighborhood in London. Did people live in Knightsbridge? Did I know the name of a single street? Had I actually been to London with Olivier, or just to a bed somewhere?

My fantasy of being found out ebbed as I realized that Lydia was simply stating the fact that there was plenty of unrest to notice these days in London. She was not making an inquiry of me at all. Surely, I had remarked something askew there. Anyone would. She did not wait for a response.

"So," she handed me the *Granta* issue, "read through this and maybe you can discuss it with Clarence. See if he mentions anything beyond his usual opinions. He's being so negative and cagey about my work on the Rushdie affair that I wonder if he's not secretly writing about it himself and not telling me because he thinks I might be working on a photo essay with another writer. Believe it or not, he's competitive that way. Have you noticed material in his study about the affair? He hasn't asked you to help him with anything extracurricular?" She gave a short bitter laugh.

With a brief eye-lock, I was punished for my sins. The room melted and reformed.

"No, no," I said. "I've not helped him with anything about the Rushdie affair. It's all about fashion."

"I have no choice but to trust you now, do I?"

"Listen, if you still want to fire me—"

"Jesus, relax." She laughed. "We're Americans, dear. We live things down. Eventually. Now, do me a favor. Read this article and maybe talk to him about it. See if anything happens to come up. If nothing else, he'll feel more included. He can feel sidelined when I'm working on something this high-profile. That's why he acts up."

I was sure that Clarence was not writing a clandestine article about Muslims. Now that Claudia was out of the picture, he was more fixated than ever on the rise of the department store in nineteenth-century Paris. The modern cathedral, Zola called it.

But as soon as I finished "In Good Faith," I went to find him. I had my own agenda.

He was in the kitchen, eating cheese. Rare winter sunlight through the window hit the glass over Lydia's famous photos and made them dazzling, if impossible to make out.

Since his impassioned plea for me to remain in Lydia's service,

Clarence had avoided being alone with me as much as possible. When we did interact, he assumed an exaggerated version of his professorial persona.

The precocious student, I played along. We were determined to act through our guilt until we forgot it.

But every once in a while I took a moment to be amazed that such major events as had recently shaken our household could be so convincingly absorbed into the stream of normalcy, that life carried on.

Until now, I had operated under the childish assumption that I was the only person in the world who had survived a trauma. My father had died and I was still alive. Wasn't that incredible? Despite the fault line in my heart, I now laughed and engaged with people and even fell in love. Miraculous, no?

Yet now I saw that I was not alone. As I watched Clarence and Lydia pushing on with manic solidity, I understood that we were all battered survivors.

Of course, there was still the question of Claudia. But I fantasized that she too must be "strong," that she had left her garret and gone away to a better life. I was glad for her to finally be out from under the thumb of her doomed love. But I missed her.

"Hi, Clarence," I said. "What kind of cheese is that?"

"Gruyère. Quite aged and sharp. Would you like some?"

"Sure. Thanks. I've been reading this Rushdie piece you might be interested in."

"Really? What does it say?"

"Well, Rushdie writes that he's been painted as something he's not," I said, "and that this false image is threatening to replace him and give him another identity. Don't you think that's interesting?"

"Well, the presumption that he knew what he was doing in *The Satanic Verses* is unfair. I'll give him that even if it is an utterly unreadable book."

"Well, maybe you should read this then? Rushdie has all this stuff about the migrant condition as a metaphor for humanity. You might like it." I pushed the magazine toward him on the kitchen table.

Instead of picking it up, he handed me another piece of gruyère. "I can't fathom why she is doing this. Why is she insisting on this Rushdie rot . . . The German photos are fantastic and of a piece. But the Muslim material is totally unrelated. Lydia's a great artist, but she's not always spot-on with the conceptual stuff." He paused and mashed his lips around. "She's offtrack, I'm afraid."

I shook my head. "I think the connection with Germany is supposed to be totalitarianism. Rushdie says it's all about who calls who a devil."

"What exactly are you trying to convince me of, Katie?"

"Maybe you should write the catalog notes for Lydia's show. I'm sure you could figure out how all the photos work together if you put your mind to it. It would be so amazing if you two collaborated."

He laughed. "Oh, believe me we've tried before and it's not pretty."

"But she liked your title for the banana pictures, the deceit one. I'm sure she'll end up using it. She's only—" I was about to say "She's only punishing you," but I caught myself.

"'Habits of Deceit' is one thing. But I'm telling you I think the connection between the Berlin Wall and English Muslims is nowhere but in her mind. Or else someone else has talked her into it. She hasn't mentioned anyone has she? Another collaboration, perhaps?"

"No, Clarence. There's no one else. Now, can't you come up with something? Can't you work with the theme of totalitarianism? Can't you do something with intellectual tyranny?"

"Are you saying I'm a tyrant, Katie?" He winked.

"I know you can do it."

"And you think Lydia would be amenable?"

"I think she'll be delighted to have you in her camp."

As I watched him contemplate my proposal, I glimpsed victory. Perhaps I could hold people together after all.

• • •

It was peach Kir time.

"So, that's truly what he's working on? Department stores? *Grands magasins?*" Lydia laughed. "That's all you've seen at his desk?"

Clarence was out running errands.

I wished he would come back and have a drink with us and make his catalog proposal to Lydia in person.

"I like what you said about the Rushdie," said Lydia, "about how he strives to change his condition, but he still inhabits it. That's very dignified."

"That's it!" I said. "Clarence would love that. Inhabiting the changing condition. That's something he could write about."

Her voice curdled. "I thought you said he wasn't writing about the affair."

"He's not," I floundered. "He's not, but if he were to write your catalog notes—"

"He'd never do that."

"But he said he would! We were sort of thinking you could do a big photo essay together, publish it somewhere after the show. Remember, you were saying about the *New Yorker* changing soon to print photographs? That would be a perfect venue for you two."

"Listen, you can't breathe a word of this. I have a very well known British writer doing my catalog. It's going to cause quite a stir, and I know Clarence is going to be upset when I tell him. So let me handle it."

"Who's the writer?"

"I cannot say yet. It's much too early, and dangerous."

Damn. With Salman Rushdie doing Lydia's catalog notes, I was powerless to bring her and Clarence together.

Lydia took a critical sip of her Kir. "Dear, would you pour me a little more Sancerre? Despite everything that's happened, I still manage to adore you, but you made this drink too sweet. Where's our man to mix when we need him? Why does he keep doing errands at Kir time? He must be so absorbed in his book that he doesn't think of things until the end of the day, and then he rushes off in that funny way of his, doesn't he?" Her suspicion twinkled and popped. She sipped from it at will.

I poured her more wine. Then I served myself.

"Tomorrow, Katherine, we finalize the guest list. *Sans faute.* You've got to keep me in line. And no matter what I say, no more spring rolls."

forty-two

Christie was sobbing. "This is why they rent to Americans. We have no recourse. They can put us out in the street whenever they want. They're not allowed to do that to their own kind."

"Christie, you're not going to be in the street. What about staying with Bastien or Christian or Pierre-Louis?"

"I can't be dependent on them. It would change the dynamic too much."

"You could tell them you were in between apartments. They're your friends. And you know you can stay here if you need to. You're a little long for the futon, but we could extend it somehow."

She stretched her neck, exposing her endless throat to the outrageousness of fortune.

"No," she sniffled. "Thank you."

Christie's landlord had a daughter who was moving to Paris for a new job, and Christie had to uproot by next week.

"It all feels so barren," she said. "You think you have a cushion, then suddenly, whoosh!" As she flung her arms toward my window as if to throw herself out, there was a rocky clattering. I had given her one of Étienne's bracelets for her birthday and the Wall chips were jangling.

I hugged her and one caught on my sweater.

I pulled away, clapping my hands. "I have it, my friend! I have it!" There *was* something I could do. "This is such a rush! Put your boots on. Let's go out to the *cabine* and call my cousin."

237

She looked at the chunks of concrete around her wrist. "Your jewelry cousin? That guy?"

"He has an extra bedroom. And I think your senses of style will totally meld. This could be beautiful."

She blew her nose into an ancient handkerchief of my father's that I kept by my bed.

"You're funny," she said.

Within a few days, Christie had moved into the Bastille apartment. Étienne helped her paint her bedroom purple and began to steal toiletries for her. On nights when she wasn't "cheating on him" at Les Bains Douches, the two of them went to Queen. Once in a while, I joined them, but I couldn't stay out late right now. I couldn't afford to be tired. Lydia's show was almost upon us.

Lydia and I spent long hours in her office, mostly on correspondence. To relieve bouts of anxiety, we went through the occasional envelope of old proof sheets in her to-be-archived files.

Every day, we walked to the gallery on the rue du Four to make sure the walls were being painted the right shade of white, to adjust lighting, to reconfirm with the owner that there would be Taittinger champagne at the opening and not Veuve Cliquot, which she couldn't abide. There was something oversweet and ubiquitous about Veuve Cliquot, unless, of course, it was vintage, said Lydia one day when we had stopped for lunch at La Palette on the way home from one of our trips. It was early March, the first day warm enough to eat outside. There was less than a week before her opening.

"I never knew how much better vintage champagne is," I said. "Until these French boys taught me to drink it. They say a lot of it is the carbonation."

"I love it when the *terraces* start to fill in Paris." Lydia was scanning the menu. "You realize how outward-looking the whole city is, how it's laid out for 'scoping' as they say. Look at the way we're all facing the street. Shall we have salades composées? You should try the *auvergnate* one. I would, but I can't have it because of all the cheese. It's the best thing here."

"I enjoy chicken liver salad though. It's the first salad on the list, see?"

"How French of you. Can you imagine an American girl ordering foies de volaille? Did your cousins teach you that?" Her eyes passed over me, searchlights on an empty street. "You should get the foies. I will take the niçoise. And is it terrible if we have a glass of wine with lunch?"

forty-three

Clarence and I met in the courtyard. He had switched from his winter coat into a brown corduroy blazer with tan leather elbow patches. He looked distracted and mildly annoyed.

We had been speaking so little lately, after my gaffe over the catalog notes, that we had grown shy. I felt confined to small talk.

"So, I hear Portia and Joshua are going to make it for the opening."

"Well, we'll get Joshua, but maybe not Portia after all."

"Really?" I tried not to sound too hopeful.

"You haven't heard? It's disgusting. She's reduced herself to begging that Olivier fool to get back together with her. She says she needs him to, and I quote, 'rescue her' until she finishes out the school year. Otherwise she might not 'make it,' whatever that means. And I wouldn't be surprised if he condescended to do it. He's not above using her for sex or for our our New York connections. That boy is such an opportunist."

Suddenly all I wanted was to talk to Étienne, to cry in those skinny arms. I needed him to tease me back to life.

I found him at his kitchen table reinforcing the rose cloak on his Prince poster. Some of the petals had come loose and the *nudité* was *indécente*. With a tiny brush, he was judiciously dabbing glue.

"Lovely," I said. In the shape of his back as he leaned over his

240

work, I saw the outline of the boy who had rejected me, sprawled in the grass at Versailles. It had been months since I had thought of him in this old incarnation, and I was shocked by how vivid the memory was.

"This poster is one of the few objects I will always keep." He pressed a petal over Prince's right thigh, then looked up at me. "Why the tears?"

Before I could get my tongue around my story, Christie burst upon us with a basket full of vegetables from the farmers' market. She thought Étienne's pallor might be a vitamin deficiency and she was cooking him lots of leafy greens.

She and Étienne kissed on both cheeks.

"Katie, what's wrong?" She put a hand on my shoulder.

"I need to talk to Olivier. Clarence says that Portia is begging him to get back together with her and that he might be considering it."

They sat me down and brought me the phone.

"Morgan!"

"Hi, it's me."

"Oh, hi. How are you?"

I took a breath. "Clarence told me Portia is not coming for Lydia's opening because she's hoping you'll take her back."

He sighed. "She's threatening to kill herself."

"I believed you when you said it was over with Portia. I trusted you."

"You can. I'm not going to touch her. Believe me. She repels me right now. But she's suicidal. I can't turn my back on that."

"I know Portia. She will never kill herself. If you agree with her when she says she's pathetic, she'll stay that way. It's disrespectful—to *both* of us."

"I'm sorry, it's complicated." His voice was shuddering. "It will take time, but it will all blow over."

I walked across Christie's tapestry-draped bedroom to the limits of the phone cord, turned around. She had covered a lampshade in tortoiseshell beads. I fingered them.

Olivier was going to have to feel my hope through the sternness of my words. "I guess I'm disappointed," I said. "I thought you were more separate already. I thought you could resist the craziness."

"I'm sorry," he said. "But she feels like she's been cast off. Even if she drives me nuts, I can't stop caring what happens to her."

"Neither can I. But Portia's not some insane person. She's self-dramatizing and upset and you're not helping by letting her drag it out. You're making it worse for her because you won't tell her to get over herself."

"No, her parents are driving her insane. Do you realize how manipulative Lydia can be?"

I laughed. "Believe me, I'm catching on."

"She's told Portia basically that she will cut her off if the girl doesn't show up in Paris for this gallery opening and spend her spring break there. It's hell."

"It's not hell, Olivier. It's the Sixième." Then it hit me. "You mean she *is* coming?"

"You have to understand," he sighed, "that Portia doesn't reason like us. *You* grasp the fact that real life is hard and that nothing actually kills you until it does. You and I have the same perspective on all this. It's like we're realists *and* romantics."

Technically, I hadn't been betrayed, but I was angry and hurt. I couldn't picture what was happening in New York beyond the broadest of outlines. The shading was infuriatingly suspect.

"Olivier, I have to go now. This call is going to cost my friends a fortune."

Late that night, feeling sad at Les Bains Douches, I drank countless glasses of vodka from Bastien's private bottle. Gallant as always, he ordered me more tonic and extra ice to suck on when I got too hot dancing.

You could tell people's level of sophistication by how well they pretended not to be looking at Naomi Campbell and Christy Turlington.

I asked him if there was any news on his parents and their separation.

242

He shook his head. He was becoming more *fataliste*. "My father says now that he wants to come back to my mother, and I find myself wondering, in reality, if it's a good idea. I never thought I would feel this. But, seeing my mother without him, I understand that she is happier, more *épanouie*. She is laughing more and she is making plans and traveling with her friends. A little like an American woman, I suppose, adventurous, not so worried about what people will think.

"And my father, he and I meet for dinner once a week *en tête-à-tête* and we have true discussions. I've been learning so many things about him. Admitting he has been some kind of failure makes him more open, and now he knows he loves my mother. I see the dynamic. I have a privileged relationship with each one of my parents. There are things you could never imagine, because they are too horrible, until they happen, and then they are fine." He sneaked a glance at the supermodels.

"They have to be fine," I said. "And you do look happier. I'm glad. But I hope you won't stop playing the *Sonate Claire de lune*."

"I will always play anything you desire."

Christian and Jean-Pierre came from dancing to sit with us. "Private Dancer" was booming through the club, and everyone agreed, loudly, that Tina Turner had extraordinary legs for her age. Bastien poured drinks all around from his bottle.

The boys were looking disapprovingly at Christie, who was across the small dance floor in a vaguely ethnic spangled tank top, jumping up and down with a more alternative crowd, even though she had come in with us and was drinking Bastien's alcohol. She looked carefree, and I felt a wave of gratitude at having finally been able to help somebody by putting her together with Étienne. That, and a titillating glimmer of social mastery.

Christian and Jean-Pierre finished their vodka tonics and went back to dance. Christie saw them, widened her circle and pulled them in. They moved uncomfortably in this foreign group, where the boys wore ripped t-shirts and had asymmetrical hair.

With silver tongs, Bastien slid ice into fresh drinks and slipped a piece into my mouth with his fingers. "Don't you think Christie has changed since she moved to the Bastille? I'm worried about her. And living with this wild *pédéraste,* with all these stories of contaminated blood. *Le sang contaminé.* It's frightening, this world now. And she shares a bathroom with him. I understand about Americans and the tradition of rebellion, how you are supposed to have a period of pretending to be poor. But this is extreme. It's a little disgusting too, no? Look at how she acts and how she dances with the *drogués.* It's not good."

"Bastien, the *sang contaminé* had nothing to do with gay people. That was a blood bank for hemophiliacs that got contaminated and gave all these poor people AIDS. It also has nothing to do with Étienne, who happens to be my perfectly healthy cousin."

He looked at me with something akin to pity. "You are so very naïve, and protected from aspects of life."

"Me, protected?" That's right, Sébastien. I'm sheltered and you know all about life and about suffering because your father left your cotton-candy-haired mother for a few weeks and you had to spend Christmas like an orphan in one of several *résidences secondaires.* You are familiar with hard knocks while I am oblivious. You know all about life, all about biology in particular, all about getting AIDS from the toothbrushes of people who don't even have it.

"You are completely wrong," I said.

"Not about Christie. *Elle change.*"

Never had I found Bastien more repellent. But, unlike Olivier, he had not let me down.

I kissed him. I can remember thinking, quite dramatically, that I was as reckless as those plague victims you read about, partying through their last evenings on earth with nothing to lose.

We stayed enmeshed for at least an hour. Bastien's ardor redoubled whenever Naomi Campbell came into view. ("When they are beautiful, the black women, they are stunning.")

Christian and Pierre-Louis looked on with sanctioning smiles.

My body told me I would never sleep with him, but I liked his weightless lips.

From time to time, Christie came over to fill her glass and arch her groomed eyebrows at us. This was what she had been envisioning for me all along.

"Don't sweat it," the eyebrows said. "What you need now, at this *phase* of life, is someone who will treat you well. Not some complicated head case who is going to drag you down. A guy who will be good to you *au quotidien*. That's all. You've finally understood."

Forty-four

Over the past months, I had made peace with my electric toilet, but I thought it might be a problem for Portia. She had come up the *escalier de service* for my very first dinner party. She had exclaimed about how creative I had been with my little space and how charming the view was from my dormer window. "I'm so jealous you can see the Luxembourg!" She had even eaten one of my blue-cheese-and-fig canapés. Wasn't this great? We were all going to sit around a tablecloth on the floor to have our pasta. Such a pretty tablecloth. Yes, of course she wanted a glass of wine. Things were going swimmingly until she asked if she could use the bathroom and I pulled open the vinyl accordion door to reveal the airplane toilet. She said she would be right back. She had forgotten something downstairs.

Why had I invited her? As soon as her mother chose to reveal her father's indiscretions, and my part in them, I figured I would be a goner in her affections and that she would look back on this evening in disgust. And even though I was upset with Olivier for humoring her antics, he hadn't gotten back together with her. Had she known that he and I spoke of her as lovers discuss a cast-off, she would have wanted to kill me. All emotional logic should have excluded her from my party.

But the fear of offending her in the moment outweighed it all. I couldn't bear the thought of her hearing the footfall of my friends on the stairs while she was left below. Not when she still thought I was kind.

246

Besides Portia, my guests were Étienne, Christie, and a couple of college friends, boys, who were coming through town and could not believe I was hanging out with Christie Brown. Wasn't she a preppy snob?

Not at all, I said. Wait and see. And within a few minutes of their arrival, Christie and Étienne were entertaining us with their ironic version of *le rock*, the *BCBG* dance *par excellence*. Even though she was taller, he spun her fluently in and out, dipped and twirled her like the proudest of Gallic alpha males. As their moves got more and more burlesque—they had a swirling, butt-bumping figure eight—I realized they must practice a lot.

We all fell down around the tablecloth laughing. The boys were disarmed. Christie was great. She was totally self-mocking about the whole French thing. And her roommate Étienne was unreal.

We heard Portia's heels clattering in the stairwell. "It's the return of the hothouse flower," whispered Christie.

"Shush! She's just a little clueless, you guys. I don't think she has a lot of friends her own age, but she's trying. Give her a chance."

"Feeling a little guilty, Katie? A little compromised?" Christie's sternness plunged the room into silence. "You shouldn't be nice to her. You'll regret it. You know you will."

The Yale boys looked puzzled.

"De quoi vous parlez?" asked Étienne. What were we talking about? Since his English wasn't very good, Christie and I spoke French when the three of us were together, but the presence of our American friends tonight made that seem rude. So, we translated when we remembered to.

"Christie se moque de moi," I explained, escaping into French to diffuse the moment. Christie is teasing me.

As the dinner progressed, I was surprised at how sensitive Portia was to the fact that Étienne might feel excluded from the conversation. She kept coming out with slow, blanket statements to him in a mix of both languages. "So, Kate says you are a *bijoutier.*" "The Bastille is a very interesting *quartier* of Paris. *Très interessant.*"

"My mother's *vernissage* for her show is *demain soir.*" She looked better now than she had at Thanksgiving. She was still thin, but not as ghostly. Perhaps her heart was slowly mending?

"Give her a break," I told Christie with my eyes. "No one is really bad here. Just weak." But my pleading looks were lost. I could see that Christie couldn't stand Portia.

"I'm going to go use your fabulous electric bathroom," said Christie, loud and drunk after dessert. "I would pretend I was so rad as to be on a plane to Paris if I weren't already here." She pulled the accordion door shut, then immediately opened it just wide enough for her leg to shoot out in a cancan kick, and slammed it back. We could all hear her peeing. Then we heard the beginning of the suction flush, a quick inhale, followed by a loud clanging and a series of "Oh my God!'s."

She had flushed one of her lipsticks, a creamy pink Chanel that Étienne claimed he had risked his life for in Bon Marché. The boys tried to fish it out. One depressed the toilet's metal center with a wooden spoon while another scooped around with a ladle. But they had no luck. Once we had determined the lipstick was lost, we decided to try to flush the toilet again. This was a bad idea. The bowl filled with water. None of it went down. The level stopped rising right before we had a flood on our hands.

I said not to worry. Since most of the maids' rooms on my floor didn't have bathrooms, there was a communal one down the hall. I would be fine.

The dinner party was over.

Portia did not say a word about the lipstick. She sat through the whole affair flipping through her father's book on the English Romantics. And she made no reference to my near inundation as she said goodbye. Instead, she told me she was impressed with my meal. All prepared on a single electric burner! I was an inspiration. My chocolate mousse was better than at La Truite Dorée, honestly. No wonder I had cured her daddy with it. Where had I learned to cook?

I didn't technically know how to cook, I said. But when the French cousins I lived with when I was younger realized how much I liked chocolate, they taught me this recipe. It was very simple, all about beating egg whites. You needed dark chocolate and a little coffee, a shot of alcohol. I could show her if she wanted.

Yes, she would like that because she'd spent her whole life thinking that La Truite had the world's best mousse, and here I was proving her wrong. "Really, it was *extraordinaire, n'est-ce pas, Étienne?*"

"Always keep an open mind, Portia," said Christie.

forty-five

The next day, I went down to work as usual, telling Lydia my toilet was broken, but that fixing it wasn't urgent. She did not seem to hear me and proceeded to rattle off a list of errands for tonight's big opening in St-Germain.

I took Orlando on my rounds, stopping only for a sandwich. I was back at the apartment a little after two.

I knocked on Lydia's door.

Rather than calling me in, she opened it herself and stood blocking my way.

"Where the hell have you been? How long can it take a person to perform three simple tasks in the outside world? Jesus! I've been looking everywhere for you. I even climbed all your stairs. I have to talk to you very seriously, right now. I must say, I'm shocked, positively shocked, at how dishonest you've been. I really believed you could change after everything I've put up with from you. But this is unconscionable."

Here it was. The bomb was dropping. She must have found out about Olivier. As with the Claudia fiasco, I couldn't believe I wasn't already dead. I hadn't been able to envision this moment, and now that I was in it, I still couldn't. I had no idea what shape things were taking. My heart was pounding and I was very, very hot. Maybe I *was* dying. I was certainly melting. I couldn't talk. Like an idiot, I stared at her.

"The plumber told me. I had to hear it from the plumber, for Christ's sake!"

I opened my mouth. It seemed I still had a voice. "Hear what from the plumber?" What plumber could know about Olivier?

"When you told me this morning that your toilet was broken, you never mentioned anything about a lipstick. Did you think it was going to disappear? We could have had a major flood, thousands and thousands worth of damage. This is not the sort of thing you hide. This is not a white lie. I'm furious, and I don't think it's at all fair or reasonable for me to have to pay a plumber for something you damaged and then tried to cover up. The bill is for three hundred francs. Add it to your rent next time. And then there will be no need for us to discuss this anymore. Let's put it behind us."

Remember, says Mom, it's the little things that get you. Planes are generally safe. You die in the taxi on the way to or from the airport.

"Wait a second, Lydia, you must have figured out by now that I can't afford—"

"This is not a question of money. It's a question of ethics."

"It was an accident."

"Why did you lie about it?"

"I'm sorry. I thought it would disappear. Most toilets could handle a lipstick."

"Don't start playing the princess now. You've got the only maid's room with a bathroom on your whole floor. We put that in at our own expense."

"Thank you."

"Listen, you're not getting out of this. It's a good lesson for you."

At least Portia hadn't ratted me out. I was grateful to her for this until she took me aside to say she knew her mother was angry and it was too bad I had to pay for the toilet, but it was a very symbolic three hundred francs to her mother. It had nothing to do with the actual money and everything to do with fairness. I had to understand that, no matter what Portia thought, she herself could not get involved. Her mother and I had a working relationship. It would be inappropriate to interfere.

Later, I sat in the garden in lingering evening light, doing letters on an electric typewriter. I had devised a system of extension cords up the back steps into the kitchen. It was one of those evenings where members of the family were keeping to themselves, secretly waiting for someone else to wonder aloud what was happening for dinner.

I was obsessed with one thought. Should I ask Christie for the money? A few months ago, I certainly would have because, even though it was an accident, it was her accident and I was broke. But I was developing a sense, strong if not fully articulated, that when you invited someone as a guest you did not hold them responsible for such things. Call it a code. I knew Mom would say I was being pretentious and unstraightforward, but I could not agree with her here. No, I would not mention the plumber's bill to Christie.

Still, three hundred francs, symbolic as they might be to someone like Lydia, were going to hurt.

What had gotten into Christie? What a clumsy thing to do. But that, as Lydia would say, was neither here nor there. The point was that the gracious action here was to not tell Christie about it, even though she made twice as much money as I did and Étienne had probably already stolen her another lipstick.

Did this mean that rightness and fairness were not exactly the same thing?

I was losing my daylight and had to type faster. Focus, Katie.

Hesitantly, Clarence started down the garden steps toward me. He tripped on my extension cord, almost fell.

"Blast! Katie, you have to do something about your wire here. Get a bright orange one or some such thing. Something we ancients can actually see. You're going to break one of our necks."

No, *you* are going to break your neck on my cord. I will not be the neck-breaker per se. There's a difference, I thought, a subtle shift in responsibility. "Sorry," I said.

He was holding an envelope, something for me to mail perhaps. He glanced around. No one.

"Here, take this," he whispered. "Put it right in your bag. It's the money for the plumber. Lydia's not thinking clearly. It's shameful. You shouldn't have to pay. She entirely misses the significance of making you pay. She's lost sight of what it means. But we all know she has other virtues."

"Are you sure, Clarence? I mean, my friend's lipstick did break the toilet."

"Of course I'm sure."

"Thanks for this." I slipped the envelope into my bag. It seemed to me that he partook of my new code, that just as it would have been tacky of me to ask Christie to pay, it would have been negligent of him not to make sure I didn't either. It all made sense. My newfound ethics were confirmed. "Really, thank you. It helps a lot."

"Please, never mention it."

I thought he would leave me to my typing, but he stood there looking at me, eyes beginning to water.

"Can I—do you need something, Clarence?"

"It's not for me," he spoke under his breath. "She's—I'm worried about her."

"About Lydia?"

He shook his head.

"About Portia?"

"God, no."

"Oh, then, it's—"

"Yes."

"You want me to go and see her?"

"Your friendship means the world to her," he mumbled. "Day after tomorrow, at ten A.M. She's still in the same place. She'll be waiting."

253

forty-six

Lydia's opening went off with barely a hitch, the only off-note being Joshua's drinking too much of the Taittinger, vomiting on the sidewalk outside the doorway, and categorically refusing to attend the celebratory dinner of *intimes* at the Truite Dorée.

Lydia was delighted. Sally and I had both been assigned to eavesdrop on the various invited journalists for her, and we were able to report nothing but praise. Even Clarence said that, despite the "unfortunate" Rushdie element, the show was a triumph.

The following morning, I left Lydia, Portia and Clarence at the breakfast table, half-joking about the hangover Joshua was sleeping off and his insistence that he wasn't going back to high school because it was bullshit and he had passed the equivalency test and no one could make him.

I set out with Orlando for the Île St-Louis, promising myself I would carry no missives, play no further active role. I wanted to see how Claudia was doing. And I had to tell her that Clarence had sent me, that he was staying with his wife because that was what one did, but that he was not a heartless bastard. Mostly, though, I was going because I missed her.

In the streets, I had the impression that someone was shadowing me, a guilty phantom wafting through the budding trees and silk scarves that brightened the city. It was a windy day, alive, rustling.

To make matters stranger, Orlando kept sniffing the air and

craning his neck backward as if he were catching something disturbingly familiar, the rush of odor released by the thaws of late March. Newborn rats and turning soil and the pee of a million nervous poodles. Spring fever.

The only way to get him to move forward was to bribe him with bits of the croissants I had bought for Claudia. By the time I reached her building, there were none left.

I had to knock several times before she opened, peering drowsy and confused through a crack in the door. "Ah, it is you!" She draped me in an exhausted embrace. "Are you all right? Can you survive in that house?"

"Sure, I'm okay. What about you?"

She didn't answer.

When she let go of me, I saw that she was wearing a lime green nightshirt that barely covered her underpants. Her hair was a mess and her eyes were stony and sunken.

"Wait," she said. "I will fold the bed so we can sit."

Without bothering to straighten her tangled sheets, she forced them into the mattress, then pushed the mattress into the sofa frame and closed it hard.

As she leaned over to shove, the backs of her thighs thick and curved, I saw pubic hair.

We sat, bits of bedding overflowing between our legs, as on a messy sandwich.

"Tell me," she said. "Tell me what is going on. How are the children? How is the lost boy?"

"Pretty lost." I chuckled, immediately cringing at my own meanness. After all, Joshua was the only member of the Schell family who had ever spontaneously thanked me for anything. Granted, it was a plate of Thanksgiving dinner, but he had been sweet about it, and here I was sounding cynical for the sake of hollow amusement. I tried to backpedal. "I mean, it's not easy for a boy like him in that family. I'm sure he has all kinds of stuff going on that we know nothing about."

"Of course he does. He wouldn't be human if he didn't have

secrets," she said, shaking out her hair and blinking her eyes into something like alertness.

"I'm afraid I can't tell you anyone's secrets," I said, hastening to add, "because I don't know them."

"When did Clarence ask you to come find me?"

"Yesterday. I've tried to call a couple of times, but it's been crazy at the house with Lydia's show. I assumed you were gone."

"I wanted to leave Paris. But I could not stay away. And, no matter what he tells you, he does not wish me to go."

"Oh, Claudia, please don't take it that way. He didn't ask me to come because he hopes to be with you. He's worried about you, but he can't be with you anymore."

"So that is why he fucks me?"

"What?"

"Oh, he can be with me! Believe me."

I had been trapped. For a second I thought to ask her if she wasn't imagining being fucked by Clarence, but I knew she wasn't that crazy. Clarence had had me completely fooled. I wondered if Lydia knew.

"Claudia, I can't help you anymore. I mean, I can't be a messenger anymore. I'm not a spy."

"I do not need *you* to spy! I can see Clarence on my own. But we are friends, no, you and I?"

"Of course we are."

I managed to avoid being alone with Clarence for two days before he cornered me in the garden again.

It was a strange time, what with the letdown after the opening. Joshua insisted with mounting vehemence that he was not returning to boarding school but staying in Paris to be "a thorn in all of your sides, and because it's pretty here." Lydia stopped arguing with him, which Portia interpreted as passive acceptance and yet another piece of evidence that her brother was a spoiled brat and it was "totally unfair, but I've learned to expect that over the years." She spent most of her time in her room, writing in a lime green leather-bound notebook which she locked with a tiny bronze key, and changing clothes.

Clarence clucked and shook his head a lot. He and Lydia had a couple of private conversations, from which he emerged trembling and mumbling, as though he had been told in no uncertain terms to deal with the situation of his son and were testing out various threats under his breath.

When he caught me, I was typing again at the the wrought iron table. My first thought was that he would make some mock-curmudgeon comment about the threat to his bones posed by my extension chord snaking down the steps. But when I looked at his face, there was no trace of professorly twinkle, only a dour and secretive purpose.

He did not beat around the bush. "Katie," he whispered, "I have to ask you one more favor. And I promise it will be the last."

"I don't mind seeing her. I've told her I can't ever carry messages again though."

"This is the final one." He laughed in mild self-deprecation. "The message to end all messages. This is the one to tell her I can never see her again, that she has to go, that the situation is untenable."

"But didn't you already tell her that? And then you got back in touch?"

"She got back in touch."

"She told me you have been *with* her again."

"I had no choice."

My grin must have betrayed a certain irony because although my answer was a simple, "I see," he proceeded to accuse me of a sarcasm that was unlike me. He said he was disappointed.

I said I thought Claudia would be fine if he were honest with her.

He agreed, which was why he was giving me one last letter to carry to her, telling her in no uncertain terms that he could not see her again and that if she would not leave Paris then he would. He and Lydia were talking about returning to the States in a few months anyway. He would simply precede her if he had to. But he suggested Claudia go to Berkeley or to Morocco, somewhere she could stop hiding.

"Clarence, I'm not sure I should do this. I mean, Lydia . . ." I looked for some kind of sign in the budding rose vine on the garden wall, but it was a maze.

"We're doing this *for* Lydia. Carrying this letter is the most important thing you could possibly do for Lydia right now, don't you see? But if you can't do it, you can't do it. I'll drop it in the mail. It's simply that coming from your hands the letter has more meaning. You lend it weight because she trusts you. *And* you soften the blow, Katie."

His face was still thin from his illness. His skin cragged around his eyes and pulled back from his pillowy lips so that he had a sort of tubercular pout which I found both repulsive and irresistible, as though I could cure it.

"Really," he pushed out a smile, "it's rather important, this last letter."

"Okay," I said.

Sadly, I watched him walk away. I had to betray his trust. I could not deliver his letter without first telling Lydia what was going on.

Was I choosing the stronger, healthier parent over the one who really loved me? Was that horrible? No, I told myself. I was learning to sort through experience, to find where loyalty lay, to be straight. From now on, I was determined to do a good job no matter the sacrifices.

Then I was hit with a further layer of compunction. The truly straight thing to do would be to explain myself to Clarence before I told Lydia. I wasn't sure I could manage it, but I should. And Clarence, because he was a grown-up and a father, would ultimately understand my need to blossom into an honest human being. He would allow himself to be sacrificed. It would be bittersweet for him, but he would forgive and admire me in time, because that's what fathers do.

forty-seven

Étienne did not call Lydia "Madame Papaye" anymore. He called her *la salope* because of what had happened with his Berlin Wall pendants.

I had brought her a few of them to look at, but she had balked at the price of two hundred francs apiece. "That much! For something so essentially junky!" She couldn't bring herself to do it. But maybe I should talk to Sally Meeks because Sally had so many connections with stylists. You never knew. The jewelry might work in a photo shoot. Sally was doing something with Japanese *Vogue* these days. This kind of kitsch might appeal to the Japanese. "Actually," Lydia had said, "let me handle Sally."

So, Lydia had passed the "moonbeam" pendants on to Sally, and Sally had returned them to her, unceremoniously, a couple of weeks later. No interest from the magazines. Thanks, but no thanks.

"I wonder," Lydia smirked, "if she didn't secretly get a commission for them in Asia and pass them off as her own find. She probably told *Vogue* she picked them up on the streets of Berlin, where she has never set foot, by the way. I wouldn't put it past her for a second."

Étienne now suspected that his designs were splashed all over Tokyo, touted as "found," as the stuff of street vendors and delinquents. "No, I *found* the story of the Wall and I *made* this. This is what I will leave behind of my life."

259

He had been so dramatically angry at first that I had written him a letter of apology, which he had thanked me for.

"I don't blame you for the sins of your *salope* of a boss, like I don't blame Americans for their president, but it's nice that you wrote to me all the same. I will remember that. Just don't forget to bring me back the *bijoux* because there are people who do want to pay for them."

A week after Sally's rejection, Lydia still hadn't given me back the pendants. She said she wanted to think about buying one for herself. And maybe one for Portia. Anything to amuse Portia these days. If only they weren't so overpriced, she hinted.

I asked Christie if she thought Étienne would be offended if I suggested a discount for Lydia. After all, she knew a lot of people, and could give him publicity if she chose.

Christie interrupted me. "That's just it. If she chooses. I don't think Étienne should be relying on her good graces. Now if Lydia were willing to cut a clear deal, that would be one thing. But it doesn't sound like she operates that way."

"No, I'm learning that she's only clear when it suits her."

"So, I assume she hasn't told Portia about her father having an affair yet?"

"I guess she hasn't."

We were on the tiny terrace of a bar on a pedestrian street near the Bastille, having blond beers late in the afternoon. Étienne was supposed to be with us, but he was still asleep after clubbing all night. He was feeling less *résistant* lately, not so young.

I still had Clarence's "final" letter to Claudia, and was getting up the nerve to tell Lydia about it and avoiding the question of how to let Clarence know about my decision.

"Christie, I want you to know that I'm going to come clean in all this."

"All what?"

"Clarence gave me another letter for Claudia. A letter telling her he can't see her again and that one of them has to leave Paris, and I told him I would give it to her, but I'm going to tell Lydia about it, because she's my boss and my loyalty should be to her, and I know I have to start being honest and I'm working on it. Do you think that's right?"

"I can't believe I ever envied you your fancy job."

"I'm going to stop the double-dealing. I am."

She looked skeptical but tried to sound supportive as she said, "More power to you."

"I can't keep lying."

"Then why didn't you tell Clarence you couldn't deliver his letter when he asked you?"

"You're right, I should have said no, but I couldn't resist at the time, and I thought, at least this means it will really all be over soon. Besides, Clarence will understand. As soon as the skies clear, he'll see I've done the right thing."

"Are you ever going to tell Portia about Olivier?"

"That's different. It's private."

She took a pert sip of her beer. "Do we know he never got back together with her?"

"Yes." I drank. "Although I do wish he'd stop feeling sorry for her, but I can't control everything. I'll go nuts if I try. He's promised to try to cut off all contact with her. He says I've made him see that it's better that way. The Schells are tough though. He's doing his best."

"You've fallen hard, haven't you? Cutting him all that slack. I thought you were going to let Bastien into your heart. After that night at Les Bains. But no dice, right?"

"I know it sounds weird after so little time together, but I feel close to Olivier. I can't help it. I have this running dialog with him in my mind that's comforting. Everywhere I go, I feel him picturing me. He's the only person who gets the life I'm living now."

"Wait a second. What about Bastien? What is he, chopped liver? You know he told me the other day he thinks you take him a little for granted. And what about Étienne and me? We're there for you, right? We'll make you feel grounded any time you ask."

"I love you guys."

"Étienne is such a doll, by the way. He's so brave. Smell this."
She flexed her wrist under my nose. "It's Guerlain. He stole it for me
at Bon Marché the other day. He's getting more and more brazen."

"I know, he is." I smiled. "He called yesterday to say he's spotted
this gorgeous Annick Goutal display for me and he's promised to get
me a huge bottle. He asked me what my favorite perfume was and
all I could think of was Eau de Charlotte."

"That's Portia's perfume."

"How do you know?"

"I saw it in her room that time you stayed there. Isn't that a
little psycho on your part to be coveting the same perfume?"

"No. Portia has about twenty bottles of perfume and my own fa-
vorite happens to be one of them. That's not so strange. It's not like
I'm wearing white foundation and bright red lipstick or anything.
It's a random preference. *Anyone* could like Eau de Charlotte.
That's not weird. No, you want to know what's really weird?"

"Sure. Tell me."

"You know that letter I wrote to Étienne to say I was sorry about
the snafu with Lydia and his jewelry? He told me it meant so much
to him. He brought it up again the other day. So, I teased him that
he should frame it and he told me in all seriousness that he had
thrown it away. He said he needed to keep everything that was
truly important to him inside his emotional memory and that he
was throwing away all the important reminders in his life. He gets
so dramatic. My feelings were hurt that he tossed my letter. Because of course he's going to forget it someday long after this Zen
master persona is gone."

"You don't get it, do you? You don't understand your own cousin
when he tries to tell you something. You know you can be so naïve
sometimes, hard-knock life and all, Katie. Bastien's right, you've
been very sheltered."

I was annoyed. Who was she to be calling me an innocent? If
it weren't for me and my family, she would be out on the street.
I wanted to say this to her, but I bit my tongue and took a long,
greedy, un-French swig of beer. I looked down at my ring. The sides

of the concrete chip were beginning to wear away. There was a scratch in the paint. Maybe Lydia was right. Maybe the ring was an expensive piece of junk. I allowed this thought for about a second before I began to cry.

Christie softened, but not all the way. "Just get him his pendants back."

Brave with drink, I went home and wrote Clarence a note:

> *Dear Clarence,*
>   *After a lot of thinking I've decided that while I want to deliver your letter to Claudia, I can't do it unless I tell Lydia first. I'm hoping everyone will understand. You all mean so much to me.*
>
> *Affectionately,*
Katie

Tearfully, I slipped it under the door of his locked office. I tried to squelch the fear that I was killing something between us, to remember what Étienne had taught me about my *Death of the Virgin*. You have to fully take a picture in, pain and all. Blind reflection isn't seeing.

That evening, I was in Lydia's office slipping Étienne's jewelry back into its velvet pouches, when Lydia came in, high from a couple of Kirs.

"So your cousin wouldn't give me a press discount?" She laughed.

"He shouldn't devalue his art."

She laughed harder. "Well then, I'm glad you're getting that stuff out of here. We have to declare war on clutter in this office. I can't take it anymore."

My heart began to pound. I had to tell her about the letter, now or never.

I looked straight into her large round watery eyes and took my first real step toward what I hoped was a grown-up moral compass. The moment felt epic.

"Lydia, I have to tell you something."

"My goodness, has someone died?" She was in a disconcertingly unserious mood.

"No, it's not that bad. But I've really been thinking about what you said when you decided I could stay after, you know, the whole thing when I messed up with the amulet—"

"Yes, yes, what is it?" Her tone stayed decidedly light.

"I, my priorities, I'm trying to be honest, and I don't know, I mean this is going to come out wrong, but there's another, I mean, Claudia, Clarence's old Claudia, she's in Paris again and she's been in touch and he needs to tell her that it's over, and he needs me to take another letter and I just can't do it without . . . I want to come clean . . . You, my loyalty has to be to—"

Her expression remained unaltered. "Oh, that, of course. You really are still rather naïve, Katherine. I basically wrote that letter for the poor man. He relapsed once or twice. Guilt. Par for the course. But he came to his senses such as they are. We drafted the letter together. I suppose he didn't mention that. I knew he'd give it to you. He likes to think he can still keep a secret or two. Makes him feel manly. So utterly like him. Of course you should deliver the letter. Do us all a favor."

"But—"

"Good of you to ask, dear. But really you should be onto us by now. Kir?"

forty-eight

The following morning, Portia left to return to school. As she thanked me again for my dinner party, she told me she hoped I would help cook for her twenty-first-birthday dinner in June, when she would be back. If Olivier kept refusing to even speak to her, she would be in a horrible state, and it would be good to see me, she said, averting her eyes from her parents, who stood with us beside her taxi, shaking their heads.

Her final words to them were, "If Joshua becomes a full-blown monster here in Paris, you'll have only yourselves to blame. There is such thing as parental authority, you know."

"At least we can keep something of an eye on him here," mumbled Clarence as we crossed the courtyard back to the apartment.

"We can, can we?" Lydia snapped. "Do you have any idea where he is now?"

"Sleeping off last night's pot?" Clarence attempted a playful sigh.

"His room is empty," said Lydia.

"Well, it *is* noon," said Clarence. "Perhaps he's gone to a museum."

Crestfallen from my conversation with Lydia, I put Orlando on his leash and carried Clarence and Lydia's joint letter to the Île St-Louis. Again, I had the sense that I was being watched.

Get over yourself, Katie. Nobody cares enough to follow you anywhere.

I was loath to see Claudia in her final disappointment. So, I knelt to slip the note under her door. Then I caught hold of myself, stood up and prepared to knock. Wasn't I here to comfort her? Before I could touch the door, though, she swung it open. In her solitude, she must be attuned to every passing shadow. She grabbed the envelope from me, and, motionless, read its contents before she even asked me in so that I stood blocked in the doorway by her rigid little body. I waited, noticing and renoticing the few details the room had to offer, the unmade sofa bed, the sludgy coffee cup on the tiny table, the silky mass of her clothes through the open door of an armoire of compressed wood chips, the moldy view from her window. My eyes made the rounds of these sad little facts while she read and reread the words on the the pearly page. Typed words with a signature at the bottom. All the while, Orlando sat patiently at my feet.

When she finally looked up, I don't think she saw us. Her eyes were roasting in their own private fury. Nothing else mattered.

"This is not what he truly wants. He did not write this alone."

"Even if he didn't write it alone, Claudia, he put his name to it. He signed it, so I think we have to believe him."

She backed into her room with an exaggerated slowness, her anger swelling into an eerie calm.

"I will rise from the ashes of this."

"That's great, Claudia. That's all he wants for you."

"Fuck him. I will leave Paris when I am ready. I will live my own life. He will never hear from me again. Not directly. Perhaps he will hear of me." She flashed a devilish grin. "But I will leave Paris when it is time for me to leave Paris. You can tell him that if he is interested. And tell him his bourgeois marriage has nothing left to fear from me. His fucking fortress. Let him rot in it. He is dead to me."

She didn't ask me whether or not I would come and see her again. But neither did she say goodbye as though I wouldn't. When she offered me a coffee and I said I had to be getting back, she did not insist.

Orlando and I were barely outside Claudia's door when he bounded up the street, so quick and delighted that his leash slithered and flew from my hand. He was headed for the sunlight at the corner of the dark street where a familiar figure stood against a wall, licking an ice-cream cone. That figure was Joshua.

"Hey."

"Joshua! What are you doing here?"

"I came to get some ice cream, dude." He ran his tongue over a scoop of what looked like rum raisin.

At a total loss, I said the first thing that popped into my head.

"You know ice cream isn't vegan."

"Oh yeah, you're right." He turned his cone upside down and dropped it into the street, where Orlando inhaled it.

"I'm sorry, Joshua, that was a bitchy thing to say. You've always been so sweet to me. I guess I'm having a bad morning. But I'm still sorry."

"So, tell me, what's she like?"

"What's who like?"

"My dad's lover. His mistress. Whatever you people call her. What's she like? Is she hot?"

"That's all over, Joshua."

"Okay, let's say I believe you. You can still tell me if she's hot."

"I, I, it's really not my business. Please. Can you ask your dad if there's something you want to know? I'm just the messenger, okay?"

"Don't kill the messenger?"

"Something like that."

I was scared he was going to ask me which apartment Claudia lived in, but instead he asked, perfectly friendly, if Orlando and I were heading home, and when I said we were, if he could walk with us.

He offered to take the leash, and together we loped through the streets of Paris, discussing the fact that he wasn't exactly a

Republican but that he was sick of his parents hypocritical knee-jerk liberal bullshit and there had to be something else out there worth fighting for.

Once we had exhausted the subject of his personal politics, he asked me how I had learned to speak French.

I told him about my cousins and about my dad's prolonged death forcing me to stay with them here in Paris longer than anyone thought I would. I talked about Étienne and our school and how proud his parents seemed to be of me when I took to the language and the culture, how it gave me a feeling of belonging that I've pretty much hung on to ever since. "French has kept me connected to my dad even though it was the thing that once kept us apart."

So what were my cousins doing now, he asked, as we started up rue St-André des Arts, the narrow *crêperie*-lined street that would take us from St-Michel to St-Germain?

Well, Étienne was in Paris, making jewelry. I showed him my ring.

Cool. And Étienne's parents?

They were retired in a town called Orléans.

What was Orléans like?

I had no idea. But I would go to see them soon.

"Whoa! Weren't they like your adoptive parents? Why would you want to blow them off like that? Haven't you been here for like months and months already?"

"Eight months." I shriveled. "I'm not blowing them off. It's just that working for your mom and this whole situation, it's pretty consuming."

"You mean it's glitzy."

"I *am* going to see my cousins."

My voice must have cracked because he softened his tone. "Listen, if you're worried my mom won't let you get away, I'll talk to her. I'll tell her they're your adoptive parents, for Christ's sake, not her and Dad, but these real people out in wherever they are. She'll let you go if I ask her. She's so freaked out that I'll do something insane, in case you haven't noticed, that I have some leverage. If you want, I'll do it for you. Just say the word."

"Thanks, Joshua. You're really kind. I've got to learn to stand up for myself though."

"Yeah, tell me about it." He gave me a pale, searching look, then broke into a grin and said these crêpes smelled too fucking good and he didn't care if they had eggs and milk in them he was going to get one and he'd buy one for me too if I wanted.

I asked for chestnut.

"Thank you," I said as he handed me the crêpe, folded into a triangle in a wax-paper sleeve. "You know, Joshua, this may sound like a cliché, but you're not nearly as harsh as you seem to want to come off. Are you really angry or are you acting rebellious for the fun of it? Because you're obviously a sweetheart."

"Don't call me that," he spoke through a mouthful of Nutella.

"Sorry." I laughed.

"I'm not angry for no reason, you know. Do you have any idea what it's like growing up in a house full of phonies? You'd be pissed too."

"Maybe, but I wouldn't want everyone to think I was an ass-hole."

"Well, you have a nicer personality than I do, don't you?"

I thought for a second. "Granted, but it doesn't mean I'm really any nicer, just a friendlier package, which some could call phony. In fact, people have."

"Nah," he said, "you're okay."

"Thanks, Josh. This crêpe is awesome by the way."

"Don't mention it."

As we approached the doorway to our courtyard, I seized my last moment with him to ask how he had found out about Claudia.

"Not so hard to miss," he said. "There's information floating around our family like poison gas. Unless you're a total idiot like my sister, all you have to do is sniff."

"You won't do anything crazy, will you Joshua? The Claudia thing is over. You won't try to see her?"

"Don't worry about me. I'm a big boy." He laughed. "I'm full of surprises, but I'm not stupid."

forty-nine

That evening, from the apartment, I called Solange and Jacques. I pictured her, aproned, running to the phone with a wooden spoon in her hand, a light spray of béchamel in her wake. Or perhaps it would be Jacques, who was fingering one of the precious Pléiade editions that he kept locked with a tasseled key in a glass cabinet. I envisioned their smiles when they heard it was me. They would stand together by the phone and ask again when I was coming to visit.

No one picked up. And, as Étienne had warned me, there was no answering machine either.

"If they wish to speak with us truly, then they will call back later, no?"

The spring progressed. Lydia took a trip to photograph the Jewish cemetery desecrations in a town called Carpentras in the South of France. While she was gone, the patio furniture was finally cleaned and painted white, and Clarence and I started to do all our work outside.

The climbing rosebush was beginning to flower after much fretting that this might be a barren year.

On a particularly bright afternoon, clipping my newspapers at the table, I looked over at the beautiful roses, at Clarence writing nearby, Joshua asleep on a blanket in the grass.

A companionable cynicism was growing between father and son, smirks and asides about the French, quips about Lydia, eye rolls, the occasional passing of a joint. I could tell that this rapprochement was making Clarence unspeakably happy. And I found a comfort in it reminiscent of last fall, the innocent time of Claudia's couscous and the Moroccan house painters.

Joshua rolled over, stretched, went into the house, and came out again with a baguette, which he brought to the table. He and Clarence began to pick it apart like two seagulls, talking with their mouths full about how relieved they were that Olivier was sticking to his guns about cutting off all contact with Portia. She would of course be a basket case when she arrived, and her twenty-first birthday would be about as much fun as a wake, but at least that creep was out of the picture.

Pretending to be completely absorbed in my work at the other end of the table, I clipped furiously, an article in *Le Monde* about skinheads in Marseilles. I was supposed to keep Lydia abreast of far-right activity in the south.

"Olivier's a cretin," said Clarence.

"He's an asshole," said Josh.

"One and the same."

"Stop eating all the bread!"

"You stop!"

"You!"

"You know what Olivier is"—Clarence laughed through his mouthful—"he's a striver, a vulgar little striver."

"Nice vocab, Dad."

My scissor work was eerily straight. The tips of my fingers unfurled into perfect leafy points, alive, precise. Like me, I thought, Olivier is becoming true. He's doing what he promised he would do. He's making Portia let go.

But my satisfaction was clouded with bewilderment at Clarence and Joshua's hatred. It seemed to go deeper than simple jealousy of Portia's affections or a desire to protect her. Did they truly think Olivier was a bad guy, or were they simply put off by his hunger? Did they find his ambition threatening? Couldn't they see, from their private garden in the Sixième, that, at some point in time, someone had to fight to get them there? Did they not recognize the dignity in that fight? We couldn't all be aristocrats all the time.

Fifty

As the days passed, the air softened.

Portia arrived. She was skinnier than ever and monosyllabic.

On her birthday, Umberto Eco sent twenty-one bouquets of white tea roses. He wished he could be here, but he was stuck in Bologna. Portia's disappointment that the flowers had not—and would never again—come from Olivier was only heightened by everyone's fascination with their famous giver.

To my chagrined surprise, Olivier also sent a present. Granted it was only a simple card and a book, but he was supposed to be keeping silent.

"Cheap bastard," said Clarence. He had wandered into the kitchen where Lydia, Madame Fidelio and I were cooking for the birthday dinner.

"Clarence, please. She'll hear you," said Lydia. "Besides, it was thoughtful of him to send a small gift. Why on Earth would you want him leading her on with expensive presents? That would be criminal. I think a book is appropriate, very well judged. Olivier knows what people need. He's attuned. But I wonder if that's something *you* can understand."

I nicked my finger on a mussel shell and swore under my breath.

Olivier's gift was a paperback edition of *Swann's Way*. Portia had been saying lately that she felt Proust was a big hole in her knowledge. She was now in the living room, reading avidly.

"We already have Proust in the house, and he can't not know

274

that," Clarence went on. "He's certainly spent enough time squatting here to remember we have the complete Proust. I've been telling Portia she should read it for years."

"So, be happy. Be grateful. She's reading it as we speak. You may not hear from her until she's done. Taste this."

Lydia was making a crème anglaise to have with berries because Portia did not want a birthday cake. ("Cake is boring. It has always struck me as a waste of calories.") She force-fed him a spoonful.

I had volunteered to make a couscous and was scrubbing the mussels for it, because, as Lydia said, they simply wouldn't do it for you in Europe like they would in the States. Assumptions were different here.

So, I was at the sink, Madame Fidelio was slicing strawberries and Lydia was watching Clarence swallow her custard.

"That's delicious," he said. "You're all working so hard. I hope you can get her to eat."

"She better eat. The saffron for Katherine's couscous is worth its weight in gold. By the way, Katherine, we're all so impressed that you know how to make couscous, especially Portia. Where did you learn such a thing?"

Clarence cleared his throat.

"From my mom," I said.

Lydia did not miss a beat.

"How nice for you." Her voice was syrup. "I'd love to teach Portia to cook, but she has no interest. Still she's touched, you know, that you're doing this for her. Don't you think, Clarence?"

"Of course she's touched." Clarence took another, nervous, bite of crème anglaise. "But do you see what I mean about him giving her Proust when we already have it? He wants to bloody own Proust. It's insidious. It's undermining."

"Clarence, let it go. And stop eating all of Portia's birthday dessert. What kind of father are you?"

Madame Fidelio asked if Madame Lydia was happy with the strawberries. Madame Lydia said beautiful, but maybe a little smaller.

275

I asked if "debeard" was a word.

Clarence was sure it took a hyphen.

Lydia disagreed. She asked him to find a lemon. Now.

Then Portia burst through the kitchen door, Olivier's book and one of her twenty-one white bouquets pressed to her chest. She was crying.

"I have to get some air. I have to take a walk. I am suffocating."

"Why don't you take Katherine with you? Madame Fidelio and I can manage the rest of the mussels. And you've prepped everything else, haven't you, Katherine? The chicken and the vegetables? Portia, you're in for quite a feast."

"Mother, a feast is my vision of hell right now." She looked so uncomprehendingly at all our preparations that I felt there was something obscene about them.

"Well, you won't see things that way after a nice walk," said Lydia. "Go, go. Why don't you girls take Orlando to the Luxembourg?"

"No, Mother. Kate, I know you'll understand that I need to be alone. It's this book. It's heartbreaking. He's waiting and waiting for the kiss that will never come." She threw her flowers down on the floor and was gone.

"Portia's missing the point," Clarence huffed. "Young Marcel is waiting for his mother to kiss him, not his ex-boyfriend."

"Clarence," Lydia pushed him aside to open the refrigerator, "you are alarmingly literal-minded." She put her crème anglaise on the top shelf and closed the door. "There. I've done my bit."

I picked up Portia's flowers. I said I thought it might be pretty to float the bouquets in big bowls around the house.

Everyone agreed. We all dropped what we were doing and started hunting for bowls because the roses were starting to suffer.

Lydia could not find the silver punch bowl, the Edwardian one. Those Moroccan painters last fall must have stolen it.

"What a ridiculous accusation," said Clarence. "Talk about racist!"

Everything smelled like saffron. Dinnertime was only an hour away. Still no Portia.

The phone rang and I picked it up.

"*Allo?*"

"Yes, hello, is Portia there please?" It was Olivier. What the hell was he doing calling this house? At the sound of mine, his voice shook.

"No, I'm sorry," I said, cold to mask my hurt. "She's out." Then I decided to punish him. "Wait, is this Joshua? Joshua, are you messing with us?"

Clarence looked up from his *New Yorker*. "Joshua's gone out on his sister's birthday? Will wonders never cease?"

"No," bleated Olivier. "It's not Joshua. It's Portia's friend Olivier. I called to wish her a happy birthday."

Clarence was gesturing for the phone.

"It's not Joshua," I whispered, "it's Olivier."

He frowned and flopped his head back into the magazine.

"Well, I can give her the message." It was all I could do to keep my voice from cracking. "We expect her back any minute."

Lydia stuck her head through the living room door. "Is that Olivier?" she asked.

I nodded.

"Tell him to hold on a moment. I'll take it in my study. Tell him not to hang up."

"Can you wait a moment, please? Lydia would like to speak to you. " I hoped the effort to steady myself wasn't apparent.

"Christ almighty," said Clarence. "What next?" He grunted off the sofa and said he was going to shower and dress.

As soon as he left, I took his spot, staring up from the cushions at the clock mired in its elaborate bronze tree, its snake, its servile nymph. It was a few minutes past five.

At quarter past, I was still gazing stupidly at the time when the phone rang again. I jumped to answer, but Lydia beat me to it.

"Katherine," she called out a moment later. "It's a French boy for you. Take it in the kitchen."

I sighed. It served me right that I should have to talk to Bastien right now, to put on a show within a show.

The portraits over the kitchen table were steamy. The air was fragrant with the fabulous meal to come, but I felt no anticipation, only an overwhelming sense of having to keep up appearances while reeling from broken trust. Tricked by Olivier's shading, by the shortcuts and the symbols he used instead of giving a full picture, I had been left in the dark. In my mind's eye, I crumpled the sketch he had done of "me" in the Place des Vosges. My hand balled into a fist.

I took the phone from Lydia.

"*Ça va, Chopin?*" I tried to make light.

"*C'est qui, Chopin?*"

It wasn't Bastien's voice, but neither was it totally unfamiliar. Perhaps another member of the *bande,* but none that I could place.

I apologized and asked who was calling.

"This is Michel, from the Fer à Cheval bar. I have a message from your boyfriend. He says he can't go another hour without hearing your voice. He's begging you to call. He's in the office."

fifty-one

I thought I would have to wait until after the couscous and berries with crème anglaise to excuse myself and race to my St-Sulpice phone booth to hear what Olivier had to say for himself. The irony of the fact that I was now as shaky as Portia was not lost on me, but awareness is not always a steadying force. I didn't know if I could keep myself from crying through the meal. Luckily, Lydia liberated me much sooner than expected.

Moments after I had hung up the phone, as I was staring at Yoko Ono through the cooking condensation, Lydia came rushing to me. She had a crucial errand. How could she have almost forgotten? Where was her mind? It was Portia's being so upset, throwing everything off balance. She couldn't take it anymore. But that was neither here nor there. Could I please go to this address immediately? It was in the Sixteenth, on the Square Alboni. No. 8. I should take the Métro to Passy. The package would be all ready for me, with the concierge. It was urgent she have it for tonight. If I hurried, I could probably get home for the beginning of dinner.

This was the same doctor's office where Olivier and I had stopped on our way to the Marmottan to see his mother's Monets back in September. Lydia was sending me out at seven o'clock on a Friday evening for diet pills.

This meant I was free to return Olivier's call, but I wasn't ready to modulate my anger or express my confusion. I was going to have to take a blind leap.

From the vestibule, I heard Madame Fidelio announce that she had found the silver punch bowl. We could put mademoiselle's roses in water now, before they faded.

Was she sure, Lydia wanted to know, that it was really the Edwardian one?

I closed the apartment door behind me and ran through the courtyard, then down the street and into my phone booth.

As if to soothe me, the glass of the *cabine* walls took me in like a home. I felt the city refracting from all sides, the shimmering trees, the metal café tables with their dirty glass ashtrays and half-empty carafes, the dust on passing shoes, the dripping ice-cream cones, the parked cars, the shop windows drowsy with oncoming summer. Paris was flowing unfiltered through my body.

What might I have looked like to my father, poured into this *cabine*, unable to sort out the meaning of this day even as it swirled inside me? Would he still be proud of his brave accentless little girl?

If only I knew what he would have wanted, I thought I could unravel into a real person. Yet so far all I had to go on were memories, ideas, family myths, visions of the life we might have had together with him directing movies and Mom not having to be so serious and the three of us taking family vacations to Paris to visit Jacques and Solange and Étienne. I couldn't hear his real voice, only the strains that ran through my head, as much my creation as his. He was the Old Master I was trying to copy. But copying, I thought, looking through the glass to the doors of the church, is not the reflex I have always assumed. It is a choice.

It was time for me to take a stand, to shape my own life. But how? I was not giving up on this city. That much I knew. I had had enough disappointment. No, I was going to start setting my boundaries with Lydia and Clarence. And with Olivier. Slowly, slowly, I would become forthright and clear of head. And begin untangling my experience.

I dialed the operator.

"Morgan!"

Olivier accepted my collect call.

Breathlessly, before I could ask any questions he began to apologize. He knew it looked bad, but he couldn't be rude to a family that had housed him. Portia hadn't been remotely led on by his present, had she?

Grateful to have something concrete to respond to, I answered that Portia had been upset by his book. I wasn't going to go into the details, but it contributed in large part to the ruin of her birthday. "I thought you had cut off all communication. What were you doing talking to Lydia?"

"I'm almost free of them, but it's common decency to acknowledge someone's birthday when you've lived with their family. At least while it's so fresh. I agree with you that by next year she will have forgotten all about me."

"What about Lydia? Is Lydia forgetting you?"

"Don't tell me you're jealous of a middle-aged lady who's addicted to papaya pills and spring rolls?"

"Olivier, this isn't funny. I don't think—I don't know if I should see you again."

"Don't you want to?"

"Of course I do, but—"

"Do you think you can ask Lydia for the third week in August off?"

"Why?"

"Well, I've done something a little presumptuous."

Feeling my resolve shake, I tried to be forceful. "Look, Olivier. This isn't working. You promised you wouldn't talk to her and you're calling the whole family and sending birthday gifts."

"Don't you want to know what I've planned?"

"Planned?"

"I knew I'd get you curious. I know you like I made you." He told me I should get that week of vacation time because he had booked us a hotel in Versailles where he thought I would like to return because of the memory I had so vividly described to

281

him of my day there with my cousins so long ago. He could tell Versailles was an important place to me. Was he right? Would I like to redeem it? He laughed gently. Would I give him one more chance?

Through the glass, I nodded a slow yes at the passing city.

Fifty-two

Christie's internship at the law firm was over at the end of July. Throughout our time together, this moment had seemed so distant that we had hardly mentioned it to ourselves, and now it was only two weeks until Christie was bound for law school. We were suddenly inhabiting the horizon.

There were two *soirées d'adieu* in the works, one with Étienne and some of his clubbing friends from Queen, one with Bastien and *la bande*.

"If this were America," said Christie, "we would mix them all up and figure the various people could get along, but it would be easier for the different French social classes to mingle with someone from mainland China than to mingle with each other. And the funny thing is that the disdain is mutual. It's beyond politics of left and right. It's virulent on both sides. Ah, the French! How are you going to figure them out, Katie, without me around to explain them to you?"

I did not know.

Bastien and I met on the leafy *terrace* of a bar he liked on the Avenue Foch, outside the entrance to the Bois de Boulogne, to talk about Christie's party. Afterward, he wanted to take me to the Jardin d'Acclimatation, the children's amusement park in the *bois*, where he used to go all the time as a child.

"The French," Christie had told me, "make no distinction between nostalgia and romance. Remember that when I'm gone."

I told Bastien I felt like a glass of red wine, maybe a Côtes du Rhône, slightly chilled. He said that a woman drinking red wine without food in the afternoon was categorically depressing. People might think I was an alcoholic. *Á la limite,* white wine was much better. Champagne or a light beer or a citron pressé, a coffee (but no milk in the heat of the day), these were all fine. Now, what did I want?

Water, I wanted water. No bubbles.

Plain water was too sad.

Okay, then, white wine. Any white wine he thought I should have.

I was annoyed at his particularity until I tasted the Montrachet.

Bastien had very specific ideas about Christie's farewell. We should have drinks *chez lui* then go out to Neuilly, where there was an outdoor restaurant overlooking the Seine. Then Castel. Then Les Bains. Then coffee and croissants back at his place.

I said this pretty much followed the arc of every night we had ever spent together. "Maybe Christie would like something a bit more *original* for her last night out? Maybe we could go find some jazz in one of the clubs near Les Halles?"

"Les Halles? With all the backpackers?"

"Christie loves live music. Have you even asked her what she wants? It's her party, you know."

"Katie, I do not like this attitude. You used to be so much softer. You are changing, Katie. Be careful."

But I did not want to be careful. I needed to change.

When he asked if I was ready to go to the *bois,* I said the Montrachet had made me so sleepy and relaxed that I hoped he wouldn't mind if we did it another time.

"But, Katie, we had a plan. I want to show you the Jardin d'Acclimatation. It will be charming after the wine." He weighted the word "charming" with all the tragedy of his parents' divorce. I melted and agreed.

I had been to this amusement park already, twice. With Cousine

Solange, we had come once for Étienne's birthday and once for mine. We had both turned ten here. We were each allowed to invite two friends, no more, because the Jardin d'Acclimatation was very expensive and only for special occasions.

Recalling Solange's descriptions of rare and extravagant pleasures as Bastien fished for two 10-franc coins for our admission to the park, I started to view the *bois* as one giant, barely attainable artichoke. I must be drunker than I realized.

Inside, I asked Bastien for cotton candy, called barbe à papa. I ate it on a small wooden train that did a circuit through the trees outside the jardin, ending up at a fairy-tale station back at the center of things.

This train ride used to be epic. While Solange knitted on a bench, Étienne and I rode through the forest, pretending we might never come back.

Now the ride was dull, constrained and short.

I had eaten my cotton candy and was still hungry. Right by the train station, there was a guimauve cart, looped all around with thick strands of fancifully colored marshmallow taffy. I would like a yellow one please. Because I could. Because I no longer had to hold to a seven-franc candy budget.

"*Petite gourmande!*" Bastien seemed delighted at my childlike embrace of the sweets. His enthusiasm sent a wave of affection through me, even though the guimauve had grown a lot sweeter over the years and I could barely stand it.

"Thank you for my nostalgic treat," I smiled, "but I'm not sure I can finish it."

"Then throw it away. All the pleasure is in the first few bites anyway."

Bastien wanted to go on the bumper cars. He remembered his mother watching him drive with such *adorable angoisse maternelle* in her eyes every time someone ran into him that he had a *certaine tendresse* for the experience. So, we got in line for ride coupons. My childhood fear of limited tickets kicked in. Solange had doled them out so carefully. How many would he buy?

When he bought more than we could possibly use so that we wouldn't have to wait in line again, my gratitude was disproportionate.

He said that, when we left, we would give the leftovers to a child, make his day. "In fact, Katie, why don't you pick the lucky child? That would make me very happy."

I moved to throw the yellow guimauve away, hesitated by the *poubelle*, took one last bite and let go.

Was this rich French boy defiling my childhood?

No, I thought. As I evolved, whole parts of me were dissolving. This felt strange and it was sad. It was probably also normal. In any case, I couldn't blame Bastien.

After the amusement park, we wandered the sandy paths through the woods. He held my hand too tightly for comfort. When he pressed me against a tree and moved up inside my t-shirt, I asked him gently to stop.

"But why?"

"I love being your friend, Bastien. I'm with someone else, though. I can't keep kissing you."

"But," he did not take his hands away, "you are not the only girl I kiss. You can kiss other boys. Kissing is like eating. There is variety. And I want you, Katie."

He pushed into me.

I ducked away, scraping my back against the bark.

"I am perplexed." He frowned.

I almost told him I couldn't have everything on the menu anymore, but I simply said that he was lovely and I treasured him but that I had made a choice.

He shrugged, took my hand again, and led me out of the woods.

fifty-three

In late July, right before Christie was to go, Joshua abruptly left Paris. He said he had something important to do at *home*, a word he invested with a quavering, weirdly patriotic fervor.

Lydia and Clarence did not seem worried. They had been dealing with his antics for years now. Besides, they had gotten him to promise, in a manner of speaking, that he would return to school in the fall to do the second semester of his senior year. After all, he *was* eighteen. As long as his education moved forward at some kind of pace, they were appeased.

"Sure, I'll go back to school. If I'm around."

While this answer seemed to satisfy his busy parents, it gave me the creeps. Joshua and I hadn't spent much time alone together since our walk back from the Île St-Louis, but he would occasionally accompany Orlando and me to the park, always offering to take the leash, for which I was inordinately thankful. The day before he took off, I asked him if he would come along to the Luxembourg.

"How lovely to be invited somewhere," he said in a stage whisper so that his father, having tea and toast at the kitchen table, could hear.

"Don't be facetious, young man," laughed Clarence, with a grateful wink at me.

Once we were outside, I asked him what it was he was planning to do back in the States and why it was so sudden and urgent.

287

"Hey, it's nice that you're worried and all, but I know what I'm about."

"I realize that, Josh. No offense, but you're at a weird time in your life. I am too. That's how I can tell. In my art, the only thing I've ever been comfortable with is pitch-perfect imitation, and now I'm trying to find a style, and I keep screwing up."

"What are you trying to say?" He jerked Orlando's head out of a flower bed. The dog looked surprised and hurt.

"Okay, I don't want to invade your space, but can I ask you to write me or call me if you think you might do something self-destructive? I know your parents think your nihilism is just a pose, but sometimes posing can get real. Don't look at me like that! I'm not calling you a poser. Okay, I'm putting my foot in my mouth. I'm just hoping you'll get in touch if you start to think about harming yourself because it's not worth it. Not to prove a point."

"So why do you put up with all this shit in our house? Is that worth it?"

"I'm betting it is. I'm like some endurance athlete, a long-distance runner. I'm suffering for a cause. I'm learning."

We both smiled sadly.

"I'm not asking you to take me as a role model," I continued. "I know I suck as a role model."

"I didn't say that."

"How about this? If I'm thinking of doing anything I think might be dangerous, I'll get in touch with you, and vice versa?"

"Deal."

Only days after Josh had gone, it was time to say goodbye to Christie.

But, on the date of Étienne's going-away for her at Queen, Lydia had a crisis. She realized she left behind several rolls of film in a hotel room in Marseille, where she had gone to shoot a rally for the far-right party of Le Pen, and she said I had to be the one to go get them. These pictures were crucial at the moment because Le Pen was deceiving the French into thinking that immigrants were a plague, and deception and racism were shaping into the themes of the nineties. Hence the vandalism in the Jewish cemeteries. Lydia sensed that it was all interconnected.

"You can take the overnight train, Katherine. Make sure you sleep on your backpack—those night trains are crawling with thieves."

"Mother," said Portia, who was on a rare visit to the office, "the least you could do is buy the girl a first-class ticket so she won't have to be with all those gross people."

"When Katherine is my age, she can ride first-class, but Katherine's not soft, are you, dear? A first-class ticket would be an offense to your youth and vigor."

Portia looked confused. "But, Mother, I'm young and *I* always travel—"

"Enough! The train leaves at nine tonight."

"But, Lydia," I stammered in protest, "my close friend is leaving Paris in a couple of days and tonight my cousin is throwing her going-away party. Couldn't I go tomorrow morning?"

"Katherine, this is the wrong time to assert whatever you are trying to assert lately. My film has to be at the printer's day after tomorrow. This is a critical moment in the history of French ideas. This is at the heart of your responsibilities. It's not as though I'm asking you to go to the grocery store or take Orlando for a stroll."

I had been about to say that taking the train to Marseille for forgotten film felt more like an errand than an important mission, but I held my tongue. Lydia had finally given me an admission that there was a scale of importance in the tasks she assigned. This was information to store and use. And it was true, the cemetery vandalism was scary and potentially telling in its threat. I should assume my roll as guardian of her Le Pen photos. Besides, there would be another going away party for Christie in a couple of days, the one Bastien and the *bande* were planning.

So, I took the overnight train and I slept on my backpack. I rode a taxi to the hotel, where the film was in an envelope at the front desk, and then took the same cab right back to the train station. In Paris, I delivered the film straight to the printer's.

Then I went home and got up the nerve to show Lydia a sketch-book of fledgling portraits of my friends, bits of Paris and copies from the Louvre. After looking for a long time, turning pages back and forth, she said that she was impressed with my effort, but that my framing was weak. I hadn't given it enough thought. And, without framing, you had no sense of time. You weren't autho-rial enough. For instance, look at this one of the child touching the Rodin (she recognized the Balzac sculpture from the garden instantly). The kid and the statue were right in the center of the picture, with a pretty border all around. Everything looked good, but there was no sense of anything coming in or out of frame, no evidence of the passing moment. No time stamp. Nothing.

"But, Lydia," I said, "what if I want the image to be sort of time-less? I'm not going to be a journalist. I'm going to be an artist."

"You can only achieve that if you're willing to commit to a cer-tain moment in time. Otherwise it's bullshit." She peered again into my Rodin drawing, then flipped to a profile of Étienne. "I need to qualify what I'm saying for you. You don't need to choose your frames or define your moments, you need to admit that you are doing so. What you have here is a hell of a talent contorted into a surreptitious naiveté. Be bolder."

"Thank you," I said.

I was there for Christie's very last night in Paris, her blowout with *la bande*.

Since her flight was at ten the following morning, there was no point in her sleeping, was there? And we should all accompany her through the night. These boys were nothing if not loyal in their festivities.

When Portia asked what I was doing, I didn't think to lie. She was so depressed that it never occurred to me she would invite her-self along. But she said a mindless night out with people she didn't really know might be just the thing to distract her.

"I'll check with Christie," I said, dreading the call. "I have to see what the plans are."

Sensing the discomfort in my phone voice, Christie sighed and said fine, bring her along. Nothing was going to ruin her good time.

But when Portia and I showed up at Bastien's apartment for drinks to kick off the evening, Christie pawned her off on Christian, pulled me into the leather couch and grilled me.

"Is it because you feel guilty or because you want to get close to her? I don't know which is sicker." She folded her knees into her chest.

"You know I still have to be nice to Portia."

"There's a difference between being nice and pretending to be her friend. You're *still* acting like the boundary is not there."

"There are no boundaries in that house, no real ones anyway, none that get any respect. I've been trying to set them here and there. No luck yet."

"Oh yes there are. And you're on your way to the wrong side of one. I'm telling you, the Schells could still all turn on you."

"But they seem to have completely forgiven me for the whole Claudia debacle."

"The Claudia debacle might not be over yet."

"But she's gone for real now. And I wish she weren't sometimes. She was totally in the throes of her Clarence obsession, and it could make her a bad friend. But mostly, she saw straight to my heart. I think she cared about me. And Clarence and Lydia still care about me. You know, people do the best they can. So they can't always control their passions."

"Katie, I love you. Étienne loves you. Lydia and Clarence and Portia and Joshua do not love you. You are their *domestique*. They have a lot of affection for you, and that's it. Face it. And you don't really love them either."

Although I began to sense that Christie was right about the quality of the Schells' attachment to me, I wasn't quite ready to admit that that was all there was. "Okay, I don't really love Portia.

But I do feel for her. I mean, she's sad. It's tough being Lydia's daughter. Perks aside, jokes aside, it's tough. But look at her over there flirting with Christian. For once, she's having a good time. Why shouldn't she have a good time? Why shouldn't she realize that she's perfectly capable of fun? After all, she's been nice to me."

"What are you talking about? She makes you nervous and she talks your ear off and she drives you nuts with her clothes. And you hate it when she calls herself a 'daddy's girl'—remember you said it was like a slap in the face? And she won't ride the Métro. Remember all those taxis she's made you split? And, for Christ's sake, she's obsessed with your boyfriend, or you're obsessed with her boyfriend. It's still unclear."

"No, it's very clear to me that Olivier is with me now." I looked across the room at Portia, holding an untouched glass of champagne, still porcelain pale in August, in a brand-new short black dress. In another week, she would leave Paris again. For a late-summer internship in New York. Would I miss her at all as the relief sunk in? Or would she fade gracefully back into the role of the fragile daughter? Would she finally disappear?

"Anyway," I said, "she's leaving."

Once Portia was gone, I would go to Versailles. Clarence was on the verge of finishing his book. Lydia was plunging headlong into a new era of reportage. Time was speeding up.

Christie looked bleak for a moment. Then she took herself in hand, deciding to enjoy her last night in Paris, and went to find a boy to fill her glass.

I looked around the living room. I had developed a perverse affection for the beige and the leather, the wall-to-wall carpeting and for the bad blue orchid painting. The first time I had been here, I had floated above it all in indignant sympathy with Olivier, who had to work so hard and could not afford to be in Paris taking this lifestyle for granted, who had nothing but his *chevalière* to symbolize his loss. His image had been so strong in me that there had seemed no point in bothering to create other memories with other boys. And yet I had.

I could not completely recognize the person I had been when Christie first dragged me into this living room. Shades of her were missing now. Or maybe I had had too much champagne, vintage champagne no less, customary in this particular corner of my life. I felt the growing pressure of experience, but no ability to stop time and think.

I headed for the bathroom. Just as I was about to step out into the corridor, I heard Portia's voice, soft and conspiratorial. "I'm sure Kate had never tasted champagne millésimé in her life before meeting your group." I peered through the doorway just long enough to see she was still talking to Christian. "She's a fast learner, but she's definitely not one of us."

Loudly, I cleared my throat and headed straight past them.

At dinner under an awning in Neuilly, Bastien, Christian, Jean-Pierre and a couple of the others stood up and asked for silence.

"Oh God, they're going to sing," Christie whispered in my ear.

Sure enough, they had changed the lyrics to a French pop song to memorialize their friend Christie's time in Paris. The gist of their version was that Christie had almost become one of them, but she still danced *le rock* like a cowgirl. The new refrain was, *"Et Christie danse le rock! Quel choc!"* as they spun each other in and out, then drew imaginary pistols from their impeccable leather belts.

"This is what they all do at weddings. They call it a 'sketch.' It always involves changing the words of a song that they all know, and it's usually terrible."

I looked over at Portia, who was picking at her appetizer, faintly appalled. Why the hell had I brought her?

"You realize," Christie said during the applause, "that there were two counts and at least one duke in that group. Not bad for a Yankee upstart like me."

293

• • •

Portia was trying to go home before we headed to Castel. Knowing she had shown her true colors back in Bastien's hallway, she could not look me in the eye, and I could tell she wanted nothing more than to get away from me. The boys were trying to talk her into staying.

"What's going on here?" asked Bastien.

"Portia says she's too tired to dance," Christian said.

"Christian"—Bastien was drunk—"take this girl and put her on the back of your motorcycle!"

As Christian led Portia away by the hand, Bastien informed me that my *copine* Portia wasn't very *marrante,* but that she was *assez classe.*

By morning, we were rid of her.

"What does she know about champagne anyway? I'm glad you finally have concrete proof that she's a bitch. Must be a relief," Christie said. "You should call Étienne. He was so disappointed when you didn't show up at *his* goodbye party for me."

I ripped my chocolate croissant and gave her half. She almost smiled. We were finally alone, outside the Bastille apartment, sitting on her suitcases, waiting for her taxi to the airport. Étienne had gone to spend a few days with his parents in Orléans. He had said he didn't want to be here at the moment Christie left. It would be too hard to watch her disappear.

"Are you excited about Stanford?" I asked. "You seem like part of you is already there, or already gone from here anyway."

"You're such a nut. I'm going to miss you." She looked up. Last night while we were dancing, thunderstorms had washed the sky. She shook her head and kept looking into the pale blue, but she did not find what she was after because she finally turned back to me and said, "Katie, I'm at a loss."

"No you're not. It's only the transition. You feel like you're making this break, but you're still going to be you and we'll all be friends and Étienne will steal you all kinds of great things and I'll mail them to you. Life will go on."

I could tell she was going to tell me something terrible, and all I wanted was to stave it off.

"Do you remember when Étienne destroyed the letter you wrote him?"

"Destroyed? I thought he threw it away. What do you mean, destroyed?"

"He burned it. He burned a lot of things."

"See, he has a cruel streak. I keep trying to tell you. Ever since we were kids. He used to torture me those years I spent here. He and his friends used to tease me in the playground, on the street, everywhere. I mean I know he's grown up into a fine upstanding person, but that nasty little boy still peeks out sometimes. I'm not surprised he's torching people's letters."

"Katie, Étienne has AIDS."

"What?"

"He's HIV-positive. And he's starting to get sick. That's why he's so tired all the time."

"That's impossible."

"I'm sorry."

Frantically, I scanned the street for some sign that this wasn't the real world, that I was going to wake up and life would fall back into place. But the street held no answers.

I grabbed Christie's shoulders.

"Breathe," she said. "You're not breathing."

"It's not fair. It can't be true."

She touched my ring.

"Why didn't you tell me before?" I moaned. "Why didn't I guess?"

"I thought he would tell you himself when he was ready. It felt like it wasn't my information. But I think now that he's waiting for me to tell you. I hope he is. I hope I'm not wrong."

We cried in each other's arms until the taxi took Christie away.

fifty-four

It was eight-thirty in the morning. Raw with sleeplessness, I stood outside Clarence's study with two notes that I had forgotten to deliver the day before, one from him to Lydia, one from her to him.

Étienne was going to die, and here I was nudging a missive under a doorway with my big toe.

Next I went to Lydia's office, still locked at this early hour, with the letter from Clarence, the first he had dictated in a while. I hoped she would not realize it had been delivered late. I had been in such a rush to get to Christie's going-away night that I had let things slide.

There was a big space between Lydia's door and the floor. Clarence's message sailed through.

Lydia's was in a fat blue envelope from one of the beautiful handmade paper stores in the Fifth Arrondissement that she patronized. It was a list of things that needed to be fixed in the apartment and garden.

Clarence's was in a thin white business envelope. It was a stream of discussion points that I had taken down on a legal pad. "These are in no particular order," he had assured me, "1: Replace Joshua's therapist; 2: Throw book party for Harry Mathews in New York or Paris this fall; 3: Insurance for the wine in the cave here; 4: . . ." These talking points persuaded me that he was not envisioning leaving Lydia anytime soon, that the story with Claudia was truly over. Folding the paper and slipping it into the thin envelope, I had had the impression of finally sealing her doom.

It was the thin envelope that I had just pushed under Lydia's door, wasn't it? I lay on the floor and peered, but the letter had glided far into the room and I couldn't be sure.

Mom had a particular affection for a silly Danny Kaye picture about the Middle Ages called *The Court Jester*. We watched it whenever it ran on TV. There was a scene where our hero, the knight (Mr. Kaye), was trying to remember which vessel had the poison in it so as to hand the right one to his enemy and not die himself. "The chalice with the palace has the pellet that is poison, the flagon with the dragon has the brew that is true." I think that's right. But could I be absolutely sure? Who was that philosopher, long ago, freshman year, who talked about radical doubt?

This was ridiculous. I would never have confused those envelopes, and the fact that I entertained the idea that I might, and that such a slip could be my downfall, was some kind of sign. And not only that I was living in a farce. Mom would say it was a proof that I wasn't taking care of myself. "You're overtired," she would say, "and you've lost perspective. *You* shouldn't be worried about swapping messages in a house full of people who can't be bothered to talk to each other."

Even if I had mixed up the damn letters, it was of no great importance. Not Berlin. Not a fatwa or an act of anti-semitic violence. Not the life and death of someone I loved.

Quietly, I went to the kitchen and filled myself a big bowl of yogurt with muesli. I sprinkled on the last of the raspberries in the refrigerator. Then, at the garden table, before the house had woken up, I spooned my breakfast slowly into my mouth.

I had almost finished when Lydia came upon me in her bathrobe. She looked at me eating as though I might be a rat. Under her gaze, I saw that I had been hiding out back with my pilfered food. I had made it, furtively, for myself, and I was eating it alone, wanting nothing more than to stay unseen. This glare of hers was precisely what I had been avoiding. Was I nothing but an animal, afraid of getting caught scavenging? And was Lydia a beast too for being so territorial about the contents of her kitchen? Was Mom right to say that Lydia was exploiting me, because that's what animals do to each other?

My stomach lurched.

Maybe it was time to go and make my own way.

Lydia peered into my dish. "Did you leave enough food for Portia?"

I blushed at the image of the empty raspberry carton in the garbage.

"You know that muesli and yogurt mixture is practically the only thing she can eat." Lydia was whispering. A sudden delicacy on behalf of her daughter had taken hold of her. "She's lost so much weight. She's so very weak. I hope you've left something for her breakfast."

A tear for Étienne ran straight onto one of Portia's precious berries. Then another and another.

Lydia first looked incredulous. Then she took a beat to soften her eyes, cocking her head to reframe the scene, to recast me. "Oh, Jesus, you silly girl," she put her hands on her hips and half-smiled. The tone of the moment was as changed as by a sunburst over the garden.

She walked over and put her hand on my shoulder. It was the first time she had ever touched me, besides the occasional drunken double peck at the end of an evening. There was a tremor to her fingers.

"Not you too," she said gently. "First my New York daughter is sobbing because she's had a big night out in Paris and all it does is make her miss Olivier. And now my Paris daughter is crying into her breakfast, God knows why, probably for this French boy who has been dropping off flowers for you with Madame Fidelio. What is it with you girls of today? When I was young, in the sixties, we didn't take sex this seriously at all. Not remotely. Come on, Katherine, look on the bright side. It's a beautiful morning in Paris."

"Lydia, it has nothing to do with boyfriends. It's my cousin, my cousin Étienne. The one who makes the Berlin Wall jewelry. I found out he's HIV-positive. He's one of my very oldest friends.

And he's my flesh and blood. And it's hard to care about anything else right now."

"That's terrible, dear. I'm sorry. Is he sick yet?"

"He's getting sick. He's with his parents right now. Maybe he's telling them."

"Are you going to Orléans then?"

"Of course."

"I hope so." She looked at me, my tired features, my empty bowl. "Katherine, you do have your own family, you know."

"You're right," I murmured. "I should have gone to see them forever ago. But being here," I gestured around the secret garden, "has been—"

"Go during your vacation."

My time in Versailles with Olivier? I couldn't bear to cancel it. I needed his empathy now more than ever. But I had to see Étienne. And Solange and Jacques.

"Can I take another week? You and Clarence will be in Italy. And Orlando is boarding, right?"

"I can't promise you that. You have your time off set already. I may well need you here to hold down the fort. I don't like to leave the place empty that long, especially with Madame Fidelio away. You should choose what is really important to you. Hanging out with dime-a-dozen boys? Or seeing your cousins whose son has AIDS? You can't always have everything all at once. Think about it."

fifty-five

I had never seen Lydia and Clarence so united as they appeared in the kitchen when I returned from photocopying early fashion magazines at the Bibliothèque Nationale on a sticky afternoon. Side by side at the table, they had rounded shoulders and unsteady hands. Their fury, taut over their despair like the skin of a bubble, gave fresh vibrancy to the room.

"We've had terrible news," Clarence told me. The gray of his skin was two shades deeper. He had not shaved. There was a fungal quality to the sprouting on his chin. He looked ill again.

Lydia nodded, letting him speak for her. As he shook his head, she steadied her fingers on his silver curls.

I put down my stack of photocopies.

Clarence inhaled deeply. "Our son has enlisted in the army. He has the bloody insane notion that he will go to Saudi Arabia to defend American interests in the Middle East. He says he hopes they send him to Kuwait for an invasion. It's a death wish."

"A death wish," echoed Lydia, grimacing at a sip of dissolved papaya mixture. I could tell she hated herself for continuing in this rite when her son's life was at stake. And yet, one must go on.

"How awful," I said, realizing how much I missed Joshua. I could not believe that this wasn't another of his black jokes. He would have let me know if it was real. "I'm sure you can talk him out of it, though. He doesn't mean it."

"But he's done it."

Gone was their debate about how to respond to Saddam Hussein's invasion of Kuwait. Ever since the attack of August 2, Lydia had been calling Clarence a hawk for saying that we should "bomb the daylights" out of Saddam. Did he actually believe all these nonsensical Hitler comparisons? Couldn't he see that this was nothing more than a war to keep the price of oil under control? Did he honestly think that Saddam was suddenly the "world's most dangerous man," "the butcher of Baghdad?" Christ, Clarence sounded like Bush himself, talking about "land grabs" and "naked acts of aggression" when we had been supporting Saddam against Iran for years. No one was arguing that Saddam was good, but to suddenly cast him as our worst enemy? Didn't Clarence see the hypocrisy? Where did all this anti-Arab "nipping in the bud" rhetoric come from? Who was racist now? Who had she married anyway?

Clarence's insistence that an unambiguous show of force was required when a crazy tyrant attacked had vanished.

"It's bad enough," he bleated, "that Joshua might be sent to Saudi Arabia, but there's going to be a war in Kuwait. It's obvious. And that will be terrible."

"He's right," said Lydia, brushing lint from his glasses with something like affection. "Saddam has completely miscalculated the effects of what he's done. He's insane. He doesn't realize that his transgression is immediately felt around the world. Everything affects everything these days. There are no isolated acts."

"Yes," said Clarence. He cleared away her murky glass for her, carried it to the sink. "Joshua has been trying to tell us, in his inarticulate way, that now that the Cold War is over, there's a new world order, with all kinds of power poles. We can't be angry with him. He's taking his own argument to the point of absurdity, poor child."

"But it's not his argument!" Lydia stiffened. "He's had a terrible influence."

"That fucking bitch," said Clarence.

"Bitch?"

They both looked at me like I was an idiot.

"Claudia," said Clarence. "Serpent. Killer. I've always sensed.

She told our own son that it was the right thing to follow his instinct to betray us, that enlisting would be good for him. Can you imagine? She told him it would be a truer way to see the world than anything our son could experience with us. The whole thing was transparent and despicable."

"Can you believe this woman ever pretended to wish Clarence well?" Lydia patted his hand. "Can you imagine anything so heartless? Our son told us she is like a sister to him. Bitch."

I shook my head, recalling Joshua's silhouette on the Île St-Louis. The ice-cream cone smashed on the street. He must have gone to see her after following me. How many times?

With all the blood sport drained from their marriage, Lydia and Clarence's bond was revealed. They were terrified of losing Joshua.

How could Claudia have done this? I had felt sorry for her, helped her. What the hell? My image of her was utterly confused. Where I was concerned, she had been calm and insightful, about my family, my art, my feelings. How could someone this sensitive do something so patently bitter and blind? I felt myself knocking hard against the limitations of our friendship, a bird banging into the glass of a lovely window.

But worse than my own disappointment was the dawning fear that Joshua might take this prank to its extreme. What if he really did go to war?

"When is he supposed to leave?" I asked.

"Next week. In theory."

I decided to fax him a short letter.

Dear Josh,

I don't mean to belittle your beliefs even if I don't share them, but I wanted to let you know that I personally don't think you should put yourself in the way of a war in the Persian Gulf. You have a lot to give to the world, smarts and insight. We all make mistakes trying to assert ourselves, especially people like you and me who aren't very practiced at it. You tend to affect cynicism and I tend to contort myself

into dishonest poses in order to please, but we're both groping,
aren't we? And if there's one thing I've learned, it's that when
lately I've been off the mark, my real true friends have been
there to point it out. You've been one of those friends. I hope I
can be one to you at this time.

Love,
Katie

Lydia and Clarence's fear for Joshua and fury at Claudia were
displacing the drama of Portia's departure this evening, but she appeared stoic about it while she packed, except for a tremble in her
lips that was typical of Clarence, the expression of a paternal gene
under duress.

"Can you please help me zip this suitcase?" Portia asked me
softly.

"Do you want me to sit on it?" I supposed she was never going to
acknowledge what I had overheard at Bastien's. But I did not care.
I knew what I knew.

"Listen," she said. "I'm not supposed to tell you this, but you
can stay here as long as you want. My mother and father like you
a lot and they don't want you to have to feel like you're outgrow-
ing the job. Mother is thinking of different ways to give you more
responsibility. She may even teach you to print negatives and
maybe have you start traveling with her. Nobody wants you to go."

"Thanks" was all I could manage.

Even through the fog of her privilege, she was able to sense and
exploit my desire for family.

She looked up toward her moldings. She glanced at a small
yellow and gold shopping bag on her dressing table, then at me,
then at the overstuffed suitcase, then back at me. More trembling
lips. A widening of the eyes.

"I—I have a present for you. I wanted to get you a gift to say
goodbye. I know that our relationship is a little awkward sometimes because you work for my mother, but I want you to know I
consider you a friend."

She handed me a bag with a bottle of Annick Goutal perfume in it. I almost took it, accepting the warmth of the gesture out of context because anything you framed could be beautiful. The foot of a murder victim could be sublime. Ethereal blond bitchy Portia's giving me the Eau de Charlotte perfume I had coveted ever since arriving in Paris, the perfume that Étienne had promised and failed to steal for me, was, in isolation, a beautiful thing. But I did not want it from her.

"You told me you liked it on me, remember? The night you had me over for dinner? I hope you'll use it. I love it, although it's not very strong. Olivier thinks it's too ephemeral, that it only works in intimate settings." As she saddened at the thought of him, her eyes became her mother's.

"I hate to say it, but maybe Daddy was right about Olivier. Maybe he is a horrible opportunist who has finished using us and wants to close the door. Maybe he's an egomaniac. So, why can't I stop loving him?"

"Portia, thanks but I am getting my own perfume. I mean, my cousin Étienne is getting it for me. I'm not in a position to accept this."

"But why?"

"It's not my style."

The doorbell rang. "Darling," Lydia's voice came down the hall, "it's Henri. He's come to say goodbye to you."

As Portia glared at me with uncomprehending suspicion, the two of us went to greet Henri. Lydia's voice floated from the living room. "Poor thing," she was explaining to Henri, "we haven't paid nearly enough attention to her leaving Paris today and going back to New York on her own, to work no less, with this whole Joshua fiasco. She must feel terribly sidelined, but she's being quite mature about it. She's grown up a lot this summer."

"Yes, she has," Clarence agreed.

Portia ran in front of me and put her arms around Henri's neck like a little girl.

"I planned my walkabout today so as to be able to stop by and give you a kiss," Henri said to her.

"You've always been the loveliest of men," said Portia, letting go of him to stand resolutely between her parents. "What do you think about the terrible news?"

"We can have no idea where this decision will lead him," said Henri, lowering himself gently onto the ottoman as we all sat. "He may never go overseas. He's at the very beginning of the process, you know."

"Yes," sighed Clarence, "but this is the kind of process that sweeps you along. The boy is in way over his head."

"I wish I could soothe you." Henri's eyes were clearer than ever. There was an absolute modesty to him. Despite all his experience of life and war and tumult, he had nothing but respect for a family centering on its own crisis. For me, he had a kind smile, but no touch. Our *géométrie* was a distant, half-invented memory. There was nothing now but the grief tightening in this room, nothing but the nuclear family and its age-old friend, Henri.

The doorbell rang again. I went to answer it.

"Hi, Harry." I smiled.

"Hello, you. I've come to say goodbye to Portia."

You too? Come for her? No joking with me today about the umbrella I still haven't managed to buy?

As I led him to the living room, he did not speak to me directly, but began to stage-whisper about Kuwait and Saddam Hussein. "Obviously, we're going in! I'm sure even our friends Clarence and Lydia are stunned at this chain of events. Turns out our worst enemy is one we didn't know we had until this moment! Fascinating. It honestly comes as a complete surprise to some, but perhaps not to all, ahem, that Mr. Hussein is a full-fledged criminal." He winked charmingly into a passing mirror.

I thought about trying to communicate to him how unfortunate his joking around might sound in light of Joshua's enlisting. I considered putting a finger to my lips, but I felt slighted enough by his coming only to see Portia that I let him go on with his loud teasing about the CIA to see how badly it would all turn out. Besides, he was not even looking at me as we walked but toward the gaping living room door through which his audience was, presumably, entertained. He would not have been able to read a sign from me even if I had given one.

"Oh, shut up, Harry!" cried Clarence as we came into the room.

Lydia burst into tears.

Harry sunk into the couch and looked to Portia for help.

"Harry," she trembled, "we can't joke about the war right now because Joshua may be in it."

Before Harry could respond, Henri stood up from his perch on the ottoman. "I was just leaving," he said, shaking hands with Harry and Clarence, embracing the sobbing Lydia. He gave me a quick double peck. Then he turned to Portia, the real object of his visit. "Dear Portia, we'll miss you," he said.

She put her arms around his neck again. "I'll walk you out."

Henri and Portia had not seen each other more than two or three times this summer. All their affection rested on years of intimacy. There was history to their embrace, and I was outside of history.

I was sure these two men with whom I thought I had become friends, Henri Cartier-Bresson and Harry Mathews, wished me well. But I saw now that they did not love me. For a second, I felt as if I had no past. But there is a difference between no common past and no past at all. I *did* come from somewhere, had memories all my own, places to revisit and people who would hug me this warmly were I ever to go to them.

The final person who came to pay her respects to Portia was Sally Meeks, slimmed to waifdom by a diet of bio-lite, the Frenchwoman's secret potion that Christie had spoken of all those months ago at Les Deux Magots. Sally was wearing heavily constructed black linen. She felt bloated after last night's farewell dinner for Portia at La Truite, where she had broken her diet, "shattered it so to speak, and today I can barely move." Artichokes were in season again. There was a lethal new chestnut soufflé on the menu. No one had told me about the meal.

"I'm so glad we had our *grande bouffe* before you got so very upset about Joshua," said Sally. "Otherwise it would have been ruined for you. Such a low, low blow."

Lydia, who had dried her eyes by now, grimaced.

"Portia, darling," Sally continued, "you can't wear those teeny pumps on the plane. You won't be able to get your feet into them by the time you land."

"My daughter doesn't swell," said Lydia, with the first hint of levity I had seen from her today.

Sally laughed too loudly. "I'm glad you haven't completely lost your sense of humor. This Joshua business looks bad, but I'm telling you he'll come around. And the one who'll be sorry is that Claudia woman. She's obviously delusional." She giggled.

"Sally, Sally," sighed Clarence. "What matters here is Joshua. It's not as though he's made some silly gaffe or bad fashion choice. This is bloody serious. Stop taking it so lightly."

"You know, Clarence, I'm not taking it lightly. I'm refusing to believe in Joshua's idiotic pretend decision. That's my position. Because the most intense truths change on a dime, and it's 'in with the new!'" She gestured feverishly up and down her own altered body. "You, of all people, Clarence, should know that it's all fashion in the end."

After Portia had gone to the airport and Lydia had taken a sleeping pill, Clarence came to find me in her office, where I was fiddling with carbon copies of correspondence about sales from the show in April. Every photo had gone to a buyer. The banana diptych was slated to appear in the *New Yorker*, but not unless they paid "us" more. There were several letters from the new editor, who had, as foreshadowed, opened the magazine to photographs. The letters needed filing. I was labeling a new manila folder.

"Excuse me, Katie," said Clarence. "I've been waiting for a

moment to tell you that Lydia mentioned that your cousin has AIDS and I'm terribly sorry."

"Me too."

"Such bad news all around," he said. "Can you believe Claudia was desperate enough to do this to us? To poison my son in order to punish me."

"Clarence, you only know what Joshua told you. It couldn't have been Claudia's idea. He wanted to do something like this all along and it's possible she just talked it through with him, let him figure it out on his own. Claudia may be obsessive, but we can't blame her for everything. Joshua is responsible for his own decisions. He's not a baby. He's awfully smart."

"Come on, you know how persuasive she is!" He pulled at his chin. "It is deeply ironic that *she* has such a massive ego, and that everything ultimately reverts back to her and her concerns, because the ego is the creation of her despised bourgeoisie."

Claudia had once told me that I was very skillful at clothing my own ego but that it was going to peek through more and more. If I didn't allow myself to become an individual, it was going to grow powerful in hiding and start to betray me, she warned. I had to be careful. She wanted me to start being myself.

But I was coming to understand that, even more than she desired my personal fulfillment, she wanted Clarence to learn something by realizing that I was, in fact, a separate being, with my own problems unrelated to his. And so was Joshua. She was using us to teach Clarence a lesson.

Clarence began fidgeting with a pen in his breast pocket. "Katie, I don't know what to do. There's no point in trying to find her, is there? In asking her to try to change his mind?"

"No," I said. "That's up to you and Lydia now."

"You may be right."

"Clarence?"

"Yes?"

"I might be ready to leave, really soon. I think I'm going to try New York. Most of my friends are there. And there's a hard-core classical art academy that I'd like to enroll in once I can get my portfolio together. I need to waitress or something to make money, a job I can walk away from and do my own work. It's time for me to learn to paint." I looked at him for approval, then said, half to myself, "I hope they'll accept me."

"Not yet, Katie. Please not with everything that's going on. She'd never forgive you if you went now. She'd leave you high and dry. You don't want this all to have been a waste of time, do you? Stay a few more months and I'll help you get in anywhere in the States you want to go. I promise."

A couple of days later, he and Lydia left for a vacation with friends in a villa near Siena.

fifty-six

"Étienne, it's me, Katie. Are you okay?"

"What do you mean? It's paradise here. It's the inside of a Balzac novel. It's a forest of symbols and rich sauces and knick-knacks. When are you coming?"

"I'm so sorry, Étienne."

"We can talk when you come. I hate the telephone."

I told him I had a week off soon and a plan to see Olivier, that I would tell Olivier I was meeting him later or leaving him early. Anything. What did Étienne want me to do?

Étienne decided I should see Olivier first. "Finish that story and then come to me."

"What do you mean, finish that story?"

"It's only a figure of speech."

"Yeah, right."

Next, I called Mom and asked her to sell my only valuable possession. On the wall of my room at home was a present from my godfather. He had sent it when I was born. It was a cel from *Bambi*, a simple image of the young deer, probably close to the beginning of the movie, before his mother gets shot by the hunters. He looks carefree and the flowers in the woods around him are kindly and cheerful.

My godfather was a movie producer who used to work for Disney, still did perhaps. I had not seen or heard from him in years.

He was one of the many people who faded from our life once Dad got diagnosed. Dad said you couldn't necessarily blame them. They were all too young at the time to face their own mortality by looking at him. There was no point in being angry. Perhaps, I thought, but there was no point either in nostalgia for the baby presents of a lapsed godfather.

Still, the cartoon image was part of the fabric of my childhood. From across the world, I could see its details, the three puddles of grass, the twinkle in Bambi's right eye, the white spots on his fur, the childish spread of his skinny legs.

Mom and I had always told each other this cel must be worth five hundred dollars.

"Mom, I hope there will never be a time in my life when five hundred dollars will mean this much to me again. I'm going on vacation with Olivier, from New York, the guy I wrote you about, and I don't want to be completely dependent on him." I hadn't realized this was true until I said it.

"Of course you don't. But you're sure about this boy? Is he worth Bambi?" She was at her desk. I could hear her typewriter clanging as she talked to me.

I didn't answer.

She didn't press. "Well, then, I suppose I have to trust you on this one. We certainly don't want you beholden to any boy."

When, two days later, Mom wired me exactly five hundred dollars, I knew that she hadn't sold Bambi for the precise amount we had imagined, that she had supplemented from her own savings for the sake of my independence.

fifty-seven

"Olivier, can we please rent bicycles to ride through the gardens? I've always wanted to do it over."

What about taking a rowboat out on the Grand Canal? That was what his mother dreamed of at Versailles. She loved the idea that the canal was in the shape of the cross.

"*Maman* is very spiritual. But she's never had anyone with her at Versailles who could row the boat. Just me as a little boy. The two of us used to take carriage rides around the canal instead, lame plodding carriage rides. You didn't even get to decide where the carriage went. You just sat there, passive."

Olivier stood behind me, arms wrapped around my chest, chin nestled in my shoulder. We gazed through the central *allée* of the formal gardens behind the château of Versailles, down a stretch of sand, bordered by cypress trees manicured to perfect points, then out a long rectangle of bright grass and on to the canal. The alignment was flawless. From up here, the canal appeared short, even though I knew it was over a kilometer in length. And it was packed with Sunday boaters on a classic summer weekend. Crowded, with no room to move.

To me, the water didn't look freeing at all. I didn't want to row up and down in a toy basin, no matter how long. I wanted to get away from this spectacular geometric part of Versailles, onto the windy gravel paths farther out, the paths I remembered. I wanted

312

to find the little farm in the distance where Marie-Antoinette and her friends got back to nature.

But we still had three more days ahead of us here, hiding out in this pretty Parisian suburb, and I could afford to wait. This rowboat was a crux in Olivier's memory. If anyone should be sympathetic, I should.

"You're sure you're a big enough boy to row now?"

He bit my earlobe, whispering, "You know, I've told my mother about you."

I was supposed to feel bathed in grace by this honor, but I was annoyed. I didn't want to hear any more about his mother. Patience, I told myself. There would be time to forget her once this boating episode was behind us.

We started down the *allée*. I had given myself a hasty pink pedicure in the early morning while Olivier slept. My polish wasn't quite dry, and a coating of fine dust settled into the toenails of my sandaled feet.

"*Maman* says you sound like a lovely girl."

We had reached the border of the lawn by now and had to pick a path on one side or the other in order to continue toward the water. Olivier seemed unable to go forward, so I steered him gently to the left.

Slowly, we moved through this old garden in the lingering summer, each of us feeling daylight from a different time.

I dreamed that we were going to engage with this place, that we were going to explore it instead of only exploring our respective pasts, or each other as we had in London. I hoped that these few days at Versailles, staying in an *hôtel de charme*, wandering the château and its surroundings, would be the beginning of our specific history. And part of me wished that he would come to Orléans with me to meet my family, although I still hadn't told him I was cutting our trip short to see Jacques and Solange and Étienne. I didn't yet know how open I wanted to be.

We strolled silently, arm in arm, toward the rowboats. We heard water spraying. Bronze horses reared from the fountains at our backs. Before us, huge urns of flowers draped the path, reds and purples and dark pinks, each with their own yellow center.

The longer I went without saying anything to Olivier about my dying cousin, the stranger it would be to bring up. So, the fact stayed in a private chamber in my heart, a chamber I both inhabited and ignored. I was in two places at once, not remembering and not forgetting. I wanted to become whole, to mingle Olivier with Étienne, to be the consistent person I was meant to be, but my resolutions kept dissolving.

"Where's my Kate? What are you daydreaming about?"

"Nothing. Come on. Let's get boating."

The water was still and cramped with tourists. Olivier's beauty grew stony as he sunk into thought, pumping the oars with a rhythm that made me wish everyone else would disappear and we could lie down together right here in this boat.

He was gazing at the massive three-tiered blocks of the château in the distance.

"Olivier, what are *you* thinking about?"

"I'm thinking, 'So this is what you can have if you're the Sun King.'"

"Only until the revolution comes, my sweet." I pushed my naked big toe into his inner thigh. His jeans were very soft.

"Kate," he said with a theatrical breath, "when will we say '*l'état c'est nous?*' When will it ever all finally revolve around us?"

"But, it does, in a way. And it also doesn't at all, does it? I mean, don't you think everyone feels like they are at the heart of their own universe? That's how our brains work. Even if we're wrong, that's what we think."

He sighed, gave me an appraising look that trailed off in disappointment. "That's not what I meant."

I felt distinctly imperfect. This was not turning out to be the boat ride of his dreams. We bumped into a family of five.

"*Putain*," said the father. "Watch where you are going. *Merde!*"

Olivier ignored him. "Actually, to get back to what you are

saying about being self-centered, I think I'm more attuned to other people's self-centeredness than my own."

The question "Who the hell is this guy?" surfaced in my consciousness like the gaping, toothy mouth of an ancient fish, only to vanish with Olivier's touch. He dropped the oars and leaned over to take my shoulders.

"Let's stop trying to talk." He sighed.

We docked and hurried back to our room.

There were no bicycles that afternoon.

The next morning, it was pouring rain. We sat in the breakfast room of our hotel. I craned my head back to rub against the chintz padding in the wallpaper. I took the last miniature croissant from an ornate basket. They weren't particularly good, but they were here, and Olivier, recovering again from overwork in the bank, had slept through dinner last night so I was starving.

"More coffee?" he asked. There were flecks of golden sleep in his eyelashes that reminded me of our first meeting in Paris, flooding me with vanished warmth.

"Yes, please. I like this hotel. It has all these quirky little touches of decadence."

It was called La Bergère, the Shepherdess, after poor Marie-Antoinette's fantasy role. The faucets in the bathroom were all sheep's heads. Her toy farm was the prevailing motif of the toile.

Olivier said we should go inside the château today, because of the weather. I agreed and went to get my sketchbook, my bicycle dream receding.

Sharing an umbrella with La Bergère's gold imprint of a frilly shepherdess complete with ribboned staff, we walked across the wet cobblestones of the Cour d'Honneur toward the château's main entrance. The slate roofs and gilded balconies shone sadly in the rain.

At Olivier's suggestion, we headed for the Hall of Mirrors.

La Galerie des Glaces, connects the Salon de la Guerre with the Salon de la Paix, war with peace, and the queen's chamber with the king's. It drips with gold. A hideously impressive display of aristocratic waste, it is at once endlessly dazzling and profoundly silly.

Standing on the outskirts of a guided tour, Olivier and I learned that there were 357 mirrors there and that at the time they were produced only Venetian craftsmen could make mirrors. Since everything in the palace had to be produced in France, the craftsmen were hired away from Venice to a French factory, only to be poisoned by Venetian envoys for their desertion.

We peeked through the crowd at our reflections. He wanted to know if I thought people were looking at us.

I drifted off to one of the gilded statues of women holding crystal candelabras that lined the windows of the hall, and I pulled out my sketchbook. The statue was standing like the figure of Prince in Étienne's poster. I drew her quickly, much too quickly by some standards, with tricks of shading, dark, light, dark, to evoke her contours. It felt good, and not necessarily dishonest. I had a vocabulary now and I let it flow. After I had the body, I began to drape her in flower petals.

"Isn't she Baroque enough already?" Olivier whispered over my shoulder. "Why are you adding that crazy cloak?"

I had forgotten about him while drawing and found his intrusion not altogether welcome.

"It's for a friend who's into kitsch."

"A friend?" He laughed with waning confidence. "Should I be jealous?"

"No. He's my cousin, and he's encouraging me to have style. Or to admit that I can't not have style. I think it's going to be fun." I closed my pad and took his hand. His family ring was heavy. "Let's go see the queen's room."

We stared dumbly at the overflowing bouquets, ribbons and peacock feathers embroidered onto the silken walls, looked up at the flounces and tassels and bunches of golden berries and grapes, at the impossibly tall candles. Like all commoners, we were set off from the royal bed by a gilt railing.

Could I picture myself a queen, he asked?

I shook my head.

Could I imagine, he gestured at a suite of inlaid furniture, the heartbreak of having to walk away from all of this?

I bit my tongue.

At dinner, Olivier told me he thought it was a good thing that Joshua was going into the army. Maybe he'd be less stoned and pimply and whining if he finally climbed into one of the beds he made and dealt with the consequences. "If there's any character in that boy, this may be his only hope of finding it. He called me to ask me what he should do, and I called his bluff."

"You're kidding. You would do that to Josh? Tell him it was cool to risk his life? Just to prove some point. You've got to be joking!"

"No."

I said I was getting the feeling that I was disappointing him, and that I wasn't what he expected, was not as graceful, not as feminine, not quite "it." I sensed he was pulling away. Was I right?

He sighed. "There's something—I can't explain it—there's something missing."

Let him think he was breaking up with me. I didn't care. In fact, I preferred it.

"Do you ever feel," I ventured, "like moments of growing up are sometimes weirdly about remembering who you used to be?"

He ignored me. "I've always had this ideal of perfection," he said. "It's from my mother and from the idea of the life she lost. I don't know what the perfection is, but I know that when I find it, I won't have any doubts. That's what Portia couldn't understand, poor thing."

Could you blame her?

"But you're different, Kate. You're stronger. I'm sorry. You're amazing. It's me who has a problem. I'm sympathetic to all of you, but sympathy isn't love even if it looks like it sometimes." He frowned dramatically. "Let's go. I'm not hungry."

His beauty was suddenly lost on me.

"I'd like to finish my duck if you don't mind," I said.

"Do you still want to ride bikes tomorrow if it's not raining?" he asked, as though gracing me with some kind of favor.

"Sure."

That night, sex in our plush if tiny canopied bed was decadent. Olivier kept sighing. Why couldn't he love me when I felt this good? It was ridiculous. Obscene. Sleep was pointless. We were now officially running out of time.

Nonetheless, he managed to doze late into the morning while I scoured the streets of the town of Versailles for picnic foods.

By the time we rode to the path where I remembered Étienne speeding so cruelly away from me, eyelashes cutting by, shoelaces whipping, my redemption fantasies were all but snuffed. I wasn't going to find any kind of love here. But maybe I was going to escape from the geometry of Versailles into the leafier, more mysterious back roads of memory.

Olivier was demonstratively melancholy. He kept crying and apologizing. I felt weirdly secure in our decision to part.

Sleep deprivation infused the woods beyond the formal gardens with magic.

"That's it! That's the spot! I remember this place so clearly."

We were riding out into a clearing in front of Marie-Antoinette's *hameau*, the play farming village with the exposed beams everywhere, where handmaidens used to wash the chicken shit from the eggs before nestling them in clean hay for the queen and her friends to collect.

I made us a picnic in the spot where Étienne had once splayed himself on the grass, ignoring me so very gloriously. I had forgotten that there was a stone bridge here arching over the lazy stream.

We laid our bicycles down. Once we were not moving, we were immediately cold, hit by an early waft of autumn. Huddling in Olivier's denim jacket, we ate quickly, baguettes with cheese and pears, madeleines.

When we had finished, I said I wanted to do something.

I took an empty Perrier bottle down to the stream and held

it with the opening against the faint current so that it filled with water. The water flowed past my bottle, but the very same water was also trapped inside. Time and events went on regardless of the glass. And yet the glass was stopping time. Constantly.

I thought I was appropriating Proust's crystalline image of young Marcel holding a glass jar in a stream.

In dipping myself briefly into a stream of Parisian lives, had I changed anything? Had I mattered in this monumental world I had hoped to enter into? Perhaps, but Paris would still be standing just fine without me, thank you very much, and its cast of characters would be in a virtually identical mess. I was barely more than an eavesdropper, an observer who would fade as I had appeared. What did I myself contain that year and what flowed inevitably by?

As these questions formed, I grew sure that my time here was ending.

"Kate, what are you doing? Isn't that water kind of dirty?"

It was indeed muddy, not exactly the sparkling stream amid young Marcel's nettles. But I defended it.

"It's no dirtier than the water in your fancy Grand Canal. In fact, it's all the same water. It's all part of the very same irrigation system, I'm sure."

Of course it was all the same water. It's the same water everywhere. And of course this part of Versailles with its windy gravel paths and shadowy plantings is no wilder or less contrived than any other. It is simply portrayed in a different style.

The ghosts out here aren't any more potent or true to life than the ghosts back in the palace staring at themselves in endless mirrors.

Getting back to nature indeed. What a joke. You never got back to anything.

"I'm going to leave here tomorrow. I have some family to see. It's important."

"I'm sorry. I thought I could truly care for you."

Well, think again.

I poured the water from my glass bottle slowly back into the stream under Marie-Antoinette's phony bridge.

fifty-eight

Étienne came to meet me at the train station in Orléans. His leather pants sagging, he was waiting on the *quai*.

He saw the worry in my eyes and preempted me.

"I like being skinny! I've been *au régime* here. It's driving Maman crazy. She makes me eat her choucroute and I puke like a super-model. My Mick Jagger ass is growing more and more pubescent with each passing day. Don't try to pretend you aren't jealous."

As soon as we sat down in the car, I started to cry.

My tears did no good, he said. He said that if I wanted to make him feel better, I should talk about my life. *Ta vie absurde chez la famille papaye.* He needed *distraction*.

But I was sorry for all the times—

Not yet! *Distraction!*

So I told him all about breaking up with Olivier.

"Finally you leave that silly boy! *Mon dieu*, Katie, you can be so slow."

"I'm a slow learner. My mom always said I was a late bloomer, a long-term slow-growth investment."

"What's going on with *la salope* and the mad family?"

I did not answer.

We drove in silence, stopped at a light, then he looked at me through those sharp lashes. "Why do you look so culpable?"

"I keep flipping back and forth between feeling like I haven't done anything wrong and this horrible guilt that I've been bad to

320

this family and wasted my time and my money and my future. Remember when Lydia found out about the letters I was carrying for Clarence and Claudia?"

He nodded, shifted into gear.

"Lydia basically kept saying I wouldn't amount to anything, but then she asked me over and over if I'd made my decision about whether or not to stay. It was so manipulative. And it made *me* feel manipulative too because I kept apologizing. And I'm still doing it, every day. Only halfway through the apologies I want to scream because I don't understand why *I'm saying sorry* to *them*."

"*Arrête!* Confession is only masochism. Can't you see with these letters and her husband's silly affair she knew exactly what was in store for her? All victims of deceit, they know on some level. Portia, she knows too. Believe me!"

"No, she can't know!"

"It won't kill her, or she'd already be dead. Every time I've been cheated on, I realize afterward that I knew. And Portia, I can tell from the smells in her room, from the wardrobe, from every little sign I read that she is like her mother, and her mother, she's such a liar, a professional liar. It's all completely controlled, always. And of course they want you to stay with them, these people. They are begging to be infiltrated. They want you in their devil's pact. And you are not critical enough. All you have to do is look at the bitch's photographs to know what she is."

"You didn't tell me you hated her show that much."

"I didn't want to hurt your feelings at the time, but I did despise that stupid West German biker with the bananas who let her take his picture because he thought he looked generous, and she did it, cynically, to make him look like a fool with no grasp of the situation. That one in particular was arrogant. But they all were, I thought. She was the only one who knew the story. The people in the pictures, they were all clueless and vain-looking."

"That's not true! She found those images. She may be a lot of things, but she's a great photographer. She is such a good artist that the rest of her hardly matters. Her crazy children and her stupid possessions and her papaya diet, all is forgiven because of what she makes. I believe that. She frames her images, with a time stamp, but they are not chosen. Can't you see? You can't not see just because you can't stand her."

"Okay." He shrugged. "So, she is something of an artist."

"Thank you. But I know that doesn't mean that I should take everything she dishes out. If I were to stay, I would do things differently."

He accelerated around a curve into a suburban housing development. The houses were white with red mansard roofs and metal shutters. I wondered which one would prove to be ours.

He drove past a senior recreation center, turned onto a street called the rue Racine. All the while, he spoke about Lydia. "Why are we fighting about some voyeuristic egomaniac?"

"Because life is about people, not hard facts, right? And I've learned a lot from her."

"For example?"

"How to use chance as a tool."

"*Quoi?* If you learned that, it was from living, not from watching her. Stop defending her. Admit that you're angry because it's frustrating and ugly if you don't."

I felt my weight sink into my shoes, my shoes push through the shallow carpet of his tiny car to feel the steel below.

"You're right. The whole reason I got into such a mess is that all I ever want is for people to like me, to give them back beautiful reflections. I sensed it was going to be crazy, from the very beginning, and I wanted too badly to be someone and to be seduced and to have the kind of adventure my dad would be proud of. I wanted experience. I thought experience would teach me who I was and that I would like me once I finally knew me. I had no foresight."

"Foresight?" He laughed. "If there were such a thing as foresight, would I be like this today?"

We pulled into a carport.

Through panes of frosted glass, I recognized the fast-approaching forms of Solange and Jacques. I broke into a run. But before I could reach the front door, they burst out and took me in their arms. They had grown old, but they felt the same.

"*La petite Parisienne, la Rastignac américaine,*" they called me without a hint of irony. I had grown. I looked smart now, too sophisticated to be wearing a ripped t-shirt. Solange said she would sew it for me. Help hide my bony shoulders. Why was everyone trying to be so thin these days? I must be starving.

"Stunning but true, Solange has cooked you lunch," said Jacques.

"We are all stuffed!" Étienne laughed. "*Maman* is stuffing me." He kissed her lightly on the cheek. She flushed. "Everything is '*comme chez Hédiard*' these days, right, my dear parents. You can feed me until they find a cure. *C'est quelque chose.*"

Jacques took Solange's hand and, for a second after we emerged from our embrace, they stood very still in their doorway, staring at me. The young woman they saw knew in this moment that she loved them unconditionally. And they loved her. They were her family. She did not have to perform. The simplicity was stunning.

I looked around. So this was the house they had been building since their youth, salting away the money year after year from their teachers' salaries, first for the land, then the foundation, the construction, the kitchen, the bookshelves for *The Human Comedy,* the marble staircase, the conversion of the attic into a sewing room for Solange. They might be socialists, but their faith in the concrete on their little plot of land in the city of their birth was the most bourgeois, sentimental, beautiful thing I had ever seen.

At lunch, which was delicious, they asked me all about Mom. Her job? Her home? Her prospects for retirement? Simple basic questions that Lydia had never bothered with.

When Solange brought out her chocolate mousse, I told her I had made it for my new boss to great success.

"You see, Maman," said Étienne, "your fame rings deep in the heart of the Sixième."

After lunch, Étienne carried my suitcase up to a small guest room. Solange had made up my bed with the same ruffled pillow

I had slept on as a girl. And she had framed a photo of Étienne and me at Versailles, looking much happier than I remembered. Jacques had left me a copy of *Le Père Goriot*, which he had had me read aloud with him when I was a kid, discussing its finer grammatical and descriptive points in order to teach me "real" French.

"Étienne," I said as he sat down beside me on my bed, "it's good to be here. You and Jacques and Solange are my home. I should have come sooner."

"I know." He sighed. "After all my rebellion, they are the ones who will take care of me and ask no questions. It would be cruel, if it weren't so lovely."

"I'm sorry I wasn't nicer to you after that movie about Jesus dying. I'm sorry I didn't think things through. I hope I haven't been hurting your feelings, but you didn't tell me. Why? I must have seemed very callous. I was calling you a drama queen and you were really sick. I feel like an idiot."

"No, I wanted to believe that you knew and were pretending you didn't to cheer me up. I'm perverse. You know that. It's part of my charm. Stop crying."

He sat down beside me on the flouncy twin bed. I thought he might put his arm on my shoulder, but he simply stayed within touching distance.

"I said, stop crying."

"Étienne, I forgive you for every time you were ever mean to me."

"For the lice?" he asked.

"For the lice."

"For the chocolate éclair?" he asked.

"That too."

"For the time I ignored you at Versailles?"

We had the same memories. How rare.

"Almost. I almost forgive you for Versailles."

"You know it was because I thought your papa had died that day and that they were going to tell you and I wouldn't have any idea how to act?"

"No, I didn't know that."

"I was very uncomfortable with you because you were such a tragic little girl and they were all so worried about you. It's a hard place for a young boy. So, forgiveness?"

"I said, almost."

"Then I suppose my Mick Jagger ass can rest in peace."

"You know, Clarence met Mick Jagger at a party the other night with Lydia. He said Mick was surprisingly smart and well read and 'not at all what you'd think.' Mick talked to Clarence for a long time about fashion."

"Oh, I am so relieved that my idol is *cultivé!* I was deeply worried about his mind for a while there. Please tell Clarence when you next see him that I want to lick him all over."

"You really don't."

Étienne hummed a few bars of "Sympathy for the Devil."

"You haven't heard from Christie either, have you?" he asked.

"No, but I'm sure we'll hear from her as soon as she's settled. You know Christie. She'll have to get the whole lay of the land in her new world. Then I'm sure she'll be in touch. She won't forget us."

"Oh, she won't forget us, but she won't be in touch for about five years. That's what I predict. She needs time away. In five years, she'll glide back into our lives in a fabulous lawyer outfit as though nothing has been and no time has passed and she doesn't owe us any explanation."

fifty-nine

"What's the matter, Katie?" asked Solange. "You're not eating like you usually do. Don't you like my beef?"

"It's August," said Jacques, gently mocking. "Beef bourguignon is perhaps a bit rough in August."

"No, it's not that," I said. "It's delicious. Any time of year. I'm just sad to be leaving here. I'm not ready to go back to Paris yet. I feel like I've only just come home."

"Doesn't matter," said Étienne. "Sadness is never reason enough to waste food. Not when there is china to collect."

I smiled and looked up at the glassed-in shelf where Solange displayed her collection of porcelain pillboxes. There was a pea pod, a violin case, a hat box, a bread basket, a bright blue egg with gold trim, a perfume flask, none measuring more than a couple of inches.

"Katie, you are nervous about something, no?" A pearl onion suspended at her lips, she searched me. "Is it very upsetting, this situation?"

"I don't think I can go back to Lydia."

"What will your mother say?"

"I don't know, but something about being here makes me realize I need to change. It's been fascinating working for her, but I can't be in her house without feeling like a liar all the time."

"They make you lie!" Étienne put down his fork.

"Étienne," said Jacques softly, "this is beautiful meat your mother has bought and prepared. Please try."

Étienne looked into his plate as at an unfordable river.

I forced down a stringy bite.

"I'll finish Étienne's," I tried to laugh. "Just give me some time."

Solange began to tear. "It is difficult for us to understand the rejection you young people feel. When you are upset, you reject things. We spent our life with not enough. The war when we were children. It's unimaginable to leave a plate of beef. But what do we know about today?"

"We're trying," said Jacques.

"You're amazing," I said. "We're sorry—right, Étienne?"

"No, you're flawed actually. If only you'd made veal, I'd be devouring it. It's August, Maman."

She pretended to slap him.

"So, Katie, if you have decided not to go back to the Sixième, then perhaps you can simply call them," said Jacques. "Or do you have work to finish?"

It wasn't until Jacques said it that it became real. In a burst of gratitude, I grabbed his hand. I couldn't work for the Schells anymore.

"I have to do one more thing before I can leave," I said. "I spoke to Lydia yesterday. She wants me home tonight to help get ready for a photo shoot. She and Clarence cut their vacation a few days short because *Libération* is coming to take her picture tomorrow, for a feature article about her work. And she must have gotten into some kind of fight with Clarence again because she said they weren't speaking and she didn't want him there because she doesn't want to look angry in the photos."

"I thought they were all harmonious in their fury about the son," said Étienne.

"So did I. But things change fast."

I tried to picture the *entracte* between the old marriage and the future, during which each player was mostly alone in his or her study. It was hard to know if they were finished or if they were pausing for breath.

"Perhaps she has decided to punish him," said Étienne.

"It all sounds so decadent." Solange sighed. "You are better off without them, Katie."

"They probably throw away food all day long!" Étienne lit up with impish glee. "They hurl it all over the furniture and call the concierge in to clean it up once they've had their fun."

Jacques and Solange both shivered and dug into their beef.

That very night, I found myself in Lydia's office, ready to tell her about Olivier, to say that I had to leave. I would see her through the photo shoot. Then I would go to New York and learn to paint. I was trembling to join the world of talkers instead of staring dumbly up at it from the underside of a puddle.

But she beat me to the punch.

"Katherine, tell me something. Do you have a conscience?"

"Of course I have a conscience."

"Then write to Portia and apologize for what you've done. She knows now about the dalliance with Claudia and how it was managed by you. You cannot imagine how devastated she is. Especially since we've all found out what kind of fiend Claudia is—what she has done to our family. Portia thought you were her close friend."

"But, isn't she upset with Clarence?" Lydia ignored the anger in my voice.

"Of course she is. She won't speak to him now that she has the details. At first, she thought his little indiscretion might be yet another reason to feel sorry for the man. But finally, the girl understands what I've been going through all these years while she's been siding so blindly with him, and I'm getting a few moments of her sympathy. Maybe because she herself knows now what it is to be betrayed? By Olivier, of course. Anyway, she's shattered. Still, she sees why her father tried to keep his sordid life a secret from her, to shelter her. But, you, you had no business lying to any of us. She needs to hear from you that you do care about her and value her friendship, otherwise her faith in friendship itself is destroyed. She needs this now with all this craziness about Joshua and her father. It's no skin off your back to show her you care."

"Lydia, there's nothing I can do for Portia. What could I possibly say?"

"Don't pretend to be so naïve. You know what to say."

"I can't write to Portia, Lydia. I haven't been her friend."

"Oh, don't be so dramatic. You're starting to sound as mopey as she does."

"Lydia, the whole time I've been here I've been seeing Olivier. It's over, but—"

I lost my voice. Her face went out of focus. I tried to steady my gaze on it as I sunk into a chair beside her. I waited for her to grow fangs, to rise, to strike.

But she kept a marble silence.

Then she began to laugh. "You idiot, idiot girl," she said. "You really need some tough love, don't you?"

"What?"

"Listen, I know you could use some kind of recommendation for a job or an art school. I mean, do you know *anyone*? I could give you a handful of names, people I know at magazines and galleries back home, depending on what you want to do, although you have no idea, do you? But Portia will have her letter from you first."

"Did you hear what I just said? Until a few days ago, I was seeing Olivier. I'm not writing Portia a letter. I am not her friend." I was laying myself stark naked, and she didn't seem to notice.

"I'm not asking you to tell Portia about Olivier," she said with an eerie plainness. "I'm asking you to apologize to her for what you did to us, with Claudia. Olivier is neither here nor there. I've known about you two forever. My dear, how do you think I found out about those letters in the first place?"

"Oh my God."

"Olivier tells me everything. He can't help himself."

"He called you after I told him about Clarence and Claudia in London?"

"He called me from Heathrow, before his flight took off, to tell me Clarence was sleeping with Claudia and you were 'stuck' in the middle. He couldn't even wait until he got home. He hates

Clarence more than he ever liked you. The boy is obsessed with his mother and hates his father. He's a pretty transparent case, my dear," she said.

"Did he tell you about Versailles?"

"After you left him there, he came into town and brought me some spring rolls, the naughty thing. How was your family in Orléans?"

"I think I have to go now."

"Just be here for me for the shoot tomorrow, and then you can do whatever the hell you want. But if you care about your future, I have one simple request and you know what it is. Now get out of here. Go sleep on everything."

sixty

I had been in Paris for a year, and it was drizzling again. I had packed up and spent the night in Étienne's apartment and was making my way to the Schells' to perform my final task. The city was awash in familiar names as I walked from the Bastille toward St. Paul, across the Pont Marie to the Île St-Louis, where I would pass up a Berthillon cone, over to the Île de la Cité, around Notre-Dame and across the Seine again to the Left Bank, up the boulevard St-Michel, and through the Luxembourg. All these words were so saturated with meaning for me that I barely needed to pronounce them to know where I was.

As I turned up our particular *rue,* so embroidered now in my mind that the purring cars and the clatter of high heels seemed to originate in my ears, I saw Clarence disappear around the far corner. Banished from Lydia's photo shoot, he was probably going to take refuge with Henri. I figured it was only a matter of time before Lydia told him about my romance with Olivier and he became disgusted with me.

Rain was falling in earnest now. I reached No. 60 and punched in the door code. Madame Fidelio was standing inside. She had been on vacation for the past few weeks, and I had almost forgotten her existence. Her solid frame was reassuring. Over the year, we had grown fond of one another. Her face was a surprising relief, like the first sighting of my mom down an airport corridor after a long semester at school.

"Madame Lydia says you are leaving us. It is a shame. But I understand. *Je comprends.*"

"You do? You understand?"

"*Ce n'est pas facile.*" She motioned across the rain-dark court-yard to the marble stairway she had so cautiously led me up last September. "No, it is not easy in that family. You were *admirable.*"

No I wasn't admirable. I was an idiot for still not having bought my own umbrella despite repeated advice from an ex-pat who knew. I was soaked. "Thank you, Madame Fidelio. You're right, it is not easy, but it is sometimes very interesting and that's what I think I came for. It was an experience."

She laughed. "*Intéressant! En effet, ils font les intéressants! Ah, c'est trop bon, ça!*"

"I have to get inside. The photographers from *Libération* will be here any minute."

"Photographers? Here? *Mon dieu.*" She rolled her eyes to the wet sky.

sixty-one

Lydia told me to wait in the living room while she finished getting dressed and to answer the door for the photographer and his assistant if they came. "Just stay in here." The subtext being keep out of my study and out of my kitchen, you little rodent.

I knew she did not need me here to translate. If anyone could orchestrate a photo shoot, it was Lydia Schell. Did she want to impress upon me one last time the sort of glamour and importance I would be losing out on as soon as I boarded that plane to New York, where, she was right, I knew virtually no one who mattered? Did she want to hit me with one final image of all that I was losing out on?

After a few minutes, she returned.

"How do I look?" she asked me.

"Fabulous."

She had styled herself in a fitted black silk button-down shirt, the same one she had bought Portia in their back-to-school trip to agnès b. Her makeup was more perceptible than usual, particularly on the cheeks. And there was a chalkiness under her eyes where the shadows usually were. Her lipstick was plum.

A touch creepy to the naked eye, this look would surely translate into freshness on camera.

Below her breastbone, she wore a large pendant, jet-black with ornate golden borders that could be Middle Eastern. Or maybe Victorian. She was a compact and alluring force.

The doorbell rang.

"Go," she mouthed.

When I came back with the photographer and his assistant, Lydia explained that, since the rain appeared to have let up, the pictures would be taken in the garden and that, while we were setting up, I could be the stand-in for her husband, Clarence, who would be here any minute. I was almost his height. She had sent him out to buy a new shirt. "He's written a major book about fashion writing. It's fascinating, and I'll make sure it gets into the article because you French will love it. *Vous allez adorer mon mari,*" she said proudly, "but he doesn't own a shirt that works with his skin tone. So, I've sent him to Alain Figaret for the right shade of pink. He will be back momentarily."

Clarence in pink? Clarence in the photograph for *her* big profile in *Libération*? "But, Lydia, excuse me, I thought Clarence wasn't coming today. I thought you said—"

"Well, my dear, I'm afraid you're already out of the loop. And why would you think I wouldn't want my husband by my side in a major piece about my life in Paris?"

"Isn't it about your work?"

"My work is my life. And if my children were here, I'd have *them* in front of the camera too. Does that answer your question?"

We led the photographer down the hallway, through the kitchen and out onto the back steps down to the garden. The bright orange extension cord that I had bought so that Clarence would be able to see it and not trip when I was working in the garden was coiled now on the landing.

The sun had come out. Leaves were beginning to turn. I pictured Clarence, his new pink shirt folded in a fancy bag under his arm, rushing through the streets so that he wouldn't be late.

Lydia checked her watch as she sat down on one of the chairs she had placed in front of the beloved rose bush.

The photographer suggested he get a few shots of her alone while they waited. She got up and looked at his light meter, then returned to her place.

I had thought it might be strange for her to be the object of an image, to find herself on the other side of the camera. But she was teaching me, yet again, that art was about framing, not about where you stood.

While the camera clicked, Lydia sat still, her eyes fixed on a branch chosen for reasons known only to her.

The photographer told me to hold a black umbrella high over her head. He asked, could I move a little to the left, please? I was peeking into the shot. No, that wasn't right at all. The umbrella was drooping.

He sighed and looked sympathetically at Lydia as if to say that his own assistant was an idiot too. With a smile, she returned his sigh. Useless, all of us.

He asked his assistant, a young man with a mottled neck like Joshua's, to hold the umbrella instead. *"Ça ne peut pas être pire."* It couldn't be worse. I should simply stand back and out of the way, he said.

So, I did. I saw Lydia against the vined background of overripe roses. What did she look like?

She was a petite woman, perhaps not as thin as she hoped to be, but elegant and elongated despite the shortness of her limbs. Her rough skin was smoothed now by makeup. She had short brown hair, highlighted an expensive burgundy color. She was graceful, well dressed. Her mouth was pursed, worked into leanness by a constant movement of silent formulations. She was relaxing it now, I could tell, at great effort. Her too-prominent eyes burned with small calculations and otherworldly intelligence. She was petty and she was larger than life.

With my own blind need for sense, I stared at her. But the more I tried to read, the more abstract she became until her eyes were globes and her cheeks were fading roses and her hair was sun. And then there were only shapes and colors and webs of light. Nothing would stay literal.

"Mademoiselle! Mademoiselle! Wake up! *Merde!"* The photographer was yelling at me in disgust. I had never failed so completely to win someone over. I had lost my touch. "We are ready for you

to take the part of the husband now. Please go sit in that other chair."

But, at that moment, Lydia smiled up to the top of the garden stairs where Clarence stood in a pale pink shirt that looked great on him. We did not know how long he had been surveying us.

"Hi, Clarence!" I called out, running toward him. Would he stay my friend? Would he continue to care about me and protect me from irrational swings of fate? After all, he had an overarching mind, right? I had to say something to him, anything. "Clarence," I babbled, "I have this new idea . . ."

He looked crossly down at the steps. His lips shook.

I saw then that it was too late, that the time for us had passed, that he knew everything. But I could not stop. "Clarence, look, I got a new extension cord, an orange one. So no one will break their necks on the stairs. Remember when you said you were going to break your neck on my extension cords? Remember that night?"

Nothing.

"Check it out. It's my legacy. I'm on my way out, but the extension cord is here to stay." My fluency had deserted me. I could not make sense. "Remember what Henri said about legacies at lunch that time? About being in the way of chance and his favorite knife?"

Clarence brushed by me.

"*Voici mon mari, l'écrivain,*" said Lydia to the photographer, getting up to embrace Clarence as he came toward her. "His new book is going to be huge."

As he and Lydia walked toward their garden chairs, Clarence risked one last over-the-shoulder look at me. It was scathing.

When they were finished, Clarence disappeared into the house. I never saw him again.

Lydia dropped a final, punitive hint about Salman Rushdie perhaps coming to hide in Paris, not so very far from here.

"Lydia, no matter what, I'm not writing to Portia."

"I know. Sometimes it's best to leave a spent situation behind you without looking back. If you're going to go to New York, then don't try to remedy anything now. Don't overthink it. We will obviously be fine in this household. But as far as you're concerned, just know that some things can't be salvaged, and you're young enough for a fresh start. Burning bridges is not the end of the world. People will try to tell you it is, but they're wrong. Sometimes, bridge-burning is the best policy."

"But I don't want to forget what has happened here, Lydia. And I also want to make something clear, if you'll permit a domestic to speak her mind. I think I've done a good job. Professionally, did I ever let you down?"

"You insist on this divide between professionalism and personal loyalty that doesn't exist! Fine, I admit you did your job well, if you don't count your various betrayals, but I cannot recommend you to any of my friends, not professionally or at all. I've given you something, though, haven't I?"

"I think so, but I still don't know what it is."

"I've armed you to be ambitious, my dear."

I began to laugh. "My cousins call me Rastignac!"

"Then go forth and be hungry!"

My Métro ride from Paris to the airport was without incident. I had mailed my few boxes ahead and was traveling light.

By the time I boarded the plane, my latest version of Paris was already falling into the lightness and shadow of memory. Parts would be overexposed, parts would be stressed to obsession, parts would remain strange. Someday, I would retrace it through the dozens of letters I had kept.

As I flew west, a layer of myself calcified into something pearlier, milkier than before. I was no longer quite crystalline, no longer accent-free to the point of invisibility. There was something to me now. Perhaps, I thought with an inner wink to Lydia, it was a sharper appetite. Or a deep knowledge of trouble. You might call it experience. Although Mom would say that you couldn't yet take it to the bank.

acknowledgments

This book has many friends.

I would like to thank Lizzie Gottlieb, who first told me to write *Lessons in French*. I will always remember the sparkle of your voice and the sparkle in your eye. And Bob Gottlieb, its first reader and most prescient critic.

Shireen Jilla, nobody read it more times or lavished more light and enthusiasm than you. You cared about every word and you are a part of the book.

Margie Stohl and Rafi Simon, my wine-writing partners in crime, there from the beginning in Otranto, you are my rock and my other brain.

John Wyatt, thanks for the unshakable writerly connection and the faith.

I would like to thank Joanna Hershon for having the courage of her convictions and giving me the best of all possible insights. Your intelligence is generous and radiant, and I owe you everything.

Gretchen Crary, basking in the fierceness of your loyalty is one of the greatest pleasures of being published. Thank you, "smart woman."

I am ever grateful to my Proust group, Ann Brashares, Dave Gilbert and Amor Towles for the adventures in reading and rereading. You are my Sonate de Vinteuil.

My original female bonders, Kelli Block, Sarah Burnes, Nancy Donahoe, Kimbrough Towles, Maggie Towles, Stephanie Vogel and Fiona Watt, you are my memory bank and the light of my life.

Kimbrough, you have been running by my side inspiring me to write forever.

Sarah, you have been my loyal sounding board.

Elizabeth Bogner, Jasie Britton, Hilary Garland, Claudia Grazioso, Julia and Jon Hall, Hannah Nordhaus, Coralie Hunter, Katherine and Joeri Jacobs, Maggie Parker, Caroline and François Reyl, Gary Shapiro, and Amy Zilliax, you are the book's earliest and most constant and creative friends. It loves you back.

Julia, I treasure your cover.

Joeri, you were right about Kate.

Thanks to those of you who have gone out of your way to show support and enthusiasm for the book: Beret Arcaya, Alain and Micheline Barthe, Carl Blumstein, Stephanie Cabot, Elka, Nick, and Susan Cloke, Joan Cohen, Alex Coulter, Kimberly Cowser, Dee Dee DeBartlo, Stephanie Douglass, Monique El Faizy, Charlie and Ellie Garland, Susie Gilbert, John Gill, Latifa Haimani, Lynne Hamilton, Kali Handelman, Sebastian Heath, Astrid Herbette, Mary Herms, Paola Iacucci, Lindita Iasilli, Olivia and Daniele Jungling, Anita Kawatra, Marthe Keller, Ben Lieberman, George Loening, Dale Loy, Stephen McCauley, Paula McLain, Linda Marini, Seema Merchant, Erin O'Conner, Brian O'Neill, Maureen O'Neill, Maureen O'Sullivan, Kirsten O'Reilly, Karen Palmer, Chris Parris-Lamb, Stéphane and Véronique Perichon, Janet Perlman, Johanna Povirk-Znoy, Eldine and Dominique Reyl, Victoria Rowan, Gretchen Rubin, Rachel Scher, Andrea Scarf, Liesl Schillinger, Shannon Thyne, Maria Tucci, Klara Vogel, Jessee and Lena Wolff, and Father Ambrose Wolverton.

Stéphanie Abou, I could not have dreamed up a more brilliant, passionate or dynamic agent. You are the book's champion, a fabulous editor and friend, and my hero.

Thank you to Anjali Singh, my delightful and deeply sensitive editor, who has shed boundless intelligence on this novel. Your clarity and sense of proportion have brought it to life.

I so appreciate the tireless and ever-positive team at Simon & Schuster, Millicent Bennett, Nina Pajak and Anne Tate, Michele

Acknowledgments

Bové and Sarah Nalle, Gypsy da Silva and Fred Wiemer. Your energy is palpable and sustaining.

Katie Espiner, at HarperCollins in London, you are a joy. Thank you for bringing your warmth to bear on this book and for always letting me know how much you believe in it.

I am grateful to Renate Liesker and Tanja Hendriks at Artemis in Amsterdam, to Caspian Dennis at the Abner Stern Agency in London, and to the editors in various parts of the world who have given the book wings.

My French "family," Bernadette and Michel Perichon, Alison and Jim Clayson, Christine Coenon and Jean-Luc André, you are my French roots.

I would like to thank my family. My sister, Eleanor O'Neill, is the world's best proofreader and my soulmate and biggest fan. I'm your biggest fan too, always. My mother, Harriet Whelan, who might be more excited about this book than I am, your optimism is my lifeline. My father, Tim Whelan, is still whispering to me to "write it all down." He is smiling up from every word.

My bright and beautiful daughters, Ella, Margaux and Iris, you are brimming with wonderful ideas. Thank you for your sense of humor and your crazy enthusiasm. I adore you.

And finally, Charles Reyl, my love. This book is for you. You have never had a shadow of a doubt.

about the author

Hilary Reyl has a Ph.D. in French literature from NYU with a focus on the nineteenth century, and has spent several years working and studying in France. She lives in New York City with her family. This is her first novel.

DATE			